Every Cough Was A Crime

Clifton Wilcox

Fredericksburg, Virginia

Print ISBN: 978-1-969770-47-0

EBook ISBN: 978-1-969770-46-3

Published by Windward Publishing LLC., Fredericksburg, Virginia.

Wilcox, Clifton

Every Cough Was A Crime

Windward Publishing, LLC

2026

Dedication

This book is a warning.

Not of disease—but of fear.

Of the moment when whispers become truth,

when suspicion outweighs compassion,

and when survival demands someone to blame.

Fear does not arrive with violence.

It creeps, it spreads, it convinces—

until neighbor turns on neighbor,

and the innocent burn to keep others warm.

Remember: the plague did not make them monsters.

Fear did.

—Clifton Wilcox

April 17, 2026

Table of Contents

Books by Clifton Wilcox 6
Chapter 1: Prologue: The East Wind 7
Chapter 2: The Earl's Disgrace 41
Chapter 3: A Different Kind of Land 73
Chapter 4: The Quiet Unease 107
Chapter 5: The First Blame 141
Chapter 6: The Strangers Among Us 175
Chapter 7: Wells of Poison 208
Chapter 8: The Night of Ashes...................... 243
Chapter 9: Safety in Blood 277
Chapter 10: The Unclean 310
Chapter 11: The Animal Curse 345
Chapter 12: Marks of the Damned 378
Chapter 13: The Last Voice of Reason 414
Chapter 14: The Breaking of Edmund Harrow 451
Chapter 15: Nothing Left to Blame 485
Chapter 16: Ashes and Echoes 518
Chapter 17: Epilogue: A Town Without Names 554
Chapter 18: Afterword: The Wind Moves On 587

Books by Clifton Wilcox

Fiction

Cool's Last Stand

Where Despair Comes to Play

The Monuments Must Bleed

Keeper of the Fallen Ages

I, Monster

Harvest of Eyes

The Case Against Jasper

Crimson Plume: The Song of Corvus

Framed in Love

Echoes of the Forgotten

Blacktop Harvest

The Plagiarist Game

The Black Forest Protocol

Outcome without Appeal

Deliberation

The Lore Hunter: Brown Mountain

Pact of Shadows: The Black Orchard

The Black Ledger of Salem

The Four That Bind

The Last Star

Chapter 1

Prologue: The East Wind

The harbor woke the way it always did, with ropes creaking and gulls arguing over scraps, with the lazy slap of water against stone. Yet on that morning the sound seemed to stop short at the mouth of the bay, as if an unseen hand had pressed down over the port and flattened it. Men spoke without meaning to whisper, and then fell silent, listening for the reason they had lowered their voices.

Out beyond the breakwater a ship drifted in, its sails hanging like damp cloth. It should have come in brisk, guided by a pilot and shouted into place, but it moved with the slack patience of a corpse carried by current. No flag snapped from its mast. No call rose from its deck. The vessel turned slightly as it entered, as though it were seeking something it could not see.

Gianni, who had worked these docks since he was a boy and now wore his years like a second jacket, squinted against the pale sun. He did not like the look of that ship. He did not like the way it seemed to glide without wake, barely troubling the water. He did not like the stillness around it, a pocket of air that did not stir even when the rest of the bay breathed.

"Where is her crew?" Asked Matteo beside him. Matteo was young enough to still believe the sea behaved according to rules, young enough to expect a greeting from any ship with men on board.

Gianni did not answer at first. He listened. He heard the small ordinary noises of the port: a cart wheel groaning somewhere behind him, the distant strike of a hammer. But from the vessel itself, nothing. Not the clink of a belaying pin, not the scrape of boots, not the irritated shout of a mate.

The harbor master, a broad man named Ruggiero, arrived in a hurry, coat thrown over his shoulders, beard still wet from washing. He took in the ship with the same narrowing of the eyes Gianni had felt in his bones.

"Name?" Ruggiero called across the water, not loud, as if he were afraid to break something fragile.

The ship did not answer.

It coasted closer. Its hull was stained with long streaks where seawater had run and dried. Barnacles crusted the line near the water, suggesting it had been too long at sea or too long neglected. A length of rope trailed from its bow, dragging in the harbor like a dead thing's hair.

Men along the dock began to gather, drawn by curiosity and the unease that followed behind it. Some crossed themselves. Some spat into the water for luck, then quickly looked away as if ashamed.

A pilot boat pushed off toward the drifting vessel, its oars dipping carefully, not wanting to splash. Gianni watched the pilot's men as they drew alongside. One stood and hooked a grapnel to the ship's rail, then pulled. He waited for the ship to resist, to tug back with life and weight, but it yielded too easily. The pilot climbed up and vanished over the side.

Moments passed. The pilot did not reappear.

"Gianni," Matteo whispered, as if saying the older man's name could make him act.

Gianni's tongue felt thick. He had boarded ships where the crew were drunk, hostile, sick, even dead. He had never boarded a ship that refused to announce itself.

Ruggiero cursed under his breath and motioned to two dock guards. "With me."

The pilot boat returned without th

e pilot. It came back empty, bumping the dock with a soft, foolish knock. The men in it were pale, eyes wide and unfocused, as if they had looked at something that did not fit into their minds.

"Where is he?" Ruggiero demanded.

The oarsman swallowed. His throat bobbed. "He went up. We waited. We called. There was… no answer. There was a smell. Like…" He gagged on the word and had to spit over the side.

Ruggiero's face tightened. He was a man who believed authority was a tool that could pry open any mystery, but his hand hovered near his belt as if seeking a weapon. He looked at Gianni, perhaps because Gianni had the look of someone who had seen more than he said.

Gianni forced himself to speak. "We should not unload her until we know what she brings."

Matteo nodded too quickly, eager to agree. Another man muttered, "Maybe pirates," as though that would be easier to understand.

"Pirates leave noise," Gianni said. "They leave men tied, or they leave blood. They leave something."

Ruggiero hesitated. Behind him, the port's life waited. Merchants had schedules. Goods were already promised. There was always pressure to make a strange thing ordinary, to push it into the shape of routine so the day could continue.

"Lines," he ordered at last. "Bring her in."

The ship came alongside with reluctant grace, the wood of its hull kissing the dock with a dull thud. Men threw ropes and secured them with hands that trembled slightly. The vessel did not protest. It lay there, moored, as though it had always belonged.

Gianni stood near the gangplank when it was lowered. Up close, the smell was unmistakable, not merely the sourness of bilge or the rankness of old fish. It was sweet and rotten at once, a heavy breath that rolled off the ship and sank into the air. Men stepped back instinctively.

Matteo raised his sleeve to his nose. "Holy Mother," he murmured.

Ruggiero glanced at the guards, then at Gianni and Matteo and two other dockworkers whose faces had the hard set of men who would do what must be done. “We go up. We find the captain. We find the pilot. We see what has happened. Then we decide.”

Decide. As if the matter could be shaped by deliberation.

Gianni’s boots met the planks of the gangway, and the wood was slick beneath him, damp not with seawater but with something that clung. He tried not to look down. The smell thickened with every step, coating the back of his throat. He breathed through his mouth and tasted salt and rot.

On deck, the silence had weight. The rigging did not sway. The sails did not flutter. A coil of rope lay half-unwound as if someone had dropped it mid-task and never returned. A bucket sat on its side, its contents dried in a dark stain. There were footprints on the deck, but they were smeared and uneven, as though made by feet that had stumbled.

Matteo made a sound that might have been a prayer. Gianni followed the direction of his gaze and saw, near the mainmast, a man sprawled on his back. For a heartbeat Gianni thought he was sleeping, until he saw the skin, swollen and dark, stretched so tight it shone. The man's mouth was open, lips cracked, tongue protruding slightly. His eyes had collapsed into their sockets, lids half-raised, showing a dull gray beneath.

Ruggiero took a step forward, then stopped, the authority in him faltering. He looked around quickly, as if the rest of the crew might leap out and laugh at the trick.

There were more.

A hand protruded from behind a barrel, fingers curled as if still gripping something invisible. Near the stern, two bodies lay tangled together, their limbs twisted in a way that suggested either struggle or a final attempt at comfort. One had blackened patches along the neck and beneath the arms, and the skin there looked ruptured, as if it had split under pressure.

Gianni had seen men die. He had seen drowned sailors washed up on the shore, their faces bloated, their bellies distended by the sea. This was different. This was not the ocean's work. This was as if the body itself had turned against the life inside it.

Matteo retched and stumbled toward the rail, vomiting into the water below. The sound of it seemed obscene in the quiet.

"Find the captain," Ruggiero said, voice hoarse. "Find the pilot."

They moved, stepping carefully around the bodies, trying not to touch anything. Gianni's eyes kept darting to the shadows beneath the raised structures on deck, to the openings that led below. The hatch to the cargo hold stood ajar, its edge dark with grime and something that could have been dried blood.

From that open mouth in the deck came a sound.

At first, it was so faint Gianni thought it was the ship settling. Then it came again: a quick, skittering scratch. Something moving where no living thing should be.

Gianni approached the hatch slowly. He peered down into the dimness. The air rising from below was worse, a concentrated stench that made his eyes water. In the gloom he saw shapes, stacked cargo and hanging nets. He also saw movement, quick and low, like shadows with intent.

Rats.

They poured over the crates and along the beams, their bodies sleek and frantic. Some paused, noses twitching, then vanished deeper into the ship. Others climbed toward the light, drawn by the new air, by the promise of escape. One rat reached the edge and paused, staring up at Gianni with bright eyes. Its fur looked wet. Around its mouth was something dark.

Gianni stepped back, heart hammering. He had never feared rats. Rats were part of the port, part of every city, living where men lived. But this swarm felt wrong, not merely hungry but driven, as if the ship itself were pushing them outward.

"Rats," he said sharply.

Ruggiero looked, and for the first time the harbor master's face showed something close to fear. "Keep them in," he barked, absurdly, as if a command could pen in a tide.

The rat at the hatch edge darted past Gianni's boot and vanished down the gangway. Another followed. Then more, slipping between the legs of the men on deck, finding cracks and ropes and the small routes that led to the dock. They moved with purpose, not scattering at shouts. They were leaving.

Gianni heard a faint sound behind him, a rasping, wet breath. He turned, hand half-raised, expecting another corpse.

Near the doorway to the captain's quarters, a figure lay slumped, not rigid like the others. The man's chest rose and fell, shallowly. His skin was gray and slick with sweat, and his lips had the bluish tint of someone freezing in the heat.

Matteo, wiping his mouth, stared. "He's alive."

Ruggiero crouched, reluctant to touch the man, but needing answers. "Who are you? Where is your captain?"

The survivor's eyes fluttered open. They were bloodshot, the whites stained yellow, as if illness had seeped into them. His gaze moved slowly, not focusing at first, then locking onto Ruggiero's face with sudden desperate clarity.

His mouth worked. A sound came out that might have been a word or might have been the throat's attempt to swallow death.

Gianni leaned in despite himself, the smell and the horror and the need to understand fighting in him. The man whispered something in a language Gianni did not know, then tried again in broken Italian, the words falling apart as they left his lips.

"Sick," he breathed. "Cities… gone. Like fire, but no flame. Wind… east wind…"

Ruggiero's expression hardened, protective armor snapping back into place. "Delirium," he muttered, though his eyes did not leave the man's face. "He is fevered."

The survivor's hand twitched, fingers clawing at the deck. His nails were black at the edges. "Do not… bring…" he tried to say, but the sentence collapsed. He coughed, and the cough sounded like something tearing.

Gianni looked past the man, toward the dock. He could see the port workers below, heads tilted up, waiting for news. He could also see, in the gaps between barrels and ropes, the quick darting bodies of rats slipping onto the stone and vanishing into the maze of the harbor. Once they were in the streets, no net would catch them.

The ship sat tied like a gift. The dock waited to claim it. Trade demanded it. Habit demanded it.

Above them, the air remained too still. The breeze that should have carried away the stench did not come. It was as if the world held its breath, and in that held breath, something unseen was already moving inland.

Ruggiero straightened as if the act might pull him out of whatever foul dream clung to the deck. He wiped his palm on his coat without realizing he had touched the survivor's sweat, then looked toward the open hatch again, eyes narrowing at the movement still threading through the darkness below.

"We cannot leave this as it is," he said, and his voice was meant to be firm. It came out thin.

Gianni heard what he did not say. We cannot pretend we saw nothing. The port would demand answers. The merchants would demand their goods. And the longer they stood there, the more rats slid past their boots and down the gangplank, vanishing into the cracks between stones and the shadowed underways where a man's eyes could not follow.

Matteo had gone pale beyond the usual fear-sickness. He kept his back to the rail, as if he did not trust the deck to hold him. "Below," he whispered. "You want us to go below?"

One of the guards, a square-jawed man whose mail shirt looked suddenly too small for him, lifted his spear as if it would be useful against rot and fever. "Maybe there is a fight," he offered, searching for a familiar kind of danger.

"There is no fight," Gianni said. He listened again, and through the silence he could still hear it: the light scratch of claws, the soft thump of something dropping from crate to beam. Life where there should have been none. "Only what's already happened."

Ruggiero glanced toward the dock. Men stood clustered, craning their necks, impatient as children kept from a performance. A few had already started to untie the small boats that would bring stevedores alongside. Routine had teeth; it pulled at everything.

Ruggiero made a quick decision that was not a decision at all but surrender to what he believed the port required. "Gianni, Matteo. With me. You two, follow. We find the captain; we find the manifest. We learn what cargo she brings, and what she's brought with it."

"And the sick man?" Matteo asked, nodding toward the survivor.

Ruggiero's eyes flicked down. The man's breathing had a wet hitch now, like lungs filling with something that did not belong there. "We will bring him ashore once we know what we're dealing with. If he can talk, I want him talking to the physician, not dying on my dock."

Gianni did not like the word ashore. It sounded like permission.

They approached the hatch, stepping around the bodies with care that felt absurd, as if politeness might keep death from noticing them. Gianni forced himself not to stare at the sailor near the mast, but the image clung to his mind anyway: blackened skin stretched too tight, a swollen throat, the open mouth caught mid-breath. He had seen men stiffen like that in winter, but this was summer air, and the skin had split in places as if something inside had pushed outward.

At the hatch lip, the air changed. It was thicker, warmer, carrying the concentrated sweetness of decay. It smelled like meat left too long, like fruit rotting in barrels, like something that should have dried but had instead fermented into corruption. Matteo put his sleeve to his face again, but it did little. The stench found its way in through his eyes, through the back of his throat.

Ruggiero lifted a lantern from one of the guards. The flame inside shivered though there was no breeze. He held it over the opening. The light fell into the hold in a narrow cone, catching on beams slick with moisture and on the rounded backs of rats moving along the lower timbers.

They did not scatter from the light. They flowed around it, avoiding it only because it was in their way.

Gianni watched them for a heartbeat too long. In the lantern glow their fur looked clotted in places, as if matted by damp. Their sides rose and fell quickly. One rat climbed a crate and paused, ears pricked, then slipped down the far side. Another followed, and another, and for a moment Gianni saw the pattern: they were not nesting. They were leaving, pouring toward every crack that promised the outside world.

Ruggiero swung a boot at one that ventured too close. The rat darted aside with insulting ease and vanished into the gloom. "Damn vermin," he muttered.

"Not vermin," Gianni thought, but did not say aloud. Not today. Today they were messengers, and the message had teeth.

He descended first, because his legs knew ladders better than arguments and because he could not bear watching Matteo go down ahead of him. The rungs were slick under his hands. Whatever coated them was not seawater. It stuck slightly, as if the wood had been brushed with oil and then left to sour.

Below, the hold opened around him like a throat. Crates were stacked in careful rows, marked with symbols and names in paint that had run from damp. Burlap sacks bulged with grain or spice. Barrels were bound with iron hoops dulled by salt. Nets of fruit hung from beams, and the fruit inside had collapsed into dark mush, dripping slowly.

The lantern light moved as Ruggiero came down behind him. Shadows lurched and lengthened across the cargo, making the stacked crates look like uneven tombstones.

"Captain!" Ruggiero called, and his voice fell dead into the space. It did not echo properly. The hold swallowed it.

Gianni stepped forward. His boots squelched. He looked down and saw a thin sheen across the planks, pooling in low places. In the lantern glow it glimmered amber-brown, streaked with darker threads. He did not want to name it, but his mind did anyway. Leakage. Rot. Fluids from bodies above, or below. The ship was sweating death.

They moved deeper, and the smell worsened until Gianni felt it behind his teeth. He heard Matteo's breathing turn fast and shallow. One of the guards began to mutter a prayer, the words tumbling over each other as if he feared pausing.

A shape lay between two stacks of crates. At first Gianni thought it was a coil of rope. Then the lantern swung and the shape resolved into a man on his side, knees drawn up, arms wrapped around himself like a child hiding from a storm.

His skin was darkened in patches, mottled black and purple. Around his groin and under his arms the swelling was grotesque, as if knots had formed beneath the skin. His shirt was torn open at the neck, and his chest was marked with ruptures that looked less like wounds and more like the body breaking under its own pressure.

Matteo made a strangled sound.

Ruggiero went closer, lantern held low. "That's not the captain," he said, as if the identification mattered.

Gianni crouched, careful not to touch. The man's face was turned toward the planks, mouth pressed to wood. A thin track of dried foam ran from his lips. His fingers were curled, nails dark at the tips like the survivor's.

"Plague," Matteo whispered, the word tasting forbidden.

"Hush," one guard snapped automatically, as if the word itself might call it nearer.

Gianni looked past the corpse to the cargo. He had handled enough shipments to know what he was seeing. Silk bales wrapped in oilcloth. Spices in sealed jars. Furs packed tight in crates with straw. Goods from far coasts and crowded markets, from cities where men lived packed together like grain.

"How long," Ruggiero murmured. He was no longer speaking to them; he was speaking to the ship. "How long have you been like this?"

The answer came from a small sound near the far bulkhead. A slow scrape. Not the quick skitter of rats, but something heavier being dragged.

They all froze.

Gianni held his breath and listened. The scrape came again, followed by a wet cough, low and rattling. A man's attempt to clear death from his lungs.

Ruggiero raised the lantern, and the light wavered across the far corner. There, half hidden behind a stack of barrels, was another body. Not dead. Not yet.

He was propped against the hull, one leg stretched out, the other bent awkwardly. His head lolled, then lifted as the light touched his face. His eyes were open but unfocused, the whites yellowed. Around his neck and jaw the skin looked stretched, as if swollen from within. He wore a pendant that might have been a saint or simply a token, and his fingers kept worrying at it in a small repetitive motion, as if he had been doing it for hours.

"Captain?" Ruggiero called again, quieter now.

The man's mouth moved. A thread of saliva hung there and snapped. "No," he rasped. The word was barely sound.

Gianni edged closer, lantern light catching on the man's lips. They were cracked and dark. There was blood at one corner, dried and black.

"Where is the captain?" Ruggiero asked.

The man smiled, and it was the wrong expression on such a face. It was not relief. It was resignation, as if the question had come too late to matter. He pointed weakly with two fingers toward the aft, toward a narrow passage leading to the crew quarters.

Gianni's stomach tightened. He did not want to follow that gesture. He did not want to see what lay where men slept.

Ruggiero hesitated only a moment. He was a harbor master, a man whose life was built on lists and order. He could not leave a corner uncounted. "Stay," he ordered one guard, and then to Gianni and Matteo, "Come."

Matteo shook his head once, violently, but his feet moved anyway. He was young and afraid and still obedient to authority even when authority led him into the dark.

The passage was low, forcing them to stoop. The lantern threw light onto the walls, and Gianni saw handprints smeared there, streaks of dark as if someone had tried to brace themselves and slid instead. The air was hotter. The ship's wood held the heat and the stink like a sealed oven.

In the first bunkroom, they found three men piled together. Not carefully, not laid out with respect, but collapsed where they had crawled. One had bitten his own forearm, teeth marks deep, as if pain had been the only thing he could still control. Another's eyes were open, staring at nothing, and his belly was distended in a way that made Gianni think of a wineskin filled past its limit.

Matteo stumbled back and hit the passage wall. The lantern light shook wildly, making the dead seem to shift.

Ruggiero's face had gone gray. He forced himself onward, into the captain's tiny cabin at the end. The door was half shut. When he pushed it open, it stuck briefly, then gave with a soft tearing sound.

Inside, the captain sat at his desk as if still working. His head was tipped forward, chin nearly to chest. One hand lay on a ledger, fingers splayed. The other had fallen to his side, still holding a quill that had dried to a sharp brittle point.

The captain's back was arched in a strange way, shoulders hunched, as if his final breath had been a convulsion that locked him there. His neck was swollen, and dark blotches climbed up behind his ears. A stain spread across his shirtfront, and the desk itself was sticky with it, as though the illness had seeped out of him and tried to write its own story.

Ruggiero set the lantern down with a care that felt like reverence. He reached for the ledger, then stopped, his hand hovering above it. For the first time since Gianni had known him, Ruggiero looked uncertain not of what to do, but of whether anything he did would matter.

Gianni leaned in just enough to see the open page. The writing was neat at the start, then increasingly erratic. He could make out dates and ports, names of goods. He saw one word repeated in the margin, written as if the captain had pressed too hard, tearing the paper slightly: febbre. Fever. Under it, another word in a different hand, perhaps a mate's: morti. Dead.

Matteo made a small whimpering sound behind them, like a child trying not to cry.

Gianni's gaze dropped to the floor. In the corner of the cabin, where a chest sat half-open, something moved. A rat nosed through fabric, then lifted its head. For an instant it looked at Gianni, eyes bright in the lantern glow. Its whiskers twitched, and a tiny dark insect crawled along the edge of its ear, then vanished into fur.

Gianni's skin tightened as if a cold wind had found him at last. Fleas. He had seen them on dogs, on beggars, on any creature living too close to dirt. But here, on a rat that had come from a ship of the dead, the small insect looked like a deliberate thing, a drop of moving ink.

The rat slipped away, squeezing into a gap behind the chest. Gianni heard it scratching, searching, already on its way back out.

Ruggiero finally grabbed the ledger, snapping it shut as if to trap the words inside. "We take this," he said. "We take the manifest. We tell the officials. We…" His voice failed him. He swallowed and tried again. "We do what is required."

Gianni looked back down the passage toward the hold, imagining the rats threading through the cargo, through the ropes, up toward the deck, and from there into the port. Into the city. Into every cellar and granary and warm place where men slept unaware.

Required, Gianni thought. Yes. And what is required now will not be what is required tomorrow.

As they turned to leave, Matteo caught Gianni's sleeve with shaking fingers. "Gianni," he whispered, eyes wide and wet. "That man above… he said east wind."

Gianni nodded once. The words had lodged in him like a splinter. Not just the wind's direction, but the way the survivor had said it, as if the wind were a thing with intention.

They climbed back toward the hatch. The lantern light swung across the hold one last time, and in that brief sweep Gianni saw the cargo for what it truly was. Not spices, not silk, not profit in crates. A nest. A carrier. A belly full of moving life that had fed on death and was now spilling out into the world.

Above, the deck waited with its silent bodies and its open sky. Beyond that, the dock waited with men ready to unload, hands already reaching for rope and barrel and coin.

And somewhere, finally, the first faint stir of air brushed across Gianni's cheek, as if the world had decided to breathe again.

It came from inland. Warm, dry, carrying the smell of sunbaked stone and distant fields.

The wind had shifted.

When they stepped back into daylight the deck seemed even more wrong, as if the open air ought to have made it honest. It did not. The bodies lay where they had fallen and the ship's timbers creaked with the small, private sounds of settling wood, the only thing on board that still behaved like something alive.

Ruggiero climbed out last, the ledger clutched under his arm as though it could anchor the world. He blinked hard against the sun, then looked down at the dock. The crowd had grown. Men leaned on hooks and coils of rope, craning their necks. A few merchants had arrived as well, sleeves too fine for labor, their expressions already pinched with impatience at the delay.

"Captain?" someone called up. "What's happened?"

"Is there coin in her?" another shouted, trying to turn fear into a joke.

Matteo stood at the rail, pale and trembling, one hand on the wood as if it might suddenly tilt. He had the look of a man who had seen something that would never be entirely explained away.

Gianni followed Ruggiero to the gangway. On the planks, near where the first rat had slipped past his boot, he saw a smear of dark filth and a scatter of tiny droppings. There were more marks along the edge of the dock itself, as if the stone had been briefly alive with movement. Now it was still, clean in its stillness, too clean, because the proof had already run into the city's cracks and shadows.

Ruggiero raised his hands to the dockworkers before the first eager man could step onto the gangplank. "No one boards," he said sharply. "Not yet."

Grumbling rose. A guard moved to stand at the foot of the gangway, spear angled across it like a bar.

A merchant in a dark cap pushed forward. "Harbor master, my goods are overdue. That ship is chartered under contract. We have obligations."

"Obligations," Ruggiero echoed, and there was something almost bitter in his voice. He looked down at them, then at the ship behind him. "There are dead men on deck."

That did it. The crowd's noise changed shape, curiosity becoming alarm. A few men stepped back as if death could leap.

"How many?" someone asked.

"All," Matteo said before he could stop himself. His voice cracked on the word.

Ruggiero shot him a look, half warning, half gratitude, then addressed the crowd again. "There is sickness. We will summon the port physician and the magistrate. Until then, no unloading. No touching of cargo. No one takes a single crate off this vessel."

The merchant scoffed, loud enough that others heard. "Sickness? Sailors die every day. Fever, rot, bad water. We are not closing the port for a ship's misfortune."

Gianni watched the faces below, the way they shifted between fear and calculation. Men could accept danger if it was familiar, if it fit into a story they already knew. Pirates, storms, even murder. But sickness that had swallowed a crew without a fight was a different kind of threat, one that did not wear a weapon at its hip.

A cart rolled by behind the crowd, loaded with barrels, and the ordinary sound of its wheel on stone felt obscene.

Ruggiero sent one guard running and ordered another to keep watch at the gangway. Then he turned toward the survivor still lying on deck near the captain's quarters. The man had not moved much. His breathing had grown louder, each inhale a wet drag. Every now and then his fingers twitched, scraping the deck as if he were trying to hold on to the ship that had killed him.

"We bring him down," Ruggiero said. "Carefully."

Matteo flinched. "If it is plague—"

"Hush," Ruggiero snapped, but the word was already in the air now, not said by Matteo alone. It was on the dock too, in murmurs that leapt from mouth to mouth like sparks looking for kindling.

Two men approached with a canvas sling. Gianni helped, because he could not stand aside and watch someone else take the risk. The survivor's skin burned under his touch, feverish and slick. When they lifted him the man's eyes fluttered open, and for an instant his gaze found Gianni's as if pleading to be understood.

"Do not," the survivor rasped. His tongue seemed too thick for his mouth. "Do not… open. Do not… let them…"

Ruggiero leaned close. "Tell me where you came from," he demanded. "Tell me what happened."

The man coughed, a bubbling sound. "Messina," he whispered, then something else, a string of place names that meant little to Gianni. "They die… like grain… cut. Streets… quiet. Priests… no bells. East wind… carries…"

Ruggiero's face tightened at the mention of a port name he recognized. Messina was not some far-off legend. It was a real place with real ships and real trade. If the sickness was there, it was on every route.

"You are fevered," Ruggiero said, the way a man might insist a nightmare is only sleep. "You speak nonsense."

The survivor's lips pulled back, not quite a smile, more a grimace at the effort of being heard. "Not nonsense," he insisted, and there was suddenly a hard clarity in his voice that cut through the rasp. "Quarantine. Rope the ship. Burn the bedding. Kill the rats."

At that last word he jerked weakly, as if he could see them even now slipping away. His eyes rolled toward the dock, toward the city beyond, and terror widened them.

Gianni followed his gaze. A child stood at the edge of the crowd, barefoot, watching with round fascinated eyes. A moment later a small gray shape darted behind a stack of nets, so quick the child might have imagined it. The child smiled anyway, as if it were a game.

Gianni's stomach turned.

They carried the survivor down the gangplank. The crowd parted reluctantly, people pressing their sleeves to their faces. Someone spat, then crossed himself. The sling's canvas creaked with each step, and the man's breath rattled against it.

The port physician arrived in haste, a thin man with a leather satchel and the distracted confidence of someone accustomed to being needed. The magistrate came with him, heavier, dressed in a robe that suggested law could shield flesh. Two clerks trailed behind, already preparing to write down whatever version of events would be convenient.

The physician took one look at the ship and stopped, his mouth tightening. "God preserve us," he muttered, then recovered and stepped closer with professional briskness. He asked Ruggiero questions. He asked Matteo questions. He did not ask Gianni anything, as if dockworkers could not carry knowledge worth having.

When the survivor tried to speak again, the physician waved a hand. "He is delirious with fever. Let him be examined."

"And the ship?" Ruggiero asked. "We should close the dock. We should—"

The magistrate interrupted, already annoyed. "Close the dock? Do you know what that means? Trade will halt. The city will howl. You have no authority to stop commerce on the word of a half-dead sailor babbling about wind."

"He said quarantine," Gianni heard himself say. The words came out before he could weigh them. "He said kill the rats."

The magistrate looked at him as one might look at a dog that had spoken. "Rats are everywhere," he said. "If rats carried sickness, no city would stand."

The physician nodded as if that settled it. "We have seen fevers before. A ship's hold breeds foul airs. Miasma. Rot. It is unfortunate, but not unheard of."

Gianni wanted to shout that this was not the usual rot. He wanted to drag them below decks and make them smell the sweetness of death and see the fleas crawling like ink. But men like these did not accept truths delivered by hands that hauled rope for a living.

Ruggiero pressed the ledger forward. "The captain wrote of fever. Of deaths. It took them quickly."

The magistrate barely glanced at it. "Then we will note it. We will pray. And we will proceed with caution." He stressed the last words as if granting a gift. "The cargo must be unloaded. Left to sit, it will spoil, and the merchants will petition the council."

"But the crew—" Matteo began, then stopped when the magistrate's eyes hardened.

The physician bent over the survivor and pinched his wrist, listened briefly to his breath, grimaced at the sound. "He will not last long," he said, as calmly as if commenting on weather. "We should move him away from the dock, to the infirmary, so he does not agitate the men with his ramblings."

"His ramblings are a warning," Gianni said, quieter now, because he could feel how easily they might turn their impatience on him. "We saw rats, swarming out. From the hold."

"Then set traps," the magistrate said. "We will have the streets cleaned." He looked around at the crowd and raised his voice, performing reassurance. "There is no cause for panic. The ship will be inspected. The goods will be handled properly. Go about your work."

The words washed over the dock like warm water over blood, blurring what had been seen. Men began to relax because they wanted to. Merchants began to talk about schedules again. The guards shifted their spears aside, because boredom was easier than vigilance.

Ruggiero's shoulders sagged. For all his authority, he was still bound by the city's need to keep moving. He nodded once, stiffly, as if agreeing to something he did not believe in.

Gianni watched the first stevedores climb the gangplank with hooks on their shoulders. He watched them wrinkle their noses at the stench, laugh too loudly, then start rolling barrels toward the edge. A crate thumped onto the dock. Hands grabbed it, carried it to a waiting cart. Another followed. The ship was being emptied of its secrets one piece at a time, distributed like charity.

The survivor was carried away on the sling, his head lolling. As he passed Gianni, his eyes opened one last time. He mouthed something that might have been a prayer, or might have been a curse. Then his gaze drifted toward the city again, toward the alleys where rats ran unseen. His eyelids fluttered, and the light seemed to go out behind them.

Matteo stood beside Gianni, his face drawn tight. "They won't listen," he whispered.

Gianni did not answer. He could taste the ship's stench still, coating his tongue, and beneath it he imagined the dry warm breath of the inland wind that had brushed his cheek when they left the hold. The east wind, the survivor had called it, as if it were an old enemy with a familiar step.

By late afternoon the dock looked almost normal again. The dead were still on the ship, but the cargo was moving, and movement is what made men believe things were under control. The rats were gone from sight, which was even better. Invisible threats were easier to dismiss.

At dusk Gianni washed his hands until the skin reddened, scrubbing under his nails, trying to scrape away the feel of that slick ladder rung and the survivor's fevered sweat. He told himself it was enough. He told himself that filth could be removed if you worked hard enough.

When night fell, he heard shouting from down the quay. A dockworker had collapsed near the fish stalls, clutching his side as if stabbed. Men gathered, swearing. Someone said he had a fever. Someone else said his armpit was swollen, a hard knot rising under the skin like a stone.

Gianni's blood cooled. He knew the man. He had helped tie the ship's lines that morning. He had laughed when the magistrate said there was no cause for panic.

Gianni pushed through the crowd and saw the worker on the ground, face slick with sweat, eyes wide with confusion and pain. Under the torchlight a dark blotch marked the side of his neck, spreading like spilled ink.

A breeze moved through the harbor then, gentle, almost pleasant. It carried the smell of the sea, the day's fish, the smoke from cookfires. It also carried something else, something too faint to name.

The wind came from inland, and it did not feel like relief.

It felt like arrival.

Chapter 2

The Earl's Disgrace

The great hall of Harrow Keep had been built to outlast the people who lived and died inside it.

Its stones were older than Edmund's memory, older even than the lines in his father's face, laid in a time when men believed weight was the same as strength and permanence the same as right. In winter the walls held cold like a grudge; in summer they sweated faintly, as though the keep itself breathed with slow displeasure. Smoke from the hearth hung in the high rafters, caught in the beams like a dark net, and the rushes underfoot smelled of old ale, damp straw, and the sharp tang of iron where weapons rested too close to the fire.

Banners watched from above: the Harrow crest stitched in fading thread, wolves and spears and a sunburst that looked less like dawn and more like a brand. The cloth stirred only when the door opened and a draught rolled through, and even then, it felt as if the movement came reluctantly, like a dead thing shifting when prodded.

Edmund stood near the long table, hands at his sides, the way a man stood when he had decided he would not beg.

Across from him, the Earl of Harrow sat in the high-backed chair that had held his father and his father's father, his posture so straight it seemed held up by the same stone as the walls. The Earl's hair had thinned, turned the color of ash at the temples, but his gaze had not softened with age. It landed on Edmund like a thrown weight.

Between them was space filled with listening.

Servants moved quietly at the hall's edges, pretending to polish what had already been polished. A page boy held a tray he did not need to hold. Even the hounds by the hearth had grown still, heads on paws, eyes half open in the particular alertness of animals that sensed anger and learned to respect it.

The Earl did not raise his voice. He did not need to. When he spoke, the hall made room for the sound.

"You have been seen," he said, "in the village again."

Edmund did not answer immediately. He could feel the warmth of the hearth at his back, but it did nothing against the cold that came from his father's measured tone. He had known this conversation was coming. It had been coming the moment he chose to go down among the cottages without escort, the moment he chose to speak to the men in the fields as if they were men and not tools that happened to breathe.

"So, I have," Edmund said at last.

The Earl's fingers rested on the arm of his chair. The nails were clean, the knuckles thick with old strength. That hand had signed charters and ordered punishments and received oaths with the ease of a man who believed the world existed to be arranged by him.

"You have been heard," the Earl continued, "making promises."

Edmund felt his jaw tighten. "I have made none that cannot be kept."

A small sound came from the far side of the hall, quickly stifled. Edmund glanced and saw Maud, one of the older servants, her eyes downcast, her mouth pressed into a line that had once been kinder. She had helped raise him when his mother died. She did not look at him now, but he knew she was listening as if her life depended on it.

The Earl's gaze never wavered. "Do not play at words with me. You have spoken of easing rents. Of delaying levies. Of letting men keep more of what they harvest."

"I have spoken of letting them live," Edmund said, before he could stop himself.

That was the first crack. It was not loud. It was simply visible, like a hairline fracture in glass that would spread no matter how carefully one pretended not to see it.

The Earl's mouth twitched, not quite into a smile. "They live," he said. "They live because this house stands. Because men fear our name more than they fear hunger. Because order is kept."

Edmund took a step forward. The rushes shifted under his boots. Somewhere above, in the soot-black rafters, a bird stirred, trapped and silent.

"They live poorly," Edmund said. "And they die easily. I have seen a man's back split open from lashes because he stole a loaf. A loaf. As if bread is treason."

"You have seen," the Earl replied, "a lesson."

Edmund's throat tightened. The memory returned too sharply, not as a story but as smell and sound: sweat, wet earth, the dull slap of leather on flesh, the way the man had tried not to scream in front of his children until he could not hold it anymore. Edmund had been fifteen then. He had stood by the bailiff, waiting for his father's approval, and something inside him had begun to turn.

"A lesson," Edmund repeated, tasting the bitterness of it. "And what lesson do we teach when we punish hunger? That we will not allow them even the instinct to survive?"

The Earl's eyes narrowed slightly, the only sign of annoyance he allowed himself. "We teach them their place."

"That place is a grave if the winter is hard," Edmund said. "Or if the harvest fails. Or if sickness comes."

At the word sickness, a few servants shifted as if the air had changed. Not fear exactly, but the uncomfortable awareness of something that had been whispered in kitchens and stables. A peddler passing through. A monk on the road. Rumors of foreign ports, of ships arriving too quiet, of cities where bells rang until the ringers died and there was no one left to pull the rope.

The Earl waved it away with a slight motion of his hand, as if he could scatter not only the thought but the thing itself. “Sickness has always come. And always will. It is not for lords to fret like women over every cough.”

Edmund felt heat rise behind his eyes, not tears but fury. “It is for lords,” he said, “to protect.”

The Earl’s voice sharpened, a blade drawn only a fraction. “Protect the land. Protect the lineage. Protect what has been given to us by God and blood and law. That is what you were taught.”

“I was taught,” Edmund said, “that the world is made of people. Not fields. Not ledgers. People.”

The Earl leaned forward slightly, and the hall seemed to lean with him. “You speak like a priest,” he said, and in his mouth, it was an insult. “Or worse, like a boy who has not yet had to make hard choices.”

Edmund let out a slow breath. He forced himself to look directly at his father, to see the man beneath the title. It was harder than it should have been. The Earl’s presence filled the space until the man himself was difficult to separate from the stone and banners, from the idea of Harrow.

"I have made choices," Edmund said. "I choose not to squeeze the village until their bones show. I choose not to treat them like livestock. I choose not to pretend that cruelty is wisdom."

A short silence followed, heavy and deliberate. The servants did not move. Even the fire seemed to quiet, its crackle subdued.

The Earl's gaze traveled over Edmund slowly, as though taking measure of him the way a merchant measured cloth, deciding where it might tear.

"You embarrass this house," the Earl said.

The words landed harder than a shouted curse. Embarrassment in the Earl's mouth was not social discomfort. It was danger. It was vulnerability. It was the threat of laughter from other lords, the kind that turned into alliances and raids and petitions to the king.

"I do not intend—" Edmund began.

"You intend exactly what you intend," the Earl interrupted. "You intend to be seen as different. Better. You intend to draw eyes to yourself. You intend to weaken what your forefathers built because you cannot stomach the weight of it."

Edmund's hands curled, then unclenched. "If the weight of it is built on broken backs," he said, "then it should not stand."

The Earl's expression went still. Not angry, not surprised. Still, like a pond after a stone sinks out of sight.

Behind Edmund, the great door to the hall opened briefly, letting in a slip of air from outside. It carried the scent of damp earth and horse, and something else, faint and strange, as though the wind had passed over distant smoke. The banners stirred a little and then settled again.

The Earl watched the movement with an absent flick of his eyes, then returned his full attention to Edmund.

"You forget yourself," he said quietly.

"No," Edmund replied, his voice steadier than he felt. "I remember myself. That is the trouble."

The Earl rose.

He did it without haste, but the action drew every gaze. When the Earl stood, the servants seemed to shrink by instinct. The chair behind him looked suddenly too small, as if it had been made for a lesser man. He stepped down from the dais, boots striking the stone with a sound like a gavel.

Edmund held his ground. He refused to step back, even as the Earl's shadow reached him. This close, Edmund could smell his father's wine and the faint medicinal bitterness of whatever herb the physician had lately given him for his joints. He could also see the tiny scars on the Earl's hands, old nicks from falconry and blade practice, proof that the man had once been young and capable of tenderness before the title hardened him into something else.

The Earl stopped an arm's length away. "You will marry who I tell you to marry," he said. "You will take on the duties assigned to you. You will stop filling peasants' heads with the notion that they deserve more than what they are given. You will learn that mercy without restraint is not mercy. It is disorder."

Edmund's pulse hammered in his throat. This was the heart of it, the demand hidden beneath every earlier complaint. Marriage. Duty. The continuation of Harrow blood through a son who would obey.

He thought of the village again, of the faces that looked up when he spoke to them plainly. Of the way a man's shoulders eased when treated as human. Of the small startled gratitude in a woman's eyes when Edmund had ordered the reeve to reduce a fine that would have emptied her pantry.

He also thought, unbidden, of those rumors of foreign sickness. Of a ship that could drift into a harbor with no living voices aboard. Of how quickly the world could change while men argued over coin and contracts.

If something truly was moving across lands, then the order his father clung to was not only cruel. It was brittle.

Edmund met the Earl's eyes. "No," he said.

The word was simple. It should have been small. In that hall, it was a stone thrown at stained glass.

A servant inhaled sharply, then tried to swallow the sound. The hounds by the hearth lifted their heads.

The Earl did not blink. For a long moment he only looked at Edmund, and Edmund felt as if he were being weighed not as a son but as a problem.

Then the Earl spoke again, and his voice had changed. It was still controlled, but something deeper had surfaced beneath it. Not rage. Disappointment sharpened into contempt.

"Then you are of no use to me," he said.

Edmund flinched despite himself, because no matter how prepared he had been, some part of him had still hoped to be heard as a son.

The Earl turned slightly, not away, but as if Edmund was already being moved from the center of his attention to the edge. "You will not undermine this house from within," he said. "If you cannot carry the Harrow name with dignity, you will carry it somewhere else, away from my lands and my people."

"My people," Edmund echoed, and the words tasted wrong, as if ownership had become a habit of speech.

The Earl glanced back, eyes cold. "Yes," he said. "Mine. And you will learn, Edmund, that a man without a place in the order is a man with nothing. Ideals do not feed a household. Compassion does not defend borders. The world will not reward you for softness."

Edmund felt the hall press in around him: stone, smoke, banners, silence. The keep had stood through wars and famines, through kings and rebellions, and it would stand after this argument too. It would stand even if Edmund did not.

Yet as he looked at his father, Edmund saw something else beneath the certainty: fear. Not fear of Edmund's defiance itself, but fear of what it represented. That another way might exist. That the old way might not be inevitable. That the stone could crack.

Outside, the wind touched the narrow windows again, a soft pressure against the glass. It was nothing like the sea wind of the southern ports, nothing like the brine-laden breath that carried ships and rumors. This wind smelled of wet fields and distant woods, of England's steady green.

But it moved all the same, indifferent to banners and names.

And in the great hall of Harrow Keep, with servants holding their breath and a father measuring his son like a failed investment, Edmund understood that whatever was coming for the world beyond these walls, his battle had already arrived.

The Earl's words hung between them like smoke that would not lift. Then you are of no use to me. The sentence had the finality of a gate being barred.

Edmund felt his throat tighten, not with tears but with the childish reflex to explain himself, to plead the case as though this were a misunderstanding that could be corrected with patience. He had stood in battle drills. He had ridden through winter rain until his hands ached around the reins. None of it had prepared him for the way a father could look at his son and see only failure of function.

"You speak of use," Edmund said, and his voice came out lower than he expected. "As if I were a tool you mislaid."

The Earl's expression did not change. He stood as steady as the keep's pillars, and for an instant Edmund hated him for it. Not because he was strong, but because he could be strong and unfeeling in the same breath.

"I speak of duty," the Earl replied. "The same duty I bore when I inherited this hall. The same duty you will bear, if you cease this stubborn performance and become the man you were raised to be."

"A man raised to what?" Edmund asked. "To take and take until the land is bones and the people are ash? To count coin while children starve on the edge of the forest?"

A murmur moved along the walls. Servants shifted, a ripple of fear at being made witnesses. Edmund saw Maud's hands twist together beneath her apron, knuckles white. She kept her eyes down, but there was a tremor in her mouth as if she fought the urge to speak.

The Earl's gaze flicked briefly toward the servants, and the hall quieted by instinct. When he looked back at Edmund, the contempt in his eyes had sharpened into something colder.

"You forget what you are," he said.

"I remember," Edmund answered. "That is why I cannot do as you ask."

The Earl took a step closer. The firelight caught the edge of his signet ring, the Harrow crest, and Edmund felt the old weight of it: wolves and spears and a sunburst like a brand pressed into skin. When Edmund was a boy, he had traced that ring with a finger and felt proud. Now it looked like a shackle a man wore willingly.

"You will marry," the Earl said, each word measured, "Isabel of Wareham. Her father's lands border ours. The alliance will settle the dispute in the north pasture and strengthen our position with the sheriff. The contract is nearly written. Your refusal would make us a joke."

Edmund's stomach turned at the casual way a woman's life was handled like a fence line. He had met Isabel only twice, each time in a room full of watchers. She had seemed kind enough, eyes steady, hands folded as if she knew the rules and had decided not to fight them. Perhaps she had no choice. Perhaps she fought in silence, in ways no one saw. The thought made Edmund's anger twist into something uglier: shame that he had never asked her what she wanted.

"And what does Isabel want?" Edmund asked.

The Earl's lip curled slightly. "Isabel wants what her father tells her to want. As all daughters do."

"As all daughters must," Edmund said, and heard bitterness creep into his voice. "And sons, too, if they are obedient."

The Earl's eyes narrowed. "Careful."

Edmund did not step back. "No," he said again, and the word felt less like defiance now and more like a boundary. "I will not be traded like a barrel of wool, and I will not trade her. Not for pasture, not for peace with the sheriff, not for your pride."

The Earl's hand moved so quickly Edmund barely registered it. He caught Edmund's chin between thumb and forefinger, not hard enough to bruise but hard enough to force his attention, to remind him of the size and strength that had ruled this hall long before Edmund's conscience had found its voice.

"You will not speak of pride," the Earl said softly. "You will not reduce the keeping of this house to vanity. Everything you enjoy, every comfort you take for granted, was bought by men who did not have the luxury of softness. Do you think kindness built these walls? Do you think stone stands because a lord smiled at it?"

Edmund swallowed against the grip. He smelled his father's wine again, and beneath it a medicinal bitterness. He wondered, with a sudden clarity that startled him, whether his father hurt more than he admitted. Whether the body, like the land, was being taxed until it failed.

"I do not mistake cruelty for strength," Edmund said. His voice was slightly strained, but he forced the words out clean. "And I do not mistake fear for order."

The Earl released him as abruptly as he had seized him. Edmund's jaw throbbed where the fingers had been. The pain was small, but it carried a deeper insult: the reminder that in this hall, Edmund's body still belonged to the Earl's authority.

The Earl turned away half a step, as if Edmund were no longer worth the closeness. "You speak as if the world can be arranged by sentiment," he said. "As if men will work because you call them partners. As if they will fight for you because you call them friends."

"They fight now because they are trapped," Edmund shot back. "Because the law binds them, because hunger binds them, because you have made sure there is nowhere to go."

"And yet," the Earl said, "they do not rise. They do not burn the hall. They do not slit our throats in the night. That is because they know their place."

Edmund stared at him. "Or because they have been taught to believe they deserve it."

For a moment something flickered across the Earl's face. Not doubt. Never that. But irritation touched with an older memory. Edmund had seen that look only once before, years ago, after Edmund's mother had died. A messenger had come with a petition from a tenant family begging a reduction in rent because the father had been maimed. The Earl had denied it without raising his voice. Later, Edmund had heard a servant whisper that the family had lost their cottage by spring. That night Edmund had found his father alone in the chapel, not praying, simply sitting with his head bowed. Edmund had been too afraid to enter.

Now the Earl's face hardened again. Whatever softness that memory suggested was locked away behind the same stone that held the keep.

"You will cease going to the village," the Earl said. "You will stop speaking to peasants as though their opinions matter. You will stop putting dangerous ideas into their heads."

Edmund laughed once, a short bitter sound he did not mean to make. It seemed to shock the hall more than any shouted insult. A page boy flinched as if struck.

"Dangerous ideas," Edmund repeated. "That they should eat? That they should keep their children? That a man should not be whipped for taking bread?"

The Earl's voice sharpened. "That they are equal to you."

"They are," Edmund said, and felt the room tilt with the weight of the admission. "Not in title. Not in land. But in blood. In fear. In pain. In the fact that sickness takes them and would take you just as easily if God chose to notice your crest."

At the mention of sickness again, the hall's silence deepened. Edmund saw the way the servants' eyes darted, the way a few of the men-at-arms shifted their weight. Rumors did not need proof to sour a room; they only needed a name and a direction. Ports. Foreign ships. Dead crews. Whispers that traveled faster than horses.

The Earl dismissed it with a hard glance. "Idle stories."

"Are they?" Edmund pressed. "Or do you simply not like the thought that something could come for you that you cannot order beaten or hanged?"

The Earl's hand moved to the hilt of the small dagger at his belt, not drawing it, but resting there as if on an old habit of control. His voice lowered, and with it came danger.

"You have grown arrogant," he said. "You think your pity makes you wise. You think you can lecture me in my own hall."

"It is my hall too," Edmund said before he could stop himself.

The Earl's eyes snapped to his. "No," he said, and the word had teeth. "It is the Harrow hall. It belongs to the line. You are only its future if you do not endanger it."

Edmund's hands curled at his sides, nails biting his palms. "And if I refuse to become what you want?"

The Earl did not answer immediately. He looked at Edmund as though seeing him fully for the first time, not as a son to be guided, but as a man who might become an enemy. It was a terrible kind of attention, stripping and impersonal.

"You will not remain here," the Earl said at last. "You will not infect my household with this foolishness. Not in the servants' ears, not in the tenants' minds, not in the ears of other lords who already watch for weakness."

Edmund felt something cold settle in him. He had expected anger. He had expected punishment. He had not expected this calm removal, as if the Earl were simply shifting a piece on a board.

"So that is it," Edmund said. "You would cast me out because I would not be cruel."

"I would cast you out," the Earl replied, "because you would be disorder."

Edmund looked around the hall one last time. The banners. The hearth. The long table where he had eaten beneath his father's gaze. The servants at the edges, holding their breath as if even air might be punished. Maud's face remained downturned, but Edmund saw a wet sheen at the corner of her eye that she quickly wiped away with the back of her hand.

And Edmund understood then that he was not only arguing with his father. He was arguing with the keep itself, with everything the stones represented. A system that did not bend. A lineage that demanded obedience as proof of worth.

He lifted his chin, jaw still aching faintly from his father's grip. "If you drive me from here," Edmund said, "you will still face what is coming. You will still face winter, hunger, sickness, fear. And you will have taught your people only one lesson: that those with power will abandon them when it is convenient."

The Earl's gaze did not waver. "I will have taught them," he said, "to survive."

Edmund held his father's eyes a moment longer, and then, because there was nothing else to do in a hall where words had become weapons, he bowed his head. Not in submission. In acknowledgment of the finality.

When he looked up again, the Earl had already turned slightly aside, as if the argument had been concluded and Edmund had become merely another matter to arrange.

The hall breathed again in small cautious movements. A servant shifted a foot. A log in the hearth cracked and sent a brief flare of sparks upward. Outside, the wind pressed softly against the narrow windows, indifferent and persistent.

Edmund stood very still, feeling the weight of his name like a cloak he could no longer wear in this place. Somewhere beyond the keep's walls, the village waited, and beyond that the roads carried rumors like ash on a current.

His father spoke once more, without looking at him. "You will be gone before the week ends."

And with that, the final argument became something else entirely: not a battle of words, but the first step into exile.

Edmund did not speak again in the great hall. There was no point in trying to stitch words back into something whole. The Earl had already turned his attention to other matters, speaking to a steward about rents and grain stores as if his son's life had been a brief inconvenience, a candle snuffed and forgotten.

Edmund stepped away from the long table and felt every eye that did not dare look at him. He could sense the servants' listening, the way their bodies held stillness like a discipline. The hall, with its banners and soot-dark beams, seemed to exhale him, pushing him toward the door the way a throat pushes out a thing it cannot swallow.

When he reached the threshold, he paused and glanced back. His father did not look up. The Earl's profile was sharp in the firelight, carved into certainty. Edmund waited for some small sign, some last crack in the stone, but none came.

He left.

The corridor beyond the hall was colder, the air damp with the keep's age. The torches along the walls burned with a low, oily smell. His boots sounded too loud on the stone, each step a declaration he had not intended to make. The keep had always been a place that answered to him, doors opening, servants stepping aside. Now he felt the subtle shift in that deference, not vanished but strained. Respect was a thing that clung to rank even when affection did not.

Maud was waiting near the stairs that led up toward the family chambers. She stood with her hands folded, apron clean, face set in the careful calm she wore when the world demanded silence. But when Edmund drew close, her eyes lifted, and the wetness he had glimpsed earlier had not gone away. It had simply been tucked into the corners.

"They said," she began, then stopped, as if afraid the keep itself might punish her for speaking.

Edmund's jaw still ached where his father's fingers had held him. The ache felt like a mark. "He told me to be gone before the week ends."

Maud's mouth tightened. "And so it is, then."

He found himself searching her face for permission to feel what he refused to show in the hall. Anger, yes, but also something smaller and more humiliating. A child's hurt, old as his mother's absence, old as the times his father's praise had been granted like coin and withheld like famine.

"I will not ask you to risk your place," Edmund said quietly.

Maud made a small dismissive sound, but it trembled. "My place has never been safe, my lord. Not truly. Not for any of us." She glanced down the corridor as if the stones had ears. Then she stepped closer and lowered her voice. "Will you go far?"

"I don't know," he admitted. The honesty surprised him. In the hall he had been all edges, all conviction. Here, in a corridor that smelled of damp wool and torch smoke, the future was suddenly shapeless.

Maud reached into the fold of her apron and produced a small bundle tied with string. She pressed it into his hand before he could refuse. It was heavier than it looked: a little bread wrapped in cloth, and beneath it something hard and cool.

He unwrapped the corner and saw a small silver coin, worn thin at the edges.

"Maud," he began.

"Hush," she said, and the old authority in her voice resurfaced for a moment, the same tone she had used when he was a boy and scraped his knee and tried to pretend it did not hurt. "It is nothing. And it may buy you a night's roof when pride won't."

He closed his fingers around the bundle. "Thank you."

She studied his face as if trying to memorize it. "Your father is angry," she said, though anger seemed too simple a word for what lived behind the Earl's eyes. "He will not call it regret. But there are things in this world that break even stone, given time."

Edmund almost laughed, but it would have come out wrong. “Time breaks everything.”

“Aye,” Maud said. “Even those who believe themselves unbreakable.”

They stood a moment longer, then Maud’s gaze dropped to Edmund’s hands, to the way his knuckles were tight around her small offering. “You must be careful,” she added, and the words carried more than the obvious meaning. Not simply careful of roads and thieves, but careful of what a man becomes when he is unmoored.

Edmund nodded once. He wanted to say he would return, that exile was only a pause, that the keep would eventually open its gates to him again. But the hall’s finality still rang in his bones. Promises would have been a kind of lie.

He went up to his chambers to pack what little he could claim without argument. The room looked as it always had: a bed with heavy coverings, a chest for clothes, a narrow window that let in the smell of rain-wet fields. Yet now it felt borrowed. The objects seemed to hesitate under his touch, as if unsure whether he had the right to lift them.

He took simple things. A change of tunic. A cloak thick enough for travel. A knife with a handle worn smooth by his own hand. A small book of psalms that had belonged to his mother, its corners softened, its pages marked with faint stains where fingers had turned them in private grief. He hesitated before placing it in his bag, then did so as though stealing.

Below, the keep continued. That was the strangest part. Somewhere a cook called for more onions. Somewhere men-at-arms laughed at a crude joke. Life moved forward with the same indifferent rhythm as the tide, as if one young lord's exile could not interrupt the machinery of a household built to endure.

On the third day, a steward summoned him to the solar. The Earl was not there. Only the steward and a clerk with ink-stained fingers, and on the table a small pouch that lay like an accusation.

The steward did not meet Edmund's eyes. "His lordship has provided you with a sum," he said, voice careful. "For travel. For your establishment elsewhere. It is… modest."

Modest. The word landed with calculated restraint. Enough to avoid the appearance of cruelty. Not enough to build anything impressive. A leash length, not a gift.

Edmund picked up the pouch and felt the coins shift inside, heavy and cold. “And the terms?” he asked.

The clerk cleared his throat. “You are not disowned,” he recited, as if reading from a script. “You remain of the Harrow blood. But you are not to return without invitation. You are not to speak in your father’s name. You are not to interfere with the estate’s governance or the village’s affairs.”

“Interfere,” Edmund repeated softly. As if mercy were meddling.

The steward finally looked up, and there was something almost apologetic in his eyes. “It is best this way,” he said, though he did not sound convinced. “A clean separation.”

Edmund slid the pouch into his bag. “Clean,” he said, and thought of the ship in the southern port from the rumors, the way officials always wanted things clean and ordinary, even when rot was already in the hold. He forced the thought away. Dorset was far from those waters. Far from those whispering roads. And yet the wind moved wherever it wished.

When he left the solar, he found his horse already saddled in the yard. The stable boy stood by its head, holding the reins too tight. The boy’s eyes were wide, full of the eager fear of someone watching history happen. To Edmund's surprise, a few servants had gathered near the well. They did not approach, but they watched. Not with celebration. With the strained attention of people who understood that what happened to a lord's son could happen, in smaller ways, to anyone.

Maud stood among them, hands folded, face composed. When Edmund met her gaze, she gave a single slow nod. Not farewell as a tragedy, but farewell as an instruction: go, and do not be swallowed.

Edmund mounted and felt the familiar strength of the horse beneath him. The animal shifted, impatient to move, unaware of the human meaning draped over its shoulders. Edmund's breath steamed faintly in the cool air. He looked up at the keep's walls, at the narrow windows like blind eyes. Somewhere behind those stones his father sat at a table, signing orders, pressing his ring into wax, shaping lives with the same certainty he had used to cast Edmund out.

Edmund could not decide which hurt more: that the Earl had done it, or that he had done it so easily.

He rode out through the gate without ceremony. The portcullis did not crash behind him. No dramatic sound marked the end. The gate simply remained, and the road opened, and the fields stretched on as they always had. That was exile: not a thunderclap, but a quiet shift in what you were allowed to call home.

The village lay a short distance down the slope, smoke rising from chimneys, roofs hunched against the sky. Edmund slowed his horse as he passed the edge. He saw a few familiar faces turn toward him, people who had spoken to him in low voices when he came without his father's men. Some lifted hands, hesitant. One old man bowed his head not in servility but in recognition. A woman clutching a basket watched him with a guarded expression that softened slightly as he rode by.

He wanted to stop, to speak, to tell them something true. But the steward's terms echoed. Not to interfere. And he could almost feel the keep's gaze on his back, the invisible reach of the Earl's authority.

So, he rode on.

By midday the keep was no longer visible. The land rolled gently, hedgerows dividing fields like stitched seams. The road was rutted, still soft from recent rain. A cart passed him, its driver giving a cautious greeting when he saw

Edmund's clothes were better than a common man's, but not so fine as a lord traveling with escort. Edmund returned the nod and felt the strange in-between of his new state: too noble to be unremarkable, too cast out to be secure.

As the day lengthened, he became aware of how much of his life had been held up by other hands. Food had appeared when he was hungry. Doors had opened. Beds had been made. Now each need rose like a practical threat. Where would he sleep? How far could coin stretch? What kind of man was he when no one was required to obey him?

A thin wind moved across the fields, carrying the smell of wet soil and distant woodsmoke. It brushed his face like a touch meant to comfort, but it did not. It reminded him of the hall's narrow windows, of banners stirring reluctantly, of the sense that the world beyond the keep's walls was shifting in ways no crest could command.

He rode until dusk, then found a small inn by the roadside, more a farmhouse with ale than a true hostelry. The owner eyed him carefully, weighing his accent and his cloak. Coin decided the matter. Edmund was given a corner of the common room near the hearth, not private, but sheltered enough to close his eyes.

He lay there with his bag under his head and listened to the room's voices. Men spoke of crops and rents. Someone complained about a cough that would not leave. Another swore he had heard from a traveler that sickness was spreading in France, that towns there were closing their gates. The words were thrown into the air like harmless gossip, met with laughter and superstition, someone spitting for luck.

Edmund stared at the low rafters stained with years of smoke and thought of his father's certainty. Order. Duty. Survival.

Outside, the wind shifted again, sliding around the inn's corners and finding the cracks like fingers. Edmund pulled his cloak tighter and felt, for the first time, the full shape of his uncertainty.

He had rejected his inheritance. He had done it with conviction, with words that sounded clean in a stone hall.

Now, in the rough warmth of an inn that smelled of ale and damp wool, with strangers laughing at distant rumors, Edmund understood that exile was not only being sent away.

It was being sent into a world that did not care why you had been right.

Chapter 3

A Different Kind of Land

The road out of Dorset did not change all at once. The hedges were still hedges, the mud still clung to the horse's fetlocks, and the sky still had the same low English temper that could not decide whether to grant sun or rain. What changed was Edmund's relationship to every mile. Each village he passed was no longer something he owned by birthright or could influence by his father's seal. It was simply a place that might feed him, refuse him, rob him, or ignore him.

He learned quickly how thin a modest sum could become when every need had a price.

In the first days he traveled as he had always traveled, with the unconscious expectation of safety. He kept to main roads, slept where coin bought him a corner by a hearth, and listened with half an ear to talk that was meant to fill silence. But his ear sharpened. He found himself watching how men measured strangers, how quickly a smile turned into suspicion when someone's accent did not match the lane they stood on. He watched how the poor moved through alehouses like ghosts, careful not to ask for too much space.

At one inn a tinker with soot under his nails spoke of ports on the southern coast where ships had come in wrong, too quiet, as if the sea had returned them empty. The men at the table laughed him down. Someone said, "We are not Italians, are we?" as if distance were a charm. They drank to England's stubbornness. Edmund drank too, though the ale tasted sour, and he thought of the way his father had waved sickness away with the same contempt he reserved for anything he could not command.

Another night a farmer complained that a peddler had refused to enter his house, had slept in his cart out in the rain rather than share a room. "Mad," the farmer said, spitting into the rushes. "Thinks breath itself carries death."

Edmund kept his face still and asked, carefully, "Where had he come from?"

"London way," the farmer said, then shrugged. "Or so he claimed. All roads lead to lies."

London way. The phrase lodged in Edmund's mind like grit. The world was wider than his father's keep had ever admitted, and wider meant porous. Rumors did not respect county lines.

He rode east because the steward's pouch, though modest, was not nothing. It was enough to choose direction. Dorset held his father's shadow. Every mile near Harrow Keep risked becoming an argument again, and Edmund had no desire to fight a battle already lost. Essex, by contrast, was a word he knew mostly through maps and casual talk of wool and marshlands, of villages growing fat off trade that moved toward London's hungry mouth. It was far enough to feel like a beginning, close enough to remain within a world whose language and laws he understood.

As the weeks passed, the land subtly shifted beneath him. The hills softened. The fields grew broader and more crowded with work. Villages lay closer together, their churches rising like stubborn knuckles from the earth. The roads were busier too, carts creaking with goods, drovers moving cattle in slow reluctant lines, men with knives at their belts traveling in pairs as if the world had grown less friendly than it pretended.

Edmund's horse began to show the wear of constant travel. So did Edmund himself. His cloak grew stained at the hem, his boots cracked at the seams, and the clean edges of his identity blurred. More than once an innkeeper eyed him as if trying to decide whether he was a gentleman down on his luck or a thief dressed in stolen cloth. Each time, coin resolved the question, but coin also dwindled.

He began to look for land not as an idea, but as a necessity.

He had imagined, in Dorset, that leaving would be an act of moral clarity. He had not imagined the daily arithmetic of survival. How much oats cost. How quickly a night's shelter could swallow a day's worth of money. How humiliating it felt to bargain with a man who knew you had no other option.

Yet each humiliation burned away another layer of inherited ease. Edmund found, to his surprise, that he did not resent it as much as he had feared. There was a strange honesty in having to ask, to weigh, to choose.

He reached a larger village near the edge of a broad stretch of workable land, not far from a road that carried merchants toward London. It was not a town, but it had the beginnings of one:

a small market square, a smithy whose hammer rang from morning to dusk, and a mill whose wheel churned steadily in the river's patient flow. The smell of bread and tanned leather mingled in the air. Men shouted prices. Women argued over fish. Children ran between carts, quick as rats.

Edmund dismounted near the alehouse and tied his horse with care. He stood for a moment and simply watched. No one bowed. No one stepped aside because of his name. They did not know his name. He was only another man with a horse and travel-worn clothes.

He went first to the reeve, because he had learned that land did not belong to the earth so much as to the men who claimed authority over it. The reeve's house sat near the church, solidly built, with a small, enclosed garden that suggested comfort. The reeve himself was a thick-bodied man with a wary face. His eyes took in Edmund's cloak, his accent, his hands.

"You're not from here," the reeve said, not a question.

"No," Edmund replied. "I'm looking to buy."

The reeve gave a short humorless laugh. "Buy what?"

"A tract of land," Edmund said, and forced himself not to let the word tract sound like something spoken by a lord who believed the world was divided into portions for his choosing. "Enough to farm. Enough to build a house. I have coin."

"Coin runs out," the reeve said, and leaned back as if the conversation amused him now. "What then?"

Edmund met his gaze. "Then I work."

That answer shifted something. Not trust, but a crack in the reeve's assumption. He looked Edmund over again, slower this time, as if seeing the difference between a man who claimed virtue and a man who might actually dirty his hands.

"You'll find land," the reeve said, "but it will not be the land you want. The best fields are held already. Lords and abbeys. Men with papers. Men with swords."

"I don't need the best," Edmund said. "I need enough."

The reeve's mouth twitched. "Enough is a dangerous word. Everyone wants enough."

He sent Edmund to speak with a local landholder whose holdings were not grand but spread enough to have a few awkward corners, strips of land that did not fit neatly into profitable fields. Edmund found the man in a yard behind a barn, arguing with a tenant over a broken fence. The landholder was older, his hair thinning, his clothes good but not fine. He looked tired in the way men did when their wealth was not inherited but managed day by day, always at risk of slipping.

When Edmund introduced himself, he did not give the name Harrow. He said only, "Edmund," and watched carefully what that did. It did nothing. The man nodded, waiting.

They walked the land together the next morning. It lay just beyond the village, a patchwork of usable ground and stubborn difficulty. A low slope that could be ploughed if one worked it. A strip near the river that flooded in hard rain. A small copse that might provide wood if tended. The soil was decent, not rich. The location was what mattered. Close enough to market that surplus could be sold, far enough from the village center that a man might live without constant eyes on his door.

Edmund listened as the landholder spoke. He asked questions not as a formality but because he needed the answers. Where did the water run in winter? Which neighbors were inclined to dispute boundaries? Who collected what dues?

What did the church expect? Each question felt like another thread binding him to reality instead of ideals.

At the end of the walk, the older man halted near a half-collapsed fence and said, "You've no family with you."

"No," Edmund said. "Not yet."

The landholder's eyes narrowed slightly. "Why come here? There are easier places to waste coin if that's what you mean to do. Plenty of men buy land thinking they'll become lords by spring. By harvest they're begging."

Edmund considered lying. It would have been simpler. But something in him resisted simplicity now. "I left home," he said. "I won't be going back."

The man studied him, then spat into the grass. "A fallen son, then."

"Something like that."

"Or a proud one," the man said.

Edmund felt the sting of it because there was truth in the accusation. Pride had been part of his defiance. Pride and disgust and a need to be clean of his father's world. But pride did not plough a field.

"I'm not looking to play at goodness," Edmund said. "I'm looking to live. And I'd prefer to live without grinding other people into dust."

The older man gave a small snort as if the sentiment were foolish, then looked away toward the river. For a moment Edmund thought he would dismiss him. Instead, the man said, "This strip floods. You'll lose planting some years."

"Then I'll plant something that tolerates wet," Edmund said, surprising himself with the steadiness of it. He had been reading the land as they walked, imagining what could be done rather than what could be extracted.

The landholder's gaze returned to him. "And the dues?"

"I'll pay what's required," Edmund said. "I'm not asking for exemption. Only the right to work and to be left alone."

They bargained, because that was how the world moved. The older man pushed for more. Edmund countered. Each coin weighed against the next month's needs. At last, they settled on a price that felt like a bruise. Edmund handed over the pouch and watched the older man's fingers disappear into it with practiced speed.

The agreement was written later in the reeve's presence, on parchment that smelled of animal and ink. Edmund signed with a hand that did not shake, though inside him something did. Not fear of the land, but the quiet terror of finality. A signature was not an idea. It was commitment. It was a door closing behind him.

When it was done, he walked back alone to the edge of his new holdings. The afternoon light lay across the uneven ground, catching on wet patches near the river and turning them into dull mirrors. The wind moved through the grass in small waves. It smelled of water and turned soil, of smoke from the village hearths. For a moment it brought back the cold corridor of Harrow Keep, Maud's trembling voice, the steward's careful terms.

He was truly away now. Not visiting rebellion, not making a point that could be withdrawn when it grew uncomfortable.

He crouched and picked up a handful of soil. It was darker than he'd expected, damp beneath the crust. It clung to his fingers. He rubbed it between thumb and forefinger, feeling grit and life. There was something grounding in the touch, something that did not care about names.

Behind him, the village's noises carried on the air: a distant hammer, a shout, a dog barking. Life. Ordinary, stubborn life.

Edmund stood with dirt on his hands and looked over the land he had bought with the last of his father's coin. He did not feel triumphant. He felt exposed. A man could be kind here, perhaps. A man could be fair. But fairness did not stop storms. It did not stop hunger. It did not stop sickness if sickness truly was moving, carried on roads and breath and unseen creatures that slipped between walls.

Still, he thought, he could build something better than what he left. If not a refuge from what was coming, then at least a place that did not teach cruelty as law.

He turned toward the village and began to walk, not as a lord returning to his hall, but as a man going to meet the people whose lives were now tied to his in ways title could not protect.

The next morning Edmund went back to the village before the sun had burned the mist off the river. He had slept in the alehouse again, not out of comfort but out of necessity; the small house on his land was more idea than shelter, a place in his mind where a roof would someday stand. When he stepped outside, the air smelled of damp thatch and last night's smoke, and the road was already marked by cart ruts freshened with mud.

He found the men first, because men were easiest to find. They were in the fields, bending and straightening in a slow rhythm that matched the waking day. A boy walked behind an ox, tapping its flank with a stick and looking bored in the way children looked when labor was the shape of their childhood. A woman at the hedge line gathered fallen branches into a bundle that would be carried home and counted as fuel as carefully as bread was counted.

Edmund approached without announcing himself, because he had learned on the road that the quiet approach made people less defensive than the lordly one. He stopped at the edge of the nearest strip of worked land and watched long enough to see who led and who followed. He noted the way eyes flicked toward him and then away, measuring his clothes, his posture, the fact that he came alone.

A man with a sun-browned neck straightened and wiped his hand on his tunic. He was not old but worry had already settled into the lines around his mouth. "You're the one bought the flooded strip," he said. It was not accusation, but it carried the weight of gossip already moving faster than Edmund could.

"I did," Edmund replied. "Edmund."

The man hesitated, as if waiting for a surname that would tell him how deeply to bow. When none came, he swallowed and offered, "I'm Walter. Walter Thorne."

Edmund held out his hand before he could overthink it. Walter stared at the gesture as if it were another kind of trap, then wiped his palm again and took it. His grip was firm, callused. The contact was brief, but Edmund felt something in it that he had not felt in Harrow Keep: the simple fact of being touched by someone who did not need to pretend they were not a person.

"I'm not here to give orders," Edmund said. "I'm here to ask questions. And to work, if you'll have me."

Walter's eyebrows rose. He looked past Edmund, as if expecting a rider or a retinue to appear and reveal the joke. "Work?"

"I've no mind to starve on principle," Edmund said, and tried to make it sound like plain truth rather than a performance of humility. "I'll need help building. I'll need to learn what grows well here. And I'll pay fairly for labor. Not in promises."

The word fairly made Walter's mouth tighten. People were cautious of kindness the way they were cautious of sudden quiet in a forest. Kindness could be bait. It could be the soft part of a trap.

"Talk to the reeve," Walter said at last, falling back on the safe answer. "He'll tell you what you can and can't do."

"I've spoken with him," Edmund said. "He told me enough to know the rules. I'm asking about life. Which bits of land always go sour. Which neighbors quarrel. What the river does when winter breaks."

Walter's gaze shifted. Behind him, two other men had slowed their work, listening openly now. They did not pretend not to watch. Their faces were guarded, but there was curiosity under it, and something else: the wary hope of people who had been disappointed too often to trust the shape of hope.

Walter spat into the soil and rubbed the back of his neck. "Winter floods, you'll lose anything you put near the bank," he said. "But the wet'll grow you good reeds, if you're clever. For thatch. And beans don't mind damp so much. Barley'll rot if you plant it too low."

Edmund nodded, storing it away. "Will you show me?"

Walter let out a short breath, half laugh, half disbelief. "Show a lord his mud?"

"Show a man his mud," Edmund corrected.

That was when the first crack in the village's suspicion widened. It did not become trust, not yet, but it became a story they could not fit neatly into the old categories. A man with a horse, a man who could read and sign his name, standing with dirt under his nails and asking how beans grew.

Walter led him to the edge of Edmund's strip, where the ground sloped toward the river and the grass thickened with damp. He pointed out the line where last year's flood had left pale debris caught in the hedge. He showed him where the soil turned heavy and sticky, where a boot could be swallowed if you stepped wrong in spring thaw. Edmund crouched, touched the earth again, and this time he imagined more than survival. He imagined thatch bundles stacked and dry. He imagined a small kitchen garden up on the higher ground. He imagined a ditch dug proper, a channel coaxed into carrying the water where it was wanted, not where it pleased.

By midday Edmund had a hoe in his hands. Someone had brought it out half as a joke, and then the joke had stalled when he took it without offense. The tool's handle was worn smooth from other hands. Edmund's palms were not soft from idleness, but they were not shaped by constant labor either. The first hour made itself known in blisters that burned under his grip. He did not stop. Pain was honest; it asked nothing but endurance.

A woman came to the field's edge with a basket of bread and cheese, and she watched him as though expecting him to tire, to throw the tool down and retreat to his coin. She was broad-shouldered, her hair tucked beneath a scarf, her eyes sharp with the quiet authority of someone who had kept a household alive through lean seasons.

"That'll break you," she called, nodding at the way he used the hoe.

Edmund straightened, breathing hard, and tried to smile without looking foolish. "Then tell me how not to break."

She hesitated, then stepped forward and took the hoe from his hands with the confidence of someone used to taking what is needed. "You're fighting it," she said. "You can't fight earth. You guide it."

She showed him how to set the blade, how to lean his weight instead of muscling through. Her hands moved with practiced ease. The soil turned. The furrow opened clean.

"What's your name?" Edmund asked.

She eyed him. "Alice Hobb."

"Alice," Edmund repeated, as if fixing it into memory mattered. "Thank you."

She handed the hoe back. "Don't thank. Just learn. If you're set on living here, you'll need to."

That afternoon Edmund did something that made people stare harder than his labor had. He spoke of the coming harvest, not as an accounting to be squeezed, but as a shared problem.

"I've no granary yet," he admitted, standing with Walter and Alice and two others near the hedge line. "And I've no wish to build one alone when the weather turns. If we wait until the grain is cut, we'll be stacking it under the sky."

Walter scratched at his beard. "We've the church barn," he said. "But Father Griffiths'll want his share for the space."

"I'll speak with him," Edmund said. "And I'll pay what's fair. But I'm thinking beyond storage. If my land yields, and I have surplus, I don't want it sitting while a neighbor's children eat thin porridge."

There was a silence, the kind that came when a man said something that sounded like a dream. Alice's expression did not soften, but her eyes sharpened, as if she were trying to see the trick in it.

Edmund continued anyway, because he had learned that courage was sometimes only continuing after a room went quiet.

"In Dorset," he said, and felt the familiar tightening in his chest at the name of home spoken like a wound, "I watched men lose everything because one field failed. Here, if we set aside a portion when the harvest is good, a common store, then when a winter comes hard, we don't have to decide who deserves hunger."

Walter's gaze flicked to the others. He looked uncomfortable, not with greed, but with the danger of being seen to agree. "That's not how it's done," he said, voice low.

"No," Edmund replied. "It isn't. That's why people die when luck turns."

A younger man, Thomas, spoke up reluctantly. Edmund had noticed him earlier for his limp, the way he kept working despite it, jaw clenched as if pain were an old companion. "If you set aside grain," Thomas said, "someone'll say it belongs to them. The reeve'll say dues. The landholder you bought from'll say rights. The sheriff's men'll sniff it out like dogs."

Edmund nodded. Thomas was not being difficult; he was being accurate. "Then we do it openly," Edmund said. "We keep accounts. We agree together what is set aside and why. If dues are owed, we pay them. But we do not let fear turn us into animals who tear at each other the moment the cupboard thins."

Alice made a quiet sound, not agreement, not mockery. Something between. "And who keeps these accounts?" she asked.

"I will," Edmund said. "And anyone who wants to see them may. I can read and write, yes, but I won't use that to hide behind ink. If you cannot read, I will read it aloud."

That was another crack. The village had men who could scratch their name, a reeve who could sign documents, a priest who could read Latin he barely understood. But the idea of a landowner reading accounts aloud to those who could not read was strange enough to unsettle even those who wanted to believe him.

They did not agree in that moment. People rarely agreed quickly to anything that threatened the usual order. But they listened, and listening was the first bond.

Over the following weeks Edmund's land became a place people stepped onto without being summoned. Not in crowds, not as a march, but in small ordinary ways. Walter came with a spade and helped Edmund mark where a ditch could be dug to guide floodwater. Alice arrived with a bundle of reeds and showed Edmund how to bind them for a temporary roof over the small lean-to he built first. Thomas, limping, taught him how to set stones so they held rather than shifted under frost.

Edmund paid them. Not with the delayed, grudging coin of a lord who treated wages like charity, but promptly, counting it into their hands. Once, when Walter refused an extra penny Edmund pressed at him for working past dusk, Edmund said quietly, "Take it. Or I'll spend it on ale and make myself useless tomorrow."

Walter stared at the coin, then at Edmund's blistered hands, and finally took it with a grudging shake of his head. "You're strange," he said, and it was almost fond.

The warmth that grew around Edmund's holding was not the warmth of wealth. It was the warmth of shared work and meals eaten from the same loaf. One evening Alice brought a pot of stew and insisted Edmund eat before he collapsed into sleep on his half-built pallet. Edmund offered coin. She refused with a glare.

"You'll pay by not dying," she said. "Dead men don't finish houses, and they don't plant beans."

He laughed, surprised by the sound of it. It felt rusty, unused. "Agreed."

After she left, Edmund sat in the lean-to with the stew's heat in his belly and listened to the village beyond his land. Dogs barked. A child cried and was hushed. Somewhere a man argued with his wife, the words blurred by distance until they became only the shape of worry.

He thought of Harrow Keep's stone hall, of servants holding their breath while he fought with his father. Here, people spoke. They complained. They laughed. They corrected him when he worked wrong. They did not treat him like a banner to fear.

And because of that, Edmund felt the first true bond tighten around his life: not the bond of lineage, but of names learned and hands known.

It was not peace. He could already sense the edges of it fraying where others watched. He saw the reeve's narrowed eyes when he passed, saw the way certain men in the market looked at Edmund's growing circle as if it were a threat disguised as neighborliness. He heard a muttered remark once, thrown like a stone, about a man who tried to make peasants forget their place.

But in the evenings, when the work was done and Walter and Thomas and Alice sat on the ground near Edmund's lean-to, sharing a loaf and a little ale, the mistrust eased enough for stories to be told. Not heroic stories. Small ones. A winter when the river froze and a cow had to be dragged from the ice. A summer when the wheat had grown so tall it looked like gold before the storm flattened it. A child's fever that took two siblings in a week, years back, leaving a mother silent for months.

Edmund listened more than he spoke. He learned the village's old pains and small triumphs. He began to understand that fairness was not an idea to announce; it was a habit to practice until it became ordinary.

And yet, every now and then, a traveler's name slipped into conversation. London. Dover. Calais. A merchant who refused to shake hands. A peddler who would not sleep in a crowded room. A rumor that sounded too much like the ones Edmund had heard on the road, the ones men laughed at until they stopped laughing.

The wind off the river came cool at night, sliding under the lean-to's roof and brushing Edmund's face as he lay awake. It carried the smell of water and earth and distant smoke. He told himself it was nothing more than the usual English weather. He told himself he had time to build, time to make this place solid.

But as the bonds between him and the village tightened, Edmund could not help thinking of how easily bonds could become chains when fear arrived.

For now, though, there was work to do. There was land to coax into yielding. There were people whose names he now knew well enough to worry for.

And for the first time since he rode out from his father's gate, Edmund felt something that was almost like belonging.

By late summer the lean-to on Edmund's strip had become something that could almost be called a house. Not a lord's hall, not even a proper cottage by village standards, but four walls that did not flap in the wind and a roof that did not drip directly onto his face when the rain came hard off the river. The thatch was uneven, and the packed earth floor held the prints of boots like memory, but it was shelter earned by blister and stubbornness.

People came to it the way they came to a place that was beginning to matter.

Walter arrived most mornings with news that moved faster than the river: which fence had fallen, which cow had wandered, which child had been caught pinching apples from the priest's small orchard. Alice came less predictably, usually when she had decided Edmund was about to do something foolish, like set a beam without bracing it first or dig a ditch too close to the soft bank. Thomas came when his leg allowed, limping in from his own strip with a quiet grimness that made his rare smiles feel like coin.

Edmund paid as promised. He read aloud what he wrote down, even when it felt awkward, even when the words seemed too small to carry the weight he was trying to build: three days' labor, one penny each, an extra farthing for work done in rain; reeds bundled and brought, a loaf exchanged, not counted as debt. It was not generosity he performed for praise. It was a habit he forced himself into until it felt less like a statement and more like the only sensible way to live.

That was what unsettled people most.

It began with glances. The kind that slid away when Edmund looked up, as if eyes could be caught and punished like theft. A man in the market who had once nodded now stared at Edmund's hands as if expecting them to be clean and soft, then seemed faintly offended when they were not. A woman who bought eggs from Alice spoke less freely when Edmund passed, her mouth tightening, her basket held a little closer to her hip.

Edmund noticed because he had learned to watch people the way he watched weather.

One afternoon he went into the village for nails and a length of rope. The smith's yard was hot and metallic, the air thick with the smell of soot and sweat. The smith, a broad man named Hugh, had warmed to Edmund at first, not out of affection but out of interest. A man building needed iron. Iron meant coin.

Today Hugh's face was guarded.

"You're wanting more again," Hugh said, not accusing, but weary, as if Edmund's requests were a sort of inconvenience to the natural order.

"I'll pay," Edmund replied, setting coin on the anvil's edge. "Same as before."

Hugh glanced at the coin without moving to take it. His eyes flicked toward the lane, where two men stood pretending to examine a cart wheel while watching the smithy. One of them was the reeve's nephew, a narrow-faced fellow with a habit of smiling without warmth.

"It's not only about paying," Hugh said quietly, leaning closer so the sound of the hammering would blur his words. "You've got folk talking."

Edmund's stomach tightened. "Talking about what?"

Hugh hesitated, then shrugged as if he wished he did not know. "About you making the others restless. About you paying too quick, too fair, like you're trying to buy hearts. Like you're making a show of it."

"A show," Edmund repeated. The word tasted wrong. He thought of Maud pressing bread and a worn silver coin into his hand as if it were a secret kindness. There had been no show in that corridor, only necessity and fear. "I'm building a life, Hugh. That's all."

Hugh's mouth twisted. "Aye. But you're building it in a way that makes other men look bad. Not just here."

Edmund followed his gaze past the smithy yard, toward the road that led out to the holdings beyond the village. Beyond those fields were other strips owned by men who did not live among the people the way Edmund did. Men who visited when rent was due, who left their bailiffs to do the ugly work so their own hands could stay clean.

On his way back to his land Edmund saw one of those men.

Sir Aldwin Ferre, a minor knight with more pride than land, was riding in from the west with two men at his back. Their horses were sleek, their bridles well kept. Sir Aldwin's surcoat was stained by travel, but it still bore a faded device stitched across the chest, the sort of ornament that announced, even in mud, that he was not to be spoken to casually.

He pulled up near the village green where a few children were chasing a hoop. The children stopped as if a string had been yanked and backed away, eyes wide. Sir Aldwin watched them, then looked toward Edmund as if Edmund were another bit of refuse on the road.

"Master Edmund," he called, stressing the title as though tasting its inadequacy. "Or is it Lord

Edmund today? I hear you've taken to calling yourself simply a man."

Edmund slowed but did not bow. "Sir Aldwin."

The knight's smile did not reach his eyes. "You're settling in, then. Digging, building, eating from the same pot as the folk who ought to be kept in their places."

The words were spoken loudly enough to carry. Men nearby pretended not to hear, but their bodies angled toward the exchange, alert and hungry for it. Conflict was a kind of entertainment when work had worn a man down.

"I'm living," Edmund said evenly. "And I find it easier to live among those I depend upon."

Sir Aldwin clicked his tongue as if disappointed. "Depend upon. There's the poison in it. You speak like they hold you up, like you're one misstep away from falling without them."

"I am," Edmund said, and surprised himself with the bluntness.

Sir Aldwin's brows rose. "So, the Harrow boy has grown humble. Or has he grown desperate?"

A few of the onlookers shifted, uneasy. They knew Edmund had come from somewhere important; it was in his accent and in the shape of his manners, even dulled by travel and labor. But the name Harrow was not commonly spoken here, and Edmund had not offered it. To have it thrown out now felt like being stripped in public.

Edmund held Sir Aldwin's gaze. "If you mean to mock me, do it plain. If you mean to threaten me, do it plain. I've no taste for riddles."

Sir Aldwin's smile widened slightly, a sign of teeth rather than friendliness. "Threaten? No. I'd have to consider you worth the trouble." His eyes slid past Edmund, toward the village and the fields beyond, measuring. "I came to see what kind of trouble grows when a man decides the old order is optional."

Edmund heard the careful wording. Not only insult, but reconnaissance. Sir Aldwin was not alone in his curiosity; he was simply the one arrogant enough to voice it.

"You've seen enough," Edmund said. "Go back to your lands."

Sir Aldwin laughed softly. "My lands are not the only ones watching. You think you can keep men loyal with kindness. You think you can make them forget what they owe."

"What they owe," Edmund echoed. "And what do you think is owed, Sir Aldwin? Obedience? Fear?"

Sir Aldwin's face hardened. "I think it is dangerous to teach a man he deserves more than he was born to."

Edmund felt the old anger stir, the same anger that had filled the stone hall at Harrow Keep until his father's eyes went cold and final. "It is dangerous," he agreed. "Dangerous to those who profit from keeping him small."

The knight's cheeks colored. For a moment Edmund thought Sir Aldwin would strike him, and perhaps he thought it too, because his hand moved toward the pommel of his sword before stopping. There were too many eyes. A knight drawing steel in the village over words would make a story even Sir Aldwin could not control.

Instead, Sir Aldwin leaned forward in the saddle, lowering his voice just enough that Edmund had to step closer to hear. "You don't understand what you've stepped into," he said. "Men like you start fires. You tell the folk there's another way, and then when winter bites, when hunger comes, when a fever takes a child, they will remember your words and they will expect miracles. When you fail them, they'll turn. And they won't turn on you alone."

Edmund's throat tightened. "Is that a warning?"

Sir Aldwin's eyes were flat. "It's amusement, mostly. But if you're clever, you'll stop before you force men of worth to intervene."

He sat back and raised his voice again, letting the village have the ending. "Enjoy your little experiment, Master Edmund. Try not to drown when the river rises."

He spurred his horse and rode on, his men following, hooves thudding over the packed earth. The children did not resume their game until he was out of sight.

Edmund stood for a moment, feeling the heat of eyes on his back. When he turned, people looked away too quickly.

Walter found him later, near the ditch line by the river. Edmund was knee-deep in mud, trying to set a small barrier of woven branches to guide water away from the lowest patch. Walter watched him for a moment with a troubled expression.

"I saw Ferre," Walter said.

Edmund kept working. "And?"

Walter spat into the mud. "And now folk'll talk more. Not because he spoke. Because he bothered to come at all."

Edmund pushed a branch into place, hands slick with river silt. "Let them talk."

Walter's jaw tightened. "You don't understand how talk works. Talk's like mice. Quiet until it isn't. Then it's everywhere and you can't catch it."

Alice arrived not long after, carrying a bundle of reeds. She set them down harder than she needed to and looked from Edmund to Walter.

"You've stirred them," she said bluntly.

Edmund straightened, wiping mud on his trousers. "By paying you on time?"

"By making it look easy," Alice replied. "By making it look like a man can be treated decent and still work."

"That's the point," Edmund said.

Alice's eyes were sharp, but there was worry beneath. "Aye. But it makes other men nervous. And when men like that get nervous, they start telling themselves stories that make them feel in control."

Walter nodded, grim. "Already heard one," he said. "Down at the alehouse. Said you've got money because you stole it. Or because you're running from something. Said you came here to hide."

Edmund felt a coldness creep into him. Not fear of the lie itself, but recognition of the shape of it. He had heard that shape before, in Dorset, when his father spoke of disorder as if it were a disease. He had seen it on the road, men laughing at rumors of sickness because laughter was easier than admitting vulnerability. People needed a reason that fit their world. When something did not fit, they made it fit by force.

"Let them think what they like," Edmund said, but his voice lacked conviction.

Alice studied him. "You keep thinking you can outwork this," she said. "Like if you dig enough ditches and read enough accounts aloud, folk'll stop being afraid of what you mean."

"What I mean," Edmund repeated.

Walter looked away toward the village, where smoke rose thin from chimneys. "You mean change," he said quietly. "And folk don't like change unless it comes with bread in the same hand."

Edmund looked down at his mud-caked hands. He had wanted to build something better, something steadier than the harsh order he had fled. He had imagined resentment as something that belonged to lords and bailiffs, to men like his father who guarded power with clenched fists.

He had not imagined it would seep in from the edges like damp, quiet at first, then stubborn, then everywhere the stone met the earth.

That night, lying under his uneven roof, Edmund listened to the wind moving along the riverbank. It slipped through the gaps in the thatch and made the reeds whisper together like low voices.

He could not tell whether the sound was only weather, or the beginning of something else: the village murmuring in its sleep, the talk spreading from mouth to mouth, the first thin threads of resentment tightening as his little experiment began to look, to those who feared it, less like kindness and more like a threat.

Chapter 4

The Quiet Unease

The talk did not arrive in the village like a messenger with a sealed letter. It came the way weather came, first as a shift in the air that made men glance up from their work without knowing why.

In the days after Sir Aldwin's visit, the road seemed busier. That might have been Edmund's imagination, sharpened by the sour taste of being named and measured in public. Or it might have been that the harvest season drew wagons as blood drew flies, and people with goods to sell moved sooner, anxious to get coin before the first frosts tightened the lanes. Either way, strangers passed more often at the edge of the fields, and with them came stories.

Edmund began to notice who stopped at the alehouse and who did not. The ones who dismounted and drank were usually the loud ones, men who believed the world was exactly as large as their own hunger. The ones who kept moving, who took water and left without sitting, were the ones whose eyes never settled, whose hands hovered near their mouths as though they feared what the air might carry.

Walter brought him the first of the new rumors while Edmund was splitting damp wood behind the house. The log resisted, heavy with river moisture, and the axe bit with a dull sound. Walter watched a moment, then said, too casually, "Heard from a carter out of Colchester. Says there's sickness on the coast."

Edmund paused with the axe half raised. "Which coast?"

Walter shrugged, as if direction did not matter and yet mattered enough that he did not want to say it plainly. "South. Over the water, too. Says ports are turning ships away."

Edmund set the axe down and wiped his hands on his trousers. The mention of ports made his mind pull up old scraps of talk from the road, and behind those scraps, the shape of something worse: the stories of silent ships that drifted in wrong. He had dismissed them then as distant, as gossip that did not belong to a man trying to build a roof before winter. Now the rumors had edged closer, like the river's floodline creeping up a bank.

"Who told him?" Edmund asked.

Walter's mouth tightened. "He said a monk. Or a priest. One of them traveling men. Could've been lying for a bowl of stew."

"Aye," Walter said, but he did not look convinced. He spit into the dirt and added, quieter, "Folks don't lie about something that makes their faces look like that."

Alice arrived later with a basket of onions and a stern look that suggested Edmund had been forgetting to eat again. She set the basket down on his rough table and said, "There were two strangers in the square. Said they wouldn't sleep indoors."

Edmund frowned. "Who were they?"

"Cloth men," she replied, peeling an onion with practiced speed. The knife flashed and disappeared again. "One had a wagon. The other walked beside, like he didn't trust wood to keep him safe. Wouldn't drink from a shared cup. Wouldn't touch coin without spitting on his fingers after."

Edmund felt a prickling at the base of his neck. "Did they say why?"

Alice's eyes flicked up to his, sharp and searching. "They said there's death in the towns downriver. Called it a swelling sickness. Said men get knots under the arms, in the groin, and then they're gone."

She said it plainly, without superstition, but the words had the heavy simplicity of a blow. Edmund's mind supplied images he did not want: skin stretched too tight, darkened patches, bodies twisted as if even death had been uncomfortable. He had never seen such things, not with his own eyes, yet his imagination, fed by travelers' half-whispered tales, made them vivid.

"And what did the village say?" he asked.

Alice snorted. "What villages always say. 'God's will.' 'Foreign curse.' 'Not here.' Hugh laughed at them and called them fox-sick. Father Griffiths said we ought to pray for the souls of those in distant places and be thankful for our own health."

"And you?" Edmund asked.

Alice's knife paused. For the first time she looked less like a woman scolding him into eating and more like a mother watching the sky for a storm. "I said," she answered, "that men don't refuse a roof unless they've seen something that makes a roof feel useless."

That night Edmund went to the alehouse himself, not for ale, but for ears.

The room was thick with the smell of sweat and spilled drink. Rushes on the floor had been trampled into damp rot. Men leaned close together, voices rising and falling like a single creature breathing. As Edmund entered, a few heads turned. Some faces softened with the familiarity he had built by sweat and coin paid on time. Others tightened, still holding the shape of Sir Aldwin's contempt as if it had branded them.

Walter was at a table near the hearth, Thomas beside him, leg stretched out stiffly. Alice sat with two women, her back straight, her eyes moving across the room the way a guard's eyes moved, never resting too long. Edmund took a bench near Walter and let the heat of the fire settle into his bones.

A stranger sat at the far end, a man with road dust ground into his boots and a strip of cloth tied around his wrist as if it were a charm. He was speaking loudly, enjoying attention. The words rose above the general murmur.

"I tell you, I saw it with my own eyes," the stranger insisted, slapping the table hard enough to make cups jump. "A whole house nailed shut.

Not by thieves, not by soldiers. By the neighbors. Like they were sealing in a nest of rats."

Someone laughed uneasily. "Nailed shut? For what?"

"For sickness," the stranger said, and spat, as if he could spit the thought away. "A family took ill, and the reeve ordered them shut in. Said it was the only way. But you could hear them inside. Crying. Scratching. Begging for water."

A low murmur ran through the alehouse, discomfort rippling even among the men who wanted to treat everything as entertainment. Edmund felt Walter's shoulder tense beside him.

"Where was this?" Edmund asked, not loudly, but with a tone that carried. The stranger's eyes turned toward him.

The man looked Edmund up and down, taking in the better cloth, the steadiness. "Down Kent way," he said. "Or near enough. Can't remember the village name. Doesn't matter. Could be any of them soon."

Father Griffiths, who had been drinking watered ale at a small table with the reeve, lifted his head. The priest's face was flushed with warmth and self-importance. "Men see what they wish to see on the road," Father Griffiths said.

"And they bring tales to frighten honest folk so they might be bought a meal."

The stranger bristled. "I don't need your meal, priest. I've coin."

"Coin buys lies too," Father Griffiths replied with a thin smile. "You speak of sickness as though it is a wolf at the door. England has endured fevers since Adam. We are not punished more than our fathers were."

The reeve nodded, eager to stand with authority. "Aye. We're not some crowded port," he added. "We've clean air. Good water. God's grace."

Edmund watched the way the room leaned toward that reassurance. It was not stupidity. It was hunger for certainty. Men wanted the familiar world back, the one where fear had names you could recognize and fight.

He felt Thomas shift, heard the quiet scrape of his cup. Thomas did not speak often in crowds, but when he did, it was usually because the weight of silence had become too much.

"My sister's boy died of fever three years back," Thomas said, voice rough. "We didn't nail the house shut. We sat with him and watched him go. That was God's grace too, Father. Doesn't mean I want to sit and watch again."

Father Griffiths's smile faded. "Mind your tongue."

"I mind it," Thomas replied, jaw clenched, "because I've got to live with it. Do you?"

The reeve gave a sharp look, as if already annoyed by the hint of dissent. "Enough," he said. "We've work tomorrow."

The stranger, seeing his audience slip, leaned forward again, hungry to hold them. "You want more? I'll give you more. There's talk of a ship in the south, came in quiet as a dead thing. Whole crew blackened. Rats pouring off it like water. And the officials, what did they do? Unloaded it. Because coin must move."

A few men crossed themselves. Someone muttered, "That's foreign nonsense."

Edmund felt his stomach tighten. The image was too close to the older rumors he had heard on the road out of Dorset, the ones he had tried to shrug off. He realized, with a cold clarity, that these stories were not changing. They were repeating. Different mouths, same shape. Like the same wind touching different fields.

He looked around the room and saw not just curiosity, but irritation beginning to coil beneath it. Men did not like being made to feel small. They did not like the idea that their work, their harvest, their careful little lives could be undone by something that traveled in a stranger's breath.

Walter leaned toward Edmund and spoke under the noise, his voice tight. "This kind of talk makes folk restless."

"It makes them afraid," Edmund murmured back.

Walter's eyes were hard. "Aye. And fear's got to go somewhere."

Edmund watched Father Griffiths and the reeve return to their murmured conversation, already smoothing the edges of what had been said. He watched the men laugh too loudly, trying to chase the chill from their spines. He watched one young mother at the door shift her child higher on her hip, the movement protective and automatic.

When Edmund left the alehouse later, the night air felt sharper than it should have. The wind off the river had turned cool, carrying the smell of wet reeds and distant smoke. He walked back to his small house along the dark lane, listening to the quiet as if it might speak.

Behind him the alehouse noise faded, swallowed by the village's sleeping walls. Ahead, his roofline rose crooked against the sky. It should have been comforting, proof of work done and shelter earned.

Instead, Edmund found himself thinking of what Sir Aldwin had said, not as a threat now, but as a bitter truth: when men expected miracles and did not get them, they turned their hunger into blame.

The road brought goods. The road brought coin. The road brought strangers to tell stories that could be dismissed by day and returned to by night, when a child coughed in the dark and the sound seemed suddenly too loud.

Edmund stepped inside his house and barred the door out of habit more than fear. He stood for a moment in the dim, listening to his own breathing. Then he went to the small table where he kept his accounts and his rough notes about planting and ditching and repairs, and he found his hand hovering as if it wanted to write something else entirely.

Not sums.

Not plans.

A list of names, perhaps, of the people whose faces had begun to change when the rumors entered their minds. Or a list of things he could do that would matter if the stories were true.

Outside, the wind moved along the thatch, making the reeds whisper together again, and the sound no longer felt like weather.

It felt like the road speaking in a language that had finally learned his name.

In the morning Edmund woke to the sound of the river changing its voice.

It was not louder, not swollen with rain. It was the opposite, a thin quick chatter over stones that had been hidden for weeks. When he stepped outside, the air had the brittle clarity of early autumn, and the river smelled less like mud and more like cold metal.

The village was already moving. Smoke rose from chimneys in straight pale lines, and the first carts creaked toward the square. Men called greetings with the same half-hearted cheer they always used when they wanted the day to behave. If the rumors from the road had planted anything, it lay beneath their words like a seed in dark soil.

Edmund washed at his basin and dressed, then went to the edge of his strip where the ditch line ran. He had learned to begin the day by looking at what he could not afford to overlook: water, earth, animals. A man could lie to himself about many things. The land did not join in.

Near the barrier of woven branches he had set, something gray floated at the river's edge. At first, he thought it was a clump of reeds torn loose. Then it turned slightly with the current and showed a pale belly and stiff legs.

A rat.

It was large, its fur slicked down as if it had been dragged. One eye was filmed over. Its mouth hung open, teeth showing. Edmund crouched and watched it bump gently against the bank, caught and released by the little suck of the current.

Rats died all the time. The river took what it took. Still, he found himself scanning the bank for others, for any sign of a bigger kill, a dog's work or a trap. He saw none. Just this one, alone, as if it had chosen to die where water could carry it on.

He straightened slowly. His hands felt clean and useless in the cold air. For no good reason he did not want to touch the carcass, did not want to drag it away and toss it into a pit. He backed up a step as if giving the thing room.

Behind him he heard a footstep and turned.

Thomas stood a few paces away, leaning on the handle of a spade like a staff. His limp was worse in the cold. He followed Edmund's gaze to the rat and made a face.

"River's full of them," Thomas said.

"Is it?" Edmund asked.

Thomas shrugged. "Always has some. They get into the grain stores, the stacks. When the nights turn, they come closer."

Edmund wanted to accept that and be done with it. He nodded once. "Have you seen more than usual?"

Thomas hesitated. He did not like being the one who sounded nervous. "Saw two in my shed yesterday," he said finally. "In daylight. That's not usual."

Edmund looked toward the village. Daylight rats, floating rats, and the road's tales sitting in men's mouths like bitter herbs.

"Set traps," Edmund said.

Thomas gave a short humorless laugh. "We always set traps."

Edmund watched the rat bump the bank again. He had a sudden memory of the stranger in the alehouse, the tale of a ship in the south. Rats pouring off like water. It was only a story, and yet he could not shake the sense that stories and signs were beginning to line up like fence posts in a row.

He left the riverbank and walked toward the village.

At the edge of the square, Hugh the smith was already at his forge, hammer ringing, the sound bright and normal. Edmund took comfort in it until he noticed something else: a dead hen lay near the butcher's block, its neck twisted at an odd angle as if it had been flung.

Two boys stood over it, arguing.

"It just fell over," one insisted.

"You wrung it," the other accused, the kind of accusation children made because cruelty was a language they learned early.

Edmund stepped closer. The boys quieted, watching him with that quick calculation children had when deciding whether an adult was threat or ally. Edmund crouched and looked at the hen. There was no blood, no sign of a bite. The comb had turned dark at the edges.

"How long has it been there?" Edmund asked.

The older boy shrugged. "This morning. It was fine last night. Mother says it stopped eating."

Edmund glanced at the butcher, who was lifting a carcass onto his block. The man's hands were red to the wrists. He gave Edmund a brief look and then looked away again, uninterested.

"Chickens die," the butcher said, as if that settled it.

"They do," Edmund agreed. He straightened. "Has it happened often?"

The butcher's jaw tightened. He hated questions; questions were a way of taking control from a man who had built his authority on refusing to explain himself. "Two this week," he said grudgingly. "If you're buying, buy. If not, stop hovering."

Edmund did not buy. He kept walking.

Near the alehouse a cart had stopped, and a man in a brown cap was arguing with the innkeeper's wife. He was a cloth trader by the look of his bundles; his fingers stained with dye. His voice was tight, his face drawn.

"I told you, I'll pay for the stall and the water," he said. "I'm not sleeping inside."

The innkeeper's wife threw up her hands. "Then don't," she snapped. "But don't come here scaring my guests with your nonsense. If you've got fleas, keep them in your wagon."

The trader flinched at the word fleas as if it were an insult to his honor. “Not mine,” he said. “That’s the point.”

Edmund slowed, listening without appearing to listen. The trader’s eyes flicked toward him, taking in his posture, his clothes. He made a small respectful nod, not fully sure what Edmund was. That uncertainty told Edmund the village was already talking about him again, sorting him into categories.

“What’s happened?” Edmund asked, stepping closer.

The trader’s mouth tightened. He glanced around the square, lowering his voice. “You’ve not heard?”

“I hear plenty,” Edmund said. “I’m asking what you know.”

The trader hesitated. He had the look of a man deciding whether to speak truth and be mocked, or to stay silent and feel complicit. “There’s sickness in the towns,” he said at last. “Not fever like usual. Fast. Ugly. Swellings. Men drop in the street. Women, too. Children. Priests won’t go near the houses.”

The innkeeper's wife made a scornful noise. "That's down the road. We're not down the road."

The trader looked at her the way one looked at someone who insisted a roof would stop rain from falling. "The road comes here," he said. "The road comes everywhere."

Edmund felt the words settle into him with a weight he could not dismiss. "Where did you come from?" he asked.

"From Chelmsford way," the trader said, then added quickly, "Not that it matters. It's moving. Folk are shutting gates, barring doors. Some say it came by ship to the south, and now it's in the air."

"In the air," the innkeeper's wife repeated with a snort. "Then we're all dead already, aren't we?"

The trader did not rise to the bait. He only looked tired. "Maybe," he said quietly. "Or maybe not, if you stop packing yourselves together like sheep."

He turned away, ending the conversation by withdrawing from it. He began to untie his bundles with careful hands, keeping his sleeves pulled down, as if fabric could be a shield.

Edmund watched him for a moment longer, then moved on. He found Walter by the churchyard gate, speaking with another farmer whose face was drawn.

Walter saw Edmund and stepped away, as if wanting to keep the talk from being overheard too widely. "You hear about the Holts?" he asked.

Edmund's stomach tightened. "What about them?"

Walter jerked his chin toward the lane that led out of the village. "Gone. Packed in the night. Left the door hanging open and the fire cold. Took their cow. Took what they could carry."

Edmund frowned. The Holts were not close to him, but he knew them by sight: a man with narrow shoulders, a wife with a baby always on her hip, two older children who ran wild. "Why?"

Walter's eyes darted toward the church as if fearing the priest might overhear. "People say they had kin in another village, and word came. Sickness there. Or maybe just rumor. Either way, they didn't wait."

Edmund felt a chill that had nothing to do with autumn. People did not leave good land and familiar neighbors without a reason that felt like a knife at the throat.

“Did anyone stop them?” he asked.

Walter gave him a look that held both irritation and fear. “Stop them? With what? A blessing? A rope?” He spat into the grass. “Folk are already saying it’s selfish. That if the Holts were sick, they’ve carried it with them. And if they’re not sick, they’ve abandoned us out of fear.”

Edmund heard it clearly: the first shape of anger forming around uncertainty. Not yet a mob, not yet a target, but the beginning of the need to make fear somebody’s fault.

He looked toward the church door. Father Griffiths stood there, speaking with the reeve. The priest’s hands moved in small assured gestures, as if he could smooth the air with them. The reeve’s face was set in the hard patience of a man who believed that if he acted bored enough, danger would become bored too.

Edmund started toward them, because he could not help himself. Walter caught his sleeve.

“Don’t,” Walter said, low.

Edmund paused. “Why not?”

Walter's grip tightened. "Because they'll hear you and decide you're the reason folk are frightened."

Edmund looked down at Walter's hand on his sleeve, then back up at Walter's face. He saw something he had not seen at first when he arrived in Essex: not only wariness, but the instinct to protect the fragile peace they had. Walter had children. Walter had a roof that depended on staying on the right side of men with authority.

"I'm trying to prevent—" Edmund began.

Walter cut him off. "You can't prevent what you can't name. Not here. Not with them." He nodded toward the priest and reeve. "They want it quiet. Quiet means it isn't real."

Edmund let out a slow breath. He understood the impulse. He also understood the danger of it. Silence did not keep sickness away. Silence only made it easier for it to arrive unchallenged.

He turned away from the church and walked toward his small house, his mind busy with small observations that felt suddenly like pieces of a larger pattern. Rats in daylight. A dead hen without a bite. A trader refusing to sleep indoors. A family leaving in the night. Men bartering for certainty in the alehouse and priests calling it foreign nonsense, as if distance were a wall.

At his table he sat and forced himself to write, not accounts, but notes the way he had begun to do on the road when rumors first scratched at his attention. He wrote down what he had seen. The rat at the river. Thomas's daylight rats. The butcher's two dead hens. The cloth trader from Chelmsford way and his talk of swellings. The Holts gone.

The act of putting it in ink steadied him and frightened him at the same time. Steady, because it turned unease into something ordered. Frighten, because order made it harder to dismiss.

He heard footsteps outside and looked up.

Alice came in without knocking, as she often did now. Her basket was empty, but her face was full.

"You look like a man counting ghosts," she said.

Edmund held up the sheet of parchment. "Signs," he replied.

Alice stepped closer and squinted at the writing. She could not read, but she could recognize the seriousness in the way his hand had moved. "What is it?"

"Things people are pretending not to see," Edmund said.

Alice's mouth tightened. "They see," she corrected. "They just don't want to speak it aloud. Speaking makes it real."

Edmund looked toward the narrow window. Outside, the wind moved through the reeds along the riverbank. It had shifted again, carrying a faint smell that reminded him of old smoke.

"I don't think it cares whether we speak," he said.

Alice was quiet for a moment, then nodded once. "No," she said. "It never does."

She looked at him hard. "What are you going to do, Edmund?"

He wished he had an answer that would satisfy both of them. An answer that would not sound like panic, or like the kind of dangerous talk Walter feared. He tapped the parchment gently with his finger.

"I'm going to keep watching," he said. "And I'm going to start acting as if the road's stories might be true, even if the reeve laughs."

Alice's eyes narrowed. "Acting how?"

Edmund thought of the trader's words. Stop packing yourselves together like sheep. He thought of the alehouse, shoulders pressed close, shared cups, laughter forced loud to beat down dread. He thought of the village's habit of touching, of crowding, of living as if closeness were safety.

He looked back at Alice. "Carefully," he said.

Outside, somewhere in the lane, a child coughed. It was a small ordinary sound. It should have meant nothing at all.

Edmund's hand tightened on the parchment anyway, and he understood with grim clarity why the signs were so easy to ignore. Each one, alone, could be explained away.

It was only when you placed them side by side that they began to look less like accidents and more like footsteps, approaching.

Edmund began with the smallest things because the smallest things were the only ones he could move without permission.

He took the next day and did not go to the fields. That alone would be noticed, and he could already imagine the village's private accounting: the strange lord who worked like a tenant, now suddenly idle. But he was not idle. He was thinking, and thinking had become its own kind of labor.

He walked to Walter's strip first, early enough that the mist still clung to the hedgerows like wool caught on thorns. Walter was mending a broken hurdle, hands quick, shoulders set as if he could hold his world together by force.

Walter straightened when Edmund approached. "You're up early."

"I need to speak with you," Edmund said.

Walter's eyes flicked toward the lane. No one stood there, but Walter looked anyway, the habit of a man who had learned that listening ears were as common as sparrows. "Speak, then."

Edmund kept his voice low. "I want lime. If we can get it."

Walter frowned. "For the soil?"

"For washing," Edmund said. "For hands. For boards. For anything that can be scrubbed. I want water set aside for it, too, not drawn from the same bucket everyone drinks from."

Walter stared as if Edmund had suggested building a wall to keep out the sky. "What's this about? That cloth man's tales?"

"It isn't only him," Edmund replied. He did not unfold the parchment he'd written on, but he felt it in his mind, each note like a nail. "Rats in daylight. The Holts gone. More dead fowl than usual. Men refusing to sleep indoors. These are not proof, but they are warnings."

Walter's jaw tightened. "Warnings of what? You still won't say the word."

Edmund hesitated, because Walter was right. The word was a spark. It could fall into dry fear and become fire. "Sickness," he said at last. "Something that spreads fast, if the road talk is true. Something you won't see until it's already in your house."

Walter's gaze held a kind of stubborn exhaustion. "We've always had sickness."

"Yes," Edmund said. "And we've always had men pretending it was only God's mood, so they didn't have to change a thing."

Walter looked away, toward his field, toward the brown stubble and the turned earth waiting for winter. "If I start talking like you, folk will say I've gone soft in the head."

"I'm not asking you to talk," Edmund said. "Not in the alehouse. Not to the reeve. I'm asking you to help me do what we can quietly."

Walter let out a slow breath. The air steamed. "Quietly," he repeated, as if tasting whether it was possible.

Edmund nodded. "If you know anyone who can get lime, send them to me. I'll pay."

Walter's mouth twitched. "You always say that like it's the cure for everything."

"It isn't," Edmund said. "But it's what I have."

Walter studied him for a long moment, then gave a small reluctant nod. "There's a man comes through sometimes, sells chalk and salt. Might have lime. I'll ask when I see him."

Edmund felt a thin thread of relief, quickly followed by the knowledge that relief was dangerous. "Thank you."

Walter returned to his hurdle, but before Edmund turned away, Walter said, without looking up, "You should speak to Alice. She'll tell you what folk are whispering when you're not there."

"I will," Edmund replied, though he already knew. Alice always knew.

He found her behind her cottage, splitting kindling with efficient anger. She struck the wood as if punishing it for being stubborn.

"You're wearing a hole in that log," Edmund said.

Alice did not smile. "Maybe it deserves it."

Edmund stepped closer, careful to keep his posture plain. He had learned that any hint of lordliness, even softened, made people either bristle or bow, and neither was useful now. "I want to set some rules on my land," he said. "Simple ones."

Alice paused with the hatchet held low. "Rules," she repeated. "That'll go down well."

"Not village rules," Edmund said. "Mine. For anyone who comes to work here, or to share food. I want washing before eating. No shared cups. No sleeping ten to a room if it can be helped. And if someone takes ill, I want them kept apart."

Alice's gaze sharpened. "Kept apart," she said. "Like animals."

"Like someone we want to keep alive," Edmund answered. "If it's nothing, then we've wasted water and offended a few proud men. If it's something, it may be the difference between one house suffering and the whole village burning through its people."

Alice lowered the hatchet and wiped her hand on her skirt. "Folk won't like it," she said, as if Edmund still did not understand how deep dislike could go.

"I know," Edmund replied. "But I can't listen to a trader speak of houses nailed shut and tell myself it's a tale for beggars. I can't watch rats creep in daylight and pretend it's only the season. Not anymore."

Alice's expression shifted, not softening, but revealing the worry beneath her hard shell. "You're frightened," she said.

Edmund wanted to deny it, because denial was the first comfort men reached for. He forced himself to be honest. "Yes."

Alice nodded once, as if honesty mattered more than bravery. "Good. Fear's not always a curse. Sometimes it's the only thing that keeps you from walking into a ditch in the dark."

She glanced toward the lane. "But I'll tell you what fear does too. It makes people cruel. They'll do anything if they think it keeps death away. Anything."

Edmund thought of Walter's words in the alehouse: fear's got to go somewhere. He felt that sentence settle again, heavier now. "That's what I'm afraid of," he admitted. "Not just sickness."

Alice set the hatchet down and stepped closer. Her voice lowered. "They're saying things about you."

"I know," Edmund said. "What kind of things today?"

"That you're bringing bad luck," Alice replied, matter-of-fact, like naming weather. "That you've come here because you're cursed, or because you've angered your father so badly the devil himself followed you out of Dorset. Some say you're trying to turn folk against their betters. Some say you're trying to gather them to you so you can rule them when the reeve's tossed aside."

Edmund felt a slow cold spread under his ribs. He had expected mockery. He had not expected the way the village was already shaping him into a story that could be used.

"Who says this?" he asked.

Alice gave him a look that suggested he was being childish. "Everyone and no one. Mouths that whisper when they think you can't hear. Men who sit in the alehouse and want a reason they feel uneasy that isn't the truth."

Edmund nodded, forcing his breath to stay steady. "Then I'll give them less to whisper about. I'll do this quietly, as I told Walter. If anyone asks, I'll say it's for winter. For cleanliness. For common sense."

Alice's eyes did not leave his. "Common sense gets men killed too," she said. "Because common sense is what they did last year, and the year before, and it didn't save their babies then either."

Edmund looked away toward his small house in the distance, the uneven roofline that still smelled faintly of reeds and damp earth. It was not a fortress. It was barely shelter. But it was his, and what he did there was his choice.

"I'm going to build a second lean-to," he said. "Away from the main house. Not much. Just enough space to keep someone separate if they fall ill. A place to bring food and water without putting half the village in the same air."

Alice's mouth tightened. "You think folk will come to you when they're sick?"

"I don't know," Edmund admitted. "But I'd rather have the place and not need it than need it and have nothing but prayers."

Alice was quiet for a moment, then nodded toward the woodpile. "I'll help you," she said.

Edmund turned back to her. "You don't have to."

Alice snorted. "Aye, I do. Because if you build it wrong, it'll fall on someone, and then we'll have a broken back on top of whatever sickness is coming." She picked up the hatchet again. "Fetch me the straight branches. Not those crooked ones you like to pretend are good enough."

By midday Edmund had rope stretched between stakes, marking out where the small shelter would stand. He kept it downwind of his house, closer to the river where the air moved. He did not know if air mattered, only that the trader's talk of breath carrying death had lodged in him like grit.

Thomas came limping up with a bundle of old boards on his shoulder. "Walter said you're building another shed," he called. "Figured you'd make it fall down if no one watched you."

Edmund took the boards and set them carefully aside. "Thank you," he said.

Thomas grunted. "Don't thank. Tell me what this is really for."

Edmund met his eyes. Thomas was wary, but he was not a fool. He had lived with pain long enough to know denial was a luxury. "If someone gets sick," Edmund said, "I want a place to keep them apart. To care for them without putting everyone else at risk."

Thomas's face tightened. For a moment Edmund saw the memory there, the sister's boy he'd mentioned in the alehouse. "So, you believe it," Thomas said.

"I believe enough to prepare," Edmund answered.

Thomas shifted the weight off his bad leg. "Folk will say you're expecting it," he muttered. "Like you called it."

Edmund felt the trap in that, the way preparation could be twisted into accusation. "Then let them," he said. "I'm done pretending fear is worse than the thing itself."

Thomas studied him, then looked toward the village as if weighing how much trouble a man could afford. "If it comes," he said slowly, "Father Griffiths won't know what to do. He'll talk about sin and foreign punishment. The reeve will talk about keeping order. And the men in the alehouse will talk about who's to blame."

Edmund's throat tightened. "I know."

Thomas spat into the dirt. "Then you'd best be careful what you build," he said, voice rough. "Not just boards. Not just ditches. You build a place folk come to in fear; you'll be blamed for whatever happens there. Even the good."

Edmund looked at the marked-out ground, the stakes and rope and the small pile of boards. He imagined a cough in the night, a swollen throat, a mother begging for help, and the village watching from behind half-closed doors, hungry for a reason that could be stabbed or burned.

"I know," he said again, and heard how thin it sounded.

As the afternoon wore on, Edmund boiled water in an iron pot until steam filled the small house. He added vinegar, what little he had, and scrubbed his table and the bench and the handle of his knife until the wood looked raw. He washed his hands until his skin reddened, and still he felt as if something unseen clung beneath his nails, not dirt but possibility.

When he stepped outside near dusk, the river wind brushed his face and carried with it the scent of smoke from the village hearths. It should have been comforting, that ordinary smell of supper and evening.

Instead, it reminded him of the faint strange smoke-scent he'd noticed in the wind more than once now, as if the air had passed over something burning far away and brought only the memory of it.

Alice stood near the new stakes; arms folded against the chill. "You can scrub till your fingers bleed," she said. "Still won't change what folk are."

Edmund watched the reeds bend along the riverbank, whispering together. "No," he said. "But it might change what happens when the first cough becomes more than a cough."

Alice followed his gaze. "And if it doesn't?"

Edmund's answer came after a beat, because he would not offer her comfort he did not believe. "Then we'll find out what else spreads faster than sickness," he said. "And whether this village can survive it."

Somewhere down the lane, a dog began to bark, sharp and insistent, then fell quiet as suddenly as it started. The hush that followed felt too complete, as if the world itself had paused to listen.

Edmund turned back to the half-built shelter and the scrubbed table and the water pot still steaming. He had been cast out of stone halls and old authority. Here he had built something warmer, something human.

Now he was trying to build, with rough boards and simple rules, a defense against what could not be seen.

And the cruelest part was that he could already feel the village's eyes on his back, measuring not whether he was right, but whether he would make a convenient reason if he was.

Chapter 5

The First Blame

It began with a cough that would not settle.

Not the usual wet hack of autumn damp, nor the polite throat-clearing men did when smoke sat too long in the lungs. This cough was small at first, almost easy to ignore, a child's sound carried between the walls of a cottage the way laughter often was. It might have remained only that, a brief discomfort in a season full of them, if the village had not already been listening for something worse.

Edmund heard of it from Alice before he saw it himself.

She came to his door near midday, her cheeks raw from wind, her scarf pulled tight. She did not waste words on greeting. "It's the Miller's girl," she said, stepping inside as though the cold itself followed her. "Joan."

Edmund set down the hammer he'd been using to fix a loose board on the new lean-to. The shelter stood half-finished, its crude frame already accusing him of having thought too far ahead. “How old?” he asked.

“Six,” Alice replied. “Maybe seven. The one with the gap in her teeth. Always running too close to the wheelhouse, like she’s trying to be taken.”

Edmund pictured the child at once. He had seen her more than once near the river, hair escaping its ties, face smudged with flour. A bright creature, the kind that seemed to pull life toward her simply by moving through it.

“What’s wrong with her?” he asked, though the question felt foolish. Wrong could mean anything. Wrong could mean a stomach ache, a fever, a fall.

Alice’s mouth tightened. “Fever,” she said. “Hot as a hearthstone. Her mother says she won’t eat, won’t drink, just lies there like she’s listening to something none of us can hear.”

Edmund felt his stomach contract with a familiar coldness. “Has Father Griffiths been told?”

Alice let out a short sound that might once have been a laugh. “He’s been told. He said to bring her broth and pray. Same as always.”

Edmund stepped past Alice toward the door. "Take me to them."

Alice's hand shot out and caught his sleeve. "Edmund," she said, and for the first time her voice held something close to pleading. "If you go now, with all your talk of washing and keeping apart, folk will say you've been waiting for it. That you wanted it."

He looked down at her hand, at the tension in her fingers as though she could hold him in place by force. "A child is ill," he said quietly.

"Aye," Alice said. "And the village is ill in the head already. Don't feed it."

Edmund's jaw tightened. The warning was not wrong. He could feel it in the way people had begun to watch him, the way preparation had become suspicious simply because it suggested the world might change. But he also knew the other truth, the one the road had taught him: illness did not pause because a man feared gossip.

"I'm going," he said.

Alice released his sleeve with a sharp motion, as if offended by her own concern. "Then don't go like a lord," she snapped. "Go like a neighbor.

And for God's sake, don't start ordering them about."

Edmund pulled his cloak on and left his tools where they lay.

The mill stood at the river's bend, its wheel turning steady, the sound of it usually as calming as breathing. Today the water's rhythm felt wrong, like a song played too slowly. When Edmund approached, he saw the miller himself outside, shoulders hunched, hands stained white with flour as if he could not rid himself of it. Walter stood nearby, speaking low. Thomas leaned on the fence, face drawn tight, his bad leg stretched awkwardly as though he had forgotten to be comfortable.

The miller saw Edmund and hesitated. It was not friendliness or hostility, but uncertainty, the village's newest habit.

"Edmund," Walter said, a brief nod. His eyes looked tired. "You heard."

Edmund nodded once. "How long?"

"Since last night," the miller answered, voice rough. "She coughed, then she burned. My wife thought it was just chill. But it's… wrong." He swallowed, and Edmund saw the fear he tried to hide. Men were allowed to fear for crops, for rents, for weather. Fear for a child stripped them bare.

"May I see her?" Edmund asked.

The miller's eyes flicked toward the door. He did not want anyone to see his daughter like this, wanted to keep the sickness inside as if walls could hold it. But Walter murmured something, and the miller nodded stiffly.

Inside the cottage the air was thick with heat and stale smoke. A pot simmered on the hearth, sending up a thin smell of onions and something sharp that stung Edmund's nose. The miller's wife sat on a stool by the bed, rocking slightly without noticing she did it. Her hair had come loose, and a smear of flour ran across her cheek like ash.

Joan lay under a blanket, cheeks too flushed, lips dry. Her eyes were half open but unfocused, the gaze of someone staring past the room. When she coughed, her small body jerked as if pulled by string, and then she fell still again.

Edmund stepped closer, careful not to loom. He remembered the stranger's tale of houses nailed shut, the sound of people scratching and begging from inside. He remembered his own half-built shelter downwind, waiting like an unspoken confession.

"Joan," he said softly.

The child's eyes shifted, not quite finding him. Her breathing was fast, shallow. Edmund could see the pulse at her throat, too quick.

The miller's wife looked up at him, eyes bright with tears she refused to let fall. "It came quick," she said, as if defending herself. "She was running yesterday. Laughing. She ate bread and cheese. She was fine."

"I know," Edmund replied, though he did not. He only knew the cruelty of suddenness.

He touched the back of his hand to Joan's forehead. The heat startled him. It was not a gentle fever. It was fierce, unnatural, as if her body had become a kiln.

The miller's wife flinched, and Edmund withdrew his hand at once. He saw her fear shift shape: not only fear for her child, but fear of what the touch meant. Fear that he might carry something with him, or take something away, or be the wrong kind of witness.

"Has anyone else in the house taken ill?" Edmund asked.

"No," the miller said quickly from the doorway. "No one. It's only her."

Edmund's mind ran through possibilities the way he had begun to train it to do. A fever from bad water. Something in the flour dust. An infection from a cut. But the word that kept pushing forward was the same word he had avoided speaking too plainly: sickness, the kind that moved on roads and breath.

"Has she any swellings?" he asked, and watched the miller's wife tense, as if the question itself were obscene.

The woman's mouth worked. Then she pulled the blanket down slightly and showed Edmund the child's neck.

At first, he saw nothing but flushed skin. Then, beneath the jawline, a bulge like a knot stood out, not large, but wrong in a way that made Edmund's skin prickle. Another swelling showed faintly under the arm when Joan shifted, a little mound pressing up like a hidden bruise.

Edmund's throat went dry.

Walter, who had followed him inside, made a quiet sound and turned his face away as if he could avoid seeing by refusing to look.

Thomas stood near the wall, jaw clenched, eyes fixed on the floor. He did not speak. The silence that filled the cottage was heavy enough to crush.

The miller's wife whispered, "What is it?"

Edmund could have lied. He could have said it was a common fever, that children often swelled when glands fought infection, that she would either pass through it or not, as children always did. He could have offered the comfort of uncertainty. But the swelling under the jawline looked too much like the tales, and the fever's heat felt like an answer already given.

"I don't know," he said, choosing honesty even as he felt how little honesty comforted. "But I think we should keep people from crowding in. Let the air move. Keep her water separate. Wash hands often. Boil cloths if you can."

The miller's wife stared at him, and for a moment Edmund saw the flicker of anger behind her fear. How dare he speak of washing when her child lay burning. How dare he offer precautions instead of a cure.

"You speak like those strangers," she said, voice sharp. "Like that cloth man who wouldn't sleep indoors. Are you saying my child is... plague-taken?"

The word plague landed in the cottage like a dropped stone. The miller inhaled sharply. Walter stiffened as if struck.

Edmund felt the room tilt. This was the first time the word had been spoken so plainly here, inside a home with a child's fever pressing against the air.

"I'm saying she is very ill," Edmund replied carefully. "And if it is something that spreads, then a crowd will not help her. It will only make more sick."

The miller's wife's eyes narrowed. "You don't want folk to see," she accused suddenly, and Edmund understood how fear twisted. "You don't want them to know. You've been making talk about sickness, building that shed of yours, scrubbing your table like a monk. You want us all to hide away on your land like frightened hens."

Walter stepped forward. "Martha," he began, voice strained. "That's not fair."

"Fair?" Martha snapped, and her voice rose despite herself, as if her fear needed volume to breathe. "What's fair about a child dying while men talk of washing? Where's Father Griffiths? He should be here. He should be praying over her, not sitting in the churchyard telling folk it's foreign nonsense."

At the mention of Father Griffiths, the miller's face tightened with a different kind of resentment, the old village anger at authority that only surfaced when grief gave it permission.

Edmund looked at Joan again. The child's eyes were open now, but they did not see. Her lips moved slightly, soundless. Her small hand fumbled at the blanket as if searching for something that had slipped away.

"We should get Father Griffiths," Edmund said.

Walter hesitated. "He won't come," he muttered, and then, realizing what he'd admitted, added too quickly, "Not that he won't. Only… he'll say prayers from the door."

Martha let out a broken sound, half laugh and half sob. "From the door," she repeated. "So, God can hear him, but sickness can't."

Thomas spoke at last, voice low and rough. "If this is what they say it is," he murmured, eyes still down, "then prayers won't stop it."

Martha whirled on him. "Don't say that," she hissed, and for an instant Edmund saw how quickly the village might turn on anyone who dared speak what no one wanted named.

Joan coughed again, harder this time, and a faint dark fleck appeared at the corner of her mouth. Martha wiped it away with a cloth, hands shaking.

Edmund backed a step, feeling suddenly intrusive, helpless. He had wanted to be useful. He had built ditches and roofs and bonds with names and shared bread. None of it mattered in this moment, faced with a child's fierce fever and swelling flesh.

He forced himself to speak calmly. "I'll bring clean water," he said. "And vinegar, if you want it. Boil cloths. Keep her as cool as you can without chilling her. And keep visitors out. Not because you should be ashamed, but because if this is catching, the village must not become a single room."

Martha looked at him with a hatred that was not truly for him, but for the fact that he could speak and she could not bargain with what was happening. "Do what you like," she said. "Words won't pull her back if she goes."

Edmund swallowed. He glanced at Walter, at Thomas, at the miller, and saw in their faces the same dawning realization. This was no longer rumor on the road. No longer signs that could be dismissed as season and chance.

This was a child in their own village, burning alive from within.

Edmund stepped out into the daylight. The mill wheel turned. The river ran. The ordinary world continued as if it had not just been wounded. But as he looked back toward the village, he could already feel something shifting there, a collective attention drawn like iron to a magnet.

A child's sickness was not only tragedy. It was a question thrown into the square.

And the village, frightened and crowded with its own helplessness, would not endure a question without demanding an answer.

Edmund returned to his land with two buckets of water slung from a yoke and the sour sting of vinegar soaking through a cloth in his bag. The practical weight should have steadied him. Instead, it made the helplessness sharper, because what he carried felt absurd against the image of Joan's throat swelling under thin skin.

As he walked the lane back toward the mill, he saw people already drifting the same way, not in an orderly line but in the loose, curious gathering that formed whenever something happened that might become story. A woman with a basket paused mid-step when she noticed Edmund's buckets and then watched him too long, as if measuring what kind of man carried water when others carried gossip. Two boys followed at a distance until Edmund turned his head and they fled, laughing too loudly.

By the time he reached the mill cottage again, Walter had managed to keep most people outside. The miller's yard was full of bodies pretending not to crowd, each person angled as if they had simply happened to be passing. Voices kept dropping into whispers and rising again in defiant bursts, like a fire that refused to settle into coals.

Father Griffiths arrived late, breathless, his cheeks pink as if he had hurried but also as if indignation had warmed him. The reeve came with him, walking a half-step behind in the way of men who liked to appear humble while being seen. Father Griffiths lifted a hand as if blessing the air itself and then halted at the threshold of the cottage door.

He did not step inside.

He peered in as though distance were prudence rather than fear. "Martha," he called, voice carrying so the yard could hear him. "Daughter. The Lord tests us in many ways."

From within came Martha's reply, hoarse and raw. "Then let Him test you nearer, Father. Come lay hands on her."

A murmur went through the yard. Edmund watched faces tighten, watched people flinch at the thought of touch. He set his buckets down by the doorstep and did not move closer than necessary.

Father Griffiths's mouth worked as if tasting words he did not like. "We must be wise as well as faithful," he said. "There is no need for panic. Children take fevers. They swell with bad humors. This is not the end of the world."

A man in the crowd spat. Another crossed himself quickly and then dropped his hand as if ashamed of the gesture.

The reeve stepped forward, his voice brisk, managerial. "No one's to go in and out," he said, and pointed at Walter as if assigning him duty. "You, Thorne. Keep them back. We don't need every fool breathing in the same room."

Walter's jaw flexed. He nodded anyway. Edmund saw the flicker in Walter's eyes: resentment at being ordered by a man who had not lifted a finger until now, mixed with relief that someone was taking charge. Authority was a salve, even when it stung.

Edmund lifted his voice, careful not to make it sound like command. “The water is here,” he said. “Boil cloths if you can. Wash hands before and after. Keep cups separate.”

Several heads turned toward him at once. The attention felt like stepping into cold water.

A woman, one Edmund had seen in the market but never spoken to, narrowed her eyes. “Listen to him,” she said, not loud, but with a sharpness that carried. “Always with his washing.”

Another voice answered, male, older. “He’s been saying sickness is coming since he arrived.”

“That’s not true,” Walter snapped, but he sounded unsure even as he defended him, as if he feared his own words would be used against him later.

Father Griffiths looked toward Edmund with an expression that tried for pastoral patience and landed on reprimand. “Master Edmund,” he said, stressing the name with brittle courtesy. “You have been stirring anxieties in the village. Now is not the time for more strange notions.”

Edmund kept his face still. "Now is exactly the time," he replied, and the firmness surprised him. "A child is burning with fever and swelling. If this is catching, then comfort will not protect us. Cleanliness might."

A brief silence followed, thick and uncomfortable. People did not like the word might. They wanted certainties that could be held like tools.

Martha appeared at the doorway then, hair wild, her apron smeared. She held the doorframe with one hand as if the wood were the only thing keeping her upright. "Stop talking," she said, voice breaking. "All of you. Either help or go away."

No one moved. Help required knowledge. Going away required admitting fear.

From inside the cottage came a small sound, not a cough this time but a thin, strangled whimper that cut through the yard like a blade. Martha turned back at once, vanishing into the smoke-dark room, and the door swung half shut behind her.

The reeve cleared his throat, irritated by the display of grief he could not control. "We'll do as we must," he said. "We'll keep order. No one's to spread tales in the alehouse. No one's to claim it's plague and send the village into hysteria."

At the word plague, several people shifted as if the ground had moved beneath them. Edmund watched their faces and understood something he had only felt in fragments before: fear did not need instruction. It only needed a name.

Thomas stood near the fence, his body angled away from the crowd, but his eyes fixed on Father Griffiths. "If it isn't plague," Thomas said, voice low, "then why won't you go inside, Father?"

The question landed cleanly. No accusation, no drama. Just a wedge.

Father Griffiths's nostrils flared. "Mind yourself," he said. "I will not be spoken to as if I were a coward by a man who limps because God saw fit to humble him."

A few people made quiet approving sounds. The old logic surfaced easily: suffering as proof of fault, pain as moral measure. Edmund felt something cold move in his chest. This was not only about sickness. This was about what sickness allowed men to become.

Thomas's mouth tightened. "God didn't give me this leg," he said. "A cart wheel did. And it didn't make me cruel."

The reeve stepped between them, palms raised. “Enough,” he said. “We’ve no need for squabbles.”

But the squabble was not the danger. The danger was the way the crowd leaned, hungry for friction, hungry for something to hold.

Edmund bent to lift one of the buckets and carried it inside without asking permission. The heat hit him like a wall. He did not approach the bed. He set the water down near the hearth where Martha could reach it and placed the vinegar cloth beside it. Martha glanced up at him, eyes red and bright.

“I don’t need your rules,” she hissed. But her hand darted toward the cloth anyway, desperate for anything that felt like action.

“I’m not here to rule,” Edmund said quietly. “I’m here to keep more children from lying like this.”

Martha’s lips trembled, and for a moment Edmund thought she might strike him. Instead, she looked away, back to Joan, and her shoulders shook once as if the effort of not falling apart took all her strength.

Edmund left again quickly. He washed his hands outside at the bucket, scrubbing until the skin stung. When he straightened, the yard's eyes were on him.

The crowd had grown.

It always grew. Misery was a bell, and people came to hear it ring even when it made them sick.

A man pushed forward through the bodies, his face mottled with drink though it was barely midday. Edmund recognized him: Rob Baines, a tenant who had laughed too loudly in the alehouse when the stranger spoke of nailed-shut houses. The laughter had never been amusement. It had been armor.

Rob pointed at the cottage door, then at Edmund. "So, it's here," he said. "All your talk and look, it's here. You happy now?"

Walter stepped toward him. "Shut your mouth."

Rob did not. He had found something in the air that fed him, a heat that was not courage but permission. "Why'd it start with the miller's girl?" he demanded, voice rising. "Why not with Father Griffiths's house? Why not with the reeve's? Why a child who's never done wrong?"

A woman answered quickly, as if the thought had already been sitting on her tongue. "Because someone's done wrong for her. That's why. Sin travels."

"Sin," Rob repeated, and spat. "Sin doesn't make swellings."

He jabbed his finger toward Edmund again. "He's the one been talking about sickness. He's the one building that little hut down by the river like he's expecting folk to die in it. He's the one scrubbing and boiling like a monk. He brings in strangers to work on his land, pays them like they're equals, makes a show of it. Maybe this is his doing."

A hush followed, and in it Edmund heard the true shift. It was not that Rob's words were clever. It was that they offered a shape for fear to take. A direction. A face.

Edmund opened his mouth, but the reeve spoke first, voice sharp and relieved. "No one said it was Master Edmund's doing," he snapped, though the protest rang false. He looked at Edmund with a hard calculating gaze, as if weighing whether defending him served order or threatened it. "We are not an unruly pack. We will not turn on our own."

"Our own," someone murmured, and the phrase carried a question under it. Was Edmund their own? He had arrived with coin and strange manners, no kin, no father's backing. He had built bonds too quickly. He had made others look cruel by comparison. That was not belonging. That was disruption.

Father Griffiths raised his voice again, eager to seize control of the story before it chose him. "This is not the time for accusations," he declared. "This is the time for prayer and obedience. Go to your homes. Keep your children in. Do not linger at the mill like vultures."

Rob laughed, short and ugly. "Prayer," he said. "Aye. Pray it doesn't take your house next, Father. Pray from your doorway."

A few people gasped. The sound was not horror. It was fascination. Someone had finally said aloud what many had thought and swallowed.

Edmund felt the air thicken with something more potent than smoke or river damp. The fear had found its voice, and now that it had spoken, it would demand to keep speaking. It would not be satisfied with cautions and boiled water. It would want a reason. It would want a culprit.

He stepped forward into the center of their attention, forcing himself to keep his tone measured. "Listen," he said. "If this is catching, then standing here pressed together will only spread it. Go home. Keep apart as you can. Wash. Boil water. Do not share cups. If you must help, bring food and leave it at the door."

Rob's eyes glittered. "Hear him," he mocked. "Hear him order us about like he's always wanted."

"I'm not ordering," Edmund said, though he knew the distinction would not matter to men who needed him to be something. "I'm asking you to live long enough to see what this is."

A woman at the back began to cry quietly. Another shushed her with a harsh whisper, as if tears were contagious too.

Walter moved beside Edmund, solid and tense. "Go home," Walter barked, finding authority in anger because anger was safer than fear. "Go on. Leave the miller be."

The crowd shifted reluctantly. A few turned away, murmuring. But most did not disperse. They lingered, eyes darting from the cottage door to Edmund's face, then to Father Griffiths's, then to the reeve's. Watching to see who would be named.

Edmund stood very still and realized that whatever happened to Joan, the village had already been infected by something else. A need that was not for healing, but for blame. A hunger for certainty sharp enough to cut.

Behind the cottage door, the child coughed again, and the sound seemed to pull the crowd tighter, not with compassion, but with dread that demanded an outlet.

Fear had found its voice.

Now it needed a target.

The crowd did not break apart the way Edmund had told them to. It only loosened, like a fist opening without letting go.

Men drifted back toward the square in small knots, speaking low, each group a little island of certainty forming in an ocean of fear. Women pulled children by the wrist, not gently now, and the children's protests turned into frightened silence when a mother's grip tightened. The miller's yard remained busy in the way a place became busy when people pretended they were helping but were truly watching.

Edmund stayed near the mill gate with Walter, both of them angled as a barrier, not to keep the village out forever but to stop the crush of bodies pressing into the cottage as if proximity could force a cure.

Father Griffiths still stood at the threshold, hands clasped, lips moving in prayers that sounded more like performance than comfort. The reeve lingered beside him, face set in an expression meant to convey calm authority, though his eyes kept flicking across the crowd as if counting how quickly calm might be outnumbered.

Rob Baines did not leave. He prowled the edge of the yard like a dog that had tasted blood and wanted more. He spoke to anyone who would listen, and even those who pretended not to listen did not move away.

Edmund heard fragments as they passed.

"Foreign sickness."

"God's displeasure."

"Bad air from the marsh."

"A curse on the mill. Too much flour in the lungs."

"Witchwork."

Edmund's jaw tightened at that last one. The word was old, pulled from the same cupboard as charms and whispered prayers and the belief that bad things only happened when someone caused them. It was a way to make chaos personal, and thus punishable.

Walter muttered, "It's starting," as if he had been waiting for the moment a rumor turned into a weapon.

Edmund watched Father Griffiths glance toward them, his gaze sharp despite the sanctimonious set of his face. The priest did not like losing the village's attention. He needed fear to come to him for naming and discipline. But if fear chose its own names, Father Griffiths's power would become irrelevant, and irrelevance was a kind of death for men like him.

A man Edmund recognized as Hugh the smith's brother pushed forward, pale under his stubble. "What do we do?" he asked the reeve. It was not a question of health. It was a question of order. Give us a rule. Give us something to obey.

The reeve lifted his chin. "We do what we always do," he said. "We keep to our homes when we can. We keep clean. We pray."

"Keep clean," Rob echoed loudly, as if tasting the phrase. "That's his talk." His finger stabbed toward Edmund again, and Edmund felt the crowd's attention turn like a weather vane.

Edmund stepped forward before Walter could. He knew Walter's anger, useful as it was, would only sharpen the sense that something was being hidden.

“I said wash,” Edmund replied evenly. “Because filth never helped anyone. It is not my talk. It is sense.”

Rob’s mouth curled. “Sense,” he said. “And you’ve got so much of it, haven’t you? Came in from Dorset, bought land with coin no one’s seen before, started telling folk how to live, started scribbling your little notes like you’re a priest yourself. Maybe you’re the one who brought it. Maybe it followed you.”

The accusation was absurd, yet Edmund felt the way it lodged. It gave the village something solid to point at: an outsider who was close enough to be familiar but strange enough to be blamed without tearing at family ties.

A woman near the back spoke, her voice trembling. “He touched the child,” she said. “He put his hand on her head.”

Edmund stared at her. He had not even learned her name. “I checked her fever,” he said. “I did not harm her.”

“But you went in,” the woman insisted. “And now she’s worse.”

From inside the cottage came another cough, harsher than before, followed by a thin sound that might have been Joan trying to breathe through swelling flesh. Martha's voice rose in a ragged plea and then cut off abruptly as if she had bitten it back.

The crowd flinched, not with empathy, but with the instinctive recoil of people being reminded that the thing they feared was real.

Rob seized on it. "Hear that?" he said. "Hear her choking? And you think scrubbing your table will stop it?"

Walter stepped forward, his face dark. "Rob, shut your mouth before I shut it for you."

Rob spread his hands. "There it is," he said, delighted. "Threats. That's how it starts. He buys you with his coin, and you threaten folk for asking questions."

Walter's eyes flashed. Edmund caught Walter's arm, just above the elbow, hard enough to steady him. Walter shook him off, but he did not swing. He stood breathing through his nose, fists flexing at his sides.

Edmund turned to the reeve, forcing the conversation back to the man who claimed authority. "If you want to protect the village," Edmund said, "send people home. Stop them gathering here. Get water boiled. If anyone else shows fever, keep them apart."

The reeve's expression tightened. He did not like being instructed, especially not by a man the village had not fully decided how to rank. "I will handle my village," he snapped.

"Our village," a man corrected under his breath, and then looked startled that he had spoken. It was the kind of slip that revealed the pressure building in people's minds. Ownership became contested when safety did.

Father Griffiths raised his voice, eager to reclaim the center. "No one is to speak of blame," he announced. "Blame is for God to place. We are to endure."

Rob laughed. "Endure?" He said. "Like the folk in that story, nailed in their house while they scratched at the door? Is that enduring, Father? Or is that dying polite?"

A few people crossed themselves again. Others looked away, as if the image hurt to hold.

The reeve turned sharply on Rob. "Get back," he barked. "You're drunk."

"I'm not wrong," Rob replied, and there it was again, that terrible righteousness fear produced. He leaned toward the nearest cluster of men, speaking quickly now, feeding his argument before anyone could cut it off. "We need to know how it came. We need to know who brought it. You think it just falls out of the sky? Like rain?"

A man answered, uncertain. "Maybe it does. Bad air."

Rob pounced. "Bad air from where? From the road? From strangers? From those who don't live as we do? From them that won't take our bread or share our cups?"

Edmund felt the direction shifting. Not only toward him. Toward any difference that could be made to carry meaning.

He saw Thomas on the edge of the crowd, his face drawn tight with anger that did not have a clean outlet. Thomas looked at Edmund, and in his gaze, Edmund read a grim warning: this will not stop with one name.

By late afternoon, the miller's yard emptied in uneasy waves. Not because fear had calmed, but because it had found places to go. Fear was not satisfied with watching. It needed to move, to search, to pull apart the village's familiar fabric until it found a loose thread it could blame for unraveling.

Edmund walked back toward his land with Walter and Alice, leaving the reeve and Father Griffiths to their brittle pretensions. The lane felt narrower than it had in the morning. Faces appeared at windows and vanished when Edmund looked up. Two children ran past them and then stopped short, staring as if Edmund's shadow might stain them.

Walter spoke first, voice low. "They'll talk all night."

Alice's mouth was a hard line. "They've been talking," she said. "Now they'll do more than talk."

Edmund's throat was tight. "Martha accused me," he said quietly. "Not because she believes it. Because she needs somewhere to put the terror."

Alice glanced at him sideways. "Don't fool yourself," she replied. "Some of them will believe it. Belief is easier than helplessness."

They reached Edmund's small house. The half-built shelter stood downwind, its stakes and crude frame catching the slanting light. It looked less like preparation now and more like a declaration: Edmund expects sickness. Edmund has a place for it. Edmund has been waiting.

Thomas arrived not long after, limping up the lane with a grim urgency. He did not sit. He stood by the door, eyes darting as if afraid to be seen too long in Edmund's company.

"They're saying it's the well," Thomas said abruptly.

Edmund felt his stomach drop. "Which well?"

"The common one by the square," Thomas replied. "Someone said the water tasted strange. Someone else said they saw a man near it last night."

Walter's face went pale under his tan. "A man?"

Thomas swallowed. "A stranger. Or a neighbor they're ready to call a stranger. Depends who's telling it."

Alice exhaled sharply through her nose. "There it is," she muttered. "Poison. That's the story they'll like."

Edmund stared at Thomas. "Who started this?"

Thomas's expression twisted. "Rob's been barking it. But not only him. Others are picking it up. They're saying if it's poison, then it's someone's doing. Someone can be caught. Punished. And then it stops."

Walter's hands flexed at his sides. "It won't stop."

"I know," Thomas said, voice rough. "You know. But they don't want to know. They want to act."

Edmund's mind flashed to the rat at the riverbank, to the cloth trader's tired eyes, to the swollen knot beneath Joan's jaw. Poison in a well did not make swellings like that. Poison did not move from house to house on breath and touch. Poison was a story made to feel clean: one source, one culprit, one solution.

He looked toward the village, where smoke rose straight into the cooling air. In that distance lay Joan's cottage, Martha's raw grief, the reeve's brittle control, Father Griffiths's cowardly prayers.

And now, a new narrative forming in the darkening lanes.

"They'll start asking who has reason," Edmund said quietly. "Who has spite. Who is different."

Alice's eyes were flat. "They always end there," she said. "Different. That's the easiest reason."

Walter looked at Edmund, something like apology in his gaze. "You should be careful tonight," he said. "Stay in. Bar your door."

Edmund felt the bitter irony. He had tried to build a place where doors were not barred against neighbors. Now he was being advised to hide like any frightened man.

"Joan's still alive," Edmund said, more to himself than to them.

Thomas nodded, grim. "For now."

Edmund's hands clenched. "If she dies…"

Alice finished the thought without softness. "They'll need a payment for it."

Silence settled among them, thick and heavy.

Somewhere out in the village, a shout rose and fell, too far to make out words, but sharp enough to raise the hair at the back of Edmund's neck. It was answered by another voice, and then another, not a chorus yet, but the beginning of one.

Edmund turned toward his table inside, where his notes lay, ink drying on paper that suddenly felt useless. He had written signs. He had tried to prepare. None of it had prepared him for the speed with which fear turned outward.

He looked at Walter, Alice, and Thomas, the small circle of people whose names and hands he knew. "If they start hunting for someone," he said, "they'll destroy the village faster than any sickness."

Walter's mouth tightened. "Aye," he said. "But you can't tell a man that when his child's coughing. He won't hear it."

Alice stepped closer to the door, peering out as if she could see trouble coming down the lane like a cart. "They'll go to the well tonight," she said. "They'll stare into it like it can answer them. And then they'll start looking for who to drag to the edge of it."

Thomas shifted his weight, pain evident in the set of his jaw. "And when they start looking," he murmured, "they won't stop with one name."

Edmund barred his door before night fully fell. The wooden beam slid into place with a dull final sound. He hated it. He hated needing it. But as the wind moved through the reeds and carried distant voices up from the village, he understood that the search had already begun.

Not for truth.

For a scapegoat large enough to carry everyone's terror, and close enough to burn.

Chapter 6

The Strangers Among Us

The night did not bring sleep so much as a different kind of waking.

Edmund lay on his pallet with his boots still on, the barred door a wooden weight across his mind. Outside, the wind moved along the river and through the reeds, but under it ran other sounds: a far-off burst of shouting, the quick scatter of feet, then silence that felt arranged. Once, something struck wood in the distance, a hollow thud like a fist against a door. Later, a dog howled and was cut short as if someone had kicked it quiet.

Near midnight he heard Walter's voice in the lane, low and urgent, and then Alice's, sharper, the words blurred by distance. He rose, went to the window, and peered through the narrow gap.

Figures moved along the lane toward the village, not a single mob yet, but men in pairs and threes, carrying lanterns that bobbed like will-o'-wisps. Some carried tools. A shovel. A hook. One had a cudgel slung across his shoulder as casually as if he were going to drive off wolves.

They were going to the well.

They were going to look into dark water and demand it explain itself.

Edmund did not open his door. He could imagine what would happen if he did: heads turning, a sudden hush, the satisfaction of seeing him appear as though summoned by suspicion. Rob Baines would point and say, "See?" And the narrative would tighten around Edmund's throat like a rope.

He waited until the lanterns had gone.

When dawn came it came thin and gray, the sky the color of old wool. Edmund unbarred the door and stepped outside into air that smelled faintly of smoke, though no fire burned near his house. The village lay quiet in the way places lay quiet after a storm, not because nothing had happened, but because people were listening for what might happen next.

Walter came up the lane with his cap in his hand. His face looked older than it had yesterday. He did not meet Edmund's eyes at first.

"They were at the well," Walter said.

Edmund nodded once. "What did they do?"

Walter's mouth tightened. "Talked. Spat. Shouted. Drew up water and made a show of tasting it like they could prove poison by courage. No one died on the spot, so some laughed. But not easy laughter."

"Did anyone claim to have seen something?" Edmund asked.

Walter hesitated, then gave a short nod. "A boy said he saw a shadow by the well after dark. A man, maybe. Then his mother cuffed him for talking nonsense, and then she said it again herself, only louder, like she'd thought of it first."

"And who did they say it was?" Edmund asked, though he could already feel the answer taking shape. Not a name yet. A category.

Walter swallowed. "At first, they threw it at anyone not in the circle. Strangers on the road. Beggars. Then it turned."

"Turned where?" Edmund asked.

Walter lifted his eyes then, and Edmund saw raw fear in them. “Toward the old talk,” Walter said quietly. “The kind folk keep tucked away until they need it.”

Edmund’s stomach pulled tight. “Old talk,” he repeated, because naming it aloud felt like stepping onto ice.

Walter’s gaze flicked toward the village, toward the clustered roofs and the church’s squat tower. “They were saying… that some people don’t drink from the well,” he said.

Edmund stood very still. There were a handful of households in the village who drew water from their own small sources or bought it, not because of poison, but because of custom and caution, because they had learned over generations that a shared well could become a shared grievance.

“You mean—” Edmund began.

Walter cut him off with a tight shake of his head, as if refusing the word might keep it from becoming a blade. “They were saying the Jews keep to themselves. That they don’t share cups. That they wash more than we do. Like it’s wicked.”

Edmund felt a coldness move under his ribs. He had known the Jewish families by sight, if not by closeness. A small community, not newly arrived, not secret, but always slightly apart because the village insisted on difference the way it insisted on boundaries in the fields. A moneylender who kept careful accounts. A cloth dyer with stained hands. A widow who sold candles and spoke politely to everyone and was never invited to weddings. They had lived in the village long enough that children had grown up alongside them, long enough that familiarity should have softened suspicion.

Should have.

"Has something happened?" Edmund asked. "Have they been threatened?"

Walter's expression twisted. "Not yet. Not openly. But the talk's loose now. Folk are remembering things they never cared to remember before."

Edmund looked down the lane toward the village and felt, for a moment, the same helplessness he had felt in the miller's cottage. Not because of a fever this time. Because of a mind turning.

He walked toward the square with Walter a half-step behind him. The village was awake now, but not busy. Market stalls stood half assembled, their owners moving slowly as if work were something done by other people in other times. The air held a strange restraint; voices stayed low, and when someone laughed it sounded wrong, like a tool used for the wrong task.

Near the well a cluster of men stood around as if guarding it. The bucket rope had been hauled up and left wet on the stones. Someone had scattered ash in a rough circle on the ground, not as a ritual so much as a declaration: we were here, we did something. The ash looked like the residue of a fire the village had not yet lit.

Rob Baines was among them, of course, leaning against the well's stone lip as if it belonged to him. His eyes slid toward Edmund when he approached, and something brightened in his expression. Edmund could not tell if it was hostility or relief at having an audience.

"You slept well, did you?" Rob called. "With your clean hands and your locked door?"

Edmund did not rise to it. He looked at the well, then at the men. "Has anyone fallen ill from drinking?" He asked.

Rob's mouth twisted. "Ill? We're all ill, aren't we? If you believe the tales."

A man beside him, one of the reeve's cousins, spoke with false reasonableness. "We're only being careful," he said. "Water's the life of the village. If it's fouled, we have to know."

"You can't know by spitting in it," Edmund replied.

That drew a few bitter laughs. Edmund felt the laughter as hostility pretending to be humor. People were already tired of caution. Caution asked too much patience. They wanted a simpler act.

Father Griffiths emerged from the church then, moving with unusual purpose. He looked as if he had dressed for an occasion, his stole set straight, his hands lifted to call attention. The reeve walked at his side, face tight and guarded, as if he did not like what was being said in the square but feared to silence it too hard.

Father Griffiths stopped on the church steps and raised his voice. "This village will not be led into panic by whispers," he announced. "We will not turn our hands against each other like heathens. We will pray, and we will endure, and we will remember who we are."

A murmur ran through the square. Not comfort. Anticipation.

Father Griffiths continued, and Edmund heard the shift in his tone, the careful way a man steered a crowd without appearing to steer. "There are those among us who do not live as we live," the priest said. "Those who keep strange customs. Those who wash their hands as though water could cleanse the soul. Those who refuse fellowship at our tables, who will not share bread and cup as Christians do."

Edmund felt Walter stiffen beside him.

Rob called out, loud and pleased, "Aye. Those who keep their own."

A few men laughed, sharp as stones striking.

Father Griffiths let the sound settle, then said, "I do not speak to accuse. Only to remind. In times of trial, the Devil seeks cracks in our unity. He whispers distrust. He points at difference and says, 'There is your enemy.' We must be wise."

Wise. The word sounded gentle. It landed like a warning.

Edmund heard the cunning in it. Father Griffiths was not shouting for blood. Not yet. He was laying down a path the village could walk later and tell itself it had only followed guidance. He was offering the oldest comfort of all: that danger came from a person, not from the air, not from the unseen, not from God's indifferent weather.

A woman near the well spoke, voice thin. "The child at the mill," she said. "Is she—?"

Father Griffiths made a pained expression, the face of a man forced to mention unpleasant things. "She suffers," he said. "As children suffer. And we pray for her."

"And if she dies?" another voice demanded, quick and hard.

The question hung in the square, heavy as a stone held over water. Edmund looked around at the faces turned toward the church steps. He saw not grief. He saw bargaining. If a child died, something must be paid. Someone must be made to answer, because the alternative was intolerable: that children could die without reason, without cause, without a hand to strike back at.

Rob stepped forward a pace. "If the well's poisoned, it's someone's doing," he said. "And if it's someone's doing, we can stop it. We can make an example."

"An example," a man echoed, as if tasting the phrase and liking its certainty.

Edmund felt the air tighten. He thought of the Jewish widow with her candles, of the moneylender's careful ink, of the way the village had always accepted their usefulness while resenting their separateness. He remembered small things that had never mattered until now: a muttered remark at a market stall about Christ-killers, a child's rhyme half learned and half forbidden, the way the priest had once spoken of "unbelievers" with a casual contempt that needed no proof.

Old prejudices did not have to be invented. They only had to be awakened.

A man near the edge of the crowd said, not loudly, almost as if speaking to himself, "They don't draw from the well."

Another answered, "They don't have to."

"And they wash," the first man added, and the word wash now held accusation in it, as if cleanliness were a sign of guilt.

Edmund looked toward the lane where the Jewish households lay, not far, close enough to be reached by any man with a cudgel and a story. He felt the beginning of a terrible momentum, the way fear collected itself into purpose.

He leaned toward Walter and spoke low. "Go," he said. "Find Alice. Tell her to warn them. Quietly."

Walter's eyes widened. "If we do, they'll say we're in league."

"Let them," Edmund replied, though he did not believe it was that simple. Nothing was simple once a crowd decided it wanted a target.

Walter hesitated only a moment longer, then turned and moved away through the bodies, head down.

Edmund stayed in the square, watching Father Griffiths's face as the priest looked out over his flock. The priest's expression was composed, almost serene, but Edmund saw the fear underneath it, and the relief too. Fear of sickness he could not command. Relief at finding something he could.

Difference had been named.

Now it could be hunted.

Edmund did not follow Walter with his eyes. He forced himself to keep his gaze on the square, on the shape of the crowd and the way it shifted when certain words were spoken. That was the danger now, not the fever itself, but what the village did with its fear when it could not bear to hold it quietly.

Father Griffiths stepped down from the church steps as if the moment had passed, as if he had not just loosened something that would not tighten again. He moved among the men near the well, speaking in low tones, palms up in calming gestures that looked like mercy and felt like direction.

Rob Baines took the priest's place without being asked. He leaned against the well lip and addressed whoever would listen, his voice pitched to carry but not quite to shout, as if he wanted to appear reasonable.

"We're not saying they did it," Rob said, and a few heads bobbed, grateful for the lie of restraint. "We're saying we can't ignore what's plain. They keep to themselves. They don't share our water. They wash like they're trying to scrub something off their hands. And now a Christian child lies swelling and choking."

A man who had been silent until now, thin-faced and red-eyed, spoke up. "It's not their fault," he said, but his tone made it sound like a question.

Rob's mouth tightened in feigned patience. "No one wants it to be," he replied. "But wanting doesn't change what is."

Edmund moved closer, stepping into the edge of their circle. The reeve saw him and narrowed his eyes, as if bracing for trouble.

"What is plain," Edmund said, voice even, "is that sickness does not choose by prayer. It does not choose by custom. Joan at the mill is ill. That is all you know."

Rob's gaze slid over Edmund like something oily. "And you know so much," he said. "Because you've been expecting it."

Edmund ignored the bait. "Has anyone seen proof of poison?" he asked the group at large. "Has anyone seen a hand drop something into the well? Or do you only have stories passed from one mouth to another until they become certainty?"

A few men shifted uncomfortably. It was easier to talk about proof in the abstract than to admit there was none. But fear wanted motion, and when motion was demanded, proof became a luxury.

A woman at the edge of the crowd, her hair covered, her child clinging to her skirt, said, "My cousin's boy said he saw a light near their lane last night."

"Near whose lane?" Edmund asked.

She hesitated, as if the name itself were dangerous. "Near Isaac's house," she said finally, and the name, spoken aloud, seemed to satisfy something in the air. A man with a name could be pointed at. A lane could be walked down.

"I saw light too," another voice offered quickly, as if not to be left behind. "A lantern moving. They were out late."

"They're always out late," someone muttered. "Counting coin."

The old resentments rose like silt stirred from the bottom of a river. Edmund heard them, the little barbs that had always existed but had been kept dull by habit and trade. Now the barbs sharpened, and the village began to enjoy the sting.

Father Griffiths approached, hands clasped. "Master Edmund," he said softly, as if they were speaking as allies. "You are making this worse."

Edmund stared at him. "By asking for sense?"

"By challenging frightened people," Father Griffiths replied. His voice remained gentle, and that gentleness made Edmund's anger burn colder. “Fear must be guided, not fought. The village needs calm.”

“The village needs truth,” Edmund said.

Father Griffiths’s eyes tightened. “Truth is God’s,” he said, and Edmund heard the meaning beneath: truth is mine to interpret. “What you offer is confusion.”

Rob gave a short laugh. “He always offers confusion,” he said. “He makes folk question. That’s his disease.”

The word disease, used like that, made a few people smile, pleased by their own cleverness. Edmund felt the crowd’s mood tipping, the way amusement could become cruelty without changing its expression.

A man pushed through from the far side of the square, breathless, a strip of cloth tied around his wrist the same way the stranger in the alehouse had worn it days ago. This one was not a traveler. He was from the village, a carter’s brother. His face was pale, and his eyes were bright with the thrill of having news.

“They’re shut in,” he announced. “Isaac’s barred his door. Wouldn’t answer when I knocked. Wouldn’t even open the shutter. Just said through the wood, ‘Leave us be.’”

A murmur ran through the crowd.

"Why bar the door if you've nothing to hide?" someone demanded.

"Because they're afraid," Edmund said, but the words were swallowed by louder ones.

"Because they're guilty," Rob countered at once, too quickly. He pushed away from the well and stood upright, a leader made of drink and certainty. "If we're all to die, we at least deserve to know why. We deserve to know who did it."

"We deserve," another man echoed, and Edmund heard the hunger in it. Deserve was a dangerous word. It turned suffering into entitlement.

The reeve raised his hands. "No one is to touch anyone," he said, but his voice lacked force. He had enjoyed authority when it meant rents and fences and quiet obedience. This was a different kind of authority, one that required courage. The reeve looked toward Father Griffiths as if expecting the priest to take the weight.

Father Griffiths lifted his chin. "We will speak with them," he said. "We will ask them plainly if they know anything of this. There will be no violence."

Rob nodded vigorously, as if he had suggested the same. "Speak, aye," he said. "Ask. But we go together. No tricks. No lies behind shutters."

Edmund saw how easily the language shifted. Speak with them meant surround them. Ask them meant accuse. Go together meant arrive as a crowd, which was already half a verdict.

He turned and began walking, because if the village was going to their lane, he would not let them go without him.

The movement out of the square gathered quickly, like a stream fed by little rivulets. Men left their stalls. Women stepped into doorways to watch, children held back by tight hands. A few people stayed behind, not out of disapproval but out of self-preservation, as if absence could later be claimed as innocence. Most went. Fear did not want witnesses who might contradict it; it wanted witnesses who would become part of its story.

They walked down the lane that led toward the cluster of smaller houses where the Jewish families lived. The lane was not far. It had never felt far. On market days it was simply another path, another place to buy candles or cloth, another doorstep to pass. Today it felt like a narrowing corridor.

Alice appeared from a side path near the smithy, her face set, her scarf loose as if she had run. She caught Edmund's arm hard enough to stop him for half a step.

"Walter went," she hissed, eyes flicking to the crowd. "He warned them."

Edmund's breath caught. "Good," he said, though he did not know what good would mean now. Warn them to do what? Run? Hide? How did a family run from a village when the village was already in motion?

Alice's eyes narrowed. "They're calling it questioning," she said. "But they've brought cudgels."

Edmund looked and saw it clearly. A few men carried clubs, not openly raised, but held in the casual way a man held a tool he intended to use. One had a hook, the kind used for hay bales. A hook was a useful thing. It could also drag a man by the shoulder.

Walter was there too, on the edge of the group, his face hard. He avoided Edmund's eyes as if ashamed of being seen among them, or afraid that meeting Edmund's gaze would make him choose.

At the front walked Father Griffiths, spine straight, a shepherd pleased with his own role. The reeve walked beside him, sweating despite the cool air, his fingers worrying at the belt that held his knife.

They reached Isaac's house, a modest structure no different in shape from the others, except for the small marks of carefulness: a cleaner threshold, a neatly stacked pile of firewood, a shutter that closed properly. The door was shut and barred. Someone had pushed a bench against it from the inside; the outline showed in the slight bulge of wood.

Father Griffiths stepped forward and called, "Isaac. Open the door."

No answer.

Rob laughed softly. "Hear that?" he said to the men behind him. "Nothing. Like they're dead already."

"Or like they don't want to breathe our air," someone said, and a few men snorted.

Father Griffiths tried again, louder. "Isaac. This is Father Griffiths. Open, and speak with us. There is fear in the village. We must put it to rest."

A pause. Then, from behind the door, a voice answered, muffled by wood. "We have done nothing," it said, and the accent was slight, the cadence different enough that it would always be noticed by ears looking for difference. "Leave us be."

Rob stepped forward, uninvited. "Nothing?" he called. "Then why hide?"

"We are not hiding," the voice replied. "We are keeping our children inside. Like you should."

That was a mistake, Edmund realized at once. It was sensible. It was true. But truth spoken from behind a barred door sounded like contempt to men who had already decided to be insulted.

A man near Rob muttered, "Hear him. Telling us what to do."

Rob's eyes glittered. "Open the shutter," he demanded. "Let us see you."

From inside came another voice, higher, a woman's. "Please," she said, and the word was thin as paper. "Please go."

The crowd shifted closer. Boots scraped. Someone's cudgel knocked lightly against his palm, a nervous rhythm.

Edmund stepped forward until he was beside Father Griffiths. "This is wrong," he said quietly, but loud enough that the reeve heard.

Father Griffiths did not look at him. "We are only speaking," he murmured back, and Edmund heard the lie in it. Speaking had become a weapon already.

The reeve cleared his throat. "Isaac," he said, trying for authority. "You will open this door. If you do not, we will be forced to assume you have reason to refuse."

"Assume," Edmund repeated under his breath. Assumption as law. Fear's favorite tool.

From inside, the man's voice answered, strained now. "You have no right."

Rob spat. "No right?" he said loudly. "This is our village. Our well. Our children. If you've fouled it, you'll answer."

A stone struck the shutter then, thrown from somewhere behind Edmund. It hit with a sharp crack and fell into the dirt. For a heartbeat there was silence, not because anyone was shocked, but because everyone was waiting to see if this was allowed.

No one moved to stop it.

Rob smiled, slow and satisfied, as if permission had just been granted by the village itself.

Edmund felt Alice's hand close around his sleeve from behind, her grip tight with warning. He heard Walter mutter a curse under his breath. He saw Father Griffiths's jaw clench, not in disapproval, but in calculation.

The targeting had begun. Not as a sudden blaze, but as a careful testing of boundaries, each small act of intimidation offered to the crowd like a coin. If it was accepted, the next act would be larger. If it was cheered, it would become inevitable.

Edmund stepped forward again, raising his voice before another stone could fly.

"Stop," he said, and the word rang out too cleanly to be ignored. "This will not cure a child. It will only make more enemies than sickness ever could."

Rob turned his head slowly toward Edmund, and the look he gave him was almost grateful.

At last, Edmund had placed himself exactly where fear wanted him: between the crowd and its chosen prey, close enough to be struck.

Edmund held his ground, though every instinct in him urged him to step back, to unmake the moment before it hardened into something permanent. The lane felt narrower than it had any right to be, packed with bodies and breath and the stink of damp wool. Behind him, men shifted their weight, the scrape of boots against dirt like an animal pawing before it charges.

"Stop," he said again, quieter this time, not because he wanted to soften it, but because he needed them to hear the shape of the words rather than their volume. "Look at yourselves."

Rob Baines let out a short laugh and spat to one side. "We are looking," he replied. "That's the whole point. We're looking at the ones who won't open their door."

Edmund turned his head slightly, just enough to meet Rob's eyes. Rob's face was drawn and red-rimmed, not only from drink, but from the strange sleeplessness fear brought. He looked like a man who had been waiting years to be allowed to be cruel and call it duty.

"You think a barred door is proof," Edmund said. "But you're the reason it's barred."

A ripple moved through the crowd, irritation at the accusation, and yet a thin thread of something else too: recognition, quickly smothered. People did not like seeing themselves clearly. It stripped away the comfort of righteousness.

Father Griffiths stepped forward before the crowd could answer, hands lifted as if he were calming livestock. “Master Edmund,” he said, voice full of strained patience, “no one here wishes harm. We are attempting to prevent it. Your words inflame.”

Edmund felt Alice’s grip on his sleeve tighten from behind, a warning to be careful, but there was no careful way to speak truth to a crowd that wanted a lie. He looked at the priest. “You say no one wishes harm,” Edmund replied, and nodded at the stone lying in the dirt. “That stone wished harm. It was thrown by a hand in this crowd. And no one stopped it.”

A man near the front shifted uncomfortably, glancing at the others as if searching for someone to blame for the stone so he would not have to own it. Another man, holding a cudgel too casually, raised his chin. “It’s only a stone,” he muttered.

“Only a stone becomes a broken skull,” Edmund said, and heard how calm his own voice sounded. Calm did not come from confidence. It came from the same coldness he had felt in his father's hall, the coldness that arrived when a line was about to be crossed.

He stepped a half-pace toward the door, placing himself closer to it than to the crowd, as if his body could be a hinge keeping violence from swinging fully open. "Isaac," he called, not loudly, "do not open."

From behind the door came a strained breath, then the muffled voice again. "We will not," Isaac said. "We have children. We have done nothing."

Rob leaned forward, savoring the sound of fear behind wood. "Then you've nothing to fear," he called back. "Open and prove it."

Edmund turned back to the crowd. "You hear yourselves?" he said. "Open and prove innocence. Since when is a man guilty because he is frightened?"

"Since his fear threatens ours," Rob snapped.

"That is not justice," Edmund said. "That is panic."

The reeve cleared his throat, trying to regain a kind of authority that had already begun to slip. "We are not here for justice," he said, then corrected himself quickly, "We are here to keep order. There is sickness in the village. A child lies ill. The well may be fouled. We must know."

"You will not know by standing here," Edmund replied. "You will not know by forcing a door. If you want to know, you look at what is true, not what is easy to punish."

A man behind Rob scoffed. "And what's true, then? You've got answers for everything, have you?"

Edmund felt the eyes on him, not only hostile now, but hungry. His difference was being measured the way Isaac's was being measured. He spoke too well. He read and wrote. He had come from elsewhere. He had been building strange little rules on his land. To a frightened mind, any difference could be made to look like intent.

"What's true," Edmund said, keeping his voice steady, "is that Joan at the mill swelled under her jaw. Swelled under her arm. That is no poison that any man drops into a bucket. That is a sickness of the body, something that moves from one to another, like fire moves when roofs are too close and the wind is wrong."

A murmur passed through the men. Some shifted back as if Edmund's words carried the sickness on their breath. Others leaned in, angry at the implication that they were helpless against something that could not be dragged into the street.

Rob's eyes narrowed. "You speak of sickness like you've seen it," he said. "Like you know it. How do you know it, Edmund? From your notes? From your little hut by the river? From the strangers you listen to?"

Alice made a low sound behind him, almost a growl. Walter's voice rose from somewhere in the crowd, rough and warning. "Leave him be, Rob."

Rob ignored Walter and kept his gaze fixed on Edmund, as if Edmund were the true door he wanted forced open.

Edmund did not look away. "I know it because men have been talking of it on roads for months," he said. "Because traders refused to sleep under roofs. Because families have left in the night. Because I have watched rats crawl in daylight. Because all of it has been moving toward us like a storm you smell before you see. I didn't summon it. I only refused to pretend it wasn't coming."

The crowd did not like that. Not because it was wrong, but because it meant there was no simple act that would stop the storm. It meant there was no bargain to be struck with God or neighbor that would guarantee safety.

Father Griffiths's voice sharpened. "Enough," he said. "You speak as though you are a physician. You are not. You are a landowner newly arrived, and you unsettle honest folk with foreign fears."

Edmund laughed once, without humor. "Foreign fears," he repeated. "As if fear respects borders. As if sickness asks whether a man kneels at the right altar before it takes his breath."

A man near the back shouted, "So you say we do nothing? Just wash and wait to die?"

"That is not what I said," Edmund replied at once. "You want something to do? Then do the hard thing. Keep apart. Stop crowding. Stop sharing cups. Boil water. Burn rags that touched sick mouths. If someone falls ill, do not hide it and do not shove your way into their house out of curiosity. And for God's sake, stop looking for a throat to put your hands around so you can pretend you've strangled the danger."

Rob's face twisted with fury, but before he could answer, another stone flew.

This one struck the door itself, a dull thud against wood, and Isaac's wife cried out behind it. The sound jolted through the lane. For a heartbeat, the crowd went silent again, the way it had after the first stone, waiting to see if this too would be permitted.

Edmund whipped his head toward the crowd. "Who threw that?" he demanded.

No one answered. Faces turned away. The silence was an answer in itself. The crowd had become a thing larger than any one man, and within it, responsibility dissolved. That was the true horror of it: no one needed to own the cruelty for it to continue.

Walter shoved his way forward then, shoulders squared, rage burning through his fear. "Stop it!" He roared, and for a moment his voice cut through the lane like an axe. "You'll kill them and call it salvation."

Rob rounded on him. "They're killing us," he snapped. "With their tricks. Their poison. Their curses."

Walter spat in the dirt. "You don't know that."

Rob's eyes were bright now, fever-bright. "I don't need to know," he said, and that admission was more honest than anything else spoken in the lane. "I need to stop being afraid."

A murmur of agreement rose, low and dangerous. Edmund felt it like a physical pressure. This was the heart of it. It was never truly about Isaac's door, or the well, or Joan's swelling. It was about the shame of fear, the humiliation of being powerless. Violence promised to turn that humiliation into action.

Edmund stepped toward Rob, close enough that he could smell ale on his breath and sweat beneath his tunic. "If you need someone to blame," Edmund said, voice pitched low so only the men nearest heard, "then blame me for speaking. Blame the wind. Blame the road. But do not blame a family behind a door because you can't bear the truth."

Rob's lip curled. "You always offer yourself," he said, and there was a strange satisfaction in his tone, as if Edmund had finally spoken the correct line in a play. "Like you want to be the hero."

"I want you to stop," Edmund said.

Rob's gaze slid past Edmund to the door. "Open," he called again, louder. "Open or we'll open it for you."

From behind the wood Isaac's voice came, tight and shaking. "If you break in," he said, "you will not wash your hands clean again."

The words were meant as warning. They landed as insult.

"Listen to him," someone snarled. "Threatening us."

Father Griffiths stepped forward, and Edmund saw the moment the priest chose his side. He did not order the crowd away. He did not condemn the stones. He looked at the door, then at the men, and said, "Isaac. For the peace of the village, you must speak with us openly. If you refuse, you invite suspicion."

Edmund turned on him. "You are feeding it," he said, and his voice cracked slightly with anger. "You are pouring oil on it and calling it holy."

Father Griffiths's eyes hardened. "And you," he replied, "stand against your neighbors in their hour of need."

"My neighbors are behind that door as much as they are in this lane," Edmund said.

The reeve swallowed, his throat bobbing. "Enough," he said weakly, and then, as if clinging to procedure would save him, he raised his voice. "Isaac. Open the door and come out. If you do not, we will take measures."

Measures. The word was a gate opening.

Edmund felt Alice's hand slide from his sleeve to his forearm, her nails pressing into him. "Edmund," she whispered urgently, "they've tipped."

He knew. He could feel it in the way men adjusted their grip on cudgels, in the way they stepped closer to the door without realizing they were doing it. The crowd's patience was gone. Reason had become merely another obstacle to shove aside.

Edmund lifted both hands, palms out, a gesture of peace that looked foolish in the face of weapons. "Listen to me," he said, forcing his voice to carry. "If you harm them, you will not make yourselves safe. You will only teach yourselves that fear is answered by violence. And once you learn that lesson, you will use it again and again until there is no one left in this village who can feel safe in their own bed."

For a moment, it seemed some part of them heard. A man with a cudgel hesitated. Another glanced sideways, uncertain, as if seeing the scene from outside himself. Even Rob's expression tightened, not with doubt, but with the irritation of a man interrupted while building momentum.

Then someone shouted from the back, a raw voice edged with panic. "The child's dying!" Whether it was true or not did not matter. The words hit the crowd like a spark in dry straw.

A wail rose from a nearby house, or perhaps it was only the same voice again, but grief and fear answered it instantly. Men surged forward a half-step, not toward the mill, not toward prayer, but toward the door in front of them, the nearest object upon which they could spend their helplessness.

Edmund felt bodies press in. His shoulder was struck hard. He stumbled, caught himself, and saw Rob's grin flash like a knife.

Reason had been offered.

The village had tasted it and found it unsatisfying.

They wanted something else, something that would feel like control, even if it poisoned them more surely than any well ever could.

Chapter 7

Wells of Poison

The shout did what stones could not. It turned a threat into a necessity.

"The child's dying!"

Edmund did not know whose voice it was, only that it came from behind the thickest part of the crowd, thrown forward like a spear. It did not matter whether it was true. In the moment it was spoken, the village accepted it as truth because it fit the shape of what they already feared. A child burning in a bed became, in their minds, a child already dead. And a dead child required a price.

The men surged again, not as one clean wave but as a series of shoves and stumbles that added up to the same thing: pressure against the door, against Isaac's threshold, against the small pocket of air where Edmund stood trying to keep bodies from becoming a battering ram.

A shoulder hit him hard enough to numb his arm. He caught himself on the uneven stones, boots slipping, and for a moment his hands were full only of staying upright.

"Back!" Walter roared somewhere to Edmund's left, his voice raw with panic and anger. "Back, you fools!"

But the word fools landed on men who no longer thought of themselves as men at all. They thought of themselves as the village, as a single creature with a single right to survive.

Father Griffiths raised his hands as if he could calm them, but he did not command them away. He only called, too late and too softly, "Order. Keep order." The reeve's face shone with sweat; his eyes darted as if searching for the one sentence that would restore his authority without making him a target of the same crowd he had encouraged.

Edmund tried once more, not with grand argument now, but with the plain voice of a man speaking to neighbors. "If Joan is dying, then go to her," he shouted. "Do not come here. You cannot pull breath back into her by breaking a door."

"Breath won't help her if the water's fouled!" Someone shouted back.

"Yes," another voice agreed, immediate and eager. "The well. It's the well. It's always the well."

It was the first time Edmund heard the accusation with that kind of certainty: not a suspicion, not a question, but a conclusion spoken as though it had always been known.

The crowd's momentum shifted, not away from Isaac's house yet, but sideways, as if a new current had entered the stream and begun to pull it. The men nearest the front still pressed toward the door, but others turned their heads toward the lane behind them, toward the square, toward the well that sat like a black eye at the center of everything.

Rob Baines took advantage of the moment the way he always did. Edmund saw him slip along the edge of the crush, quick and practiced, avoiding the bodies in a way that suggested he was less drunk than he pretended. Rob's voice rose above the noise.

"Listen!" He shouted. "Listen, all of you. We're wasting time here."

A few men hesitated, annoyed at being told they were wasting anything, but they listened anyway because Rob's certainty was the closest thing they had to direction.

Rob pointed toward the village. "We're standing in a lane shouting at a door while our children drink poison. While Joan lies swelling and choking. You think a family hiding behind wood is the danger? The danger is in the water. In the well. And you know who doesn't drink from it."

The last line did not need a name. The crowd supplied it at once. The name had been warming in the village's mouth since the morning, since Father Griffiths had spoken of those who kept strange customs and washed too much.

Edmund felt a sick drop inside him, as if his body had recognized the turn before his mind could. He stepped toward Rob. "You don't know the water is poisoned."

Rob's eyes flicked to Edmund, and the look he gave him was not surprise but satisfaction. "Don't I?" Rob said. "Then why does it taste wrong?"

A man near the back shouted, "It was bitter!"

Another chimed in, "It made my tongue go numb."

Edmund heard the way the claims multiplied, each one adding detail, adding proof by repetition. He had watched it happen before in smaller ways: a shadow at a well becoming a stranger, a stranger becoming an enemy. Now it was happening faster, because fear had learned it could move the village like a herd.

"The water tastes like water," Edmund snapped. "You're tasting your own spit and calling it evidence."

That drew angry mutters. People did not like being told their senses were unreliable. Unreliable senses meant unreliable safety.

Rob lifted his hands, palms outward, as though he were the reasonable one. "All right," he said, "all right. Then let's make it plain. Let's ask them."

"Them" again, the word that turned neighbors into a single dark shape.

A voice from behind the door, Isaac's wife perhaps, spoke in a thin, strained burst. "Leave us alone!"

The plea only sharpened the crowd. Pleading sounded like weakness, and weakness sounded like guilt to men who needed guilt to be real.

Walter shoved his way forward until he was near Edmund, shoulders braced. His face had gone pale beneath the grime. "Edmund," he said under his breath, "this is beyond talk now."

"I know," Edmund replied, and hated how calm his own voice sounded. Calm was what he did when he could not afford to panic.

Alice appeared on the edge of the lane, her scarf half fallen, eyes bright and hard. She met Edmund's gaze for a single moment and he saw the same thought there: if the crowd turns fully, the first door they break will not be the last.

The reeve finally found his voice, or something like it. "Rob," he called. "Enough. We will not-"

Rob cut him off, not by shouting over him but by ignoring him. Ignoring was more powerful than argument. "We go to the well," Rob declared. "We draw it up. We taste it again. And we make them taste it too. If it's clean, they've nothing to fear."

The crowd made a sound that was half agreement, half relief. A test. A simple act. Something you could do with your hands. It did not require understanding swellings under a child's jaw or sickness carried on breath. It required only a rope, a bucket, and someone to force.

Edmund stared at Rob. "Make them taste it," he repeated, and the words tasted of iron.

Rob smiled. "Aye. Make them swear by it. Right there in the square where all can see. No more hiding behind shutters."

Father Griffiths stepped forward at last, his voice high with authority he had not earned. "The well must be protected," he said. "If there is corruption, it must be revealed. We will proceed with caution."

Proceed. Caution. Edmund heard the softness of the language, how it excused what it was about to permit. The priest did not say violence. He did not say force. He said reveal, as if truth was something that could be dragged out of a man by his collar.

Edmund looked at Father Griffiths and felt something harden. "You're giving them leave," he said.

Father Griffiths's eyes flashed. "I am keeping my village from panic," he replied.

"You're teaching them to panic with purpose," Edmund shot back. "That is worse."

But the priest had already turned away. He had chosen his place, not between the crowd and the weak, but beside the crowd so he could pretend he still guided it.

Rob clapped his hands once, sharp. "Move," he said, and men began to shift, backing away from Isaac's door not out of mercy but out of new focus. The lane loosened as the pressure turned toward the square.

Edmund stepped toward the door quickly, using the brief space. He leaned close, speaking low through the wood. "Do not come out," he said. "Do you hear me? Whatever they say, do not come out."

A pause, then Isaac's voice, tight. "Where can we go?"

Edmund's throat tightened. There was no honest answer. Run, and they would be hunted for running. Stay, and they would be punished for staying. "Bar it," Edmund said. "Stay away from the shutters. Keep your children back. If you can slip out the rear and go to my land, do it. But only if you can do it unseen."

Inside, a small child began to cry, a thin sound. A woman murmured to soothe him. Edmund pressed his forehead briefly against the wood, a gesture he did not mean to make, and then pulled back as if the door itself might burn.

Behind him, Rob's voice carried, calling men by name, pulling them along. "Hugh. Come on, you've got arms. Thomas Thorne, you too. Don't stand there like a woman."

Edmund heard Thomas's name and turned his head. Thomas stood stiffly, jaw clenched, his limp making it harder for him to move with the crowd. Two men grabbed his arm, not cruelly yet, but insistently, pulling him into motion.

Walter spat and followed, not because he agreed, but because if he did not, the crowd would mark his absence. The village had begun keeping a different kind of account: not who paid rents, but who stood with them when blood was demanded.

Edmund moved with them because he had no choice. If he stayed at Isaac's door alone, he would be left behind as an obstacle to be dealt with later. If he went, he might be able to pull someone back from the edge, or at least witness what was done so it could not be dressed later as necessity without stain.

They poured into the square like water released from a gate, voices rising as they went. Doors opened a crack and shut again. Faces appeared behind shutters. Children were pulled inside as if the air itself had become hands.

The well waited in the center, the rope damp, the stones marked with ash from last night's performance. Men crowded around it, hungry for ceremony.

Rob stepped up to the lip of it and looked down, as if expecting the darkness to answer him. He lifted his head and spoke, not as a drunk now, but as a man who had found his role.

"It's poison," he said, and the square quieted, drinking the words. "Not God. Not bad air. Poison. Put there by hands that hate us."

Edmund felt the word settle over the village like soot, clinging to every surface. Poison turned sickness into intent. Intent required an enemy. And an enemy, once named, could be handled.

Rob's gaze swept the crowd, then fixed on Father Griffiths, as if inviting blessing.

Father Griffiths did not smile. He only did not object.

In that silence, the accusation became more than a claim.

It became permission.

The square held its breath for a heartbeat, as if waiting to see whether the word poison would be challenged by someone with the right to do so.

No one challenged it.

Rob Baines leaned over the well again and spat, the glob striking the dark water with a tiny, obscene sound. He straightened and wiped his mouth with the back of his hand, turning to the men around him like a judge who had already decided.

"Draw it," he said.

A carter's son stepped forward eagerly, as though glad to be given a task that did not require thought. He took the rope and hauled, muscles tensing, the wet fibers creaking. The bucket rose, dripping, and as it came into the light it swung slightly, scattering beads of water onto boots and hems.

"Smell it," Rob commanded.

The boy hesitated, then leaned in and sniffed. His face tightened, not in certainty, but in the way a person's face tightened when everyone watched him and expected a conclusion. "Smells…" he began.

"Wrong," Rob supplied, and several men nodded as if the word had been on their own tongues.

"Wrong," the boy repeated, grateful for the rescue.

A low murmur moved through the crowd. Edmund saw it in the way shoulders loosened, in the way frightened men became animated the moment they were told there was something to do. It did not matter that wrong had no meaning. Wrong was a doorway, and they were already stepping through.

Father Griffiths stood near the church steps; hands folded at his waist. The stole at his neck looked too clean, too ceremonial, like a ribbon put on a blade. The reeve hovered close to him, pale and sweaty, eyes darting as if he could still find a route back to order without being accused of cowardice.

Edmund pushed forward until he stood close enough to the well to see the water trembling in the bucket. It was clear enough, a dull gray reflecting the sky. He could not smell anything beyond wet rope and old stone.

"This proves nothing," Edmund said, keeping his voice steady. "If you think it tastes strange, it is because you want it to. Your fear will season it."

A few men turned on him with the same immediate irritation they had shown on the lane. Edmund recognized the hunger in their eyes: not for truth, but for an argument they could win by force.

Rob's mouth curled. "Always with your words," he said. "You can't wash poison away with talk."

Walter stood just behind Edmund's shoulder, stiff as a post. Alice was further back, her gaze moving across faces, reading the crowd the way she read weather. Thomas had been pulled into the press near the front; he leaned awkwardly on his good leg, jaw clenched, looking like a man who had been dragged into a fight he wanted no part of but could not escape.

Rob lifted the bucket by its handle and held it up so all could see. "If it's clean," he called, "then we'll all drink, and we'll all live, and we'll all be ashamed of our fear."

The lie in it was almost impressive. He spoke as if he would happily accept being wrong. Edmund knew better. Being wrong was not in Rob's nature now; it would strip him of the authority he had built from panic.

Rob's eyes swept the square and landed on a man near the edge, a thin fellow with a scar along his cheek. "You," Rob said. "Drink."

The man flinched. "Why me?"

"Because you've got a mouth," Rob answered, and the crowd laughed, sharp and quick, pleased by cruelty disguised as humor. "Drink, and show us it's safe."

The man's gaze flicked to the reeve as if hoping for intervention. The reeve looked away, lips pressed tight, trapped between fear of disorder and fear of being the next target of it.

The man took the bucket with shaking hands. He stared into the water as if waiting for it to confess. Then, under the weight of watching faces, he lifted it and swallowed.

He coughed at once, sputtering water down his chin. A few men jeered. Someone slapped his back hard enough to make him stumble.

"There," Rob said triumphantly. "See? He choked. Poison."

"He choked because he drank too fast," Edmund snapped.

Rob turned his head slowly toward Edmund. "Or because his body knows," Rob said. "Like a dog knows rotten meat."

A murmur of assent rose. Edmund felt his stomach twist. They were not testing the water. They were testing how far they could push a man and still call it reason.

Rob pointed at another. "You too."

Then another. "Drink."

The bucket went hand to hand. Some drank quickly to be done. Some refused until they were shoved and made to. Each cough, each grimace, each splutter was seized as proof. Each steady swallow was ignored or reinterpreted as resistance to poison, as if survival itself was suspicious.

Edmund caught the rope as it swung and steadied it, trying to stop the bucket from sloshing. It was a small act, almost invisible, but he needed something to do that was not shouting into a storm.

"This is madness," he said to Walter under his breath.

Walter did not answer at once. When he did, his voice was tight. "Madness is what happens when folk think God's left the room."

Rob stepped up onto the low stone rim of the well, elevating himself. The crowd's attention fixed on him like iron filings. He raised his arms as if preaching.

"We've proven enough," he declared. "The well is fouled. And we know who doesn't drink from it."

The square went quieter, the way animals went quiet when a predator moved through brush.

Edmund felt Alice's gaze snap to him from where she stood. He saw the warning in her eyes before she could speak it.

Rob's voice hardened. "Bring them," he said.

For a moment no one moved. Not because they disagreed, but because the first step into open violence always carried a thin risk. People wanted to see who would go first, who would become the instrument so the rest could say they had only followed.

Then Hugh the smith's brother, broad-shouldered and eager to belong, stepped forward. Two others followed. A few men took up cudgels that had been carried as "just in case" and now looked suddenly necessary.

Edmund moved as well, because he had learned that absence would not keep his hands clean. If he did not witness, if he did not resist where he could, the village would later tell itself any story it liked about what had been done.

They surged toward the lane again, not with the scattered uncertainty of earlier, but with purpose. The square emptied in a slow spill of bodies. Doors shut tight as they passed. Shutters clicked. The village was becoming a place of watchers, each household hoping the mob would choose someone else.

At Isaac's house the door was still barred. The shutters were closed. The very caution meant to protect his family now served as a painted mark.

Rob arrived first and struck the wood with his fist. "Open," he shouted. "By order of the village."

By order of the village. Not the reeve. Not the Earl. Not the King. The village itself, made into a god.

Isaac's voice came from behind the door, strained. "Go away."

Rob laughed. "We've tasted the well," he said. "We've choked on it. You will come and swear on it in front of all. You will drink, and you will show us you have not poisoned it."

"You're drunk," Isaac replied, and Edmund heard the desperation in the insult. A man reached for any weapon when his children cried behind him.

Rob's face darkened. "Not drunk enough," he said, "to let my children die while you hide."

Edmund stepped forward, putting himself near the door again. “Isaac,” he said, low, “do not answer him.”

But it was too late for silence to be safety. Silence only gave the crowd space to fill with whatever certainty it wanted.

The reeve arrived, breathless, trying to look as though he led rather than followed. Father Griffiths stood behind him, eyes fixed on the door, his expression set in a pained righteousness.

“This is enough,” Edmund said to the reeve, pitching his voice so others heard. “Send them home.”

The reeve’s mouth worked. He looked at the men around him, at their hard faces, at the cudgels. He knew, Edmund saw, that if he tried to send them home now, they might decide he was the one protecting poison.

“We only want them to answer questions,” the reeve said weakly.

Rob seized the word answer and made it into a hammer. “Aye,” he said. “Answer. Like any honest man would.”

He nodded to Hugh’s brother. “Break it.”

The man hesitated only long enough to glance around and see he would not be stopped. Then he lifted his shoulder and drove it into the door.

The wood groaned.

A woman screamed inside, high and raw.

Edmund surged forward instinctively, shoving at Hugh's brother's arm. "Stop!" he snapped.

The man recoiled, more surprised than hurt. Rob's hand shot out and shoved Edmund back hard enough that Edmund stumbled into another body.

Rob's eyes were bright. "There it is," he said loudly, so all could hear. "He stops us. He always stops us."

Edmund tried to regain his footing. Walter caught his elbow, steadying him. Walter's face was white with fury, but he did not swing; he knew, as Edmund did, that if he struck now, the crowd would call it proof of conspiracy.

The door took a second blow, then a third. The bar inside held for a breath, then cracked with a sharp sound like a bone breaking. The door flew inward.

Men rushed in at once, filling the small house with bodies and noise. Edmund pushed forward, but Walter held him back for a heartbeat. “If you go in,” Walter hissed, “they’ll say you went to help them flee.”

“I’m going in because they’ll kill them,” Edmund replied.

He wrenched free and followed the crush into the dim interior.

The room was small, neat, and instantly made filthy by boots and shouting. A table was overturned. A clay cup shattered. In the corner, a woman clutched a child to her chest, her face streaked with tears. Another child stood frozen, eyes huge, as if his mind had left his body to avoid what it saw.

Isaac stood near the hearth, hands raised, not in surrender but in the reflex of a man trying to keep strangers from reaching his family. His face was gray with fear.

“Please,” he said, and the word was swallowed by Rob’s voice.

“Where is it?” Rob demanded. “Where’s what you put in the well?”

“We put nothing,” Isaac choked out.

Rob stepped close and grabbed Isaac’s tunic, hauling him forward so hard Isaac’s feet stumbled. “Liar,” Rob said, and then turned his head and shouted to the others, “Search.”

Men began tearing at the room as if poison would be hidden like stolen bread. They pulled open chests. Scattered linens. Threw aside books as though ink itself were suspicious. One man seized a jar of herbs from a shelf and held it up. “Here!” he shouted.

“It’s for cooking,” Isaac’s wife cried. “It’s only—”

Rob slapped the jar from the man’s hand, spilling dried leaves across the floor like dead insects. “Witch’s scraps,” he said, and a few men muttered agreement, eager to label anything unfamiliar as evil.

Edmund stepped between Rob and the woman with the child. “Enough,” he said, voice low but hard. “You’re terrorizing children.”

Rob’s gaze slid to him. “You care for their children,” he said softly, as if savoring each word. “But not ours.”

“I care for all children,” Edmund said.

Rob’s mouth twisted. “That’s what makes you dangerous.”

He shoved Edmund aside with his forearm, not even looking at him fully, as if Edmund were furniture. Edmund stumbled into the wall, pain sparking through his shoulder.

Someone struck Isaac then. A fist, quick, from the side. Isaac's head snapped, and he sagged, catching himself on the hearthstone. The sound that left him was not a cry, but a stunned breath, like a man whose body could not believe it had been harmed in its own home.

The first blow changed everything. Edmund felt it ripple through the room: the moment restraint died.

Men began shouting over one another, each trying to be the one to force the confession that would make their fear feel justified. The crowd pressed closer, bodies surrounding Isaac, hands grabbing, voices demanding.

"Say it!"

"What did you put in?"

"Who paid you?"

"Was it all of you?"

Isaac's wife screamed again, and the child in her arms began to wail, a thin sound that should have stopped any human heart. It did not. It only became another noise in the storm.

Edmund pushed forward again, fighting against shoulders and elbows, trying to reach Isaac, trying to put himself between fists and flesh. He caught a glimpse of Father Griffiths in the doorway, not entering fully, his face tight with the effort of looking sorrowful while allowing it. The priest's lips moved as if in prayer, but his eyes did not leave Isaac's trembling form.

The mob did not need the priest's words now. It had its own liturgy.

Pain for confession. Fear for truth. Violence for control.

And in the crush of bodies and the shriek of children, Edmund realized with a cold clarity that the village had crossed into a kind of justice that could never again be satisfied by innocence.

Someone produced a length of rope from nowhere, as if it had been waiting in the village's pocket all along. It slid across the floorboards with a wet sound where spilled water and crushed herbs had already made mud of the neat little room.

"Bind him," Rob said.

It was not a suggestion. It was a relief, offered to men who had been standing in the foul, shifting air of uncertainty for days and were exhausted by the effort of pretending they were still decent.

Two men seized Isaac's arms. He tried to twist away, not to fight them, but to keep his body between their hands and the woman in the corner with the child. His elbow caught one man in the ribs and earned him a fist in the mouth. The blow split his lip; Edmund saw the sudden bright smear of blood and felt his stomach tighten as if his own mouth had been struck.

"That's it," someone snarled. "There's your true face."

As if blood proved guilt.

Isaac sagged, blinking. The men hauled him upright again, twisting his arms behind him until his shoulders rose and trembled. Rope bit into his wrists. He made a small, involuntary sound, part breath and part pain.

Edmund pushed forward once more, forcing his way into the ring of bodies. "Stop this," he said, and the words scraped his throat raw. "You're hurting him because you're frightened. That is all."

A shoulder slammed into Edmund's chest. He stumbled back into the wall, the impact knocking air from him. When he lifted his head, he saw Rob watching him with a calm, satisfied interest, as if every protest Edmund made was a kind of confirmation.

"Look at him," Rob said, loud enough for the men at the edges to hear. "He speaks for them as if he's kin. As if their blood is his."

"It is blood," Edmund snapped, breathless. "It is the same as yours."

Rob smiled slightly. "Then let's see how much of it Isaac is willing to spill for truth."

Isaac's wife, Miriam, rose from the corner with the child still clutched to her chest. She looked smaller than Edmund remembered, not because she had changed, but because fear had changed the way the room held her. "Please," she said, voice shaking. "We have done nothing. We have children. If you must take someone, take me. Leave him."

A man laughed, the sound ugly and quick. "Hear her bargain," he said. "Like it's a market."

Miriam flinched as if struck. The child in her arms wailed louder, face red and slick with tears. Another child, the older one, stood near the hearth with his hands balled into fists, lips pressed tight in an effort not to cry. His eyes fixed on Isaac's bleeding mouth, wide and shining with horror that had nowhere to go.

Rob stepped closer to Isaac until their faces were inches apart. "What did you put in the well?" Rob asked softly.

Isaac shook his head, rope creaking as his shoulders tightened. "Nothing," he managed, thickly, blood on his teeth. "Nothing."

Rob's hand rose, slow, almost gentle, and for a heartbeat Edmund thought he meant to wipe the blood away. Instead, Rob slapped Isaac across the face, open-palmed, hard enough to snap Isaac's head to the side. The sound was loud in the cramped room. Miriam cried out.

"Say it," Rob murmured. "Just say it."

"I cannot say what is not true," Isaac whispered, and there was a stubbornness in it that Edmund admired and feared. Stubbornness was a candle in wind. It burned bright and it drew attention.

One of the men holding Isaac, flushed with the sudden power of being allowed, struck him again, this time with a fist to the ribs. Isaac doubled slightly, rope pulling his arms higher, and a broken gasp tore out of him.

"Enough!" Walter's voice cut in from behind Edmund. Walter had shoved his way into the room; his face was pale, and his eyes were wild with the effort of holding himself back from violence. "You'll kill him."

Rob turned his head. "Is that what you want?" Rob asked, almost curious. "Because if you want to stop it, you know how."

Walter stared at him. "By killing him faster?" Walter spat. "That's your cure?"

"It's not a cure," Rob replied. "It's an answer. And we're owed one."

The word owed again, that dangerous entitlement to meaning.

The men began to search more viciously, as if the room itself were lying. They tore open a sack of flour and sent a white cloud into the air. They smashed a crock of pickled onions. One man seized a small knife from the table and held it up as if it were an altar offering.

"A weapon," he said.

"It is for bread," Miriam cried. "It is for food."

"Everything's for something," the man muttered, and his eyes did not look at her. They were fixed on the others, waiting for approval.

Edmund saw Father Griffiths still in the doorway, keeping his robe from brushing the floor as though the filth might stain him. His lips moved. It could have been prayer. It could have been a rehearsed line of comfort. It did not matter. He did not step in. He did not put his body between fists and flesh. He watched like a man watching a fire he had helped light, telling himself he was only witnessing, not feeding it.

The reeve hovered behind the priest, face drawn tight. When his eyes met Edmund's briefly, Edmund saw panic there, not guilt. The reeve looked like a man realizing he had lost his own horse and was now being carried wherever it ran.

Rob leaned close to Isaac again, voice low. "If you confess," he said, "it will be quick. You will spare your wife and children worse."

Miriam made a choked sound. "No," she whispered, and the older child by the hearth whispered it too, almost soundless.

Isaac's eyes fluttered. He was breathing hard, each breath a fight. Edmund could see the tremor in his arms, the strain in his shoulders as the rope held his joints at an unnatural angle.

Rob nodded to one of the men. The man stepped behind Isaac and yanked the rope upward, forcing Isaac's bound arms higher. Isaac's body arched. A hoarse cry escaped him, the first full sound of pain Edmund had heard from him, and it made something in the room shiver.

"Tell us," Rob said, louder now. "Tell us what you did."

Isaac's mouth opened and shut. He shook his head weakly, tears running now, not from weakness of spirit but from the simple betrayal of flesh.

Rob's patience ended like a snapped thread. "Then tell us who did," he said. "Who among you. Who paid you. Who told you to do it."

Isaac's eyes squeezed shut. His voice came thin and broken. "No one," he whispered.

A fist struck his stomach. Isaac retched, choking on spit and blood. The men holding him tightened their grip to keep him upright, like men holding a post while they hammered it into ground.

Edmund tried to shove forward, but bodies blocked him. Someone's elbow caught his jaw; pain flared white, and for a moment he tasted his own blood too. He spat it out, furious, and the act felt like stepping closer to the animal they were all becoming.

"Stop!" He shouted again. "This will not change the sickness. You will only make yourselves murderers."

"Better murderers than corpses," someone shouted back.

The man behind Isaac yanked again, harder. Something in Isaac's shoulder seemed to give, not a clean break but a sickening shift that made Isaac scream. The scream cut through the room, through the shouting, through the child's wailing. For a breath, even the men doing the hurting froze, startled by the sound they had pulled from him.

In that brief silence, Miriam's sobs were loud, and the older child's breathing came in short, terrified bursts.

Rob watched Isaac with a predator's focus. "There," he said softly. "There it is. Now. Speak."

Isaac's eyes rolled, unfocused. His voice came out in a whisper that sounded like sand. "Please," he said, and the word was not for them. It was for his wife, his children, his God, anyone who might take him away from this room.

Rob leaned in. "What?"

Isaac swallowed. His throat bobbed. He turned his head slightly, as if trying to find Edmund through the crush of bodies, as if looking for one face that still held some resemblance to the village he had lived among. Edmund met his gaze, helpless.

Isaac's mouth trembled. Then, in a voice hardly louder than a breath, he said, "We… we did it."

Miriam made a sound like she had been stabbed.

The room erupted. Men shouted triumph. Someone laughed, high and giddy. The confession moved through them like strong drink, quickening their blood, turning their fear into jubilation because at last fear had a shape they could strike and call it justice.

Edmund felt cold spread through his limbs. He knew what he had just heard was not truth. It was surrender. It was pain speaking in the only language the mob would accept.

Rob's eyes shone. "Aye," he said, and his voice softened, almost kind. "There we are. Tell us. What did you put in the well?"

Isaac's eyes darted toward his wife. His lips parted. Nothing came at first, only breath and a faint sob. Then he forced words out, stumbling over them. "Powder," he said. "Bitter… bitter powder."

"What powder?" Rob demanded.

Isaac shook his head, frantic, searching for something that sounded plausible to men who did not know his herbs from his salt. "From the south," he whispered. "From a trader. He said… he said it would make you sick."

A man near the table seized on it at once. "Foreign!" He shouted. "I told you. Foreign sickness."

Father Griffiths's face tightened with something like relief. He lifted his hands and began to murmur, as if sanctifying the moment. "The Devil works through the unbeliever," he said, and the words slid into the room like oil.

Miriam's knees buckled. She sank to the floor with the child still in her arms, rocking now, not to soothe him but because her body did not know what else to do. "No," she kept whispering. "No. Isaac, no."

Isaac's head drooped. Tears ran down his cheeks, cutting clean lines through the blood and grime. He did not look at Rob now. He did not look at the men who had broken him. He looked at his wife and children as if trying to memorize them before the village took even memory away.

Rob grabbed Isaac's chin and forced his head up. "Who else?" Rob demanded. "If you did it, you didn't do it alone. Who helped you?"

Isaac's eyes squeezed shut. His body shook. The rope creaked as his shoulders trembled with the pain still hanging from them.

Edmund understood then what would happen next. Confession was never enough. It never filled the hunger. It only proved that hunger could be fed.

If Isaac named no one, they would hurt him until he did. If he named someone, they would take that person and repeat the ritual. The village would multiply its certainty by multiplying its victims.

Edmund tried to speak, but Walter grabbed him by the sleeve, hard. "Edmund," Walter hissed, eyes wide, voice shaking, "don't. Not now."

Edmund stared at him. "We can't let—"

Walter's face twisted with anguish. "If you speak now, they'll turn on you too," he whispered. "And then there's no one left to pull anyone back."

Edmund looked at Isaac, at Miriam on the floor, at the children's terrified faces. He looked at Rob, flushed with victory, and at Father Griffiths, watching like a man witnessing divine proof rather than human cruelty.

Isaac's voice came again, faint. "Eli," he whispered, and Edmund felt the name land like a stone dropped into deep water.

One name, offered like blood payment.

Rob straightened, satisfied. "Eli," he repeated loudly. "You heard him. Eli helped. Not only Isaac. Not only this house."

The men surged toward the door again, eager, the confession already pulling them toward the next doorstep. Edmund saw Thomas pressed near the wall, his face gray with horror, his mouth working as if he were about to vomit.

Miriam lifted her head from the floor, eyes wild. "He lies," she cried. "He lies because you broke him. You broke him!"

Rob stepped over her as if she were dirt. "Then we'll break the next one," he said, almost conversational, "until the truth stops hiding."

Edmund watched the mob spill back into the lane, carrying Isaac's words like a banner. Behind them, Isaac sagged in his bonds, bleeding and shaking, his confession hanging in the air heavier than smoke.

Edmund understood with sick clarity that the village had found a method. Pain could manufacture certainty. Blood could buy a story.

And now that they had learned that they would not stop at one confession.

They would bleed the village until it said whatever fear demanded.

Chapter 8

The Night of Ashes

They did not walk to Eli's house as men going to speak. They walked as men going to collect something owed.

The lane outside Isaac's door filled with bodies again, boots churning the dirt to paste. Voices overlapped in jagged fragments: "Eli," and "the dyer," and "I always said," and "Christ have mercy," said like a habit, not a plea. Someone had dragged Isaac out after them, half carried, half hauled, the rope still biting into his wrists. Edmund saw his feet scuff the ground, saw the way his head lolled as if his neck could not hold it.

Miriam's cry followed from the doorway, high and raw, until a man shouted for her to be quiet and another laughed as if it were a joke. The older child stumbled after the mob two steps before a neighbor caught him by the shoulder and shoved him back into the house, hard enough that the boy hit the doorframe. The child did not cry. He simply stared, as if sound had left him.

Edmund pushed through the press, trying to reach Isaac, trying to put his hand on the rope, to loosen it, to do something that was not only watching.

Walter caught him again, rougher this time. "Edmund," he said, his voice cracked with something close to pleading, "you cannot pull him free. Not in front of them."

Edmund wrenched his arm, but Walter's grip held. Walter's knuckles were white. His eyes flicked to the men around them, measuring the moment the crowd might decide Walter's loyalty was uncertain.

"They will kill him," Edmund hissed.

Walter swallowed hard. "They might," he said. "But if you make yourself the next obstacle, they will kill you first and keep walking. And then there's no one left who even remembers what a boundary is."

The mob surged onward, dragging its certainty toward the next door. Eli's place sat closer to the square, a small house with the sharp smell of dye that always clung to it, even when the wind turned. In calmer times, that smell had been merely unpleasant. Now it became evidence. Now it became a sign that Eli handled strange things, foreign powders, dark liquids that stained hands and cloth and, in the village's new imagining, wells.

The sun was already slanting low, the light thin and cold. Smoke from a few hearths drifted straight upward under the unnatural stillness, and that stillness made every sound louder: Isaac's hoarse breathing, the scrape of rope, a woman's sob from behind a shutter, quickly muffled.

As they moved, Edmund caught glimpses of faces that had not come to Isaac's house but now leaned out to see. Men who had stayed behind earlier stood at their thresholds with arms crossed, watching with careful neutrality. Women held children close and whispered, not prayers, but instructions: Don't speak. Don't stare. Don't give them a reason to remember your name.

At Eli's door, the crowd tightened. The house looked no different than it had yesterday. That was part of what made Edmund's stomach turn. The village was remaking the familiar into the monstrous without changing anything but its own mind.

Rob Baines arrived at the front as if he had been born there. He shoved a man aside, grabbed the latch, and yanked. The door did not open. It had been barred.

"Of course," Rob said, loud, savoring it. "Of course he bars it."

A stone struck the door and fell. Then another. The sound of wood being hit by rock was blunt and final, like a hammer finding its nail.

"Eli!" the reeve shouted, forcing authority into his voice like a man forcing breath into dying lungs. "Open, by order of—"

"Order of what?" Rob cut in. He turned, grinning at the men behind him. "Order of the well? Order of the swelling child? Order of the village that's tired of dying quiet?"

A murmur of approval rose. Edmund saw Father Griffiths at the edge, not in front, never quite in front when fists were raised. The priest's mouth moved, perhaps prayer, perhaps words meant to be repeated later as justification. His eyes stayed on the door.

Rob planted his hands on his hips, looked up at the lowering sky as if to summon patience. "Bring him out," he called. "Bring him and his wife. Bring his children if he's got them. We'll have them taste the water."

Inside, there was no answer at first. Then, muffled through wood, a voice came, strained and frightened. "Go away."

It was Eli. Edmund recognized the tone, the flatness of a man trying to keep terror from shaping his words.

Rob's smile widened. "You heard Isaac," he said. "He named you. He confessed. You think we'll pretend we didn't hear it?"

"He lied," Eli said, and his voice broke on the word. "He lied because you hurt him."

The crowd rippled, angered not by the accusation but by the implication that they could be wrong.

Rob leaned forward until his mouth was close to the crack in the door. "Then come out and say it," he murmured. "Come out and drink. Prove you're clean."

Edmund heard it, the same demand dressed as fairness. Prove innocence by submitting to humiliation and fear. And if Eli came out, they would not be satisfied. They would interpret every tremor, every cough, every flinch as proof of poison.

Someone pushed forward carrying a torch.

It was a simple thing at first: a stick with a rag wrapped at one end, soaked in fat, its flame small in the daylight. Edmund did not even know where it had come from, only that it had appeared because someone had thought ahead. The sight of fire in a crowd did something immediate. Men straightened. Shoulders squared. The torch made their purpose feel older than any one of them, like a ritual remembered by the body.

Alice stepped to Edmund's side, her voice low. "They've brought light," she said. "They'll bring more."

Edmund turned toward the reeve, desperate for any remaining structure to hold. "This has to end," he said. "Call them off."

The reeve's eyes flicked to the torch, and for a moment fear flashed there, not fear of plague, but fear of what the village had become. Then his gaze slid away. "We only mean to question," he muttered, but his words sounded thin even to himself.

Rob saw Edmund speaking to him and called out, "He's whispering again! Always whispering. Like he's planning."

A few men laughed, and the laughter was sharp with relief. Better to mock Edmund than to look at the torch and ask why it was there.

The man holding the torch lifted it higher. The flame wavered. The rag snapped quietly as fat burned.

"Don't," Edmund said, louder now. He stepped forward until he stood between the torchbearer and the door. "This is a home."

The torchbearer hesitated. Not because he felt mercy, but because he wanted permission. He looked past Edmund, toward Rob.

Rob's gaze locked on Edmund, and Edmund saw the calculation there, the pleasure of being able to choose what happened next. "Move," Rob said.

Edmund did not.

Rob stepped closer, his voice dropping. "You think you're saving them," he murmured so only those nearest heard. "But you're only showing the village who stands in the way."

Edmund's mouth went dry. He thought of his father's hall, the Earl's certainty. This was a different tyranny, but it had the same cold core: obedience demanded not because it was right, but because it was useful to power.

Behind Edmund, someone shoved. Hard.

He stumbled forward, caught himself against the door, palm hitting wood. The impact rattled through the plank, and inside, a woman screamed.

The shove came again. Not a single man now. Several. Hands on his shoulders, his back, his arms, forcing him sideways.

Walter's voice rose, "Stop!" and for a moment Edmund thought Walter might actually strike someone. But Walter didn't. Walter only shoved Edmund back, not away from danger, but away from being trampled. Walter's face was twisted with helpless rage, his loyalty stretched until it hurt.

The torchbearer stepped forward into the space Edmund had occupied. The flame bobbed near the door.

Father Griffiths spoke then, quietly, to the men nearest him. Edmund did not catch all the words, but he heard enough: "Purge," and "protect," and "if corruption hides behind wood…"

Not a command. Never a command. A suggestion that sounded like righteousness.

Rob lifted his chin. "Smoke draws rats out," he said, and several men nodded as if he had quoted scripture.

The torch touched the door.

At first, nothing. Just a smear of black where the rag brushed wood. Then the fat caught on a splintered edge left by the earlier stones, and the flame clung. It crawled, small and hungry, along the grain.

A woman inside cried out again, not the sharp scream from before but a sobbing plea, words muffled and frantic. The bar scraped. There was movement, panicked, trying to decide whether to keep the door closed against men or open it to fire.

"Open!" Rob shouted, and his voice rose with excitement now. "Open before you burn!"

The cruelty of it hit Edmund like a blow. Offer a choice that was no choice at all. Come out and be taken, or stay and choke.

The flame strengthened. It found the rag left behind, then the dry edge of a board. Smoke began to curl upward, thin at first, then thicker, staining the air.

Someone cheered. A single voice, then another. The sound made Edmund's skin crawl.

It was not the cheer of victory. It was the cheer of release, of men feeling their fear turn into heat in their hands.

The fire took hold with sudden eagerness, as if the house itself had been waiting for someone to give it permission to die.

And as smoke rose into the still evening, Edmund understood that the village had crossed beyond beating a confession out of a man.

They had discovered a cleaner pleasure.

Fire did not argue. Fire did not require proof. Fire made everything the same in the end: wood, cloth, flesh, history, all reduced to ash that could be swept away and forgotten.

Rob stepped back to admire what he had started, his face lit by flickering orange. The glow made him look almost holy, and that was the most terrible thing of all.

Because around him, men watched the flames and began to think, truly think, that burning a neighbor's house might be the first real act of safety they had accomplished.

The first crack of burning wood sounded like a sigh.

It came from somewhere deep in the door, a small surrender, and then the smoke thickened. It rolled up beneath the lintel and pressed against the still air like something alive, searching for the nearest throat.

Inside, feet pounded. A bench scraped. There was a frantic scraping sound that could only be hands on wood, trying to lift the bar while the heat rose behind it.

“Open!” Rob shouted again, his voice bright with a terrible cheer. “Open and come out clean!”

“Clean,” Edmund heard someone repeat, and the word twisted in his mind until it meant the opposite of itself.

The door shook once, then twice, not from the crowd now but from within. The bar lifted enough to clatter. The latch rattled. For a breath Edmund thought they would not open it, that pride or terror would hold them behind the burning wood until the fire took more than the house.

Then the door swung inward.

Smoke poured out first, thick and gray, carrying the bitter sting of fat and char. A woman stumbled into view, coughing hard, her head covered in a scarf that had been pulled down over her mouth like a poor shield. Behind her a man lurched, one arm wrapped around a smaller figure, a child pressed against his chest.

Eli.

His face was streaked with soot already, eyes wide and bright. When he coughed, the sound was wet and panicked. His wife made a thin, raw noise that might have been a sob if she had air enough to make it.

The crowd surged forward, not to help them away from the fire, but to close around them so the only path out of the burning doorway led straight into waiting hands.

Edmund stepped forward instinctively, reaching for the child first, because the child's smallness made the danger obscene. He got one hand under the child's arm before a man shoved him hard in the shoulder and he stumbled sideways.

"Don't touch them!" Someone barked, as if compassion itself was contamination.

Rob pushed through, face lit by the fire behind him. "There you are," he said, almost pleased. "Now. The well."

"We did nothing," Eli rasped, coughing. "We did nothing. You set my house—"

A man struck him across the mouth before the sentence could finish. Eli's head snapped. The child cried out, a thin sound swallowed by the crowd's roar.

"None of that," Rob said. "You'll speak in the square."

Edmund tried again to get between them. Walter's body slammed into his from the side, not as an attack, but as a shield. Walter's voice was low and urgent near Edmund's ear. "They'll drag them. Let them drag, or they'll drag you too."

"I can't let them," Edmund hissed back, his throat burning from smoke and rage.

Alice appeared at Edmund's other side, her eyes bright with the cold clarity she always found in chaos. "You can't stop a flood with your hands," she said, not gently. "But you can pull what you can to higher ground."

Edmund understood what she meant a heartbeat before she moved. While the crowd's attention fixed on Eli and the burning house, Alice slipped along the edge, quick as a fox, toward the back of the small yard. There were always back ways. Every house had them. Every family knew which fence rail was loose, which gap in a hedge could become a path when the front door was death.

Walter saw her go and hesitated, then followed, head down, moving like a man who had decided something without wanting to admit it aloud.

Edmund's mind raced. Isaac's house, Miriam and the children. The widow with the candles. The moneylender and his sons. Too many doors. Too many faces. And the village, drunk on the sight of flame, now believing fire could purify what sickness had touched.

The men at the front began to haul Eli away. His wife clung to his sleeve, coughing, stumbling. Rob kept a grip on Eli's collar as if leading an animal. The burning house behind them crackled louder, the flame now clearly visible through the open doorway, licking up the interior wall.

A cheer rose again. Edmund felt it like sickness in his stomach.

He turned and ran.

Not toward the square, not toward the well, but away from the noise, cutting through a narrow gap between cottages, boots slipping on damp earth. The village felt different when he moved through it alone, not because it was quieter, but because every shutter seemed to have an eye behind it, watching to see which way he ran and what that might mean.

He reached the lane that led toward his own land and saw Walter there already, half hauling someone along by the arm. It was Miriam, Isaac's wife, her face streaked with tears and grime, a child clutched tight against her body. The older child was beside her, stumbling, eyes fixed ahead as if he could not afford to look back.

Walter's jaw was clenched so hard the muscles jumped. "They slipped out back," he panted. "Alice found them. Isaac's still—" He swallowed hard. "Isaac's still in their hands."

Edmund's chest tightened. He pictured Isaac bound, bleeding, the confession still hanging over him like a curse that would never lift. There was no time to mourn it yet. Mourning required safety.

"How many?" Edmund asked.

Walter shook his head. "Not all. We can't get all. Not with them watching."

As if summoned by the thought, another figure appeared from the shadow of a hedge: the candle widow, her gray hair uncovered, her hands trembling as she clutched a small bundle of cloth. Alice was with her, one hand firm on the woman's elbow, the other holding a kitchen knife she had not bothered to hide.

"Move," Alice snapped when she saw Edmund. "Stop standing like a post. They'll come looking once they've finished their little show."

Edmund forced himself into motion. "To my shelter," he said.

Miriam lifted her head, eyes wild. "Your land?" she rasped. "They'll burn that too."

"Then they'll have to cross it to do it," Alice said, and there was something savage in her certainty. "And they'll have to say out loud what they are."

Edmund led them along the hedgerow rather than the main track, cutting across the damp edge of a field. The half-built shelter stood downwind near the river, the crude frame and roof of rough boards that had seemed like an accusation days ago and now seemed pitifully small against what hunted them.

As they approached, Edmund saw movement there already. Another family, two men and a boy, huddled in the shadow of the boards. The moneylender, Edmund realized, his face wax-pale, his lips moving as if counting prayers instead of coins. His boy's eyes were enormous.

Edmund's breath caught. More had come than he knew. Which meant more had managed to run. Which also meant the village would soon realize some had escaped.

He pushed the shelter's hanging cloth aside and guided them in. Inside, it smelled of fresh-cut wood, damp earth, and fear. It was not a true house, only a structure meant to keep rain off and wind out. Edmund had imagined using it for sickness, for isolation, for care. He had not imagined it as hiding.

Miriam sank to the ground with her child, rocking him. The candle widow leaned against a post, shaking so hard her bundle rattled. The men in the corner stared at Edmund as if he were both savior and omen.

"We won't stay long," Edmund said, though he had no plan beyond the next breath. "Just until the night gives cover. Then we can try for the road."

"The road is death," one of the men muttered, voice hollow.

Edmund crouched near Miriam, keeping his voice low. "If we can reach the woods, we can follow the river south," he said. "There are hamlets. Farms. Places to hide."

Miriam looked up at him, and grief poured out of her in a raw stare. "And Isaac?" she whispered.

Edmund's throat tightened. He could not lie. He could not tell her Isaac would meet them later when Edmund knew how the village treated confessions: as fuel. "If I can," Edmund said. "If there is a moment."

Alice made a harsh sound. "There won't be," she said flatly. Then, seeing Miriam's face crumple, she added, less cruelly but no softer, "Not tonight. Not once they've started burning doors."

Outside, the air carried sound from the village now, a distant roar that rose and fell, like a beast breathing. Shouts. A crack that might have been another door breaking, or a roof beam giving way. And beneath it, faintly, the church bell ringing once, then again, not for prayer, but as a call. A signal. A gathering.

Walter stood at the shelter's opening, peering out as if he could will the darkness to hurry. His hands shook when he thought no one watched.

Edmund stepped beside him. “They’ll come,” Edmund said quietly.

Walter’s mouth worked. “Aye,” he admitted. “They’ll come when they notice who’s missing.”

Edmund looked toward the village, toward the smoke smudging the low sky. “Someone will tell them,” he said. Not because he wanted to accuse, but because villages were made of tongues. Even those who did not throw stones still traded in information. It was how they proved they belonged.

As if the world wished to prove him right, footsteps sounded on the far side of the hedgerow. Slow. Careful. Not running with a mob but moving with purpose.

Alice stiffened, knife lifting slightly.

A man’s voice came through the leaves. “Walter?” it called, low and urgent.

Walter’s face went slack with shock. “Thomas,” he breathed.

Thomas limped into view, his hair damp with sweat, his face gray. He held his hands open, palms forward, a gesture of peace. For a heartbeat Edmund felt relief so sharp it hurt. Thomas was reason, as much as anyone left was.

Then Edmund saw it: the way Thomas's eyes flicked past Walter toward the shelter opening. The way he stared a fraction too long at the boards, at the shape of bodies huddled inside.

Thomas swallowed. His voice came rough. "They're asking," he said. "They're saying some of them ran. They're saying whoever hides them is part of it."

Alice's knife did not lower. "Who sent you?" she asked.

Thomas flinched. "No one sent me," he said, too quickly. "I came because Walter—because you—" He looked at Edmund then, and there was something in his gaze that made Edmund's skin tighten. Fear. Yes. But also calculation, the kind a man made when he stood near a mob and felt its breath on his neck.

"They're coming this way," Thomas said. "Rob's got them worked up. Father Griffiths's ringing the bell like it's Easter and the Devil's at the gate. They want to search. They want to know whose land is… sheltering."

Sheltering. Edmund heard the emphasis and understood it was not accidental.

Walter stared at Thomas as if seeing him for the first time. “You told them,” Walter said, voice barely above a whisper.

Thomas’s eyes darted away. “I didn’t,” he insisted. “Not with words.”

Alice made a cold, humorless sound. “But with your face,” she said. “With your fear.”

Thomas’s shoulders sagged, just slightly. “They would have killed me,” he muttered. “They were watching. Rob kept looking at me like he knew I’d been near you. Like he knew I wasn’t shouting loud enough.”

Edmund felt something hollow open in his chest. Betrayal did not always come as a deliberate act. Sometimes it came as survival wearing a man’s skin.

“How long?” Edmund asked, voice steady by force.

Thomas swallowed. “Minutes,” he said. “Not long. They’re gathering. And Rob said… Rob said if anyone’s hiding them, we burn that place too. Because fire shows what’s inside.”

From within the shelter came a muffled sob, quickly smothered. Miriam clutched her child tighter.

Edmund looked at the crude boards, the thin roof. He looked at the faces inside, pale and shining with terror. He looked at Walter and Alice, the only ones still standing on the right side of the line.

Then he looked back at Thomas and saw what Thomas could not bring himself to say: he had come not only to warn, but to see if Edmund would run, so Thomas could later tell the mob, "He fled. That proves it."

Thomas's mouth trembled. "Edmund," he whispered, "please. Come with me. Walk back before they arrive. If you stand here, they'll take you too. They'll say you led this."

Edmund heard the offer for what it was: a way for Thomas to save his own skin by pulling Edmund into the village's story as either penitent or guilty. There was no innocence left, only roles.

Edmund straightened, cold settling over him like armor. "Go," he told Thomas. "If you want to live, go back and tell them you didn't find anything."

Thomas's eyes filled, and for a moment Edmund saw the man he had been. Then Thomas blinked, hard, and whatever softness was there folded away.

"I can't," Thomas whispered. "They'll know."

Edmund nodded once, as if that settled it. "Then you've already chosen," he said.

A shout rose from the direction of the village, closer now. Another answered. The bell rang again, insistent.

Walter closed his eyes briefly, like a man bracing for impact.

Alice lifted her knife higher and stepped closer to the shelter's opening, planting herself where anyone approaching would have to see her first. Her voice, when she spoke, was flat and steady. "Now we find out," she said, "who the village thinks deserves to burn."

The mob arrived before full dark, but the night made them braver. Torches multiplied along the hedgerow like malignant stars, their flames tugged sideways by a faint breeze off the river. Edmund heard them before he saw them: boots in wet grass, the clatter of tools carried too openly to be called tools, voices slipping between laughter and prayer.

Walter leaned close to Edmund at the shelter's mouth. "They'll come straight for you," he said, as if the words were something he could place gently to soften the blow.

"They'll come straight for whoever stands in front," Edmund replied.

Alice did not look at either of them. She stared into the hedge like a hunter listening for the first snap of twig that told her which way death would step. "They're not hunting truth," she said. "They're hunting the feeling of being right."

Thomas had already limped back toward the village, swallowed by the dark and the reeds. Whether he would tell them nothing, or tell them enough, no longer mattered. The sound of the bell had done what no man's words could. It had gathered a single will out of many frightened bodies, and that will now moved toward Edmund's land.

Inside the shelter, Miriam rocked her child, whispering words that were not English. The candle widow's bundle shook in her hands as if it had a pulse of its own. The moneylender's boy pressed his face into his father's coat, the way a child tried to climb back into safety by force of will.

Edmund's half-built boards and posts would not hold against a crowd, not for long. He had imagined this place for isolation, for care, for the sick to be kept separate and tended. He had not imagined it as a last wall.

"Out the back," Alice said suddenly, so low it was almost breath. "Now. We go along the river."

A muffled cry rose from behind the hedge, then a man's voice. "Here! Here's his little hut."

Walter's shoulders tightened. He started to move, then froze as if his body could not choose between standing and fleeing.

Edmund grabbed Walter's forearm. "Get them moving," he said. "Take them into the reeds and keep low. If you stop to argue, we lose everything."

Walter blinked, as if waking from a blow, and nodded once. He ducked into the shelter and began pulling people up by their elbows, gentle and forceful at once.

Miriam looked at Edmund with eyes too wide. "Isaac," she whispered again, as if the name could be a rope Edmund might throw across distance.

Edmund could not answer with comfort. He only touched her shoulder briefly, a human contact that felt almost forbidden now. "Go," he said. "Go, Miriam. Keep your child quiet if you can."

The crowd broke through the hedge before the last of them were out.

Men poured into the open space around the shelter, torches held high, faces orange and distorted. Rob Baines was at the front as if the path had been made for him. Father Griffiths was there too, not in front, never in front, but close enough to be seen. The reeve hovered beside him, drawn and pale, his authority now reduced to standing near holiness and hoping it protected him from being questioned.

Rob spotted Edmund at once, still at the shelter's mouth. His grin cut bright through soot and torchlight. "There he is," Rob called. "There's our clean-handed lord."

A man behind him shouted, "Where are they?"

Edmund stepped forward, away from the shelter, so the shadow of the boards fell behind him and hid whatever movement still lingered there. "There's no one here but me," he said.

The lie was thin. It did not need to be believed. It only needed to slow their eyes for a moment.

Rob's gaze slid past Edmund to the shelter. His nostrils flared as if he could smell fear like smoke. “You built it for plague,” he said. “Now you use it for poisoners.”

“They’re people,” Edmund replied. “They’re families.”

“Families,” Rob echoed with a laugh, and the men around him answered as if laughter were an oath. “You love them, don’t you? More than your own.”

Walter’s knife flashed briefly in the torchlight as he cut through reeds along the river path, ushering Miriam and the others into the dark. Edmund heard the soft hiss of reeds parting, and then the river swallowed the sound, its slow movement indifferent.

Rob stepped closer, close enough that Edmund could see the veins at his temple, the sleeplessness turned into feverish purpose. “They ran,” Rob said, not as a guess but as an accusation. “They ran because you helped them. Because you are part of it.”

Father Griffiths lifted his hands slightly, a gesture that might have meant restraint if his voice had matched it. “Master Edmund,” he called, loud enough for the group to hear. “If you have sheltered them, you must answer for it.”

Edmund turned his head and looked at the priest. "Answer to whom?" He asked. "To you? To Rob? To a mob with torches?"

The reeve swallowed. "To the village," he managed, the phrase that had become their god.

Rob's torchbearer stepped forward, fire crackling. "Burn it," someone said from the back, eager and simple. "Smoke'll show if he's hiding them."

Edmund felt the moment tighten, the same moment he had watched at Eli's door. The crowd did not need proof. It needed ritual. Fire was easy. Fire did not ask questions.

Alice appeared then, not running, not shouting, simply stepping from the dark edge of the shelter's far side into the torchlight with her knife raised. For a heartbeat, the men nearest flinched. Alice had always been a woman people avoided crossing even when the world was calm; in chaos, her steadiness looked like something unnatural.

"Come closer," she said. Her voice was flat, almost bored. "Any of you. Come closer and see what bleeds."

Rob smiled wider. "Look," he said, delighted. "The harrow woman's dog shows teeth."

Alice's eyes did not move from the torch. "You set one flame on these boards," she said, "and you'll have more than smoke. You'll have every man on this land marked as an arsonist. And when the sickness takes you anyway, you'll have no one left to blame but your own hands."

A few men shifted, uneasy. The words landed. Not because they were moral, but because they hinted at consequence, the one thing fear hated most.

Rob saw the hesitation and moved to crush it. "He's bewitched her," he said, jerking his chin at Edmund. "He's got them all under him. That's how they work. That's how poison hides. Under fine words and clean tables."

He lunged suddenly, grabbing for Edmund's collar.

Edmund reacted without thought. He caught Rob's wrist and twisted, not hard enough to break, but hard enough to make Rob hiss and jerk back. For an instant the crowd inhaled as one body. A hand laid on a lord was not new; a lord laying hands back, on the man now acting as the village's mouth, struck a different nerve.

"You touch me," Rob said, voice low and shaking with excitement, "and you prove it. You prove you're against us."

Edmund released him. "I'm against this," Edmund said. "Against burning homes and calling it purity. Against beating a confession out of a man until he says anything you want. Against turning neighbors into prey because you're too frightened to admit you don't understand sickness."

Rob wiped his wrist as if Edmund had dirtied him. "Then we'll have a cleaner village without you," he said.

The torchbearer stepped forward again.

And then, from the river path, a sound rose. A sharp cry. Not loud, but sudden, the kind of noise that snapped heads toward it.

Alice moved like a thrown stone. She sprinted into the dark without looking back, vanishing into reeds with a rustle. Rob shouted, "After her!" and several men broke formation, chasing the sound. Their torches bobbed away, scattering light across water and grass.

Edmund understood what Alice had done. A decoy. A sacrifice of attention. She had made herself the hunted thing so the families could keep moving.

The crowd's unity fractured for a precious few heartbeats.

Walter's voice carried faintly from the river: "Now, Edmund!" a harsh whisper that cut through reeds.

Edmund looked once at the shelter. Its boards stood innocent and pitiful, already condemned in the minds of men who wanted flame. He looked at Father Griffiths, whose face had pinched into something like outrage now that control was slipping. He looked at the reeve, whose eyes begged for someone else to decide.

Then Edmund ran.

He dove into the reeds and the river cold slapped his boots through mud. Behind him, Rob's shout rose, furious and triumphant, as if Edmund fleeing was proof.

It became a night of movement and hiding and wrong turns. They followed the river south where the banks were soft and the trees leaned close, a dark corridor. Miriam's child cried once and then went silent, exhausted by terror. The moneylender muttered under his breath as he walked, prayers and numbers tangled together. Walter supported the candle widow when her legs shook too hard.

They did not stop until the sky began to pale.

And when morning finally arrived, it did not feel like a beginning.

They crouched under a stand of willows where the river slowed, and the mud held the shape of every footstep like memory. Edmund's clothes were soaked to the knee, his hands raw from reeds cutting skin. He looked back upriver, toward where the village lay.

Smoke still rose, thin and steady, straight into the calm air. Not the friendly smoke of breakfast hearths, but heavier, dirtier. It smeared the pale sky as if trying to write something there.

No one spoke for a long time. They listened, waiting for the sound of pursuit, for a bell, for the crackle of torches coming through brush. But the world held an unnatural stillness, the same stillness that had come with the ship in the prologue tales, the kind of quiet that was not peace but aftermath.

Miriam finally broke it. "Do you hear it?" she whispered.

Edmund listened harder.

Nothing. No distant shouts. No cries. No bell. Even birds seemed reluctant, their morning calls thin and delayed.

Walter's face had gone slack with fatigue. "They'll be sleeping," he said, but his voice held no conviction. "Or… counting what they've done."

Edmund pictured the square at dawn. Ash in the air. Blackened doorframes. The well sitting unchanged at the center, indifferent to blame. He pictured Eli's house as a gutted shell. Isaac bound and broken, his confession already turned into a story that made violence feel righteous.

"The silence is worse," the candle widow whispered, her voice papery. "When people are shouting, you know where they are. When they are silent…"

"When they are silent," Alice's voice finished, and Edmund startled because he had not heard her approach.

She emerged from the trees on the far side, hair damp, a smear of soot on her cheek, knife still in her hand. Her eyes were bright and hard, but she was breathing steadily. Alive.

Walter let out a sound that was half relief and half anger. "You fool," he whispered.

Alice shrugged slightly, as if she had merely stepped out to fetch water. "They chased," she said. "Not far. They're brave in lanes, not in trees."

Edmund stared at her, gratitude and horror tangled together. "Did they burn it?" he asked, meaning the shelter, meaning his land, meaning the last physical mark of the life he had tried to build.

Alice's mouth tightened. "I don't know," she said. "But I saw the glow over the village. More than one house."

Miriam's face crumpled. She pressed her lips to her child's hair, rocking again without realizing. The moneylender looked down at his hands as if expecting to find ash there already.

Edmund turned his gaze back toward the smoke. Morning light made it look almost gentle, like mist rising from fields.

It was not gentle. It was what remained after fear had been given matches.

Behind them, the river moved on, unconcerned. Ahead, the road waited, dangerous and uncertain. And upriver, the village sat in a quiet that was not repentance, not grief, but a pause between breaths.

The morning after did not bring clarity. It brought silence, and in that silence, Edmund could feel the village holding its new lesson close: that there was relief in destruction, and that once a thing was burned, it could no longer argue.

Chapter 9

Safety in Blood

They stayed under the willows until the light had fully taken the sky, because moving too soon felt like inviting the sound of pursuit to find them. The river slid past in a slow brown sheet, carrying flecks of broken reed and last year's leaves as if it had always carried such things and always would. Edmund kept his eyes upriver. He could not stop. Smoke still bruised the horizon where the village lay, and the line of it made a kind of tether in his mind, a reminder that what had burned there had not only been wood.

Miriam sat with her back to a trunk, her child heavy against her chest. The boy's crying had run out in the night; now he made only small, exhausted sounds when he shifted, like a kettle settling after it has boiled itself dry. The older child hovered near her knee, no longer frozen, but emptied, his gaze moving over the trees with wary attention, as if expecting men to step out of every shadow.

The candle widow, hunched and shaking, kept rubbing her hands together, the way a person did in cold, though the air was not cold now. The moneylender sat with his son pressed to him, the boy's face half hidden in cloth, his eyes peeking out whenever a bird moved. Walter stood at the edge of the willows, watching the riverbank as though his stare could keep it clear. Alice paced in a small, tight line, knife still in her fist, her breathing steady enough to be anger in motion.

Hours passed, and nothing came.

No bell. No shouted names. No torches bobbing through brush. The silence did not loosen Edmund's chest; it tightened it. It was the same kind of pause the village had made before each step into violence, that brief moment of stillness when men waited to see whether anyone would stop them. Only now the stillness belonged to the aftermath, and the question beneath it was different.

Had the village grown tired? Or had it simply finished what it meant to do for the moment?

Walter came back from a short walk along the river, rubbing mud from his hands. "No tracks," he said quietly. "Not down this far. If they came after us, they didn't have the sense to keep close to water."

"They had sense enough to follow torches," Alice replied without looking at him. "Sense comes and goes when it's fed by drink and Father Griffiths's voice."

At the mention of the priest, Miriam made a small sound in her throat, something between a sob and a growl. "He said words," she whispered. "While they did it. Like words could make it clean."

Edmund crouched near her. He wanted to offer comfort and found he had none that would not be an insult. He could still see Isaac's face in his mind, the blood, the rope, the moment his body surrendered truth to pain. Isaac's confession had not been believed because it was plausible. It had been believed because it was useful.

"We can't stay here," Edmund said softly, more to the group than to her. "If we don't move, we'll be found by someone else. A fisher. A farm boy. Anyone. And if news has spread, it won't matter how far we are from the village."

The moneylender lifted his head at that, eyes red-rimmed. "Where then?" he asked. His voice sounded thinner than Edmund remembered from market days, stripped of the ease that came from being necessary. "If we go to another village, will they take us in? Or will they throw stones as well?"

Edmund glanced upriver again. Smoke continued to rise, but it did not thicken. It did not boil. It stood almost steady, like the last breath of something that had already died.

"First," Alice said, "we find out what the village is doing. Then we decide if we run blind or with some sense."

Walter frowned. "You want to go back?"

"Not you," Alice snapped. "Not Miriam. Not the boy. Someone who can walk into a lane without being dragged to the well."

Her eyes slid to Edmund.

The logic of it was ugly and true. Edmund could pass, for a little while, as a man who still belonged to the shape of the village. He was their lord, their odd one, their convenient conscience. And now, perhaps, their next target waiting on a delay. But his face was known, and in England familiarity sometimes bought a moment where a stranger would be stabbed first.

Walter understood what she meant, and his jaw worked as if chewing something bitter. "If you go back," he said to Edmund, "they'll hang you in the square."

"If they meant to do it this morning," Alice replied, "they'd have chased all night. They didn't. That means they think they've done what they needed."

"Or they think we're trapped out here and can be taken later," Walter said.

Edmund looked at the faces huddled under the willows, at the way each one flinched when the river made an ordinary sound. He could not take them on the road without knowing whether the road had already been turned into another kind of weapon.

"I'll go close," Edmund said at last. "Not into the square. I'll watch from the fields. If there's a patrol, if they're searching, I'll come back at once."

Miriam's eyes fixed on him. "If you see Isaac," she whispered, and it was not a request so much as a desperate shaping of reality, as if speaking the possibility might make it exist.

Edmund's throat tightened. "If I see him," he said, and hated that the words were all he could offer.

Alice stepped forward. "I'm coming," she said.

"No," Walter said immediately. "They'll notice you. They already hate you."

Alice's mouth hardened. "They already hate me," she agreed, as if that settled the argument in her favor. Then, after a moment, she tossed the knife into her other hand, quieter. "Fine. I'll go far enough to pull you out if they take you. I won't show myself. But I won't sit under trees while you walk into a snare alone."

Walter started to protest again, but Edmund lifted a hand. "Let her," he said. "If I'm caught, I'd rather she be there than no one."

They moved in a cautious, broken line along the riverbank until the willows were behind them and the land rose slightly, giving a view across fields toward the village. They did not go close enough to see faces, only enough to see shape and movement.

The village looked quiet.

Too quiet for what it had become the night before.

No crowd swarmed the lanes. No torches remained. From this distance the church tower stood unchanged, stubborn as stone always was, and the square lay hidden behind roofs. But smoke still leaked from two points, thin and persistent, and one of the points was not the usual place of morning hearths. One was where Eli's lane lay.

Edmund crouched behind a hedge and watched. After a time, he saw men moving, not running, but walking with the careful slowness of people who had been awake too long. A few carried buckets. One carried a bundle that might have been bedding or clothing. Another bent over something and rose again, the movement of lifting debris, of clearing.

The village was tidying itself.

Even from afar, Edmund could feel the shift. The night had been a storm of purpose; morning was an attempt at order. People did not like to live in the raw shape of their own cruelty. They needed to arrange it into something that could be borne.

Alice, half hidden beside him, whispered, "They're cleaning."

"Yes," Edmund murmured. "They're making it look like an accident."

A figure emerged near the church and stood on the steps. Even at this distance, Edmund recognized the posture. Father Griffiths. The priest lifted his arms and addressed a small knot of people. Edmund could not hear the words, but he could imagine them. A sermon that turned fire into discipline, confession into truth, violence into protection.

Alice watched for a long moment. "Look at them," she said quietly. "They'll call it mercy. They'll say the houses had to burn so the poison wouldn't spread."

Edmund watched a man pause in the lane and cross himself before returning to his work. Not a prayer of grief. A sealing gesture, as if marking something done and closed.

Walter's fear had been of what the mob would do in the heat of its frenzy. Edmund realized, staring at the calm movement below, that the deeper danger was what the village would do when it was calm again and had to live with what it had done. Calm did not always bring remorse. Sometimes calm brought a story.

And a story, repeated, became belief.

Alice shifted her weight, eyes narrowed. "No one's falling in the street," she said. "No one's screaming. They'll take that as proof."

Edmund felt it too, the temptation even at the edge of his own mind: the hope that perhaps, for a day, the sickness would pause, that perhaps there would be no new swelling, no new blackened flesh. Not because the village deserved reprieve, but because the innocent under the willows did. The human mind reached for patterns the way a drowning man reached for wood.

If there were no deaths today, the village would say the well had been saved. The poisoners punished. God appeased.

Edmund could already hear Rob Baines's voice crowing over it, could already imagine the way men would straighten their backs and tell themselves they had been brave, not monstrous.

"False relief," Edmund whispered, and Alice glanced at him.

"What?" she asked.

He swallowed. "If the plague gives them a pause," he said, "they'll think their violence bought it. They'll think blood made them safe."

Alice stared down at the village, her expression unreadable in the hedge-shadow. "Then they'll want more blood," she said.

"Yes," Edmund replied, his mouth dry. "And next time, they won't need a confession."

They stayed there until the sun climbed higher and the village continued to move in its quiet, purposeful way. Once, Edmund saw a small group carry something long and heavy between them. It might have been a beam. It might have been a body wrapped for burial. From this distance, the difference did not matter. Either way, the village was learning to handle consequences with the same hands it had used to make them.

Edmund backed away from the hedge at last, drawing Alice with him. They retreated toward the river, toward the others waiting under trees.

Nothing had chased them. No shout had risen. No men had poured out of the village in pursuit.

That absence felt, to the frightened part of Edmund's mind, like permission to breathe.

And that was how the village would feel too, he realized. A morning without immediate collapse. A moment where the air did not seem to kill. A pause that could be claimed as victory.

The most dangerous thing that could happen now was not another death.

It was a lull.

Because in that lull, the village would become convinced it had been right. And a man who believed he had saved his children by burning someone else's house would not hesitate to strike the match again when fear returned, as it always did.

Edmund quickened his pace back toward the willows, dread heavy in his gut, because the relief he felt in his own lungs was already curdling into something else.

Not hope.

Foreknowledge.

By the time Edmund and Alice slipped back under the willows, the others had not moved far. They had shifted their bodies, nothing more, the way people did when the ground began to ache beneath them and still they were afraid to stand.

Walter rose at their approach, hope and dread wrestling across his face. “Well?” he asked, and the word came out too sharp.

Edmund crouched and kept his voice low. “No search,” he said. “No torches. They’re cleaning up. Father Griffiths is speaking on the steps like it’s a Sunday and not a ruin.”

Miriam’s head lifted, eyes red and fixed. “Isaac?” she whispered.

Edmund held her gaze as long as he could, then looked away. “I couldn’t see,” he said. “From where we were, there was no… I didn’t see him.”

Miriam's mouth tightened as if she had bitten the inside of it. She nodded once, not because she accepted the answer, but because she had no place to put her grief except back into her own chest.

The moneylender shifted, his son still tucked under his arm. "And the well?" he asked, as if the well might be a mouth that could be made to speak sense again.

"The well is still there," Alice said, and her voice had the flatness of someone describing a stone. "It always was. It always will be."

They sat with that for a time. The river moved, and the reeds whispered against each other. The stillness that had felt like a pause in hunting now grew into something heavier, something with edges.

Walter rubbed a hand over his face. "Maybe…" he began, and stopped as if the word might betray him. "Maybe it's passed."

Edmund heard the longing in it and hated it, because he felt the same longing pressing against his own ribs. The mind could not live without reaching for some shape of mercy, even when it did not deserve it.

"It doesn't pass like a rain cloud," Edmund said quietly. "Not once it's here."

The candle widow, who had been silent so long Edmund had nearly forgotten she could speak, made a thin sound. "Then why are they calm?" she asked. "Why aren't they dying already, if God means to punish?"

Edmund did not answer at once. He watched a beetle climb a blade of grass and thought of the ship in the tales, the one that had brought rats into a port and then into streets, the way an unseen beginning could travel quietly until it was everywhere. "Because it moves," he said. "Because it takes time. And because sometimes the worst thing that can happen is nothing at all. It teaches people the wrong lesson."

Alice snorted, a harsh, humorless breath. "They'll call last night a cure."

Walter's jaw worked. "And if no one dies today," he murmured, "they'll believe it."

They did not move until the sun began to slide down again and the light shifted toward evening. They were hungry, but hunger was a familiar pain. Fear was the thing that kept changing shape. When they finally did rise, it was not toward the road yet. They moved along the river, keeping to the trees, not daring to cross open fields where anyone might see them. The ground was soft, and their footprints filled with brown water almost at once, as if the earth itself were trying to erase them.

As they walked, they heard sounds that did not belong to their small group. A distant shout, then another. The noises came from upriver, from the direction of the village. They stopped and listened.

Walter's hand went to the small knife at his belt, a poor comfort. "They've found the trail," he whispered.

"No," Alice said, head tilted. "That's not a hunting shout."

Edmund listened harder. The shouts did not carry the same sharp rhythm as a mob calling for names. They rose and fell unevenly, like people calling from house to house, confused rather than triumphant. There was no chant. No single voice leading. Just sound scattered by wind and distance.

Miriam clutched her child tighter. "What is it?" she whispered.

Edmund's throat tightened, and the answer came before he wanted it to. "It's starting," he said.

They moved again, faster now, until they found a deeper fold of trees where the river bent and the bank rose. There, they huddled in a hollow sheltered by roots. The air smelled of damp earth and crushed leaves. Dusk gathered, and in the dim, faces looked carved from ash.

They did not see anyone that night. No one came pushing through reeds with torches. No dog barked along the bank. The village did not hunt them.

Instead, nearer midnight, they heard the church bell.

It rang once.

Then again.

Not the jubilant ringing that had called men to fire. This was slower. Measured. A bell used the way it was meant to be used, to mark death.

Walter's eyes widened in the dark. "They're burying," he whispered.

Alice leaned her head back against a root and let out a long breath through her nose, something close to satisfaction but poisoned by grimness. "Good," she said softly. "Let them ring it until their arms ache."

Edmund did not feel satisfaction. He felt only the cold weight of inevitability. The bell did not prove justice. It proved that violence had failed, and in failing, it would demand more violence to explain why.

The next morning, a mist lay low over the water. It softened the world until distance looked like memory. They ate what little they had managed to bring: a heel of bread, a few hard apples. The children chewed silently, eyes darting at every sound.

Walter stood apart, watching upriver again. His restlessness was a physical thing, a man forced to stand still while his home became a rumor.

"I'm going to look," he said finally, voice rough.

Edmund turned. "No," he said at once. "Not alone."

"I'll be quick," Walter insisted. "Just close enough to see. If folk are sick, if Rob's out, if they're searching… we need to know."

Alice pushed up to her feet. "He's right," she said. "Knowing is the only advantage we have left."

Edmund stared at them both, then nodded once. "All right," he said. "But we don't go into the lanes. We don't let anyone see us."

They left Miriam and the others deeper in the trees, with Alice's knife pressed into Miriam's palm and a few hard instructions whispered like a prayer. Then Edmund and Walter moved upriver with the caution of men crossing a battlefield after the fighting had paused.

They found the first sign before they reached the village.

A small cart stood abandoned on the track that ran toward the fields, its shaft sunk into mud. No horse. No driver. One wheel had slipped into a rut and the whole thing leaned, laden with sacks that had burst. Grain spilled in a pale fan across the earth, already damp, already attracting movement.

Rats.

Not one or two darting away at the sound of footsteps, but several, bold in daylight, their fur slick, their bodies swelling in a well-fed confidence. They moved through the spilled grain like it belonged to them. When Walter stepped closer, one lifted its head and looked at him, unafraid.

Walter froze. "Christ," he breathed.

Edmund's skin crawled. He had seen rats in barns and along the river, but not like this. Not in the open, not so many, not so unconcerned.

They moved on, leaving the cart and its silent story behind. The closer they came, the more the air changed. Not smoke now, but something sweeter, thicker. A smell that reminded Edmund of the miller's cottage when the child first sickened, but magnified, carried on damp air.

Near the edge of the village, they crouched behind a hedge and looked through a gap.

The lane was not empty. People moved, but not with purpose. They drifted. A woman stood in a doorway holding a cloth to her mouth, watching the road with wide eyes. Two men carried a body between them, wrapped in a sheet that sagged in the middle. They did not move like men bearing someone honored. They moved like men trying not to touch.

A child sat on a step with no shoes on, rocking slightly, his gaze fixed on nothing. No one spoke to him as they passed.

The bell rang again, and this time Edmund heard the answering sound: a distant wail, the kind that came from a house when someone inside had stopped breathing.

Walter's mouth hung open. "They said it was poison," he whispered, as if accusing the air itself of lying.

Edmund felt a bitter pressure behind his eyes. "Poison would not do this," he said. "Not like this. Not across houses. Not across days."

A man came into view limping, his hands held away from his body as if he did not trust them. It took Edmund a moment to recognize him: the scar-faced fellow Rob had first ordered to drink from the bucket. The man's face was gray, and he paused halfway down the lane to cough, a wet, tearing sound. When he straightened, he spat into the dirt. Dark flecks marked the spit.

He took two more steps, then folded as if his bones had turned to water. He hit the ground on his side and lay there twitching.

For a heartbeat, no one moved. People looked at him the way they had looked at the well, waiting for meaning to rise out of darkness.

Then the woman in the doorway screamed.

Men rushed toward the fallen man and then stopped short, hovering, afraid to touch him. One bent as if to help and then jerked back as if the air above the body had burned him. Another made the sign of the cross so violently his fingers struck his own forehead.

Walter's hands were shaking. "Help him," he whispered, but his feet did not move.

Edmund knew why. The distance between them and the village was a thin mercy. If they stepped into the lane, they would not save the man. They would only add themselves to the story. The village would not see Edmund as a helper now. It would see him as proof made flesh.

A second scream rose from further down the lane. Then another. The sounds overlapped, not in unity, but in unraveling. Somewhere, a door slammed hard enough to rattle shutters. Somewhere else, someone shouted a name, a desperate call that went unanswered.

Walter swallowed, his throat working. "This is the wave," he said hoarsely. "This is what you said would come."

Edmund watched the lane fill with frantic motion, bodies moving away from each other and yet unable to stop gathering at the points where death appeared. The village had bought itself one morning of calm by spilling blood. And now the sickness was taking payment with interest.

“We have to go back,” Edmund said, forcing the words past the tightness in his chest. “We can’t stay near. If they see us…”

Walter did not argue. His eyes were fixed on the lane, on the man still twitching in the dirt, on the way no one could bring themselves to lift him. “Rob will blame someone,” Walter whispered. “He’ll blame the ones who ran. He’ll blame you. He’ll blame anyone who isn’t already dead.”

Edmund backed away from the hedge, pulling Walter with him by the sleeve. As they retreated toward the river, the bell rang again. And beneath it, faint but clear even from the edge of the fields, Edmund heard another sound that made his stomach drop.

Laughter.

Not much. Not joyful. A short, brittle burst, like a man choking on his own breath. The kind of laugh someone made when the world became unbearable and the mind, scrambling for footing, grabbed at the nearest cruel thought.

Even now, even with bodies dropping in the lanes, part of the village was searching for the comfort of blame.

The new wave of death had arrived, and it did not care who had been burned or who had confessed. It moved through the village like water through cracks, indifferent to righteousness.

And Edmund knew, with a certainty as cold as river stone, that when the fear surged again, the village would not turn its hands inward and admit it had been wrong.

It would reach outward.

It would look for someone to pay.

Edmund and Walter did not run back to the river hollow so much as retreat with the careful urgency of men backing away from a fire that could leap.

Behind them the village noises tangled into something worse than shouts. Not the clean roar of a mob moving with one purpose, but the ragged sound of too many small panics colliding. Doors slammed. Names were called and swallowed by distance. The bell continued its slow insistence, toll after toll, as if Father Griffiths had decided that if the village could not be saved, it could at least be counted.

Walter stumbled once on the track, his boot catching in the mud. Edmund caught his sleeve and hauled him upright.

"Don't fall," Edmund said, and hated the flatness of his own voice. As though falling was a choice.

Walter's breath came in sharp pulls. "I saw him," he managed. "The scar-faced one. The one Rob made drink."

"Yes," Edmund said. "I saw."

Walter's eyes flicked sideways, wild. "And they did nothing. They hovered like he was already carrion."

"What could they do?" Edmund asked. It came out harsher than he intended. Then, softer, "They're afraid to touch. Afraid to breathe. Afraid to admit this isn't a thing you can beat out of a neighbor."

Walter made a broken sound in his throat that was almost agreement, almost grief.

They slipped back beneath the trees where the riverbank rose and the reeds thickened. The damp smell of earth met them like a wall. Miriam looked up at once, her face tightening with the reflex of hope and dread. Alice rose from where she had been crouched, knife no longer in

Miriam's hand but back in her own, as though the blade had returned to its rightful owner.

"Well?" Alice asked, and there was no softness in her, only readiness.

Edmund crouched and lowered his voice. "It's spreading through the village now," he said. "Bodies in the lanes. The bell's not for show."

The moneylender's son made a small sound and pressed closer to his father's side. The candle widow whispered something under her breath, not a prayer exactly, more like counting.

Miriam's eyes searched Edmund's face as if it were a page she could read. "Isaac?" she asked again, and the name was a bruise she kept pressing to see if it still hurt.

Edmund held her gaze. "I couldn't see him," he said. "I'm sorry."

Miriam looked down at her child, and Edmund watched the way her jaw clenched until it shook. She did not cry. She had already spent her voice.

Walter sank onto the damp ground, elbows on his knees, staring at nothing. "They were wrong," he said hoarsely. "They burned houses. They broke men. And it's still here."

"They weren't wrong about one thing," Alice replied. "They were afraid."

Walter flinched. "Fear doesn't excuse it."

"No," Alice said. "But fear explains the next part."

Edmund felt that next part like a pressure in his chest, the sense of a wheel turning back to the same notch. "They'll look for an answer," he said. "And if the answer isn't the well, or poison, or Isaac's confession, they'll find another. They cannot bear meaninglessness."

The moneylender lifted his head, eyes hollow. "We must leave," he said. "Today. Now."

"And walk into another village that's heard rumors?" Alice asked. "Walk into a market with our faces and our fear and our accents? They'll smell it. And if the plague is here, it will be there soon. People will be looking for someone to blame before we even cross their boundary."

Walter rubbed at his mouth with the heel of his hand. "So, we sit here until we rot?"

Edmund did not answer at once. He listened. The river moved. Birds were quieter than they should have been. And far off, as if carried by the wrong wind, he heard a faint chorus of voices from upriver.

Not screams now. Not the bell.

A chant, half formed. A group speaking together, finding the comfort of rhythm.

Alice heard it too. Her head tilted, eyes narrowing. "There," she said quietly. "That's them finding their feet again. Not with truth. With noise."

Walter pushed himself upright. "We should go farther," he said. "Before they think to search the banks."

Edmund nodded, but the chant troubled him more than a search would have. A search meant they still believed the danger could be caught like a rabbit. A chant meant they had begun to believe something else: that the danger had a will, a face, a mark.

They moved deeper along the river bend, keeping to the cover of trees and reeds until the sounds from the village blurred. Edmund guided them to a stand of alder where the ground rose enough to keep their feet from sinking. They settled there as if settling meant anything now.

Time dragged. The sun climbed, thinned behind haze, and began to slope again. Hunger sharpened, then dulled into a constant ache. The children dozed in fits. Miriam's older boy stared upriver as if he could see through the curve of trees, as if he could see his father's broken shape and will it whole again.

In the late afternoon, as light began to yellow, someone approached through the reeds.

Alice was on her feet in an instant, knife lifted. Walter's hand went to his belt. Edmund raised a palm, not to stop them but to steady the moment.

The figure pushed through and froze at the sight of steel.

It was Thomas.

His limp was worse, or perhaps Edmund only noticed it now because every weakness had become a danger. His hair was plastered to his forehead with sweat. His face was pinched, eyes too bright, the look of a man who had run from something without admitting it to himself.

Walter surged forward a step. "What are you doing here?" he demanded.

Thomas's eyes flicked over them, landing on Miriam and the children, the moneylender and his boy. Guilt crossed his face like a shadow.

"I shouldn't be," Thomas said. "But I had to tell you."

Alice did not lower her knife. "Tell us what," she said. "Quickly."

Thomas swallowed. His throat bobbed. "They're dying," he said, and the bluntness of it made the group go still. "Not one or two. It's in houses all over. The reeve's wife took sick. One of the men who carried Eli out fell in the lane and bled from his nose like a butchered pig. Father Griffiths says it's punishment."

Walter's mouth twisted. "Punishment for what? For burning?"

Thomas shook his head quickly, almost desperately. "No. Not for that. He says it's punishment for harboring wickedness. He says it's the poison spreading because the source wasn't cut out deep enough."

Edmund felt cold settle under his ribs. "Deep enough," he repeated.

Thomas nodded, eyes darting as if he expected the trees themselves to judge him. "Rob's saying Isaac confessed, and Eli denied, and that proves they're trained to lie. Rob says the ones who ran are carrying the corruption with them, and anyone who helps them will die too."

Miriam made a small sound that was not quite a sob, not quite a laugh. She clutched her child tighter, as if her arms could keep words from reaching him.

Edmund leaned forward. "What are they doing?" he asked. "In the village. Right now."

Thomas hesitated, and that hesitation told Edmund the answer before it came.

"They started with the strangers," Thomas said. "Or what they call strangers. Any house that didn't come out last night, any man that didn't carry a torch. Rob says sickness chooses cowards. Father Griffiths says sickness chooses sinners. They're… they're taking people to the square."

Walter stared. "For what?"

"To be questioned," Thomas said, and the phrase sounded like ash in his mouth.

Alice's voice went flat with disgust. "Questioned with fists."

Thomas flinched. "They need someone to hold," he said. "They can't stand it. The deaths today broke the relief they had, and now they're worse than last night because last night they thought it worked."

Edmund closed his eyes briefly. He saw it with awful clarity: the morning calm, the tidying, the priest on the steps, the village building a story in which fire had been a medicine. Then the sickness returning, indifferent and unstoppable, leaving that story with a hole in it.

A hole needed filling.

If violence had bought them one morning, then perhaps more violence would buy them another. If burning one house had not saved them, then they had burned too little, or the wrong house, or with insufficient zeal. The logic was monstrous and simple, and it ran on the same rails as every punishment Edmund had ever seen dressed as duty.

"Who are they taking?" Edmund asked, though he already feared the answer.

Thomas's eyes slid to Miriam and the others, and shame made his face redden. "Anyone they can," he admitted. "But Rob's saying it plain now. He's saying you helped them. He's saying your land was their hiding place and that proves you've been part of it since the first child died."

Walter swore under his breath. The moneylender's son began to whimper quietly; the sound pressed into cloth.

Miriam looked at Edmund, and there was no accusation in her gaze, only terrible understanding. "They will not stop," she whispered.

"No," Edmund said. His voice sounded distant to his own ears. "They won't. Because stopping means admitting they were wrong. And they would rather be cruel than wrong."

Alice stepped closer to Thomas, knife still up, her eyes hard. "Why did you come," she asked, "if you've already given them our trail once with your fear?"

Thomas's shoulders sagged. "Because I can't breathe," he said, and the honesty of it cut through his cowardice like a blade. "Because I watched a boy no older than ten dragged by his hair because his mother begged for mercy too loudly. Because I heard Father Griffiths say God loves a clean village and I knew he meant clean of people. And because Rob said tonight they'll come for Edmund. They'll come for his house and burn it proper this time, with witnesses, and hang him if they can find a beam that won't snap."

Edmund stared at him. The threat should have felt personal. Instead, it felt inevitable, the next click in the wheel.

Walter's voice shook with fury. "So, you ran here to warn us. And then what? You go back and tell them where we are?"

Thomas's face crumpled. "No," he said quickly. "No. I swear."

Alice's knife did not move. "Swear to what," she asked, "when swearing is just breath?"

Thomas looked at Edmund then, and tears stood in his eyes without falling. “I’ll go the other way,” he said. “I’ll tell them I found tracks downriver. I’ll lead them off.”

Walter barked a bitter laugh. “Now you’re brave.”

Thomas flinched as if struck, but he did not argue. “Maybe I’m only scared of the right thing now,” he whispered.

Edmund watched him, and pity rose in him despite everything. Pity, and something like dread. The village did not only burn the innocent. It burned the weak parts out of everyone it touched, leaving only fear and whatever shape fear chose to wear.

“We move,” Edmund said at last. “We don’t wait for night. We don’t wait for them to come with torches again.”

Miriam tightened her grip on her child and nodded once, as if motion was the only prayer left.

The moneylender rose, his son clinging to him. The candle widow pulled her bundle close. Walter took a breath that looked like swallowing knives.

Alice lowered her blade just enough to gesture. “Downriver,” she said. “Farther. We keep to water and tree cover. No roads unless we must.”

Thomas took a step back into the reeds, as if already half gone. “Edmund,” he said, voice cracking, “I’m sorry.”

Edmund met his gaze. “Be sorry later,” he said. “Right now, be useful.”

Thomas nodded once, sharp, and vanished into the green tangle.

As the small band began to move again, Edmund felt the wheel turning behind them, felt it in the distant bell and in the imagined glow of torches that would rise again as soon as the village needed to believe it could still purchase safety.

Violence had failed to stop death.

So, the village would try violence again, not because it worked, but because it offered the only thing fear could understand: an action that felt like power.

And once a people learned to call that feeling justice, they did not need the plague to keep killing.

They would do it themselves, until there was no one left to blame.

Chapter 10

The Unclean

By late afternoon the river widened and slowed, as if it, too, were tired of being chased. Edmund kept them under the cover of alder and willow where the bank dipped, choosing mud over open ground, reeds over roads. They moved in short bursts, then stopped, then moved again, every pause heavy with listening. The village lay upriver now, out of sight but not out of reach. Its bell had carried farther than its smoke, and even here Edmund could still hear it in his mind, each slow toll like a finger tapping the inside of a skull.

The children's feet began to drag. Miriam's younger boy, too small to understand where his father had gone, had reached the point where fear no longer made him quiet. He began to whimper with the thin persistence of exhaustion. Miriam bounced him and whispered into his hair until her voice frayed. The candle widow stumbled twice, and Walter caught her elbow both times without a word, his jaw clenched as if kindness might be mistaken for weakness.

The moneylender walked with his son pressed close, his eyes flicking to every bird and rustle. It struck Edmund, bitterly, that the man had once moved through the market with the confident pace of someone who belonged. Now he moved like a thief in his own country.

Alice stayed at the rear, knife in hand, turning her head often, watching for the wrong movement in the brush. She looked like she had been made for this: for flight, for sharp decisions, for surviving the parts of the world that did not pretend to be fair. Edmund hated that he needed her steadiness, hated that the village had made it necessary.

They had just settled into a shallow hollow where roots rose like ribs from the bank when Walter held up a hand and went still.

"Listen," he whispered.

At first Edmund heard only river and wind. Then, faintly, carried along the water in broken pieces: voices. Not the scattered cries of panic they had heard the day before. This was a chant, low and rhythmic, as if the village had put words into a single mouth. Between the chant came a thinner sound, something like weeping, and then a shout that cut it short.

Miriam stiffened. The older boy's eyes widened. The moneylender's son pressed his face into his father's side.

"They're doing it again," Walter said, his voice almost absent. "They've found another reason."

Alice's gaze did not lift from the trees. "They don't need reasons anymore," she said. "They need shapes. Bodies. Something to put under their hands."

Edmund tried to tell himself the voices were far, that sound traveled strangely over water, that it might be a farmyard or fishermen calling. But the cadence was wrong. It had the same ugly comfort as prayer, the kind spoken not to ask for mercy but to insist on it.

He thought of Thomas vanishing into reeds, promising to lead the mob away. Edmund had wanted to believe it could matter. Now he wondered whether any lie, however clever, could divert a hunger that had already turned inward.

The chant drifted on, then broke apart. Somewhere upriver, the bell tolled again, and the sound came with an answering murmur, like a crowd reacting.

Edmund closed his eyes briefly. In the darkness behind them, the village was still a living thing. Not a home. A mechanism.

"We go farther," he said. "Before night. Before they decide the river is a road they should follow."

No one argued. They gathered themselves again, dragging their small bundles, Miriam holding her child so tightly his face disappeared against her. The older boy walked beside her with a strange stiff dignity, as if he had decided that if he could not save his father, he would at least not be seen to break.

They moved downriver until the trees thinned and fields began again, the bank rising enough that Edmund could see beyond the next bend. A low copse stood ahead, a place to hide, and beyond it a track that would lead away from the water. Edmund did not want the track. He did not want any human path. But he understood that staying too close to the river would narrow their choices until the river itself became a trap.

They were halfway to the copse when Alice froze and lifted her knife.

A figure stood at the edge of the trees, not approaching, not fleeing, simply swaying slightly as if the ground was moving under him. It was a man, thin to the point of sharpness, his tunic hanging wrong on his bones. He held his hands away from his body, palms half open, and when he spoke his voice scraped like dry leaves.

"Don't," he croaked. "Don't come close."

Walter stepped forward a fraction, then stopped. Edmund felt his own instinct pull him back, the hard-earned reflex of the last days: distance was safety. But the man did not look like a pursuer. He looked like what the village had begun to leave behind.

"Who are you?" Edmund asked.

The man's eyes were red-rimmed and too bright. His lips were cracked. When he swallowed, it looked painful. "No one," he said. Then, after a pause, as if a name might still matter to someone somewhere, "Jory."

Edmund searched his memory. The name came back with the image of a lanky youth who used to hang near the edge of market days, carrying bundles for pennies, laughing too loudly, always watched by women who pulled children away. Not dangerous, just… wrong, in the way villages decided some people were wrong by nature.

"What happened?" Edmund asked.

Jory's laugh came out as a cough. He bent slightly, hand pressing his ribs. "They said I was dirty," he rasped. "Not like mud. Like… like bad. Like I made it worse."

Alice's knife did not lower. "Who did?" she asked.

Jory's gaze flicked to her blade and then away, as if the sight of steel had become a language he understood too well. "Rob. Father Griffiths. All of them. They brought me to the square." His eyes unfocused for a moment, staring past Edmund as if the memory was still happening. "They said sickness likes the weak. They said God shows it by who He takes first."

Walter's voice came harsh. "God's taking everyone."

Jory shook his head slowly, and the movement looked like it made him dizzy. "Not fast enough," he whispered. "Not fast enough for them. They wanted to make it make sense."

Edmund felt cold spread through him. He had feared they would hunt the ones who fled. He had not allowed himself to fully imagine how quickly a village could decide that the nearest enemy was the easiest.

“What did they do to you?” Miriam asked suddenly. Her voice was raw, but it cut cleanly through the men’s exchange. She stepped forward half a pace, then stopped, clutching her child tighter, as if remembering too late what touch could mean.

Jory blinked at her, as if surprised a woman like Miriam would speak to him at all. His mouth worked. “They made me stand by the well,” he said. “They made me drink and drink. Not to test. To make me choke so they could say it proved something.” He licked his cracked lips. “They said I stank. They said I’d been in the wrong houses. They said my mind was… loose. That loose minds let the Devil in.”

Edmund could hear Father Griffiths’s voice in the words, could hear the priest’s careful way of turning cruelty into doctrine. A loose mind. An unclean body. The plague as proof of moral rot rather than a thing carried on breath and flea and rat.

“And then?” Edmund pressed.

Jory’s gaze dropped to his hands. The fingers trembled. “They took Old Nan,” he said. “The one who talks to herself. They took her because she wouldn't stop praying out loud and it scared them. They took Stephen the lame, too. Said he'd been spared in other years because sickness didn't want him, and now it wanted the rest because they kept him." His voice broke on the last words, as if part of him still expected the village to behave like a village.

Walter stared, face tightening. "Stephen?" He repeated. "Stephen Harp? He can barely walk."

Jory nodded, small and sick. "They called him a burden," he whispered. "They called all of them burdens. They said the strong must cut away the weak like rot from an apple. Father Griffiths said it with his hands up like he was blessing a baby."

Edmund felt his throat constrict, not only with horror but with recognition. This was the next step in the village's logic. Once it had learned that safety could be performed through violence, it would keep performing until someone applauded. When the strangers were gone or hidden, it would turn to those who could not run.

Alice's voice was flat. "They killed them."

Jory's eyes flicked up, and for a moment Edmund saw the child he had once been in them. "Not all," he whispered. "Not yet." Then, with a shuddering breath, "They said they were cleansing. They said it was mercy."

Mercy. Edmund thought of Isaac's broken whisper, of Miriam's sobs, of Eli's burning door. Mercy was what men called it when they could not bear the weight of the word murder.

"Why are you here?" Edmund asked softly. "How did you get away?"

Jory swallowed, and his throat bobbed hard. "They didn't care if I ran," he whispered. "They said I'd die in the ditch and save them the trouble." His mouth twisted. "Rob laughed. Said the river would wash me clean."

Walter took an involuntary step forward, then stopped again. "Are you sick?" he asked, voice tight.

Jory stared at him, and something like resignation passed over his face. "Aren't we all?" He whispered.

It was not an answer. Edmund looked closer. Jory's skin had a sheen of sweat. His breathing was too quick. He kept touching his neck as if something there hurt.

Edmund felt the old conflict rise, sharp and immediate: compassion against survival. He could not forget the bodies on the ship in the stories, the way disease rode quietly until it did not. He could not forget the man collapsing in the lane, the dark flecks in his spit. And yet he could not look at Jory and see only a risk.

He saw the village's newest offering.

Miriam's older boy stepped forward unexpectedly. He held out something small in his hand: a bit of bread, crushed and damp from being carried. His face was expressionless, but his arm shook.

Jory looked at the bread as if it were a miracle and a trap. He did not take it. He only stared, lips trembling.

Edmund's chest tightened. The child's gesture was too pure for the world they were in.

Alice moved first. She stepped between the boy and Jory, not with cruelty, but with the hard decisiveness of someone cutting a rope before it dragged everyone under. She gently pushed the boy's hand down.

"No," she said, not unkindly. "Not close."

The boy's eyes flashed with something like anger, then dimmed into a familiar emptiness. He stepped back to his mother's side without a word.

Edmund looked at Jory. "Go downriver," he said. "Stay away from roads. If you can reach the marshlands, people won't follow."

Jory's mouth opened, and for a moment Edmund thought he would beg. Instead, he gave a small nod, as if begging had already been punished out of him.

He turned unsteadily, took two steps, then paused and looked back over his shoulder. "They're not stopping," he said, voice barely carrying. "Even when they're dying, they're dragging folk out. Rob says the plague picks out the sinful first."

Edmund heard the truth beneath it. The plague did not pick. The village did. It would decide who deserved to be first because deciding was easier than waiting.

Jory's gaze moved over them, lingering on Miriam's child, on the candle widow, on the moneylender's pale face. "If you go to another village," he whispered, "don't tell them you're hungry. Don't tell them you're scared. They can smell it. They'll look for the soft ones."

Then he turned and vanished into the trees with the slow, swaying gait of a man walking away from the only place he had ever belonged.

For a long moment no one spoke.

Walter's hands were clenched so tightly his knuckles showed white through grime. "Old

Nan," he said finally, as if saying it might anchor the horror to something real. "Stephen."

Edmund stared at the river beyond the copse, at the way it moved without care, carrying everything away in time. The village's chant echoed again in his memory, and now he understood what it was shaping itself into.

Not a hunt for poisoners.

A purge.

"They've run out of strangers," Alice said quietly. "So, they've decided the unclean were among them all along."

Edmund felt the wheel turning, steady and merciless. He thought of his father's cold certainty, of order enforced by pain. The village had always lived under a lord's shadow. Now it had learned to cast its own.

"Move," Edmund said, voice rough. "We keep moving."

And as they pushed on, leaving Jory's warning behind like a stone dropped into water, Edmund could not stop imagining the square upriver: the priest's hands raised in blessing, Rob's grin lit by torchlight, and the vulnerable dragged forward not because they had poisoned a well, but because the village had decided that weakness itself was the crime that had invited death.

They made camp that night in a strip of scrub between field and water, where nettles grew high enough to hide a crouching body and the ground was just firm enough that the candle widow would not sink to her ankles. The river was close, a constant sound that should have soothed, but now it only reminded Edmund of how easily a thing could travel without being seen.

No one spoke much. Even the children seemed to understand that voices were a kind of smoke.

Near midnight, the bell rang again upriver. It was farther now, softened by distance, but the rhythm was unmistakable. Not calling men to gather and burn. Counting.

Walter sat with his back against a tree, head bowed, hands locked together as if he were holding himself shut. Alice stayed awake on the edge of the scrub, knife resting across her knees, eyes on the dark line of the fields. The moneylender mouthed prayers that sounded like numbers when the wind caught them. Miriam did not sleep at all. She rocked her child in the shallowest motion, as if he were a thing that might spill out of her arms if she stopped.

At some point, long after the last bell note had faded, the sound of voices carried across the water.

Not the ragged cries they had heard before. This was steadier. A cadence that rose and fell as though practiced. Edmund had heard similar sounds on holy days when the village processed behind Father Griffiths, singing to make itself feel unified in something larger than hunger and work. The same shape of sound now, but stripped of joy.

Walter lifted his head. "That's not mourning," he whispered.

Alice's gaze stayed fixed. "No," she said. "That's ceremony."

The voices came and went with the wind. At times Edmund caught only fragments, words that might have been prayer or might have been names being answered by a crowd. It was impossible to know from this distance. Yet the shape of it made his skin tighten. A mob shouted as it pleased. A ritual did not. A ritual repeated itself until it felt inevitable.

Before dawn, footsteps approached along the riverbank.

Alice was up in an instant, blade lifted. Walter reached for his belt knife, his movement stiff with fatigue. Edmund raised a hand, palm out, for stillness.

A man emerged from the reeds and stopped when he saw them. He was not from their small band. His clothes were wrong for a traveler, patched poorly and tied at the waist with a length of twine. His hair was matted with sweat, and his eyes looked too large in his face, as if fear had pulled the flesh tighter around them.

He lifted his empty hands. "I'm not with them," he said, voice hoarse.

"Then who are you?" Edmund asked.

The man swallowed. "My name's Martin," he said. "From the next village down. I… I came upriver for my sister. She married there. I thought I could fetch her away before it took her."

He did not say plague, as if naming it might bring it nearer.

Alice kept her knife up. "And did you?" She asked.

Martin shook his head once, and the motion looked like it hurt his neck. "No," he said. Then, in a rush, as if the words had to get out before he could stop them, "They killed her."

Miriam made a small sound, a breath that collapsed into nothing. Walter's jaw tightened so hard Edmund heard his teeth grind.

"How?" Edmund asked, and hated himself for the question, but needed the shape of the truth. A death by sickness was an ending. A death by neighbors left something behind that did not rot away with the body.

Martin stared at Edmund as if deciding whether he could bear to answer. Then his gaze slid past them, upriver, toward the unseen place where bells and chanting had been born.

"In the square," he said. "They brought her out like a sinner at confession. They made her kneel. Father Griffiths stood on the church steps with a bowl of water. He sprinkled it on the ground and called it cleansing."

Edmund felt a cold line form down his spine. He pictured the priest's careful hands, the way he never quite stood in front when fists flew, but always managed to be seen when words could be turned into permission.

Martin's voice trembled. "Rob Baines was there. He had a list. Not written. He just… he just named folk, and men dragged them forward as if they'd been waiting to be told which bodies were allowed to be used."

Alice's mouth tightened. "Your sister," she said. "Why her?"

Martin's eyes shone wetly in the dim light. "Because she was slow," he whispered. "She was never quick in her head. Everyone knew it. She would laugh at the wrong time and forget names and wander. They always said she was touched. And now they're calling that unclean. Like it's a stain that draws the sickness."

Walter looked away, the muscles in his cheek jumping.

Martin went on, words scraping out of him. "They said she had brought God's anger into the village by being wrong. Like a cracked pot that lets rot in. Father Griffiths said mercy demanded they cut out the rot."

Miriam's arms tightened around her child until the boy made a soft protest in his sleep.

Edmund's voice came quiet, controlled by effort. "What did they do to her?" he asked.

Martin swallowed hard. "They hanged her," he said. "But not like the king's law. Not quick. They made it a thing everyone could watch. They made the children stand in front so they would learn what safety looks like."

The phrase hit Edmund like a blow: learn what safety looks like.

Martin's hands began to shake. He clenched them and forced himself to continue. "Before it, Father Griffiths made them all kneel. He made them say words together. He made them swear they were clean. And then Rob made the ones who swore loudest pull the rope."

Walter's head lifted sharply. "Pull it," he echoed, as if the idea itself were poisonous.

Martin nodded, face twisting. "So, no one could say it wasn't them. So, everyone shared it. They called it unity."

Edmund closed his eyes briefly and saw the village doing it with fierce relief. A shared act meant shared blame, and shared blame was easier to carry than private shame. It spread the weight until no single man had to feel it fully.

Alice lowered her knife only a fraction, not trust but exhaustion. "How many?" she asked.

Martin gave a thin, broken laugh. "Enough that the square stinks," he said. "Enough that the bell can't keep up. They've built a line of posts by the well. Like they're fencing in a garden."

A garden of bodies, Edmund thought, and felt bile rise in his throat.

Martin's eyes flicked to Miriam. "They're taking old folk," he said, voice lowering. "The ones that can't run. The ones that cough too loud. The beggars. The lame. The ones who shout at night. They call them burdens. They call them the village's filth. They say if the plague eats them anyway, better to feed them to God on purpose and be spared."

Walter made a raw sound. "Spared," he whispered. "As if God's counting."

"He is," Martin said, and there was a frightening certainty in it that did not belong to faith so much as terror. "That's what Father Griffiths says. He says the sickness is a measuring. He says if they give up the unclean, God will see their obedience."

Edmund looked upriver, into the darkness that hid the village. "And the sickness?" he asked. "Did it stop?"

Martin's face collapsed into something like despair. "No," he said. "It's worse. People are dying while the rope is still swinging. But that only makes them more certain they haven't cleansed enough. They say the unclean were deeper than they thought."

Edmund understood then the purpose of the ritual. It was not to stop death. It was to give death a reason that could be handled with hands and rope. A disease that came without meaning was unbearable. A neighbor marked as filth could be dealt with. It turned helplessness into action, and action into a kind of drunkenness.

Miriam's voice came small, scraped raw. "They'll come for the children next," she said, not as a question but as an awful prediction. "If the plague doesn't stop, they'll say the children are cursed."

Martin stared at her and did not deny it. His silence answered for him.

Alice's eyes narrowed. "How did you get away?" she asked him. "If they're building posts, they'll be watching roads."

Martin's gaze dropped. "I didn't get away clean," he whispered. "I lied. I told them I'd come to take my sister downriver and keep her from spreading it. I told them I would bind her if I had to." His voice broke. "I said anything. They let me pass because they thought I was useful."

Walter spat into the dirt, the gesture sharp with disgust.

Edmund did not judge Martin. He had seen too many men in the last days shaped into tools by fear. "Go downriver," Edmund said. "Do not go back. Not for anyone. There is nothing left to fetch that will not cost you your own life."

Martin nodded quickly, relief and guilt mixing across his face. He stepped backward toward the reeds, then hesitated. "They're saying your name," he added, and Edmund felt everyone go still. "Rob's saying the lord has harbored corruption from the start. Father Griffiths says pride invites plague, and your pride is in protecting the wrong people."

Walter's shoulders tightened. Alice's hand moved, reflexively, toward the hilt of her knife as if she could stab a name spoken in the dark.

Martin backed away, voice dropping. "They're making it a story now," he said. "Not just cleansing. A lesson. They say they will build a clean village out of ash, and everyone will know it was done by faith."

Then he vanished into the reeds and the river swallowed his footsteps.

For a long time, no one moved. The sky began to pale behind the trees, and the first thin light made the world look innocent again, which felt like another cruelty.

Edmund stared at his hands, raw at the knuckles, and thought of the square. The well at its center. The posts rising beside it. The priest's water sprinkled like absolution. Rob's list made of breath and hatred. Children made to watch so they would grow into men who mistook violence for protection.

Walter spoke at last, voice hoarse. "That's not panic anymore," he said. "That's law."

"No," Edmund replied, and the word came out colder than he intended. "It's worse. Law at least pretends to be restrained. This is worship."

Alice's eyes stayed on the upriver darkness as if she could see through miles of trees and fields. "And worship doesn't stop on its own," she said. "Not until it runs out of sacrifices."

Miriam bent her head and kissed her child's hair, once, twice, the way a person touched something to reassure herself it was real. "Isaac," she whispered again, and Edmund felt the name drift through the morning air like smoke.

He had no comfort to offer. Only the next step, and the knowledge that upriver, a village had learned to kill in rhythm. The rope did not creak as loudly when everyone pulled together. The crowd did not feel the weight of what it had done when Father Griffiths gave it words to hide behind.

Ritual executions, Edmund realized, were not simply murders with prayers added.

They were a way of teaching ordinary people to live with murder.

And once taught, they would use that lesson again and again, until nothing in them remembered the difference between cleansing and ruin.

Dawn did not bring safety. It brought shape.

In the thin gray light, the riverbank looked ordinary again: wet reeds, low scrub, the muddy scars of their feet. But Edmund could not shake Martin's words, the way they had fallen into the air like ash and refused to settle.

They're saying your name.

Rob had always wanted the village to look at Edmund as an exception, a wrong sort of lord. A lord who spoke too gently. A lord who ate with laborers and listened when he should have commanded. In calmer years, that difference had been tolerated the way a village tolerated a strange weather pattern: with suspicion, with jokes, with the certainty that it would correct itself.

Now difference was not tolerated. It was hunted.

Walter sat with his knees drawn up, staring at the river as though it might offer an answer if he watched long enough. Alice kept to the edge of the scrub, knife in hand, shoulders squared against the day as if she could physically bar it from coming closer. Miriam's child slept in fitful jerks, each breath a small triumph. Miriam herself looked hollowed out, her gaze fixed on the ground as though her eyes could no longer afford to look up and find another thing to lose.

The moneylender cleared his throat softly, then did not speak. The candle widow's lips moved without sound, a private litany. Edmund could not tell if she prayed for mercy or for forgetting.

"We cannot stay near the water," Walter said at last. His voice was rough, the sound of a man who had spent too long swallowing words. "If they decide you're the devil of it, they'll come down every path. They'll search the banks. They'll say the river carries your corruption."

Edmund nodded slowly. "They will use anything that moves," he said. "Wind, water, animals. They will turn the world into proof."

Alice glanced back toward the upriver curve, where the trees hid the village and made it harder to believe it still existed. "They've made a story," she said. “A story needs a villain more than it needs a cure.”

Miriam lifted her head. Her eyes were rimmed red, but there was something steady underneath the grief now, something like the hard beginning of hate. “Why you?” she asked Edmund. “Why would they choose you when Rob is the one who—” Her voice broke, and she swallowed the rest as if it were blood.

Edmund knew the answer and hated that he knew it.

“Because I do not fit into what they want the village to be,” he said quietly. “Rob fits. Father Griffiths fits. The reeve fits. Even when they lie, their lies sound like the old order. Mine does not.”

Walter gave a short, bitter sound. “Because you treated people like they mattered,” he said.

Edmund looked at Walter. “And because I defended those they wanted to use,” he added. “If the strangers were guilty, then their violence could be called protection. If the strangers were innocent, then the violence was what it truly was. So, they need the strangers to remain guilty in the village mind, even as the bodies pile up. And who stood in the way of that guilt? Who argued? Who tried to stop them?”

Alice's knife shifted in her grip. "You," she said, flat.

Edmund did not flinch from it. "Yes."

A bird called from somewhere downriver, a thin sound like a question. The world was still too quiet. The quiet did not feel like peace. It felt like something listening.

They moved again in short, careful stages, keeping to low cover. Edmund guided them away from the track that ran near the fields and toward a strip of trees that would bring them closer to a small cluster of farms he remembered from past seasons. Not a village, not a market, just scattered holdings. People there might give water. Might let them rest in a barn for an hour. Might not ask too many questions.

Or might ask the only question that mattered now: who are you, and which story do you belong to?

The first farm they saw had its gate shut and latched, a crude plank nailed across it as if to keep out wolves. A bundle of herbs hung by the door, and beneath it, a smear of ash drawn in a rough cross. Fear-markings. The kind that made people feel they had done something.

Edmund approached alone, hands open, keeping his distance. Alice stayed back with the others, her gaze fixed on the shuttered windows.

A woman appeared at the doorway, not stepping out, only peering through a crack. Her hair was uncovered, untidy, as if she had been too tired or too frightened to braid it. When she saw Edmund, her eyes narrowed.

"Go on," she called. Not angry. Afraid. "We've nothing."

"We're not here to take," Edmund said. "We need water. For the child."

At the mention of a child, her face softened for a heartbeat, then tightened again. "How many of you?"

Edmund hesitated, and in that hesitation he felt the trap. If he said the truth, she might picture a band that would overwhelm her. If he lied and she saw more shapes in the trees, she would label him a deceiver.

"Five," he said at last. "And two children."

The woman swallowed. "From where?"

Edmund could have lied. He could have named some other place, some other direction, and hoped distance would protect him. But lies had become the village's language, and he had seen what that language did to people.

"From upriver," he said.

The crack in the door seemed to narrow. The woman's voice changed. "From that place," she said, and the way she said it made it a stain, not a name. "They say it's burning."

"It is," Edmund replied. "And dying."

The door did not open. Instead, the woman glanced over her shoulder as if someone stood behind her. Edmund heard a man's voice inside, low and urgent. He could not make out the words, but he heard one name clearly, spoken like a warning.

Harrow.

Edmund felt his stomach drop.

The woman looked back at him, and whatever pity had been there was gone, replaced by the brittle righteousness that fear could summon as quickly as breath. "You're him," she said.

Edmund did not move. "I am Edmund Harrow," he said, because denying it would only make it worse.

The woman's eyes widened, as if she had not expected truth. Then her face hardened in relief, because truth gave her something she could do.

She raised her voice. "Get off my land," she shouted. "We don't want your sickness here. We don't want your kind."

"My kind," Edmund repeated softly.

The door behind her banged as someone inside moved. A man stepped into view behind her shoulder, clutching a hammer like a weapon. He did not come out, but he made sure Edmund saw the tool in his hand. A threat without the burden of crossing a threshold.

Edmund tried once more. "A child is thirsty," he said. "We're not asking to enter. Just water in a cup. Set it by the gate. We'll take it and go."

The woman's mouth twitched, and for a moment Edmund thought she might yield.

Then she shook her head sharply. "They said you sheltered them," she said. "They said you helped the poisoners flee. They said you stood against the village when it tried to cleanse itself. They said the plague followed you like a shadow."

Behind Edmund, a twig snapped. He did not turn, but he knew Alice would have stiffened, and

Walter would have shifted his weight like a man deciding whether to run or fight.

"Who said?" Edmund asked, though he already knew.

The woman's eyes flicked away, as if the answer embarrassed her, as if she disliked admitting how far gossip had already traveled. "A man came down the track last night," she said. "From there. He said Rob Baines spoke it in the square and Father Griffiths blessed it. He said you're a fine-tongued devil and your woman's a knife. He said you'll turn up begging for mercy and bring death to any door that opens."

Edmund held still while the words landed. Not because they were true, but because they were effective. Rob had done what Edmund had feared he would do: he had turned Edmund's difference into intent. Kindness into manipulation. Mercy into conspiracy. And Father Griffiths had given it the seal of God so ordinary people could repeat it without shame.

Alice stepped out of the trees then, just enough to be seen. She did not raise her knife. She simply let the woman see her, as if confirming the image the rumor had painted.

The woman flinched back behind the doorframe.

Edmund turned his head slightly. “Alice,” he said quietly.

“I know,” Alice replied, her voice low, controlled. “I won’t.”

Edmund faced the door again. “We will go,” he said to the woman. “But hear me. What’s happening upriver is not cleansing. It is murder. It will not stop the sickness. It will only teach people how to kill each other faster.”

The woman’s lips pressed thin. “That’s what you would say,” she answered, and then shut the door hard enough that the latch rattled.

Edmund stood for a moment, staring at the wood as though it might open again if he stared with enough will. Then he stepped back, slow, and returned to the others.

Walter’s face was tight. “They know,” he said.

“They know a story,” Edmund replied. His voice sounded strange to him, as if it belonged to someone older. “Not us.”

Miriam held her child higher on her hip. “They won’t help,” she said. It was not despair. It was a conclusion.

“No,” Edmund said. “They won’t. Not while my name buys them the feeling of safety.”

The moneylender's eyes were wide, his mouth slightly open. "How far has it spread?" he whispered.

Edmund looked upriver, though the village was hidden. "Fast," he said. "Fear travels faster than any plague."

Alice crouched beside the candle widow, who was trembling again. "We don't beg at doors," Alice said to Edmund, blunt as a blade. "We take what we need or we die."

Edmund met her gaze. "If we take," he said, "we become what they already say we are. And then every door will be barred forever."

Alice's expression did not soften. "Every door is already barred," she said. "They just showed you."

Edmund had no answer to that. He felt the world narrowing, not because the land had changed, but because people had. A village could burn itself and still cling to the belief that it was righteous. A stranger could hear a rumor and lock a gate against a thirsty child because a priest had blessed the rumor into truth.

Walter exhaled hard through his nose. "Rob's clever," he said, voice thick with hatred. "He's made you the reason. If they find you and hang you, they'll call it proof. If they don't, they'll call it proof too. Either way, you're the thing they point at."

Edmund nodded slowly. "A named enemy is easier than an unseen sickness," he said. "If they can kill me, they can pretend they've killed the cause."

Miriam's older boy looked up at Edmund then, his face unreadable in the pale light. "Will they kill you?" he asked. The question was not frightened. It was flat, like a child asking whether winter would come.

Edmund's throat tightened. He thought of his father's hall, of the Earl's certainty that blood and legacy could not be resisted. He thought of Rob's grin lit by flame. He thought of Father Griffiths sprinkling water like permission.

"They will try," he said honestly.

The boy nodded once, as if adding it to a list of things he now knew about the world.

Edmund rose. His knees ached. His hands were raw. He looked at each of them in turn: Miriam, holding what remained of her family with both arms; Walter, still trying to be a man in a world that rewarded beasts; the candle widow, who had survived long enough to see mercy turned into a rope; the moneylender and his son, learning that value was not protection; and Alice, who had always known that doors could become walls overnight.

"We keep moving," Edmund said. "But we do it differently now."

Walter frowned. "How?"

Edmund looked downriver, toward the marshlands Jory had named, toward places where the land itself was harder to cross and easier to hide in. "They want one enemy," he said. "So, I will be their enemy."

Alice's eyes narrowed. "Meaning?"

Edmund swallowed. The decision tasted like iron. "Meaning they will look for me," he said. "And while they look, you will not be found."

Miriam's face tightened. "No," she said at once, fierce in a way she had not been since Isaac was taken. "You won't leave us."

Edmund met her gaze. "I won't abandon you," he said. "But if my name is a torch they're carrying, then we cannot all walk together without being seen."

Walter's voice came low and urgent. "Edmund, listen—"

"I am listening," Edmund cut in, then softened his tone. "I have listened all my life. That is why I know what they are doing. They have turned me into the shape of treachery because I would not let them turn others into ash. If I stay in the middle of you, I drag you into the square with me."

Alice stood very still. Then she nodded once, slow. "You're thinking like prey," she said. "Split the scent."

Edmund looked at the others. "We will find cover and food," he said. "We will move in smaller shadows. And if they catch me—" He stopped, because saying it aloud made it real in a new way.

Walter's face had gone pale. "If they catch you," Walter said, "they'll do more than hang you. They'll make a lesson. They'll make you a warning."

Edmund nodded. "I know."

Upriver, faint as memory, the bell rang again.

Edmund felt it in his bones, each toll a reminder that the village's fear was becoming structure, becoming law and worship and story. And in that story, Edmund Harrow was no longer a man who had tried to build something gentler.

He was the reason the gentleness had to die.

Chapter 11

The Animal Curse

They did not separate at once.

Edmund had spoken the decision aloud but speaking it and doing it were different things. The river still ran beside them, and the trees still offered the same thin mercy. Miriam's younger boy began to fuss again, exhausted and hungry, and Miriam's whispering went hoarse. The candle widow's feet dragged. The moneylender's son stared at every moving leaf as if it might become a hand.

Walter kept close to Edmund, not quite blocking him, but moving as though his body could argue against Edmund's plan by refusing to let him out of reach. Alice walked a few paces behind, watching the line they left in mud, watching the reeds part and settle again. She did not try to soften what Edmund proposed. She only watched for the moment it became necessary.

By late morning they found a low patch of ground where the river had flooded once and left a tangle of brush and deadfall. It was not comfortable, but it was hidden. From the bank you could not see into it unless you knew where to look. Alice tested the edges, pushing through thorns, then came back with a curt nod.

"This will do," she said. "For an hour. For a breath."

They crouched among the brush. Walter broke a piece of bread into smaller pieces and handed it out with the careful solemnity of communion. The children ate without speaking. The moneylender chewed as if each swallow might be his last. The candle widow's hands trembled so badly she dropped her piece once and had to pick it up from damp leaves.

Edmund watched them eat and felt the hard shape of his choice pressing against his ribs. If he stayed, the story would find them. If he left, they might still die, only farther from his eyes. There was no clean act left, only acts with different kinds of blood on them.

Alice crouched beside him, close enough that her voice did not carry. "Now," she said.

Edmund glanced at Miriam. Miriam was watching him, as if she had known Alice would speak. Her face had changed since the night Isaac was dragged away. The grief was still there, but it had condensed into something denser, something that could hold anger without spilling.

"No," Miriam said immediately, before Edmund could rise. "If you go, they will follow you and they will still come for us."

"They will follow my name whether I move or not," Edmund replied quietly.

Walter's jaw tightened. "We go together," he insisted. "We keep moving. We keep low."

"And every farm we pass shuts its door because Harrow is with you," Alice said. "Every man who hears a rumor looks for the lord who sheltered poisoners. He's a torch to them now. Let him carry the flame away from the rest."

Walter rounded on her, fury flashing. "And if he's caught?"

Alice did not blink. "Then they'll stop looking for the others for a while. Because they'll be too busy congratulating themselves."

The cruelty of her honesty made Walter's face go pale.

Edmund touched Walter's arm, a brief pressure. "You take them downriver," he said. "Toward the marshlands Jory spoke of. Keep to cover. Don't beg at doors again unless you must. If you must, send the boy alone."

Miriam's older child, who had been silent through all of it, lifted his head slightly. His eyes had the flat steadiness Edmund had seen before. He did not ask why him. He only listened, as if storing instructions the way other children stored songs.

Miriam's mouth tightened. "You speak as if you've already been taken."

Edmund forced himself to meet her gaze. "I'm speaking as if I want your children to live," he said. "That is all I can control."

The candle widow made a small sound, somewhere between protest and prayer. The moneylender's lips moved, silent counting. Walter looked as though he might strike Edmund out of sheer helplessness.

Alice stood. "Quick," she said. "Before the day turns and sound carries farther."

Edmund rose with her. For a moment he hesitated, not from fear of what awaited him, but from the sick tenderness of leaving them in a nest of thorns and calling it protection.

He crouched by Miriam and lowered his voice. “I am sorry,” he said, and knew it was too small.

Miriam stared at him. Then, unexpectedly, she reached out and gripped his wrist. Her fingers were cold and strong. “If you see Isaac,” she said. “If you see him anywhere. If you see even his body.”

Edmund swallowed. “I will not leave him unnamed,” he said. It was not a promise to save, but it was the only promise he could make without lying.

She released his wrist.

Walter stepped forward, close enough that Edmund could smell the sweat and river on him. “You’re making yourself bait,” Walter whispered, voice thick. “This isn’t what you wanted when you left Dorset.”

Edmund almost laughed at the bitter truth of it. “No,” he said. “But this is what they’ve made.”

Walter’s eyes shone. He gripped Edmund’s shoulder hard, then released him abruptly, as if touch might break him open.

Alice started away through the brush, and Edmund followed. After ten paces she stopped and looked back once. Walter was already guiding the others deeper into the tangle, bending branches back into place, erasing their passage with the care of a man scrubbing blood from boards.

Then Edmund and Alice moved upriver along the river's edge, not running, but walking with the measured caution of people who knew the wrong kind of haste drew eyes.

They had gone less than a mile when the first carcass appeared.

A dog lay in the shallows where the bank dipped, half on mud, half in water. Its legs were stiff, its mouth slack. It had not died of sickness. Someone had cut it. The wound was clumsy, more rage than skill. Flies already found it, black dots shifting in the damp light.

Edmund stopped so abruptly Alice nearly collided with him.

Alice looked down at the dog without expression. "Not plague," she said.

"No," Edmund replied, and felt his stomach tighten. "Not mercy either."

He scanned the bank. A few paces farther, something pale bobbed against reeds. He stepped closer and saw it was a cat, bloated and drowned, its neck broken. Its fur was slicked flat, and one eye stared upward as if fixed on the sky.

For a moment Edmund could not speak. He thought of the village lanes, of cats that used to dart through scraps, of the quiet comfort of animals that did not care about sermons or blame. In his mind he saw Rob Baines's grin, Father Griffiths's hands raised, and now the same hands turning on creatures that could not argue or plead.

Alice's voice was low. "They've started blaming the beasts."

Edmund's throat felt raw. "Why would they do that?"

Alice gave him a sideways look that was almost impatience. "Because beasts can't contradict the story," she said. "And because it feels cleaner to kill what doesn't look like you."

They kept walking. The further upriver they went, the more signs appeared. A chicken with its neck wrung and thrown onto a hedge. A sack of something dark and heavy dumped by a ditch; when Edmund drew closer he saw small bodies, rats, many of them, crushed or clubbed. Someone had gone to war against what they could catch.

Edmund's mind went back, unbidden, to the prologue tales. Rats scattering from a dead ship into a port, unnoticed until it was too late. He had not said it aloud to the villagers because saying rats would have sounded like a superstition, and superstition already ruled them. But he had thought it: the fleas, the filth, the hidden travel of tiny lives.

And now, instead of understanding the danger, the village was turning that half-knowledge into slaughter.

They came upon a man in the fields, kneeling by a hedgerow with a sack at his feet. He moved in quick jerks, striking at something in the grass. When he looked up, Edmund saw the red rim of exhaustion around his eyes.

The man froze when he saw them. His gaze flicked over Edmund's face, then to Alice, then down to her knife.

"Who are you?" the man demanded, voice cracking.

Edmund kept his hands visible. "Travelers," he said. "Looking for water."

The man's suspicion did not ease. His knuckles were scraped raw. "Don't come near," he snapped. "We've had enough of near."

Alice's posture remained loose but ready. "What are you doing?" she asked.

The man jerked his chin toward the sack. "Rats," he said. "They're everywhere. Bold as lords. Coming out in daylight like they own the place. Father Griffiths says the Devil rides on them. Rob says they've been nesting under floors and in barns and carrying the sickness on their backs."

He spat into the grass. Dark flecks marked the spit, and Edmund's stomach dropped.

"You're coughing," Edmund said quietly.

The man's eyes flared with anger, as if Edmund had accused him of a crime. "Everyone's coughing," he snapped. "That's why we're cutting it out. That's why we're killing every crawling thing we can."

Edmund looked at the hedgerow and saw what the man had been striking. A small dog, not yet fully grown, lay twisted in the grass, its ribs showing. The man's stick was wet at the end.

Edmund's voice went cold despite himself. "That won't stop the sickness."

The man's face tightened into something like a sneer. "That's what you'd say," he answered.

Edmund felt the familiar chill. "You've heard my name," he said.

The man's gaze sharpened. "I know your face," he said slowly. "Harrow. The one they say sheltered them."

There it was again, the story spreading faster than breath.

Before Edmund could speak, the man lifted his voice, calling toward the distant line of trees. "Oi! We've got someone here!"

Alice moved instantly, not toward the man, but toward Edmund, her body angling as if to pull him out of sight. "We're done here," she said under her breath.

Edmund backed away, heart pounding, not from fear of one man with a stick, but from what the man's shout could summon. In the distance, another voice answered faintly. Then another. Not words yet, but attention gathering.

As Edmund and Alice slipped back toward the river, they heard the man's muttering carried on the wind, half prayer, half curse. "Kill the cats. Kill the dogs. Kill the rats. Clean it. Clean it. Clean it."

Edmund kept moving, his boots sucking at mud.

Behind them, upriver, a village that had begun by burning doors was now learning to make enemies out of everything that breathed and moved without speaking. And Edmund understood the shape of this new curse they had invented: if the plague could be blamed on animals, then any compassion could be called foolishness, any attempt to preserve life could be called treachery.

It was not enough for them to kill neighbors. Now they had to kill the world itself, piece by piece, until nothing remained that could remind them what an unafraid life used to look like.

Edmund and Alice kept to the river's curve until the reeds thinned and the bank hardened into trampled mud. The sound of the village reached them before the roofs did. Not the bell this time, not the chant of shared words, but a sharp, scattered music of terror: dogs yelping, men shouting, something heavy striking stone, and beneath it all a thin, constant squealing that made Edmund's teeth ache.

Alice slowed and raised a hand. "Not through the lane," she murmured. "We watch first."

They climbed the low rise where the alder gave way to a hedge. From there the village sat in a shallow basin of fields, its lanes like veins, its square hidden behind roofs. Smoke still rose in places where fire had eaten yesterday's certainty and left blackened ribs. But the smoke was not the most immediate thing now. Movement was.

Men ran in packs, not with torches, but with clubs, sticks, shovels, anything that could strike. Women stood at doors with children clutched to their skirts, faces tightened into the same hard shape Edmund had seen in the mob's eyes. The village was awake in a different way. Not drunk on fire, but frantic with purpose, as if it had found a new kind of work that promised to keep death busy.

A dog burst into the lane, ribs showing, tail tucked, blood dark on its flank. It skidded on the mud and tried to turn, but a man was already behind it, shouting. The dog darted toward a doorway, desperate for any shelter, and a woman who would once have opened her arms to a familiar animal instead kicked at it, shrieking as if it were a snake. The dog yelped and stumbled back into the open.

Three men fell on it at once.

Edmund watched the first blow land and felt his stomach lurch. The dog's cry rose, then broke into a gurgle. A second blow struck the skull and the cry stopped completely, replaced by the wet sound of breath failing. The men did not pause to check whether it was dead. They kept hitting as though striking made them safer.

One of them looked up, panting, and shouted toward the doors, “See? See! Kill them before they carry it!”

A woman answered with a ragged cheer that sounded more like relief than approval.

Alice’s jaw clenched. “They’re turning it into sport,” she said.

“It isn’t sport,” Edmund replied, though he wished it were, because sport at least admitted itself as cruelty. “It’s penance. They think the more they kill, the more they prove obedience.”

They moved along the hedge, keeping low where the leaves were thick enough to hide their faces. As they edged nearer, the smells grew stronger. Not only smoke and human waste and the sick-sweet tang Edmund now associated with plague, but the sharp metallic bite of blood. It lay over the village like a new kind of fog.

A cart creaked into view, pushed by two boys who were too young for this work and too old to refuse it. The cart was piled with sacks that sagged and bumped against each other as the wheels jolted over stones. A tail hung out of one sack, limp and striped. A paw, small as a child’s hand, flopped over the edge. The boys pushed with their heads down, faces fixed, while a man walked behind them with a stick, not to guide the cart but to strike at anything that moved in the lane.

A cat appeared on a low wall, sleek and black. For an instant it looked like any ordinary village creature, watching the world with indifferent patience. Then a stone flew and struck it in the ribs. The cat made a choking sound and toppled. Before it could scramble away, a girl no older than Miriam's older boy ran forward and brought a brick down on its head with both hands.

The girl's face was twisted, not with hate, but with desperate concentration, as if she were trying to do it correctly the way she had been instructed. When the cat stopped moving, the girl looked up and shouted, breathless, "Father said we must!"

Someone answered, "Good lass," and the words made Edmund feel colder than the sight of the brick.

Alice's voice came very low. "They're teaching the children."

Edmund could not take his eyes from the girl. He imagined Father Griffiths's hands raised, sprinkling water in the square, blessing rope and posts. Now those same hands were blessing bricks. Blessing small fists. Blessing a generation that would grow up with dead animals as proof of virtue.

A shout rose from nearer the square. "Rats! Under the smith's!"

Men surged toward it. Edmund and Alice followed along the hedge until the lane opened enough that they could see the mouth of the square itself. Not fully, but enough.

The well stood at the center like a calm eye, indifferent to the frenzy around it. Beside it were the posts Martin had spoken of, rough and newly set, their bases darkened as if blood had soaked into the wood. Edmund could not see bodies hanging now, but he could see the marks where bodies had swung, the ground scuffed into a hard ring by many feet. It looked used. That was the worst part. It looked like a place the village had begun to rely on.

Near the well, men had overturned barrels and crates, tearing at them with hooks and knives. They were not searching for food or goods. They were searching for movement. When a rat darted out from beneath a broken board, a man screamed as if it were a demon and brought his shovel down. The rat's body burst, and the man recoiled, then struck again, again, again, until there was nothing left but a smear.

"Careful!" someone shouted. "Don't touch it bare!"

A woman thrust a rag at the man, and he wiped his shovel like a priest wiping a chalice.

Edmund's mind returned to the merchant ship, to the rats that had slipped into streets unnoticed. He felt a sick certainty settle in him. The village had arrived at a truth by accident: rats mattered. But instead of understanding what that meant, instead of realizing that rats were not the enemy but the carrier, the host, the unnoticed road, they had chosen the simplest response.

Kill what you can see. Believe what you can strike.

Rob Baines stood near the church steps, visible even from this angle because he positioned himself as if all sight belonged to him. He held nothing in his hands, no tool, no club. He did not need one. His weapon was the way men turned their heads toward him for instruction, the way fear waited for his mouth to give it shape.

Father Griffiths was beside him, just behind, as always. The priest's face was pale, eyes bright with a fervor that made Edmund's skin tighten.

He was speaking, his lips moving steadily, and men nodded as if each word placed another stone in the wall between them and meaninglessness.

Edmund could not hear the sermon clearly, but he caught fragments when the wind shifted.

"...unclean creatures..."

"...God's scourge..."

"...cast out..."

Rob's voice cut through more sharply. "No cats. No dogs," he shouted. "Not one. They carry it in their fur, in their mouths, in their breath. You want your children to live; you kill it before it crawls to their beds!"

A murmur rose, hungry and eager, and the village scattered again, taking his instruction like a command from a lord.

Edmund felt something inside him twist. "He's going to wipe them out," he whispered.

Alice did not look at him. "He's going to wipe out anything that could make sense of the plague without needing him," she said. "Animals are simple. Kill them and you feel you've done something. Then when the sickness continues, you need a new thing to kill."

As if the village itself wanted to prove her right, a new commotion burst at the far edge of the square. A pig had broken loose from a pen, squealing wildly, hooves slipping. It barreled into a man's legs and sent him down. The man screamed, not in pain, but in outrage, and a dozen others rushed in with hooks and knives.

The pig's squeal rose into a high, impossible pitch. Men grabbed at it, missed, slipped in the mud. A woman shrieked, "It's cursed!" and that word changed everything. Cursed meant permitted.

A hook caught the pig's flank and tore. Blood sprayed, bright even through distance. The animal bucked, dragging the hook-bearer two steps before another man drove a knife in. The squeal became a choking, bubbling sound that went on longer than Edmund could bear.

He turned his head away, swallowing hard.

When he looked back, the men were already arguing about what to do with the carcass. "Burn it," one shouted. "Bury it," another countered. A third said, "Throw it in the river, let it go away," and Edmund felt his stomach drop at the casual cruelty of that solution. As if the river were not also a road to other villages, other mouths, other hands.

Alice watched the debate with a cold steadiness. “They’ll poison the water themselves,” she said. “Then swear it’s proof of poisoners.”

Edmund’s heart pounded, not only with horror but with urgency. This was not only moral collapse now. It was practical madness. Cats kept down rats. Dogs warned and guarded. Livestock fed the village. Slaughtering animals would not purify them. It would starve them, unbalance them, and leave the rats to multiply in the spaces where fear had created emptiness.

A door slammed in the lane below their hedge. A family dragged a dog out by a rope tied tight around its neck. The animal’s paws scrabbled at the earth, choking. The father’s face was wet with sweat and tears. The mother held the children back, her arms locked around them, while the eldest boy, jaw clenched, lifted a club like he had been shown.

“No,” the father sobbed, voice cracking. “No, it’s always been good. It’s always—”

A neighbor shouted, “Do it or we’ll do it for you!”

The father’s hands shook as he held the rope. The boy raised the club and hesitated, eyes darting to his father as if begging for permission to be a child again.

Then the crowd's impatience pressed in, and the club came down.

Edmund felt a wave of nausea. The father made a sound like something tearing inside him. The mother turned her face away and whispered something Edmund could not hear, perhaps a prayer, perhaps an apology.

The dog twitched, then went still.

The neighbor clapped the boy on the shoulder. "That's it," he said. "That's a clean house now."

Clean. Edmund thought of the word being used like a knife, cutting life into acceptable and unacceptable pieces.

He backed away from the hedge, breath shallow, because staying longer meant being seen, and being seen meant dragging the village's new hunger onto the river path where Miriam and the others hid.

Alice followed him without being told. They retreated into the alder shadow until the village noises dulled, though they did not disappear. Even at this distance, the yelps and shrieks and thuds continued in broken rhythms, like a grotesque bell of their own.

Edmund leaned against a tree and closed his eyes for a moment, fighting the tremor in his hands. "They're killing the wrong creatures," he said, and the words felt too small for what he had witnessed.

Alice's voice was hard. "They're killing anything they can," she replied. "Because they can't kill the plague."

Edmund opened his eyes and stared toward the river, imagining rats slipping through grass, fleas riding unseen on fur, the village's cats and dogs disappearing one by one. He saw what would come next as clearly as if it had already happened: the grain stores overrun, the bodies unburied because men were too sick or too afraid, the rats feasting without competition, multiplying in the warmth of chaos.

The village believed it was cleansing itself.

In truth, it was removing the last small barriers that had kept the real carrier in check.

Edmund pushed himself upright. "We have to warn them," he said, though even as he spoke he knew how the village would respond to a warning now. Warning was treachery. Warning was the voice of the enemy.

Alice's gaze flicked to him. "You can't cure madness with sense," she said. "You can only survive it."

Upriver, a dog screamed once, then went abruptly silent.

Edmund flinched, not only for the animal, but for the sound of what the village was becoming: a place where silence was manufactured, one body at a time, until there was nothing left to make the world feel familiar.

They turned away from the village at last and followed the river's edge again, moving quickly, because every moment they lingered near those lanes was a moment the story might find them.

Behind them, the slaughter continued, and Edmund understood that the village had found a new kind of righteousness: one that required no proof, only a corpse.

And the rats, bold in daylight, would inherit the streets.

They followed the river down beneath the alder and willow until the village noises became only a dull smear, as if the sound itself had been thrown into water and held under. But even when the yelps and the blunt thuds were no longer distinct, Edmund could still hear them in his mind, each struck body turned into a prayer, each corpse turned into an argument.

Alice led without looking back, choosing the softer ground where footprints filled with brown water and did not hold their shape. Edmund kept glancing upriver, half expecting to see men spilling out of the lanes with clubs raised, half expecting to see nothing at all and feel the worse fear of being hunted without knowing it.

The river narrowed where reeds grew thick again. The air there held a sour sweetness, not smoke now, but rot beginning its slow work. The scent did not come from one place. It came from everything: damp earth, stagnant puddles, and, Edmund suspected, bodies that no longer had hands to carry them to churchyard ground.

Alice stopped at a bend where the bank rose a little and the trees thinned enough to see across a strip of pasture.

"Look," she said.

At first Edmund saw nothing but grass moving in the faint breeze. Then the grass parted near a low stone wall and something small and brown slid through, quick as a thought. A rat. Then another behind it. Then, as he kept watching, more: not a sudden swarm, not a dramatic flood, but a steady traffic of them, crossing the pasture in daylight as if the sun no longer meant danger.

Edmund's throat tightened. "Where are the cats?" he asked quietly.

Alice gave him a flat glance. "Under bricks. In sacks. In the river."

Edmund's mind supplied images he did not want: the girl with the brick, the boys pushing a cart of sagging sacks, the neighbor calling it a clean house. He had grown up hearing sermons about order and obedience; he had not grown up imagining a village could decide that mercy meant slaughtering anything that purred.

A black shape moved near the wall and for one foolish heartbeat Edmund thought it might be a cat, some stubborn creature that had lived through the frenzy. But it was only a crow, hopping closer to something in the grass. The bird pecked once, twice, and lifted its head to stare around as if waiting for permission.

Edmund shifted his weight and felt his boot sink slightly into the bank. When he pulled it free, a thin film clung to the leather, not mud exactly, but the slickness of soil churned by too many feet and too much panic.

"They think they're cutting the sickness out," he murmured.

Alice's voice was quiet, almost weary. "They're cutting the village out," she said. "Piece by piece."

They moved again, keeping to the edge where willow roots broke the bank into pockets of shadow. Edmund tried to picture Miriam and the others downriver, huddled in brush with nettles catching at their clothes, the children too tired to cry. He had told himself splitting away would make them harder to find. Yet the farther he walked from them, the more he feared that what he had really done was leave them alone with a world that had learned to lock its doors.

Ahead, the path along the river met a narrow track that ran toward a cluster of barns. Edmund remembered the holding: a farmer who traded barley at market, a sour man but not unkind. The barns sat low and dark against the field, their thatched roofs damp with the last rain. There were no people visible. No smoke from the chimney. No cattle in the yard.

Alice slowed again, knife low at her side. "We don't go in," she said. "We look; we keep moving."

They approached through the hedge line, careful to keep their bodies broken by leaves and branches. As they neared, the quiet became a different kind of quiet, not peaceful but emptied. Then Edmund heard it: a dry, constant scratching, like fingernails on wood.

It came from the barn.

Near the threshold lay a dog. Or what had been a dog. Its body was stiff, its coat rough with dried blood. Someone had struck it and left it where it fell, as if even the act of dragging a corpse away had become too risky. Edmund felt his stomach turn, but he forced himself to keep looking, because looking was the only way to know what the village was doing to itself.

The barn door was closed but not latched properly. A gap at the bottom showed darkness inside. From that gap came movement: a whisker, a snout, then the quick flash of teeth. A rat slipped out, paused with its body half in the light, and then darted away toward the hedge.

Then another followed.

Alice's hand tightened on her knife. "They're nesting in there," she said.

Edmund crouched by the wall and peered through a crack between boards. The barn smelled of grain and damp and something fouler beneath, the sharp stink of small bodies and waste. In the dimness he saw sacks piled near the back, some torn open. The pale spill of barley made a bright scatter across the floor. And in that scatter, shapes moved in and out like waterbugs: rats, too many to count, bold enough to climb the sacks in plain sight.

A low sound came from deeper inside the holding, not from the barn. A cough. Wet, ragged, followed by a thin moan that might have been a man trying to speak and failing.

Edmund's chest tightened. "Someone's alive," he whispered.

Alice's eyes narrowed toward the house. Its door was shut, but the shutter on one window hung crooked. "Alive doesn't mean safe," she said.

"I know," Edmund replied, though the words tasted like ash. He could not stop himself from edging closer to the house, keeping low beneath the window. The air near the wall smelled of sweat and sickness. Another cough came, closer now, followed by the unmistakable sound of vomiting.

Edmund pressed his face nearer the cracked shutter and saw a figure on the floor inside; a man sprawled on straw. His skin had the gray sheen Edmund now recognized, the look of a body losing its argument with fever. Beside him sat a bucket, stained dark. No one tended him. No one held water to his mouth. A bowl lay tipped on its side, empty.

A small shape moved near the man's shoulder. At first Edmund thought it was a child, and his heart seized. Then he realized it was a rat climbing over the edge of the straw, sniffing at the man's sleeve as if deciding whether flesh was already available.

Edmund jerked back, bile rising hard. He clapped a hand over his mouth to keep from making any sound.

Alice stepped close, her voice low. "Now you see," she said. It was not a rebuke. It was a grim statement, like naming weather. "They killed the dogs and cats, and now the rats have no reason to fear the open. They'll be in every barn, every storehouse. In beds, if there's warmth."

Edmund swallowed, trying to steady his breath. "And fleas," he said, thinking of the ship, thinking of the unseen riders on fur. Thinking of the way the disease moved without needing permission. "If the rats multiply—"

"They will," Alice cut in. "And the village will call it a curse and swing another rope."

Edmund stared at the closed door of the house. In his mind he saw the farmer in the square days ago, laughing at Edmund's warnings about isolation and cleanliness, the comfortable arrogance of someone who believed sickness belonged to other places. Now he lay on his floor while rats walked the walls of his barn.

"We can't help him," Edmund said, and the admission hurt even as it felt inevitable.

Alice watched the yard with quick, sharp glances. "If you go inside you'll come out carrying more than pity," she replied. Then her gaze flicked back to Edmund. "And even if you saved him, he'd still die when the village found out you were here. If he lived long enough to speak, he would name you to buy himself a moment of mercy."

Edmund closed his eyes briefly, and in that darkness he saw Thomas's face, wet with sweat and shame, promising to lead the mob away. Survival wore too many masks now. It could look like warning. It could look like betrayal. It could look like a man dragging his own sister to the square because the priest told him it would cleanse the village.

They backed away from the holding and slipped into the reeds again. The scratching from the barn faded, but Edmund could not shake the image of rats moving through spilled barley like it was meant for them.

As they walked, Edmund noticed more signs, small and easily missed if a man were not looking for them. Burrow holes at the base of hedges. Droppings on stones near the water. A half-eaten egg lying in mud, its shell broken like a mouth.

The village would not see these things as consequence. It would see them as confirmation.

Edmund heard Rob's voice in his imagination, loud and certain: See, they were everywhere. See how the creatures came when we spared them. See how the plague hides in fur and feather.

And Father Griffiths would lift his hands and bless the story, because a story that made sense was more precious than truth.

Alice stopped once more, listening.

"What is it?" Edmund asked.

She tilted her head toward the wind. "No dogs," she said quietly.

Edmund frowned.

"In a village," Alice continued, voice low, "even dying, you hear them. Barking, fighting, begging. Even if men are sick, dogs still make noise. Now it's… nothing. Just crows."

Edmund listened, and she was right. The air held no barking at all. Only the river's slow movement and the distant, occasional calls of birds.

A silence made by hands.

Edmund felt a chill spread through him that had nothing to do with damp clothes. He understood then what the village had done beyond cruelty. It had removed its own alarms. Dogs warned of strangers. Cats kept vermin down. Livestock meant food when roads closed. By killing its animals, the village had not purified itself.

It had made itself easier to overrun, easier to starve, easier to rot.

And the worst part was that the consequences would not arrive as a single dramatic punishment. They would arrive as a series of ordinary failures: stores ruined, wells fouled by careless disposal, fields left untilled because hands were busy swinging clubs and pulling ropes. Each failure would feed the next fear. Each fear would demand a new killing.

Edmund looked downriver, toward where Miriam and the others hid in marsh-bound cover. His choice to split away had been made to keep them alive. Now he wondered if anything could keep anyone alive when the land itself was being turned into an enemy.

"We should go farther from here," he said.

Alice's expression remained hard, but there was something in her eyes like agreement edged with warning. "They won't stay busy with beasts," she said. "Not once the beasts are gone. Then what's left?"

Edmund knew the answer. What was left was always the same.

People.

He started walking again, keeping to the river's edge where reeds hid his legs and the mud stole the sound of his steps. Behind him, upriver, the village would keep killing what it could catch, convinced that each corpse was another stone in a wall against plague.

But the wall they were building had cracks everywhere, and through those cracks the unseen consequences were already slipping: rats growing bold, filth spreading, hunger nesting in barns, and sickness moving with the calm patience of a thing that did not care what stories men told to excuse themselves.

Edmund felt the wind shift slightly off the water and carry with it the faintest hint of the village again, not the screams now, but the noise of work. Clubs striking. Shovels scraping. Men keeping busy.

He imagined them congratulating each other for their resolve.

And he imagined, with a cold certainty that tightened his ribs, the moment they would look up from the animal carcasses and realize the deaths had not slowed.

When that moment came, they would need something else to kill.

Something that could answer their accusations with a human voice, so that silencing it would feel even more like victory.

Chapter 12

Marks of the Damned

The river bent away from the village and carried Edmund and Alice into a stretch of bank where the reeds grew tall, and the mud took sound into itself. Even so, the village clung to them. It clung as a smell, faint and sour on the wind. It clung as memory: the dog struck until it stopped being a dog, the girl raising a brick because someone had told her God wanted it.

Alice moved ahead, picking places where the bank broke into pockets of shadow. Edmund followed, watching the water, the grass, the small movements that now meant more than they should have. Every rat track looked like a warning. Every burrow hole felt like an omen the village would twist into scripture.

They had gone far enough that the roofs were hidden behind trees when Alice stopped so suddenly Edmund nearly stepped into her back.

Voices.

Not the village's roar. These were fewer, close, speaking hurriedly through brush.

Alice sank into a crouch and held up two fingers. Wait. Edmund mirrored her, lowering himself into the reeds. He could see the edge of the track beyond the riverbank: a narrow strip of packed dirt that would carry carts in better days. Now it carried people.

Three villagers came into view, moving fast. Two men, one woman. They were not armed with clubs. They carried bundles, hurriedly tied. The woman's hair had been covered with a cloth, but it had slipped back, exposing loose strands that stuck to her face with sweat.

"They're saying it's in the hair," the woman said, voice tight with disbelief and terror. "As if God counts the color."

One of the men spat into the track. "Father Griffiths says the plague marks what it wants," he muttered. "That it chooses. Like it's got eyes."

"It doesn't choose," the other man snapped, as if arguing against a thought inside his own skull. Then, softer, "But Rob says he saw it. Swears on his mother's grave. Says he saw three sick ones with the same pale eyes staring like fish."

The woman made a sound that might have been a laugh in another life. “Half the village has pale eyes.”

“That’s why it’s spreading,” the first man replied, and the words were so perfectly circular Edmund felt cold under his ribs. “That’s why we must be careful. Rob says if you’ve got the wrong look, they’ll take you. They’ve already taken Cuthbert’s girl. Said her eyes were too blue, like water gone bad.”

The second man’s face twisted. “She’s ten.”

“She’s alive,” the first man said, and there was a terrible logic in the emphasis, as if being alive was now the only accusation that mattered. “At least she was when they dragged her. They said she carried the mark. They said she’d been spared when better folk died, and that proved it.”

The woman’s bundle shifted as she walked, and Edmund caught sight of what she was clutching: a child’s cloak. Too small for any grown body. She hugged it close as if the cloth could be made into protection.

“They’ll start with eyes,” she whispered. “Then they’ll say hair. Then they’ll say a mole. A scar. Anything.”

"A birthmark," the second man said, voice dropping. "I heard them in the square. A birthmark means the Devil kissed you before God did."

The woman shook her head hard, as if trying to shake words out of her own mind. "We're leaving," she said. "We're going to my sister's downriver. She'll take us. She has to."

The first man snorted. "No one has to. That's what this has taught me."

They hurried out of sight down the track, their feet raising little puffs of dust that settled quickly, as if even the earth did not want to remember them.

Edmund's breath felt trapped in his chest. He turned his head slightly toward Alice, careful not to rustle the reeds.

"They're moving beyond enemies you can name," he whispered.

Alice's eyes stayed on the track, sharp and unreadable. "They ran out of strangers," she said. "Then they ran out of beasts. Now they'll run out of mercy."

Edmund watched the empty track and tried to fit what he'd heard into a shape that didn't make him sick. Blue eyes. Hair. Birthmarks. It was madness, and yet it was a particular kind of madness, one he recognized from the way the village had always worked when it wanted certainty. It took a thing that could not be controlled and pretended it could, by turning it into a test.

A test meant there were answers. A test meant there were categories. A test meant there were people who could be sorted into safe and unsafe, clean and unclean, damned and spared.

He thought of the first child who had died, how quickly fear had demanded a reason. Poison had been simple because it pointed to hands. Then the strangers had been simple because they were already different. Then the vulnerable had been simple because they were already despised. Now, with difference exhausted, the village had begun to manufacture it.

Alice began to move again, keeping low. Edmund followed until the track curved and the brush thickened. The river narrowed and then widened again, the water sliding past in a way that made time feel unreal. Somewhere in the distance, the bell rang once. It was faint, but it carried.

They came to a place where the riverbank rose and a thin stand of trees gave a glimpse of fields beyond. Far off, near the line where the village would be if the land stayed honest, Edmund saw movement: a knot of people on a path, too small to be a crowd, too organized to be panicked wandering.

Alice saw it too. She lifted her chin, listening.

A shout carried, broken by distance. Then another. Not chanting this time but questioning.

Edmund and Alice moved closer through the trees until they could see the group more clearly. Four men, walking in a line, with a fifth behind them carrying something long. A pole, Edmund realized. A staff like the ones used in processions, except this one had rags tied to it in strips, fluttering like pennants. Not holy. Signaling.

They stopped a man on the path. A farmer by the look of him, shoulders hunched, hands stained. The four men surrounded him, and even at this distance Edmund could read the posture: the contained excitement of men granted authority they had never earned.

One of them held the staff out and pointed it toward the farmer's face, as if the pole could sense sin.

"Show your hands," a voice carried faintly.

The farmer lifted his hands, palms up.

"Turn your head," another shouted. "Look at me."

The farmer did.

One of the men leaned in close, so close it looked almost intimate, and then jerked back as if startled. He shouted something Edmund couldn't make out. The others reacted immediately, tightening their circle.

They were not looking for symptoms of illness, Edmund realized. Not for swelling, not for fever. They were looking for signs that could be read without touch. Signs that could be seen and agreed upon by any frightened eye.

Marks of the damned, in the language Father Griffiths would use, because a mark meant God had chosen a side.

The farmer's shoulders sagged. He seemed to plead, his mouth moving, but the men did not listen. One grabbed his arm. The farmer tried to pull away, and then the pole-bearer swung the staff down hard across the man's back. The farmer folded to his knees.

Edmund's hands clenched in the reeds. It was not the violence that shocked him most, though it turned his stomach. It was the efficiency. The men had become a moving court, a traveling square, carrying judgment to wherever fear could reach. The village had begun to patrol itself, not for sickness, but for difference.

Alice touched Edmund's sleeve, a warning. "We don't intervene," she murmured.

Edmund swallowed hard. "That's a man," he whispered.

"And if you step out," Alice replied, voice like stone, "you'll be a named man. The one they already want."

The patrol began to drag the farmer off the path, toward the village. The farmer stumbled, resisting only weakly now, as if the first blow had taken more than strength. The staff's rags fluttered behind them, bright against the dull field, a flag made from scraps.

When they were gone, the field lay still again. But the stillness had changed. It held the knowledge that any path could become a tribunal.

Edmund backed away from the trees, breath shallow. "They're making it random," he said. "So, no one can defend themselves."

"It's not random," Alice answered. "It's convenient. Randomness is what it feels like when the rules change faster than people can learn them."

Edmund thought of the farmer's hands held up, obedient, as if obedience still mattered. He thought of Rob Baines shouting about no cats, no dogs, and the village rushing to comply. Obedience had become a drug. It promised safety in exchange for participation. The more people obeyed, the more they proved they belonged to the side that lived.

He felt the anatomy of it laying itself out in his mind, piece by piece, like a body opened on a table.

First, the plague. An unseen killer, indifferent to prayer and punishment.

Then the need for a reason, because meaninglessness was worse than death.

Then a target that was already different, because the village could strike without fearing it might be striking itself.

Then a ritual to make the striking bearable.

Then a story to make the ritual holy.

And when the story failed to stop death, the story did not die. It evolved. It shed its old proof and grew new proof in its place.

Blue eyes. Pale hair. A mole. A birthmark. A scar from a childhood fall. Anything that could be pointed to and agreed upon by a crowd that wanted the relief of certainty more than it wanted truth.

Edmund's mouth went dry. He pictured Miriam's older boy, his steady gaze. He pictured the moneylender's son, eyes wide and frightened. He pictured their faces being weighed by strangers for the color of iris and the shape of brow.

"We have to get back downriver," he said, and the urgency in his voice surprised him. "If they start measuring people like livestock, it won't stay in that village."

Alice nodded once. "It never stays," she said. "Fear is a traveler."

They turned away from the field and pushed through the reeds, moving faster now, not caring that the mud sucked at their boots, not caring that thorns snagged at sleeves. Behind them, upriver, the village was no longer only killing what it could catch.

It was learning how to see enemies in faces.

And once a people learned that trick, every glance became an accusation, every familiar feature a risk. The plague might have arrived on rats and wind, but the village was building something that could outlive disease: a way of looking at each other that turned the ordinary into evidence.

Edmund kept his eyes on the river and tried to breathe through the tightness in his chest.

He had thought the village's cruelty had limits, that it would exhaust itself on strangers and beasts and the already despised.

He had been wrong.

The village had discovered the most inexhaustible source of targets it would ever have.

Each other.

The reeds closed behind them as Edmund and Alice pushed downriver, faster now, their careful quiet traded for the harsher need to put distance between themselves and the thing the village had become. Mud gripped at Edmund's boots as if trying to hold him in place. The river slid alongside, dark and patient, accepting whatever the banks gave it without question.

They moved until their lungs burned and the last glimpse of field patrols was swallowed by trees. Only then did Alice slow, lifting her head as if scenting the air.

"We're close," she murmured.

Edmund knew what she meant. Not close to the village upriver, but close to the hollow of brush and deadfall where Walter had taken the others. Close to Miriam and the children. Close to the thin, trembling thread of lives he had split himself from in the hope that splitting would spare them.

A branch snapped somewhere ahead.

Alice dropped into a crouch, knife sliding free with barely a sound. Edmund followed, lowering himself into the wet shadow of the reeds.

Another snap. Then hurried footsteps, not trying to hide, coming straight along the bank as if whoever approached had stopped caring whether the world saw them.

A woman burst into view, hair loose, skirts muddy to the knee. A boy followed her, perhaps twelve, his face sharp with fear. Behind him came a man carrying a bundle wrapped in a blanket, held awkwardly against his chest like a sack of grain that might shift and spill. The man's eyes were wild, fixed on the ground as if he feared the sky was watching.

When they saw Edmund and Alice, they froze.

“Stay back,” the man barked at once, and the words came out like an order he had practiced. He tightened his grip on the bundle.

The woman’s gaze flicked to Alice’s knife and then to Edmund’s face. Her mouth worked as if she recognized something and wished she did not.

Edmund held up his hands. “We’re not following you,” he said. “We’re only moving along the river.”

The boy swallowed hard. “Are you from there?” he whispered, jerking his chin upriver.

“From near,” Edmund admitted.

The man’s nostrils flared. “Then you’re sick,” he said, and fear made it certainty. “Or you’re carrying it on your clothes.”

“We’ve been away from the lanes,” Edmund replied, keeping his voice low and even. “We’re not here to bring you harm.”

The woman stepped forward a half pace despite herself, her eyes searching Edmund’s face like someone reading a prayer for the right line. “They’re checking people,” she said, and her voice shook on the last word. “On the roads.

They're stopping folk and looking at them like cattle."

Edmund nodded. "We saw."

The man's jaw clenched. "They stopped my brother," he said, as if spitting the sentence might make it less true. His eyes darted to the boy. "They said his eyes were wrong."

The boy flinched as though struck.

The woman's voice broke. "His eyes are his eyes," she whispered. "He was born with them."

The man's bundle shifted. A thin wail seeped out, high and weak. Edmund's stomach tightened. Not a sack of grain. A baby.

The man adjusted the blanket, and Edmund caught a glimpse of a small face, gray with exhaustion, a mouth opening and closing in feeble protest. The baby's eyes were wide and very pale, like watered milk.

The boy stared at the baby and then looked away quickly, as if the sight itself was dangerous.

"They said it starts in the family," the man went on, voice hoarse. "That marks run in blood. Father Griffiths says God shows Himself in the flesh."

Alice's gaze stayed fixed on the man's hands and the blanket. "So, you ran," she said.

The woman nodded sharply. "We ran because our own—" She swallowed. Her throat bobbed hard. "Because my mother said we should hand the baby over."

Edmund felt something cold move through him. "Hand the baby over to whom?"

The woman's eyes filled, but the tears did not fall. "To the men with the staff," she whispered. "To take back to the square. She said if we gave them the marked one, they wouldn't take the rest."

The boy made a small choking sound, a sound that was half sob and half laughter of disbelief. "Grandmother said it like it was bread," he whispered. "Like it was a tithe."

The man's face tightened into something like fury, but underneath it Edmund saw the crack of grief. "She's frightened," he said, as if defending the act and hating himself for it. "We're all frightened."

Edmund took a careful step closer. The man stiffened but did not retreat. Fear held him in place as firmly as any rope.

"Your mother," Edmund said gently. "She wanted to give up the child to save herself."

The woman shook her head hard, and the motion flung damp hair across her cheeks. "Not herself," she insisted. "She said to save the house. To keep the others. She said sickness takes what it's pointed at."

Edmund thought of the posts by the well. Of ropes made into lesson. Of children made to watch so they would learn what safety looked like. He looked at the baby's pale eyes and felt an old, bitter understanding sharpen inside him.

"It isn't only the village that's fracturing," he murmured. "It's families. It's the inside of the home."

Alice's voice came flat. "That's always next," she said. "When the mob runs out of strangers to blame, it eats its own table."

The man swallowed, and his gaze flicked past Edmund toward the bend in the river, as if expecting pursuers to appear at any moment. "They're saying mothers should watch their children," he said. "They're saying if a child has the wrong mark, the mother hid it, and hiding is proof of guilt."

The boy's face twisted. "They made Mrs. Cuthbert pull her girl's hair back," he whispered, words tumbling out as if he could not hold them. "Right in the road. They said her hair was too fair. They said fair hair means the Devil can see you better."

Edmund's throat went tight. "And did they take the girl?"

The boy nodded once, small and terrified. "Her father tried to stop it," he said. "He grabbed the staff. Just for a moment." His eyes went distant. "They hit him until his hands stopped moving."

The woman let out a thin sound, a breath that collapsed. "That's why I ran," she whispered. "Not because they'd take the baby. Because if they took him, they'd make us do it. They'd make us hand him over so we couldn't say we were innocent."

Edmund could see it: the village's genius for shared guilt, the way Rob and Father Griffiths had turned participation into proof of belonging. If a mother carried her child to the square and surrendered him, then she could never again claim the village was wrong. She would be tied to its story with her own hands.

The man's eyes hardened suddenly, and he stared down at the baby as if seeing something new there. His voice dropped. "My brother said… he said maybe it's true. He said maybe the baby is wrong and we're fools to risk the rest for him."

The woman's head snapped up. "Don't," she said, the word sharp as a slap.

The boy stared at the man with horror. "Father," he whispered.

The man's jaw worked. For a heartbeat Edmund thought he might deny it, might pretend the thought had not existed. Instead, he exhaled hard and looked away, shame moving across his face like shadow.

"I didn't say I believed it," he muttered. "I said he said it."

But the seed was there. Edmund saw it plainly: the village did not only kill bodies. It planted ideas that turned love into suspicion. Once planted, the ideas did their work even far from the square.

Alice shifted her weight, knife still low. "If you keep talking like that," she said to the man, "you'll leave this river with three and arrive with two."

The man flinched as if she had struck him. The woman tightened her grip on the edge of the blanket, pulling it closer around the baby.

Edmund felt his chest ache with something that was not only fear. It was a kind of grief for the ordinary world, for kitchens and hearths where a child's cry meant hunger, not accusation.

He looked at the boy. "What's your name?"

The boy hesitated, then whispered, "Will."

Edmund nodded. "Will, listen to me. No one can see plague in the color of an eye. No one can read God in a birthmark. They're lying because they need a rule that makes them feel safe."

Will's mouth trembled. "But they believe it," he said.

"Yes," Edmund replied, and the honesty tasted like iron. "They believe it because believing is easier than being helpless."

The woman's gaze clung to Edmund, hungry for certainty. "Where do we go?" she whispered. "If we go downriver, they'll stop us. If we go to another village, they'll look at the baby and—" Her voice cracked. "They'll do the same."

Edmund thought of Walter's instructions, of marshlands and cover, of sending a child alone if one must beg at a door. He thought of his own small band hidden in thorns, already marked by rumor. He could not take these strangers with him. More bodies meant more sound, more tracks, more chances for fear to turn hungry again. Yet leaving them felt like stepping over a drowning man because saving him would wet your sleeve.

Alice watched Edmund's face and seemed to read the struggle there. "You can't carry every broken family," she said quietly. "Not when the whole country is cracking."

The man's eyes sharpened. "Who are you?" he demanded again, suddenly suspicious, as if realizing too late that gentleness could be a trap. "Why do you speak like that?"

Edmund held his gaze. He could lie and perhaps gain their trust for a moment. He could say he was only a traveler. But he had heard his name carried to barred doors already. Names traveled whether you offered them or not.

"Edmund Harrow," he said.

The reaction was immediate. The woman's hand flew to her mouth. Will's eyes widened. The man took a sharp step back, clutching the baby tighter as if Edmund's name itself could infect the blanket.

"Harrow," the man whispered, and it was not a name now. It was a warning. "They said you're the reason. They said you sheltered them and the plague followed you."

Edmund did not argue. He only nodded once, because arguing would only make the story more real to them.

The woman's voice came out as a thin plea. "Is it true?" she asked. "Did you… did you bring it?"

Edmund felt the question strike a tender place inside him, not because it had power, but because it revealed how completely the village had succeeded. Even here, on the riverbank, a mother could be made to doubt her own eyes and ask if a man's presence could summon death.

"No," Edmund said, forcing steadiness into the word. "I didn't bring it. But they need someone to point to. That's what they do when they can't point to the sickness itself."

The man's breathing was quick now. "Then you'll be hunted," he said, and there was a strange relief in it, as if the idea of one hunted man made the world feel simpler again. "They'll come for you."

"Yes," Edmund replied.

The man's gaze flicked to the baby, to Will, to the woman. He seemed to wrestle with a thought, and Edmund saw the village's new logic grinding inside him: If Harrow is hunted, then standing near Harrow is danger. If danger can be avoided, it must be.

The woman saw it too. She stepped closer to the man, her voice urgent. "Don't you dare," she whispered.

The man's lips parted, then closed again. His eyes flashed toward Edmund, anger and fear braided tight. "Get away from us," he said, voice thick.

Edmund nodded. He did not step forward. He did not plead. He simply took one step back, then another, because he had learned what pleading did in a world that had decided fear was wisdom.

Alice moved with him, keeping her body angled between Edmund and the family, as if expecting the man to change his mind and strike in the name of safety.

Will stared at Edmund, and in the boy's face Edmund saw something that made his chest tighten: not hatred, not even fear exactly, but the hollow look of a child watching adults betray each other and learning that love could be negotiated away.

The woman's eyes followed Edmund as he retreated, and her mouth moved silently. Perhaps she wanted to apologize. Perhaps she wanted to ask again where to go. Perhaps she wanted to ask whether her own mother's suggestion had been the first crack in their family or only the most obvious one.

Then the man tugged her arm, and they hurried on downriver, leaving Edmund and Alice in the reeds.

They stood in silence until the family's footsteps were swallowed by the bend.

"That's how it spreads," Edmund said finally, voice rough. "Not only the sickness. The suspicion."

Alice's expression was hard, but there was something like weariness beneath it. "When a village teaches people that survival is proof of innocence," she said, "love becomes a bargain. Everyone starts asking what they can sacrifice to keep their own skin."

Edmund looked downriver, toward the hiding place where Walter and Miriam waited. He imagined Miriam's older boy with his steady eyes, and the thought of those eyes being called a mark made Edmund's stomach twist.

"We have to reach them," he said. "Now. Before the road patrols drift this far. Before the story teaches Walter to doubt Miriam, or Miriam to doubt her own children."

Alice nodded once. "Families fracture," she said, as if naming it made it a known enemy. Then she turned and began moving again, fast and low, along the river's edge.

Edmund followed, and behind them, upriver and downriver both, the land filled with people running from each other while carrying the ones they loved. The plague moved unseen, patient as the river. But fear moved in plain sight, and it had learned how to slip between husband and wife, between parent and child, until a family that had once been a shelter became another square where someone had to be chosen to pay.

Edmund and Alice moved with the river tight to their left and the reeds brushing their legs like cold fingers. The family they had just met was already gone around the bend, swallowed by the same trees that had hidden Miriam and the others. Edmund kept expecting to see Walter's shape ahead, crouched and waiting with that tense, half-anger he carried when the world refused to make sense. Instead, there was only the water's slow drag and the wet suck of mud underfoot.

“Slow,” Alice murmured once, not looking back. “Listen.”

Edmund slowed, breath shallow. The world had taught him too quickly that hurried feet became a signal. He tried to sort sound from sound: river, wind, a distant crow. Then, faintly, something else. Not footsteps, not voices. A repeated knocking, like wood on wood.

Alice stopped and crouched, and Edmund followed. He peered through the reeds toward the brushy hollow where Walter had led the others. The deadfall and nettles sat as they had before, tangled and ordinary. But the knocking continued, irregular, impatient.

A low hiss came from within the hollow, sharp as a warning. “Don’t move.”

Walter.

Edmund’s chest loosened by a fraction. He shifted his weight, careful, and whispered, “Walter. It’s me.”

Silence. Then Walter’s voice, tight and disbelieving. “Show your hands.”

Edmund froze. For a moment he thought he had misheard, that fear had changed the words in his mind. But Alice had already lifted her hands slightly, palms out, a gesture that was both compliance and caution.

Edmund raised his hands, fingers spread. “Here,” he said softly. “It’s Edmund.”

There was movement in the brush, and Walter’s face appeared between branches. His eyes were bloodshot, his cheeks hollowed as if the last day had scraped flesh away. He stared at Edmund’s hands as if expecting to see blood there, or some mark that would explain the world.

Alice stepped in first, parting reeds with her forearm. “You’re making noise,” she told Walter. “That knocking.”

Walter’s jaw clenched. “It’s the widow,” he said, and the word widow sounded newly literal now, not a label but a sentence. “She won’t stop. She says it keeps her from hearing them.”

Edmund slipped into the hollow and felt the air change, warmer and closer, thick with sweat and damp leaves. Miriam sat against a root with her younger boy limp in her lap, his face turned inward toward her chest. The older boy crouched beside her, watching Walter rather than Edmund, as if Walter’s body was the measure of whether danger had arrived. The moneylender sat with his son pressed close; his arm wrapped around the child so tightly the boy’s ear was flattened. The candle widow rocked slightly, tapping a small stick against a stone over and over, eyes fixed on nothing.

Miriam looked up, and for a heartbeat Edmund saw relief in her face. Then it was gone, replaced by the·hard guardedness that had been growing in her since the night of fire.

"You came back," she said. It was not gratitude. It was assessment.

"I said I would," Edmund replied.

Walter stepped closer, still blocking part of the entrance with his body. "And you brought her," he said, and the way he said her made Alice a risk rather than a person.

Alice's gaze sharpened. "I didn't drag him," she said. "He can still choose."

Walter's eyes flicked to her knife, then away. "Choice," he muttered. "A luxury."

Edmund moved further into the hollow so no one could claim he was hovering at the threshold like a stranger waiting to be admitted. "We saw patrols," he said, pitching his voice low. "They're stopping people on the paths. Not for sickness. For… marks."

The moneylender lifted his head, eyes wide. "Marks," he echoed.

"Eyes," Edmund said. "Hair. Birthmarks. Anything they can point to without touching. They've made it into a test."

Miriam's older boy's gaze flicked to Edmund, then immediately dropped, as if he had been taught not to invite attention. Miriam's arm tightened around her younger child.

Walter gave a short, bitter laugh that held no humor. "So that's what they're doing now," he said. "Good. Good. Soon they won't need plague at all."

"Walter," Edmund began.

Walter cut him off. "Don't," he said, voice rising just enough that Miriam hissed for quiet. Walter swallowed and forced it down again, but the anger remained in his face, hot and close to the surface. "Don't come back with your calm voice like it's only a matter of explaining. We've had visitors."

Edmund's stomach tightened. "Who?"

Walter hesitated, and the hesitation was its own kind of answer. "Thomas," he said at last.

Alice's posture changed instantly, a small shift of weight that made her look looser and more dangerous. "He found you," she said, and it was accusation wrapped in a statement.

"He came in from the reeds like a ghost," Walter replied, eyes never leaving Edmund's face. "Said he was leading them off. Said he'd told them downriver, like he promised."

"And did he?" Edmund asked.

Walter shrugged one shoulder, sharp and resentful. "How would I know? I only know he knew where we were."

The moneylender's son made a small whimper and buried his face deeper into cloth. The candle widow's tapping sped up, knock-knock-knock, like a heartbeat trying to outrun itself.

Edmund looked at Miriam. "Did he threaten you?" he asked.

Miriam shook her head once. "He cried," she said flatly. "He said the village was worse. He said they were taking children now, looking at their eyes like they could see sin." Her gaze went to Walter. "He wanted to stay with us. Walter told him to go."

Walter's lips pressed thin. "Because if he stays, he's a trail," he said. "And if he goes, maybe he's a trail somewhere else."

Alice let out a slow breath through her nose. "And you let him go," she said, and Edmund could hear in her voice that she meant it as both question and judgment.

Walter's eyes flashed. "What would you have done?" he demanded. "Stabbed him? Is that how you keep us safe?"

Alice did not answer immediately. She looked at each face in the hollow, taking inventory the way she always did: who was ready to run, who would freeze, who would scream. "I would have made sure he couldn't speak our hiding place to anyone," she said at last.

Miriam's head snapped up. "And if he didn't mean to?" she asked, her voice suddenly fierce.

Alice met her gaze without flinching. "Meaning doesn't matter when fear is squeezing your throat," she replied. "You heard the family on the riverbank, didn't you? How fast a father started talking like he could trade his own baby for safety."

Miriam's face tightened, and Edmund saw the truth of it land in her. Not because she agreed, but because it matched what she had already watched happen in the square.

Edmund tried to pull them back into quiet, into something that could be managed. "We have to move again," he said. "Patrols were close. And rumors are flowing downriver. A farm woman knew my name. Knew yours too, Alice."

The moneylender swallowed, his throat working. "If they know your name," he whispered, "they'll know ours. They'll say we were with you."

"We were," Walter said, and there was a bite in his tone, as if the admission itself was a trap closing. He looked at Edmund. "That's the point, isn't it? Your name is a sickness now. It carries faster than fleas."

Edmund felt the words hit, not because they were unfair, but because they were true. He forced himself to keep his voice steady. "That is why I split away," he said. "To keep you from being seen with me."

Walter's laugh was quiet and ugly. "And while you were away, Thomas found us anyway," he said. "So, what did it buy?"

Edmund opened his mouth, then shut it. He had no honest defense. He had chosen the least bloody option he could see, and the world had shifted so that even the least bloody option still bled.

Miriam spoke, her voice low. "It bought us time," she said, and Edmund looked at her in surprise. She did not meet his eyes. Her gaze stayed on her child's face, on the rise and fall of his breath. "Time to see what we are becoming."

The candle widow's tapping stopped abruptly. In the sudden quiet, the river sounded louder, like water rushing through a narrow throat.

Walter stared at Miriam. "What do you mean?" he asked.

Miriam lifted her head then, and her eyes were dry. "I mean when Thomas came," she said, "I wanted to let him stay. Not because I trust him. Because I was lonely. Because I wanted another adult voice that wasn't fear." She swallowed. "And then I thought, what if he coughs? What if he wakes my boys? What if he tells someone? And I hated myself because I realized I was thinking like them."

Walter's face flickered, something like shame trying to break through anger. He looked away.

Edmund felt a cold weight settle in his stomach. This was what he had been trying to outrun: not only the village's ropes and posts, but the way the village's thinking seeped into anyone forced to live near it. Suspicion as reflex. Mercy measured like a ration. Safety bought with someone else's risk.

"We met a family running downriver," Edmund said, voice softer. "A grandmother tried to give up a baby because his eyes were pale. The father didn't do it, but the thought was already in the house. That's what's spreading now. The plague kills bodies. Fear kills what holds people together."

The moneylender lifted his head, and Edmund saw in his eyes not only terror but calculation. "If we go to a village," the man said slowly, "we must decide who speaks. Who approaches. Who looks least… suspicious."

Alice's gaze snapped to him. "You're already sorting us," she said.

The moneylender's face flushed. "I'm trying to keep my son alive," he hissed, and the edge in his voice made the child flinch.

Walter turned on him. "And if someone has to be left behind to keep him alive?" Walter demanded. "Will you decide that too?"

The moneylender's jaw worked, and for a second he did not answer, which was answer enough.

Edmund felt something inside him go cold, not from surprise but from inevitability. The village did not have to reach into this hollow with torches to destroy them. It only had to teach them its language, and they would begin doing the work themselves.

Alice crouched near the hollow's edge and listened. "We can't argue here," she said. "Not now."

Walter took a step toward her. "Don't tell me what we can do," he snapped, then immediately lowered his voice again as if remembering sound could kill. "You don't own us."

Alice's eyes hardened. "I don't want to own you," she said. "I want you to live. But if you keep spitting at each other, you'll hand the patrols a chorus to follow."

Miriam's older boy shifted closer to his mother, his face closed. Edmund watched him and realized with a sick twist that the boy was learning the same lesson the village children were learning, only in a different way. Not how to swing a brick, but how to watch adults become unpredictable.

Edmund knelt, making himself smaller, trying to lower the temperature of the air. "Listen," he said. "We move before midday. We go to the marshlands. We don't take roads. We don't take tracks. If we see anyone, we hide. If we must ask for help, we do it through the smallest risk."

Walter stared at him. "And who is the smallest risk?" he asked, voice flat.

Edmund hesitated, and in that hesitation, he felt trust evaporate like breath on cold stone. Every answer meant choosing a sacrifice, even if the sacrifice was only the chance to be seen.

Alice answered for him, her tone matter-of-fact, almost gentle in its brutality. "Not Edmund," she said. "Not me. Probably the boy."

Miriam's head snapped up again. "No," she said, immediate and fierce. "No more children as tools."

Walter looked at Miriam, then at Edmund, and his face twisted with something that might have been pleading if he still believed pleading mattered. "You hear it?" he whispered. "This is what they've done. They've turned us into a village."

Edmund felt his throat tighten. He wanted to tell Walter that they were not like them, that they could still choose differently. But he could not deny what he had just seen: the moneylender measuring faces for suspicion, Walter searching Thomas's visit for betrayal, Miriam confessing the instinct to shut a crying man out of shelter.

Even here, among nettles and deadfall, under the cover of reeds, the village had reached them.

Not with fire.

With doubt.

Outside the hollow, the river slid past, indifferent and soundless. Somewhere upriver, beyond trees and smoke and stories, a bell might have been ringing. Edmund could not hear it now. But he could feel its rhythm in the way everyone held their breath, in the way no one quite met anyone else's eyes for too long, as if eye contact itself might become a mark.

They began to gather their things in silence. The candle widow resumed tapping her stick, slower now, as if trying to make the sound behave. Miriam shifted her child higher, her arms locked tight. Walter took position at the edge, watching the reeds for movement that wasn't wind.

Edmund rose, and when he looked at the faces around him, he understood the new danger with a clarity that made his stomach sink.

It was no longer only the patrols on the paths, or the ropes by the well.

It was the thinning thread between one person and another, stretched until it frayed.

And once it snapped, there would be nothing left between them and the village's lesson except the raw instinct to survive, no matter what had to be handed over to buy it.

Chapter 13

The Last Voice of Reason

They left the hollow before the sun climbed high enough to burn the mist off the river. The candle widow's tapping ceased only when Walter took the stick from her hand and tucked it into his belt as if it were a blade. She did not fight him. She only stared at the place where her fingers had been, as if sound had been the last thing she owned.

Edmund walked at the front, choosing ground that broke their outlines: reed beds, low willow, patches where floodwater still lay and would swallow footprints. Alice ranged out and back in short arcs, returning with brief looks that meant either nothing had moved or something had and she didn't want to name it yet.

Behind them, the village remained out of sight, but it rode the air anyway. Not as smoke now. As a habit. A way of tightening the jaw at every rustle. A way of holding a child closer and resenting the weight of him.

They followed a narrow strip of land where the river slowed and widened into a marshy plain. The ground changed underfoot, from mud that sucked to grass that gave, to water pooled in shallow bowls covered with slick green skin. Reed heads whispered against each other like gossip. Somewhere out in the wet, birds called and then fell silent again, quick to stop announcing themselves.

"This is where people disappear," Alice murmured, scanning the line where water met land. "If they don't know it."

Edmund nodded. He had hunted once in marshes like this with his father's men, long ago, when the world had still been only cruel in ways that were familiar. You could lose a dog in this, lose a man. A body could sink and be found seasons later, hair woven with reeds like a crown.

Walter eased Miriam over a softer patch where her foot would have gone through. Miriam did not thank him. She was past the point of spending words on anything that did not keep her children upright.

The moneylender kept his son close enough that the boy's shoulder rubbed his hip with each step. The child's eyes were wide and glassy, too dry, as if tears had been used up. Edmund watched him and felt the same cold knowledge he had felt watching the village children with bricks: whatever this boy survived, it would live in him.

They found a raised island of firmer ground; a hump of earth crowned with stunted thorn and a half-dead alder and stopped there to breathe. From the crest Edmund could see the marsh stretching, broken by channels of dark water. The river itself had become less a line and more a spread, as if it was unsure where it belonged.

Alice crouched and tested the soil with her fingertips. "This holds," she said. "For a little while."

They sank down, backs to scrub and roots. Miriam's younger boy began to whimper immediately, the sound thin and persistent. Miriam pressed her mouth to his hair and whispered until the whimpering softened into hiccupping breaths.

Walter sat with his elbows on his knees and stared out over the reeds as if he could see patrols moving through them. His hands opened and closed once, twice, a restless motion that did not know where to go.

Edmund looked at the small circle of faces and felt the weight of his own name sitting among them like a stone.

"We can't keep moving like this," he said quietly.

Walter's head snapped toward him. "You want to stop?"

"I want to think," Edmund answered. "Before thinking becomes another thing we're too frightened to afford."

Alice's gaze did not leave the marsh. "Thinking won't feed them," she said, but there was no contempt in it. Only the blunt knowledge of a woman who had spent her life watching plans fail when stomachs grew empty.

Edmund acknowledged it with a nod. "No. But without thinking, we become the village. We already hear it in ourselves." He looked at Walter when he said it, then at the moneylender. "We are starting to measure each other for risk like they measure eyes for sin. That is how they win without ever finding us."

The moneylender swallowed and looked away.

Walter's voice came harsh and low. "They're hunting children now. They're hanging the weak.

They're killing beasts until the rats own the barns. And you want us to talk about what's in our hearts?"

Edmund held his gaze. "Yes," he said. "Because what's in our hearts is the only thing they can't swing from a post unless we hand it to them."

Silence settled. Even the widow stopped rocking for a moment. The river made small licking sounds against the marsh channels, patient and indifferent.

Edmund shifted closer, lowering himself so he was not towering over anyone. It was an old habit from when he worked his Essex fields beside laborers. Stand as a man among men. Not as a lord with answers.

"We need rules," he said, and heard how cold the word sounded after everything that had happened in the village. He forced himself to continue. "Not laws like theirs. Not rituals. But agreements, so when fear rises, we don't make decisions with teeth."

Walter gave a short, bitter exhale. "Agreements won't stop a rope."

"No," Edmund said. "But they might stop us from putting a rope in our own hands."

Miriam's head lifted slightly. "What agreements?" she asked, her voice raw but steady. She had been the first to admit the thought that shamed her. That admission had changed her. It had made her dangerous in a different way: less easy to manipulate by shame.

Edmund counted them off carefully, each one like laying a plank across water. "We do not abandon anyone because of a rumor. Not eyes, not hair, not a mark. Not because they cough." He saw the moneylender's flinch and added, "If one of us grows sick, we isolate as much as we can without leaving them to the rats. We do what the village refused to do: we accept sickness as sickness."

Alice's mouth tightened. "And if you isolate one," she said, "someone has to bring water. Someone has to be near."

Edmund nodded. "Then we decide it together. No one is volunteered by another man's fear."

Walter's jaw worked. "And if patrols come?"

"We hide," Edmund said. "We don't bargain with them. We don't try to prove we're clean by offering someone else."

The candle widow made a small sound then, the first she'd made that felt like more than breath. "They made the children watch," she whispered, and her eyes stared at nothing. "They said it was for their souls."

Edmund felt something tighten in his chest. "Yes," he said softly. "And now those children know how to pull a rope and call it safety."

A movement flickered at the edge of the reeds below the island, and Alice's knife came up so quickly it seemed to appear in her hand. Walter shifted forward, readying his own blade.

"Hold," Alice murmured, eyes narrowed.

A man stepped into view, hands raised, breathing hard. For a heartbeat Edmund did not recognize him. Then he saw the familiar slope of the shoulders, the way shame lived in his posture.

Thomas.

His face was streaked with mud and sweat. His eyes were red, not with fever but with crying that had gone on too long. When he saw Edmund, relief and fear crossed his face in quick succession, as if he could not decide which was more dangerous.

"I didn't lead them here," Thomas blurted, voice cracking. "I swear I didn't. I went downriver like I said. I told them you were gone the other way. I told them you'd crossed fields toward the road. I lied, Edmund. I lied until my tongue felt like it would split."

Walter made a sound like a growl. "And yet you found us," he said.

Thomas flinched. "I followed the river," he whispered. "I thought… I thought you'd do the same. I had nowhere else. They won't let me back. Rob said if anyone helps Harrow, they're helping the plague."

Edmund watched Thomas's hands, half expecting to see a weapon. They were empty and shaking.

Alice did not lower her knife. "You came to beg," she said.

Thomas's mouth opened and shut. "Yes," he admitted. Then, with sudden desperate force, "And to warn you. They've made a band. Six men. They carry a staff with rags like a banner. They're stopping people beyond the fields now. Beyond the farms. They're saying they'll cleanse the whole hundred. They're saying Harrow's hiding with a pack of corrupters and that anyone who shelters him will be burned out."

Walter spat into the reeds. "Burned out," he muttered. "Like foxes."

Thomas's eyes flicked to Miriam and the children. He seemed to shrink at the sight of them, as if seeing what had been carried and not dropped made his own failures heavier. "I saw them take Cuthbert's girl," he whispered. "Not just take. Make her mother hold her still while they looked at her eyes in the road. Father Griffiths was there. Not with the staff but watching. Nodding."

Edmund felt the marsh air turn cold in his lungs. "He left the church," he said.

Thomas nodded miserably. "They go where the fear is now. The church steps aren't enough."

Miriam's older boy stared at Thomas with a flat, unreadable expression that made Thomas look away.

Edmund made a decision then, not because it was right, but because standing still was becoming its own kind of death.

"We can't outrun this forever," Edmund said.

Alice finally lowered her knife a fraction, just enough to show she was listening. Walter's face hardened, anticipating what Edmund would say next.

Edmund looked at them all, one by one, forcing himself to meet eyes that wanted to slide away. "There are still people in that village who haven't pulled a rope," he said. "People who are frightened but not yet drunk on it. If anyone can be gathered, if anyone can be given another way to think before Rob's story becomes the only one left, it must be now."

Walter shook his head immediately. "No," he said, the word sharp. "You go back and you die. Or worse. They'll make you kneel in the square and Father Griffiths will call it mercy."

"I know," Edmund replied.

The moneylender's lips moved as if counting again. The candle widow began to rock, faster now, caught between wanting a plan and fearing what plans cost.

Thomas took a step closer, stopping when Alice's gaze warned him. "Edmund," he whispered, "they're not listening to reason. They're listening to who shouts loudest."

"That's why I need more than my voice," Edmund said. He looked at Walter. "That's why I need the faithful few."

Walter's eyes narrowed. "Faithful," he echoed, and there was pain in it. "To what?"

Edmund swallowed. He thought of Essex fields. Of shared harvests. Of laughter in a hall that had not been built on fear. He thought of the moment the village learned to call violence control.

"To the idea that we are still human," he said at last. "That's all."

Miriam held her child tighter, and her voice came low. "And if your faithful few are wrong?" she asked. "If you go and you fail?"

Edmund did not lie. "Then we will at least fail trying to keep something from rotting inside us," he said. "Because if we only hide, if we only run, then fear will do its work anyway. It will turn us against each other in this marsh, and no patrol will need to find us. We will hand ourselves over piece by piece."

Walter's throat bobbed. For a moment Edmund saw the man he had been before the village: stubborn, decent, capable of kindness without feeling it was weakness. Then the hardness returned, not because Walter did not feel, but because feeling had become unbearable.

"You can't ask us to walk into that," Walter said.

"I'm not asking all of you," Edmund replied. "The children stay out of sight. Miriam stays with them. Someone has to keep them alive if I don't return." He forced the words out, each one tasting like blood. "But I need witnesses. I need men who can still look at a neighbor and see a neighbor, not a mark."

Alice's gaze sharpened. "You're going to stand in front of them," she said, understanding finally. "Not to fight. To speak."

"Yes," Edmund said.

Thomas's face crumpled. "They'll kill you."

Edmund nodded. "They might. But if no one speaks against Rob while speaking is still possible, then the only voices left will be his and Father Griffiths's. And then this will not be one village. It will be every village the wind touches."

Silence again. The marsh held them in its wet hands, offering hiding but not comfort.

Walter stared out over the reeds for a long time. Then he looked at Edmund with an expression that was half fury, half something like grief.

"You always did think words could mend what men break," Walter said.

Edmund met his gaze steadily. "No," he replied. "I think words are the last tool left before the breaking becomes all there is."

Walter's eyes closed briefly, as if he were bracing himself against an oncoming blow. When he opened them again, his voice was hoarse.

"If I go with you," he said, "it's not because I believe they'll listen. It's because I can't bear to watch them turn you into a lesson without someone remembering you were a man."

Edmund felt his throat tighten, and he nodded once.

Alice sheathed her knife with a small, decisive motion. "Then you don't go alone," she said.

Miriam's breath caught, but she did not argue. Perhaps she had learned that some arguments only delayed what was already moving.

Edmund looked at the small group on the island of earth: a farmhand with torn loyalty, a woman made sharp by survival, a man whose goodness had been beaten into grimness, and a handful of frightened souls clinging to them like driftwood.

The faithful few.

Not faithful because they were sure they would win, but faithful because something in them still refused to call slaughter cleansing.

Edmund rose slowly. The ground under his feet felt unsteady, as if the marsh itself did not trust what he intended.

"We go at dusk," he said. "We go quiet. We speak once. And if they refuse to hear it, we leave before they can make our bodies part of their story."

Walter gave a short, humorless laugh. "And if they don't let you leave?"

Edmund looked upriver, toward the unseen square with its well and posts and rags on a staff fluttering like victory.

"Then," he said softly, "at least the last voice they silence won't be begging them to be merciful. It will be telling them what they are."

Dusk came slowly, as if the sun, too, hesitated to look upon what the village had made of itself.

Edmund spent the afternoon on the marsh island in a state that was not quite waiting and not quite prayer. He checked the straps of his boots and found his hands shaking when he tried to tighten the buckles. He forced them still. He went to Miriam once, crouching near where she sat with her younger boy against her chest, the child's breath shallow but steady.

"You stay hidden," Edmund told her.

Miriam did not look up at first. She stared at the reeds, at the thin channels of water, as if the marsh might be persuaded to swallow every road and erase every village. "We will," she said. Then her gaze lifted, and Edmund saw something hard set behind her grief. "If they don't come here first."

"They won't," Alice said from behind him. "Not unless they already know."

Miriam's mouth tightened. "They know everything," she replied, not to Alice but to the air itself. "They know your names, your faces. They know where to look for a reason."

Edmund wanted to promise safety. He had learned, too late, that promises were only another kind of lie when the world was this hungry.

Walter stood apart, sharpening his belt knife against a stone with slow, deliberate strokes. The sound was small, but Edmund felt it in his teeth. Thomas hovered near the edge of the island, eyes scanning the marsh as if expecting the reeds to part and reveal pursuers at any moment.

"It'll be worse than you think," Thomas said quietly when Edmund approached him. "They're different now. They're… proud."

Edmund nodded. He had seen the pride in the way men wiped blood from shovels like cleansing oil, in the way a neighbor congratulated a boy for killing the dog that had once guarded his door.

"How far do the patrols reach?" Edmund asked.

Thomas swallowed. "They walked out past the farms today," he said. "They stopped anyone on the tracks. They made folk turn their heads. Made them show their eyes in the light. They're calling it God's inspection."

Edmund felt his stomach turn. "And Father Griffiths blesses it."

Thomas's face twisted. "He blesses everything Rob puts in front of him," he whispered. "Or maybe it's the other way round."

Alice moved close enough that her voice would not carry. "We don't go in like visitors," she said. "We go in like shadows. The fewer see us before we speak, the better."

Walter's knife paused mid-stroke. "And once we speak?" he asked.

Edmund held Walter's gaze. "Then we take whatever opening remains," he said. "If there is one."

They left Miriam and the children in the reeds as the light began to thin. Miriam did not cry. She only held Edmund's wrist once, briefly, as she had before, as if reminding herself he was solid. Her older boy watched without blinking, his face too composed for a child, as if he had already learned the uselessness of pleading.

The moneylender did not ask to come. He sat with his son tucked against him, and Edmund saw in the man's eyes an ugly relief mixed with fear. Relief that someone else would go toward danger while he stayed with what he still possessed. Edmund did not judge him for it. Judging had become too easy, and too similar to what the village did.

Edmund, Alice, Walter, and Thomas moved off the island and into the marsh channels, following Thomas's memory of the land. The reeds grew taller as they went, heads brushing Edmund's shoulders. Water seeped into his boots. The ground gave underfoot in places, and Walter steadied him once with a hand on his elbow, not gentle, but necessary.

By the time they reached firmer land, the village lay ahead as a smudge of dark shapes against the dimming sky. No bell rang now. The silence felt like a held breath.

They skirted the outer fields, staying low by hedgerows. The air was wrong near the village, thick with a sour sweetness and smoke that had settled into everything. Somewhere a crow called, and another answered, and Edmund realized how little other sound remained. No barking. No lowing cattle. No cats yowling in alleys. A village without animals sounded less like peace and more like something dead pretending it still lived.

A torch flared near the square, then another. The light moved like restless eyes.

"They're gathered," Thomas whispered.

Walter's jaw clenched. "Always gathered," he muttered, as if the village could no longer bear being alone with itself.

Edmund felt the old, familiar stone of fear in his chest, but beneath it was another weight, heavier and calmer: the knowledge that whatever happened in the next hour would not be undone. If Rob had truly made Edmund into the shape of corruption, then Edmund's presence would not be received as a man returning home. It would be received as a story made flesh.

They reached the line of outer cottages. Shutters were closed. Ash marks and crude crosses streaked doorframes. Bundles of herbs hung like offerings. A broken cart lay on its side in a lane, abandoned mid-task. Edmund glimpsed something pale in the gutter and realized it was the stiff body of a cat, half-crushed, left as if disposal itself had become too much trouble.

Alice touched Edmund's arm and pointed toward a back path that ran between two barns. "That way," she murmured.

They moved through the narrow passage. The smell of spilled grain and rat waste hit Edmund sharply. He heard scratching inside a wall, confident and constant. The village had killed what it could see, and in doing so had fed what it could not.

At the edge of the square, they paused behind a stack of firewood. The well stood at the center as it always had, a familiar shape made monstrous by what surrounded it. The posts were still there, dark at the base. The ground around them was scuffed into hard earth, a ring worn by many feet. Torches cast light that trembled across faces.

The staff with rags stood near the church steps, propped upright like a banner. Men held it with the solemnity of pilgrims carrying a relic.

Rob Baines was in the open, his face bright with torchlight, his posture loose with power.

Father Griffiths stood near him, hands folded, eyes shining. The priest's mouth moved in a quiet murmur, not to calm the crowd, Edmund realized, but to tune it, the way a man tuned a string before a performance.

Rob raised his arms, and the murmur stilled. Not fully. Never fully. But enough to listen.

"We've cut out the rot," Rob called. "We've burned what was foul, and we've named what was false. And still the scourge bites, because the rot ran deeper than we knew."

A voice from the crowd shouted, "Marks!"

Another answered, "Eyes like river glass!"

Laughter rose, then died, replaced by a tighter sound that was almost prayer.

Father Griffiths lifted one hand. "The Lord reveals," he said, and the crowd quieted further, hungry for revelation.

Edmund's throat went dry. This was not a meeting. This was not even a mob, not in the old sense. This was ritual made portable; fear made into religion.

Alice leaned close. "Now?" she whispered.

Edmund looked at Walter and Thomas. Walter's face was pale and hard. Thomas trembled.

Edmund stepped out from behind the woodpile.

For one heartbeat, no one saw him. The torches shifted, smoke curled, the crowd's attention still held by Rob. Then a woman near the well turned her head, and her eyes widened.

"Harrow," she breathed.

The name moved through the square like a spark in dry straw.

Heads turned. Bodies angled. Men leaned forward as if pulled by a rope.

Rob's face changed, not into surprise, but into something sharper and pleased, as if the night had delivered him a gift. "Well," he said loudly, and the single word carried amusement like poison. "Look what crawled out of the reeds."

Edmund walked forward a few steps into clearer light, hands visible, empty. He felt every gaze latch onto him. It was not the gaze of neighbors seeing a man. It was the gaze of people seeing a verdict.

Father Griffiths's expression remained almost gentle, but his eyes were bright and intent.

"Edmund Harrow," he said, voice carrying, "you return to us at last."

Edmund forced his voice steady. "I return because this has gone beyond fear," he said. "It has become murder dressed as cleansing."

A murmur rose at once, not confusion but outrage, as if Edmund had spoken blasphemy.

Rob smiled wider. "Hear him," he called to the crowd. "Hear how he speaks. Always the same. Always calling evil good and good evil. Always defending filth."

Edmund raised his voice slightly. "You killed your own animals," he said. "You have made the rats bold. You have fouled your barns and your stores. You think you are purifying, but you are feeding what carries the sickness."

A shout cut through: "Liar!"

Another: "He wants us sick!"

A third voice, higher, trembling with conviction: "He speaks for them!"

Edmund felt the square tighten around him. Walter stepped out into view behind Edmund's left shoulder, and several men in the crowd hissed at once, recognition turning into accusation.

"There," Rob said, pointing. "He brings his faithful with him. Come to preach while we bury our dead."

Edmund tried again, pushing against the rising tide. "This plague does not choose by eye color," he said. "Not by hair, not by birthmark. You are hunting marks because you cannot bear not knowing. But the sickness does not care what stories you tell about it."

Father Griffiths's face tightened, as if pained by Edmund's stubbornness. He lifted his hands, palms outward, the gesture of a man offering patience. "Listen to him," the priest said, voice soft and deadly. "He says your faith is fear. He says your obedience is madness. He says you cannot see God's hand in what is happening."

The crowd's anger flared hotter at the priest's framing than at Edmund's words. Edmund felt, with sudden clarity, what he was up against. He had not walked into an argument. He had walked into a sermon, and in a sermon any dissent was not difference of thought. It was betrayal.

Rob's voice sharpened. "He stands here and tells you your eyes are nothing," he shouted. "He tells you the marks God shows are lies. Why? Because he wants you blind. Because blind men are easy to poison."

A man near the posts yelled, "He sheltered them! He's the root!"

Edmund heard his own heart in his ears. He spoke anyway. "If you need a root," he said, "look to the ship that brought rats into ports. Look to the fleas and filth. Look to the dead that were not buried. Not to children's faces. Not to a woman's hair."

A stone struck the ground near his foot. Another followed, thudding into the dirt.

Rob raised his hand, not to stop it, but to savor it. "There it is," he called. "He blames ships. He blames wind. He blames everything but the corruption he carried into our streets. He would rather you fear a rat you cannot see than the traitor you can."

Edmund's stomach sank. Logic was not landing. It was being seized and twisted into proof of his treachery. Every explanation he offered gave Rob another handle.

Father Griffiths leaned forward, his voice carrying with quiet certainty. "You stand before your people and call their vigilance sin," he said. "You tell them to open their doors to sickness. You urge them to spare what God has marked. Why should we believe you, Edmund Harrow, when every word you speak would loosen the only bonds holding this village together?"

The crowd roared then, not with the chaotic rage of panic but with the unified anger of a congregation defending its creed.

Edmund understood, in that roar, what the subtlest cruelty of it was. In calmer days, reason had been admired as a lord's virtue, a sign of steadiness. Now, reason sounded like treason. It sounded like a man choosing the plague over his neighbors' comfort. It sounded like betrayal because it threatened the only thing the village still had: the certainty that their violence meant something.

Walter's voice rose behind Edmund, harsh and ragged. "You're not holding anything together," he shouted. "You're tearing it apart!"

A man in the crowd surged forward, face red with torchlight. "He speaks too!" he yelled. "They're all with him!"

Edmund saw hands tightening around clubs. He saw faces that had once been familiar hardening into shapes made for punishment. He had come to speak once and leave before they could turn his body into part of their story.

But the story was already closing around him.

And in the village's eyes, his calm insistence on truth had become the final, unforgivable act: not simply disagreement, but a betrayal of the comfort their madness provided.

For a moment the square became nothing but sound. The roar rolled through bodies and bounced off stone walls and shut shutters, and Edmund felt it in his ribs as if the air itself had turned solid.

He lifted his hands higher, palms out, the gesture useless and instinctive. He saw eyes fixed on him with the bright, feverish focus of men who had found a single point to aim at. Beyond the ring of faces, torches spat and trembled. The staff with its rags stood upright like a flag planted in the earth, marking territory.

Rob took a slow step forward, smiling as if this were a performance arranged for his pleasure. "Hear how he brings his smooth words," he called. "Hear how he insults your grief and calls it madness. He would have you lie down like lambs and let the scourge eat you. He would have you do nothing."

Edmund's voice came out rougher than he intended, but it carried. "Doing something is not the same as doing right."

A few heads jerked at that, not because it convinced them, but because it sounded like judgment. Judgment was Rob's privilege now, and the village did not like to share it.

Father Griffiths moved a half step forward, hands still lifted as if holding the air between them. "Edmund," he said softly, and the softness was a blade. "You speak as if you alone are clean of fear. Yet you hid. You ran. You left others to face what came."

A ripple of assent moved through the crowd, hungry for that shape of accusation. Edmund felt it: the village's need to turn his flight into proof of guilt, as if any act of survival could be made into a confession.

"I ran because you were killing the innocent," Edmund said, and forced the words to remain steady. "Because you burned homes and called it safety. Because you made children watch a rope swing and taught them to call it mercy."

A woman near the well made a strangled sound, half rage, half something else. Edmund could not tell if it was shame trying to speak and being drowned.

Rob's smile thinned. "Innocent," he repeated loudly, savoring the word as if it were a joke. "You dare speak of innocence when corpses fill our lanes? When families rot in their beds? Where was your innocence when the plague came through our doors?"

"It did not come through our doors," Edmund snapped before he could soften it. He caught himself, forced his breath to slow. This was the moment he had come for, the last chance to make his plea before anger closed every ear.

He turned his head, letting his gaze move across faces he recognized: men he had hired at harvest, women who had brought eggs to market, boys who had once chased each other through the square in summer dust. Their eyes did not meet his. They slid away as if looking directly at him might make them complicit in hearing.

"You think I insult your grief," Edmund said, louder now. "Listen to me. Your grief is real. Your fear is real. The sickness is real. But what you are doing with your fear is not protection. It is hunger given permission."

A stone flew, not thrown hard enough to kill, but hard enough to sting if it struck. It hit the ground and spun to a stop at Edmund's feet.

Walter shifted beside him, a step forward, shoulders bunched as if ready to lunge. Alice, a pace behind, moved with the controlled readiness of a drawn bow. Edmund did not look back at them. He did not want the crowd to see their tension and use it as proof that he had come to fight.

He pushed on.

"You have killed strangers," he said, and the word strangers made some faces tighten in discomfort, because even now some of them remembered names that had been spoken in their streets for years. "You have killed the weak. You have killed the lame and the old and those who could not defend themselves. Now you kill beasts that never wronged you, and the rats grow bold because you have removed what kept them down. You have turned your own village into a feast for the very thing you fear."

A man near the posts shouted, spittle bright in torchlight. "So, you know best? You, with your fine land and your fine ideas?"

Edmund looked straight at him. "No," he said. "I know I can be wrong. That is the difference between me and this." He lifted one hand toward Rob and Father Griffiths without pointing, refusing to give the gesture the satisfaction of accusation alone. "They do not allow wrongness. They allow only enemies."

Rob's voice cut in, sharp. "You hear him? He sets himself above your priest. Above your folk.

Above God. He calls us enemies when we are the ones trying to keep you alive."

Edmund felt his chance narrowing. The crowd was turning with each sentence, not toward him, but away, as if reason were a sickness and they were learning to recoil.

He tried a different path, not argument but memory.

"Do you remember the first child?" he asked. "The one who died so quickly you could not believe it was natural? Do you remember how you stood here and begged for an answer? You did not ask for truth. You asked for certainty. And when no certainty came, you made one."

A few faces flinched. A mother clutched her own child closer, as if the mention alone could summon the death back into her arms.

"You wanted a well poisoned," Edmund continued. "Because poison has hands. Because hands can be punished. And when that did not stop the sickness, you wanted strangers to blame. And when the strangers were ash, you wanted the unclean. And when the unclean were gone, you wanted beasts. And now you want marks in the flesh."

He drew a breath, tasting smoke.

"This will not end," he said, and the words came quiet but strong, carrying in the brief lull. "Not because the plague is endless. But because you have built a machine that must be fed. Each time the sickness continues, you will say you have not killed enough. You will say God still demands proof. You will say the rot is deeper. And you will dig until you reach bone."

Father Griffiths's expression tightened, offended not by the warning but by the challenge to his authority. "Enough," he said, voice still soft, and the softness made it worse. "This is not counsel. It is temptation. You come to unmake the village's unity with your words."

Edmund turned his head toward the priest. "Unity built on blood is not unity," he said. "It is a crowd holding the same knife."

The priest's eyes flashed. "Then you deny that obedience can save," he said, and his tone made obedience sound like salvation itself.

"I deny that murder can save," Edmund replied.

A shout rose: "Blasphemy!"

Another: "He calls Father Griffiths a murderer!"

Edmund lifted his voice again, forcing it over the rising anger. "I call no man beyond repentance," he said, and felt Alice stiffen behind him at the word repentance, because it belonged to sermons, and sermons were the village's weapon now. He pressed on anyway. "If you have pulled a rope or swung a club, you can stop. You can stop tonight. You can bury the dead instead of adding to them. You can isolate the sick with care instead of dragging them into the square. You can wash your hands, burn your bedding, keep your animals where they belong and your rats out of your stores. You can do the hard work of living with fear without turning it into cruelty."

Rob laughed, a short, bright sound that made heads turn toward him. "Hear the lord," he said. "He tells you to wash while you're drowning. He tells you to burn bedding while the scourge burns your lungs. He tells you to tend the sick, as if the sick have not brought this upon us."

Edmund's jaw tightened. "The sick do not bring sickness by deserving it," he said. "They are not sinners for coughing. A child is not cursed for having blue eyes. A man is not damned for being born with a mark on his skin. These are lies. You know they are lies."

He let his gaze sweep again, searching for any sign of recognition, any flicker of the old village that had once laughed and worked and complained about weather rather than fate. He found only guarded faces, and behind them something else: fear of being the first to soften.

He understood then that the final plea was not only against Rob and Father Griffiths. It was against the crowd's terror of standing alone in compassion.

Edmund took a step closer to the well, closer to the posts, and felt the air around him tighten. It was like stepping toward a cliff edge. He could smell the old damp of the well stones beneath the newer smells of smoke and sweat and blood.

"If you need to punish someone," he said, voice carrying in the sudden hush that fell as if the square itself leaned in, "punish me. If killing a man will make you feel safe for one hour, then take that hour."

A murmur ran through them, surprised and pleased, and Edmund felt something inside him go cold. He had not meant it as offering. He had meant it as mirror.

"But do not tell yourselves it is righteousness," he continued quickly, before the murmur could become decision. "Do not tell your children it is mercy. Do not bless it with water and prayer. Say the truth, at least once before you lose even that. Say: We are afraid. We do not know how to fight an unseen thing. So, we make visible enemies and we kill them."

A woman's sob broke out, sharp and sudden, and then stopped as if someone had struck her.

Edmund pointed not with a finger but with his voice, thrusting it into the crowd. "Look at what you have already learned to do," he said. "Look at the animals gone, the silence where barking should be. Look at the rats bold in daylight. Look at your barns torn open. Look at your families turning on each other for a hair color. This is not God's work. This is ours."

Rob's face hardened, the smile finally slipping. He raised his hand, and men near him shifted as if that single gesture were command enough.

"This is the devil's tongue," Rob called, loud and sure. "He wants you to doubt your own eyes. He wants you to pity what should be cut away. He wants you soft so the scourge can finish you. Are we soft?"

"No!" the crowd shouted back, and the shout was relief. It was belonging.

Father Griffiths's voice followed, quieter but carrying, as if he were sealing a vow. "Those who speak against cleansing speak for corruption," he said. "Those who undermine our vigilance invite the plague into every home."

Edmund felt the last door closing. He tried anyway, because trying was the only remaining act that still felt human.

"Then you will have your proof," he said, voice fierce now. "You will kill and kill and the sickness will continue. And when it does, you will not blame yourselves. You will blame the next face, the next mark, the next child. There will be nothing left but ash and a story you cannot stop telling, because without it you would have to feel what you have done."

For an instant, for one thin instant, Edmund saw it land in a few eyes. Not agreement, not courage, but the flash of recognition that hurt.

Then a man surged forward from the ring with a club raised, and the moment shattered.

Alice moved like a strike of lightning, stepping in, her knife appearing and then halting an inch short of flesh. She caught the man's wrist with her free hand and twisted hard, sending the club clattering to the ground. The man screamed.

The scream did it. It snapped the crowd's restraint like a thread.

"Knife!" someone shouted. "She's got a knife!"

"They've come to cut us!" another voice cried, and the lie spread faster than breath.

Walter lunged, not to attack but to shield, shoving Edmund back a half step. Hands grabbed at Walter's arms. Someone struck him in the side and he grunted, bending. Thomas appeared at the edge of the torchlight, face white, eyes frantic, and then vanished again as the crowd swelled.

Edmund tried to raise his voice, but it was swallowed. The square became bodies pressing, shouting, grasping. Someone seized Edmund's sleeve and tore it, the cloth ripping with a sound like paper. Another hand grabbed his hair and yanked his head back, forcing his face up toward torchlight and the church steps.

Rob's face hovered above the crowd, satisfied. Father Griffiths's lips moved, perhaps in prayer, perhaps in instruction.

Edmund felt his feet leave the ground for a moment as men hauled him forward. His boots scraped, found earth again, slid.

He caught a glimpse of Alice, her knife now held low, her face set in a grim calculation: too many, too close, no clean cut that didn't become slaughter. He saw Walter on one knee, trying to rise while hands pushed him down. He saw Thomas's shape darting away along the edge, not cowardice but the instinct to survive long enough to warn the marsh.

Edmund drew a breath that tasted of smoke and terror and spoke his last words into the faces nearest him, not to persuade the leaders, not to win, but to plant something that might hurt later, when the fever of certainty cooled.

"You will not be saved by what you are about to do," he said, voice hoarse but clear. "You will only become the thing you fear."

A fist struck his mouth, bursting pain and copper across his tongue. The crowd roared approval.

As they dragged him toward the posts by the well, Edmund understood with a cold clarity that his plea had ended as all reason ended here: not answered, not debated, but silenced. And the silence that followed would not be empty.

It would be filled with the sound of a village teaching itself, once again, how to live with murder.

Chapter 14

The Breaking of Edmund Harrow

Edmund's feet scraped furrows in the dirt as they hauled him across the square. The grip in his hair did not loosen. It tightened whenever he tried to lift his head, forcing his neck back so the torchlight could find his face. The pain in his mouth pulsed with each heartbeat, hot and metallic; blood ran down his chin and into the torn collar of his shirt.

The posts waited beside the well, dark at the base where the ground had been fed too often. Edmund smelled the wet stone of the well and, beneath it, the sourness of old smoke ground into timber. The crowd's shouting layered over itself; a single animal made of mouths.

"Hold him!"

"Make him look!"

"Let him see what he's done!"

Hands shoved him to his knees. For a moment his vision blurred, and the world became the wavering orange of torches and the hard black of shadow. Someone kicked the back of his thigh to keep him down. He did not cry out. He refused them that small proof of power.

Rob Baines pushed through the bodies with a surety that did not belong to a man who owned no land. The crowd made way for him as if he carried a title. His face shone with sweat; his eyes were bright, not with fear, but with a kind of hungry delight that made Edmund feel colder than the night air.

Rob crouched in front of him, close enough for Edmund to smell ale and onion on his breath. "There he is," Rob said, loud enough for the ring of faces to hear. "The lord who would rather preach than bleed with us."

Edmund swallowed, tasting copper. "I bled," he rasped. His words were thick; one side of his lip felt numb. "Not with you. Because of you."

A murmur rose, sharp with offended righteousness.

Rob straightened, and his voice turned theatrical. "Hear that? He blames you for your own dead. He blames you for the plague." He lifted his arms as if addressing a market crowd.

"He comes back from hiding and tells you that your vigilance is murder. As if we haven't watched children swell and burst. As if we haven't buried fathers with no priest left to bless them because the priest is busy keeping the rot out."

Father Griffiths stepped into view beside the church steps, his robes dark in the torchlight. He did not shout. He did not need to. The crowd leaned toward him as if his calm were the only steady thing left.

"Edmund Harrow," the priest said, and there was sorrow in his tone carefully measured, the sorrow of a man who wished to be seen as merciful even while he sharpened the blade. "You stand before your neighbors and accuse them. You deny the signs the Lord has shown us. You deny the marks He has revealed."

Edmund lifted his head despite the hand still knotted in his hair. The motion sent a spear of pain through his scalp. "You have revealed nothing," he said, voice rough. "You've invented it."

A man in the crowd spat. "Hear him. Still talking."

Another shouted, "Ask him about the knife!"

Edmund's gaze flicked, searching the edge of the torchlight for Walter, for Alice. He saw Walter on the ground near the well, half propped on one elbow, his face drawn tight. Two men held him by the arms, not gently, like a sack they meant to drag later. His eyes met Edmund's for a heartbeat, fierce and miserable, and then a hand struck Walter across the back of the head to make him look down.

Alice was harder to see. Bodies pressed too close. Edmund caught only a glimpse: her hair dark against torchlight, her face set in a stillness that was not surrender but calculation. Someone had her by the shoulder, and the arm was wrapped around her upper chest like a restraint. Her knife was gone.

"Your woman cut at a good man," Rob called, answering the crowd's demand as if he had been waiting for it. "She drew steel in the square. In front of our well. In front of God's house."

Edmund forced his voice up, louder. "She stopped a club," he said. "Your man swung first."

A roar answered him. The sound did not deny the truth. It drowned it.

Father Griffiths raised his hand. The movement was small, yet it quieted the nearest mouths, and their silence spread outward like a ripple in water.

“Violence in the square,” Father Griffiths said, voice carrying, “is violence against the village itself. We have endured much, and the Lord has instructed us in hard measures. But those measures must be pure. They must be guided. Not tainted by the blade of a woman who keeps company with corruption.”

Alice’s mouth opened, and Edmund saw her speak, though he could not hear the words over the muttering that surged again. The man holding her tightened his grip until her shoulders jerked back. She went still.

Edmund looked back at the priest. “You bless ropes,” he said. “You bless clubs. And you call her tainted.”

Father Griffiths’s eyes narrowed a fraction. “Careful,” he murmured, so softly the men nearest him leaned in to catch it. “Your tongue has done enough harm.”

Rob’s hand shot out and seized Edmund by the jaw, fingers digging into bruised flesh. He forced Edmund’s face up toward the torches. “Look at him,” Rob said, loud. “Look how he stares like he’s still lord here. Like he can judge you.”

Edmund's jaw ached under Rob's grip. He could have bitten. He did not. He would not give them another story to tell about savagery.

Rob released him with a shove that rocked Edmund forward, and the hands behind him caught his shoulders and yanked him upright onto his knees again.

"Tell us," Rob demanded. "Tell us why the plague followed you. Tell us why you sheltered poisoners and let them slip through our fingers. Tell us why your barn didn't burn when others did. Tell us what you paid for it."

Edmund stared at him, trying to breathe through the pain. Around Rob's shoulder he saw faces in the crowd, and in some of them he recognized a flicker of uncertainty. Not enough to stop what was happening. Only enough to make them look away quickly, as if doubt itself were a mark.

"I paid nothing," Edmund said. "I fed people you wanted dead."

A man near the posts shouted, "He admits it!"

Edmund's voice rose. "Yes. I admit it. I sheltered them. Not because they were guilty, but because they were hunted."

Rob smiled, and it was a smile Edmund had come to recognize: the smile of a man receiving the confession he wanted, even if it was not the confession he had asked for. "There," Rob said, turning to the crowd as if Edmund were already finished. "He says it plainly. He chose them over you."

"That is not what I said," Edmund replied, but his words sounded thin against the simplicity of Rob's framing. Rob did not need truth. He needed a shape.

Father Griffiths stepped closer to the posts, his shadow stretching long across the scuffed ground. "Edmund," he said, gentle again, "if you would ease the village's burden, you will confess fully. You will name what you have done. You will name your companions. You will name what poison you carried into our wells and into our homes."

A laugh broke out, sharp and ugly. "The wells," someone said. "He's back at wells."

Edmund felt the absurdity of it press on his chest. The well stood there, unchanged, and yet it had become a stage for every lie the village needed. He remembered the first accusation, how quickly it had ignited. Now they returned to it like a prayer.

"I poisoned nothing," Edmund said.

Rob's face hardened. "Then you deny the confessions?" he demanded. "You deny they admitted it before they burned?"

Edmund's mouth tightened, and the split skin pulled. "They confessed under pain," he said. "Under fire. Confession is easy when the alternative is worse."

A stone struck Edmund's shoulder and bounced away. It did not hurt as much as the sound of approval that followed it.

Father Griffiths's voice grew firmer. "You see?" he said to the crowd. "He calls your justice cruelty. He calls your vigilance sin. He would unmake every hard choice you have made to keep your children breathing."

A woman near the edge sobbed, "My boy," and someone beside her hissed at her to be quiet.

Rob stepped to Edmund's side and spoke with the casual authority of a man assigning work. "Tie him," he said.

Rope appeared from somewhere, rough and dark. Edmund had seen that rope before. Not this exact coil, perhaps, but its kind. He had watched it bite into wrists in the square when the first scapegoats were dragged forward. He had watched it swing from these same posts.

Hands forced his arms back. The rope looped around his wrists, scraped skin, tightened. Edmund clenched his jaw as pain flared through his shoulders. He did not struggle. Struggle would only give them the pleasure of more restraint, more bodies pressing in, more blows justified as necessary.

As they bound him, the crowd surged closer, hungry for proximity. Edmund felt breath against his cheek, smelled sweat and smoke, heard murmured prayers mixed with curses.

"Look at his eyes," a man muttered near Edmund's shoulder, as if the earlier madness had not vanished but simply folded itself into the current moment. "Look at them. Too calm."

"He's marked," another whispered, and the word marked moved through the listeners like a familiar hymn.

Edmund's throat tightened. Calm was a mark now. Reason was evidence. The village had learned to turn any human trait into proof of guilt if it served the story.

Walter's voice cut through, hoarse with pain and fury. "He's not marked. You are," he shouted, straining against the hands holding him. "You're marked by what you've done!"

A fist struck Walter's mouth. He folded, and the men holding him laughed.

Rob lifted both hands as if blessing the scene. "Hear his man," he said, voice bright. "Even now they curse you. Even now they spit on your grief."

Edmund leaned as far as the rope allowed, trying to turn his head toward Walter. "Walter," he said, voice low, not for the crowd but for the man who had chosen to stand with him anyway. "Don't give them more."

Walter's eyes flashed up briefly, and Edmund saw in them a terrible apology: I can't stop.

Father Griffiths stepped to the well and dipped his fingers into a bucket drawn up for the purpose. Edmund watched, sick, as the priest lifted his wet hand and traced a sign in the air, the gesture slow and deliberate.

"This village is under attack," Father Griffiths said. "Not only by sickness, but by those who would weaken our resolve. We cannot afford doubt. Doubt opens doors."

Edmund felt the crowd's attention tighten like a noose. The priest's words were building the frame, laying the beams of a verdict.

Rob's voice slid in beside the priest's. "We will have truth," he said. "And if he will not give it, then we will take what we can from him. His name. His pride. His breath. Whatever the Lord requires to show us the way."

The crowd murmured assent, and the sound was worse than shouting. It was agreement settling.

Edmund's wrists burned where the rope bit. Blood from his mouth had dried in a crust that pulled when he breathed. He looked out at the faces again, searching for someone who would meet his gaze and hold it.

Most did not.

A few did, briefly, and in that brief meeting Edmund saw the thing that would haunt them later, if anything survived to haunt: recognition without courage. The knowledge that this was wrong, paired with the fear of being the next one made right by force.

Rob moved closer and lowered his voice so only Edmund could hear. His breath was warm with triumph. "You should have stayed in the marsh," he murmured. "Now you'll save us after all. Not with words. With an example."

Edmund held his gaze, refusing to flinch. "It won't save you," he said softly.

Rob's smile returned, smaller and meaner. "It'll save us from you."

He straightened and turned to the crowd, raising his voice again. "Bring him to the church steps," he ordered. "Let him answer before God and all of us. Let him confess or be shown for what he is."

Hands seized Edmund's bound arms, yanking him to his feet. Pain shot through his shoulders, white and sharp. The world tilted, steadied, and then began to move as they dragged him away from the posts, past the well, toward the church where Father Griffiths waited like a judge.

Edmund stumbled once, caught himself before he fell. The crowd pressed in on either side, a corridor of faces and torches and hatred wearing the mask of duty.

Above it all the ragged staff fluttered, its strips of cloth snapping lightly in the night breeze like a banner celebrating a victory that had not yet been completed.

Edmund tasted blood again, fresh this time, and understood with a clarity that felt almost calm: they had not brought him here to discover the truth. They had brought him here to finish the story.

And the story required him to be guilty, because if he was not, then the village would have to face something far worse than plague.

It would have to face itself.

They dragged him up the worn stones to the church steps as if hauling a sack of spoiled grain. Edmund's boots caught on the edge of a riser and his knees struck hard. Someone laughed when he grunted. Hands yanked him upright again, forcing him to stand beneath the dark mouth of the church door.

The wood behind him was marked with chalked crosses and smeared ash. Edmund remembered, absurdly, how this door had once meant weddings and baptisms, the whole village pressed close and warm, cheeks ruddy from ale and summer heat. Now it was a threshold to something colder than any winter. The church did not feel like refuge; it felt like a witness that had learned to look away.

Father Griffiths stood one step higher, so that torchlight framed his head and cast his shadow down over Edmund's bound arms. Rob waited to the side, close enough to touch, relaxed as a man at market watching a bargain go his way. Around them the square pulsed with bodies.

"Quiet," Father Griffiths said, and the word moved through the crowd in a reluctant ripple. Not silence, never silence, but a tightening. A readiness.

Edmund's jaw throbbed where Rob had grabbed him earlier. He kept his head up anyway.

"You were granted land," Father Griffiths began, voice even, almost tender. "You were given the care of souls on that land, Edmund Harrow. And instead of gratitude, you fed rebellion. You let strangers settle under your roof. You told folk that burden could be shared and that obedience was cruelty. And then the Lord sent His scourge, as the Lord does, to correct what has grown crooked."

A murmur of agreement ran through the faces below. Edmund saw people nodding as if they had always believed this, as if their own hands had not been the ones to set fire to homes.

"The Lord sent rats," Edmund said hoarsely. "And fleas. And you turned it into a story about sin because sin can be hanged."

A fist struck his ribs from the side, hard enough to steal his breath. Edmund folded slightly, then forced himself upright again. The blow bought a roar of approval.

Rob leaned in close, voice low. "Careful," he murmured, almost friendly. "You don't want them to stop at you."

Edmund's eyes flicked, searching the torchlit faces for Walter and Alice. He saw Walter dragged closer by the men who held him, his mouth split, blood dark on his chin. Walter's gaze found Edmund's and held for a heartbeat, furious and helpless.

Alice was forced forward too, a grip at each arm. Her face was pale, but her eyes were steady. Someone had tied her wrists with the same rough rope. She did not struggle. She measured.

Edmund's throat tightened in a way pain could not explain. He had come to the square to keep them from being turned into a lesson. Now they stood beside him on the church steps, ready to be used as punctuation.

Father Griffiths followed Edmund's gaze and smiled faintly, as if he had anticipated the direction of Edmund's weakness. "You brought companions," he said. "You gathered them around you like a little court in the marsh. A lord still, collecting loyal souls. That is not humility. That is seduction."

"They are not mine," Edmund said, voice rough. "No one belongs to me."

Rob laughed, loud enough to be heard. "Hear him," he called. "He speaks like a saint while his woman draws steel and his man curses a priest. No one belongs to him, but everyone bleeds for him."

Edmund pulled a breath that tasted of smoke and blood. "They bleed because you make bleeding a requirement," he said. "Because you've taught the village that guilt can be shared like bread."

That landed somewhere. Not in the crowd, but in a few faces near the back, eyes narrowing as if a thought had tried to rise and was pushed down again.

Father Griffiths's tone hardened. "We will not be instructed by you," he said. "Not after what you have done. Not after what you have hidden."

Edmund lifted his chin. "Hidden?" he rasped.

Rob stepped forward, raising his voice so the nearest could hear. "Where are the ones you sheltered?" he demanded. "Where's the widow? Where's Miriam and her brats? Where's that little rat of a money-man with his counting lips? Tell us where you've stowed them, Harrow, and perhaps the priest will grant you a cleaner end."

Edmund felt his stomach drop, not at the threat, but at the reach of it. The mob was not satisfied with a single corpse. It never was. It needed more to justify the first.

"I don't know," Edmund lied at once, and knew it would not matter. Truth and lies were both swallowed and converted into the same fuel.

Walter jerked against the men holding him. "Leave them out of it!" he shouted.

A club struck Walter's stomach and he doubled, gagging. The sound that came from him was part breath, part rage. The men holding him laughed as if they had fixed something.

"See?" Rob said, gesturing toward Walter like a demonstration. "He's loyal. Loyal enough to throw himself in front. That's what Harrow does. He infects people with loyalty."

Edmund's hands burned against the rope. He forced himself to look at Walter, to let Walter see he was seen. It was all he could give. Words had become useless.

Father Griffiths nodded once, as if in prayer, then turned his attention to Alice. "And you," he said. “You wander with a knife and no husband at your side. You have no place in a righteous village.”

Alice’s mouth tightened. “I had a place,” she said, voice clear. “You burned it when you needed to feel clean.”

The crowd hissed. Someone shouted, “Witch!”

Father Griffiths did not flinch at the word. He only let his gaze rest on her a moment longer, as if considering how best to fold her into the village’s new scripture. “You struck a man in the square,” he said. “You raised steel against God’s people.”

“I stopped him striking first,” Alice replied. “You call that sin because it interrupts your lesson.”

Rob’s eyes gleamed. “She admits it,” he said quickly, as if gathering kindling. “She admits she came armed to defy us.”

“She came armed because you’re a mob,” Edmund said, and earned another shove that rocked him against the step behind.

Father Griffiths lifted a hand, not to halt the violence, but to frame it. “The Lord tests us,” he said. “He shows us who will stand with the village and who will stand against it. Edmund Harrow has stood against it from the beginning. He has taken the sick, the outsiders, the marked, and he has sheltered them. He has spoken against cleansing. And now he brings those who would stab our men and poison our resolve."

Edmund felt the net tightening. Not only around him, but around the meaning of everything that had happened. If the village could make protection sound like sedition, then any mercy would be treason. Any restraint would be betrayal.

He looked down at the crowd and saw familiar faces, warped by torchlight into something older than hunger. Men who had once complained about taxes now waited to be told whom to hate. Women who had once offered soup to a neighbor now clutched their children as shields and stared as if hoping to see a demon in Edmund's eyes so they would not have to see a man.

Rob turned abruptly and pointed toward the edge of the square. "Bring him," he called.

A stir moved through the bodies. Someone shoved a figure forward from the dark.

Thomas stumbled into the torchlight like a man pushed out of a doorway. His hands were up, palms out, as if he could stop the world from striking him if he showed he carried nothing. His face was streaked with grime; one cheek was swelling where someone had hit him.

Edmund's chest tightened. Thomas's eyes darted, frantic, and then fixed on Edmund with a look that was half apology and half pleading.

"They found you," Edmund breathed.

Thomas shook his head rapidly. "I didn't—" he began.

Rob cut him off with a slap that snapped Thomas's head to the side. "You led us to him," Rob said, loud, and Edmund felt the crowd lean in at the neatness of it. "You said you saw him at the marsh edge. You said he's gathering poisoners like eggs under a hen."

Thomas's mouth opened. He looked toward Father Griffiths as if the priest might care about truth.

Father Griffiths's gaze stayed calm and distant. "Confession is not always spoken," he said. "Sometimes it is shown in the company a man keeps."

Thomas's eyes went wet. "I tried to help," he whispered, voice cracking. "I tried to—"

A man in the crowd screamed, "Traitor!" and a stone struck Thomas's shoulder. Another hit his ribs. Thomas folded with a small, wounded sound.

Edmund watched, sick, as the village found a new way to feed itself. They did not even need certainty now. They needed only a body that could be made to fit the day's shape.

Rob grasped Thomas by the hair and hauled his face up so everyone could see him. "This one," Rob announced, "was Harrow's errand boy. His messenger. His rat in our walls."

Thomas's lips trembled. "Edmund," he whispered, and the name was not accusation. It was desperate reaching.

Edmund tasted blood again, fresh, as his split lip reopened. He wanted to tell Thomas to be silent, to stop pleading, because pleading only gave them more sound to twist. But he saw in Thomas's face the same thing he had seen in the river family, in Miriam's confession, in Walter's fury: the frantic instinct to buy safety with words, even when words were only rope.

Father Griffiths stepped down one step, bringing himself closer to Edmund, Alice, Walter, and Thomas all at once, as if gathering a family before an altar. The thought struck Edmund with cold irony. A family, yes. Not by blood. By the simple act of refusing to abandon each other in a world that demanded abandonment as proof of belonging.

The priest's voice lowered, carrying in the hush. "Edmund Harrow," he said, "you will name those who hid with you. You will name those you sheltered. You will unburden the village of your corruption."

Edmund stared at him. "And if I do not?"

Father Griffiths's eyes flicked, briefly, toward Alice. Then to Walter. Then to Thomas, sagging on his knees. The gesture was small. The crowd understood it immediately.

Rob's mouth curled into a grin. "Then we cleanse your household," he said brightly. "All of it."

Edmund felt something in him tear, not dramatic, not loud, but final. This was how the village solved the problem of love. It made love into leverage. It turned loyalty into a weapon aimed at the loyal.

He drew a slow breath, forcing his voice into steadiness he did not feel. "You want names," he said. "You want me to hand you bodies so you can keep believing you are in control."

A man behind him yanked his bound arms higher, pain spearing up through his shoulders until his vision swam. Edmund gasped, then fought for breath again.

Father Griffiths watched without expression, as if pain were simply a tool being applied correctly. "Name them," he said again, softer now. "Spare them the worst of it."

Edmund turned his head toward Walter, toward Alice, toward Thomas. In their faces he saw three different kinds of courage: Walter's battered defiance, Alice's cold readiness, Thomas's trembling remorse. He saw what he had built in Essex when he tried to live differently than his father: not a dynasty, not a legacy carved into stone, but a handful of people willing to stand near him when standing near him meant danger.

Rob had called it a court. Father Griffiths had called it seduction. Edmund knew what it was.

It was family.

And the village was about to destroy it, not as an accident, but as proof.

Edmund lifted his chin, despite the pain, and spoke with deliberate clarity into the torchlit air.

"I will not give you their names," he said.

For a heartbeat there was silence, sharp enough to cut.

Then the crowd exhaled as one, a sound like a door slamming shut, and Rob's grin widened into something almost joyous.

"Then we begin," Rob said.

And Edmund understood, with sick certainty, that whatever happened next would be done not only to punish him, but to teach every watching soul what it cost to belong to anyone but the village's fear.

Rob did not shout again. He did not need to. The square had learned his language; a lifted hand was enough to make men move as if pulled by a single rope.

Two of them seized Edmund by the shoulders and hauled him off the church steps. The rope on his wrists jerked tight and bit deeper as his arms were forced behind him. His boots skidded on the worn stone, then struck dirt. The crowd shifted to make a lane, eager and tight, faces bright in torchlight and hungry for the next instruction.

Father Griffiths descended more slowly, as if this were a procession and he had a part to play that required dignity. He carried a small wooden cross in one hand. Edmund had seen it at burials, at christenings, at the mild ordinary ceremonies that once stitched the village together. Now it looked like a tool placed on a table beside other tools.

Walter fought when they dragged him down after Edmund. He surged forward, shoulder-first, trying to break the grip on his arm. For a heartbeat the men holding him stumbled, and the crowd's breath hitched with a thrill that was almost delighted.

Then a club struck Walter behind the ear. His legs buckled. He did not fall fully, not at first. He swayed, teeth bared, as if his body refused to accept what it had been told.

"Hold him up," Rob ordered, voice brisk. "Let him watch."

Walter spat blood and tried to lift his head. "You don't cleanse," he croaked. "You only—"

A fist drove into his belly and the rest of the sentence collapsed into a gagging cough.

Alice was dragged next. Her bound hands were lifted high enough that her shoulders pulled back painfully, but her face did not change. She looked across the square as if marking exits that no longer existed. When her eyes met Edmund's, there was no plea in them. Only a grim acknowledgement of what the village required to feel safe.

Thomas stumbled behind them, shoved forward by the men who had beaten him into obedience. He looked smaller than Edmund remembered from before the fires, as if shame and terror had peeled something away from him. His lips moved, praying perhaps, or trying to form words that might undo what his feet had carried him into. No sound came out that mattered.

Rob led them toward the posts beside the well. The same posts that had held strangers. The same ring of scuffed earth that had become familiar to the village's feet, a place used enough to stop shocking anyone.

As Edmund was dragged across it, the smell of the well rose damp and old beneath the smoke. He thought, absurdly, of water pulled up on summer days, children leaning in to look at their own faces reflected. He thought of clean mouths, laughing mouths. Then the memory broke under the press of bodies and the iron taste of blood.

"Now," Rob said. He turned slightly, as if speaking to Father Griffiths as much as to the crowd. "Now we show them what happens when a man thinks he can stand apart."

Father Griffiths stood near the well with the cross held upright, his face set into measured sorrow. "This is not pleasure," he said, voice carrying. "This is burden. This is obedience."

Someone in the crowd echoed, "Obedience," like a prayer.

Rob nodded as if the word pleased him. He pointed at Edmund. "He refused names," Rob announced. "He refused to unburden us. He chose to protect corruption over the village."

Edmund lifted his head. His jaw ached. His lip split again when he spoke. "I chose to protect people," he said hoarsely. "You are the corruption."

A hiss rose, swift and angry. Hands tightened on clubs.

Rob's smile returned, smaller now, the smile of a man pressing a hot iron to skin and watching it take. "Hear him," he said. "Still judging. Still proud."

He stepped closer, and his voice dropped so only Edmund could hear. "Proud men make good lessons."

Edmund met his gaze and felt, beneath the fear, a cold steadiness settle. The village could do what it wanted with his body. It could not make him agree with it. That was the last piece of ground left, and he held it like a nail driven into stone.

They forced Edmund to his knees at the base of the post closest to the well. The rope on his wrists was retied around the timber. The knot was practiced, quick. The hands that did it had done it before.

A man leaned close to the side of Edmund's face and muttered, "Look straight when Father Griffiths speaks. Don't make it worse."

Edmund almost laughed. Worse. As if the village had any mercy left to bargain with.

Father Griffiths stepped forward and held the cross out. "Kiss it," he said softly. "Confess your error, Edmund Harrow. Ask forgiveness. The village will see your humility."

Edmund stared at the cross. It was wood, worn smooth by generations of hands. He wondered if any of those hands had once trembled with real faith, not fear masquerading as it.

He lifted his eyes to the priest. "You used to bury the dead," he said. "Now you sell the living."

Father Griffiths's gaze flickered, a quick flash of something like anger beneath the gentleness. He leaned closer, lowering his voice. "You could spare them," he murmured, and Edmund knew he meant Alice, Walter, Thomas. The family the village had made of them. "A name. A place. Give us what we need and this will end clean."

The priest's breath smelled of wine and smoke.

Edmund swallowed, feeling the rope scrape his wrists as he shifted. "It will not end," he said. "Not clean. Not ever."

Rob stepped in at once, loud again, impatient with nuance. "He refuses God," he proclaimed.

"I refuse you," Edmund replied, and the words came out clearer than he expected, carried by something stubborn that had survived Dorset stone halls and Essex fields and the sight of a dog beaten to pulp.

The crowd surged. A woman cried out, "Make him stop talking!"

Rob lifted a hand, and the surge stilled just enough. He wanted the words. He wanted the last defiance to be witnessed.

"Then we begin with the mouth that spreads poison," Rob said.

A man stepped forward with a strip of cloth, dirty and twisted like an old bandage. Edmund saw it and understood. Not to gag him, not merely. To make speech itself look like disease that needed binding.

They forced the cloth between his teeth. The fabric tasted of sweat and ash. It scraped his split lip. Edmund clenched his jaw until his teeth hurt and refused to open his mouth for them, but the man shoved hard, fingers pushing, and Edmund gagged as the cloth filled his mouth. Then they tied it behind his head.

The crowd made a sound of satisfaction, a communal exhale.

“There,” Rob said. “Now the plague can’t speak through him.”

Edmund’s breath came hot through his nose. The gag did not stop him from making sound entirely, but it made every sound animal, stripped of words. That was the point. The village wanted him reduced to noise.

Walter struggled again when he saw it. “Cowards,” he tried to shout, but it came out broken. He lunged toward Edmund, and the men holding him dragged him back, forcing him to his knees at the second post.

Alice’s eyes sharpened. She watched the men’s hands, the rope, the distances between bodies. Then she looked at Rob with something like contempt so pure it almost looked calm.

Rob noticed. He smiled at her as if she were part of the entertainment. "Still staring," he said. "Still thinking you can slip the net. You won't."

Alice's voice came level. "You'll have to kill me," she said.

"Oh, we will," Rob replied lightly. "But first you'll watch your lord made small. That's what women like you need. A lesson."

Edmund felt the cloth bite as he tried to speak around it, a muffled sound that did not form into words. Alice's gaze flicked to him, and for a heartbeat he saw in her eyes a warning: do not waste breath.

Father Griffiths lifted his cross again. "May God forgive what we must do," he said.

The sentence was the village's final trick: to frame violence as duty, and duty as holiness.

Rob nodded to the men nearest Edmund. A hand seized Edmund's hair again and yanked his head back, exposing his throat in torchlight.

For a moment, terror surged so sharply Edmund's body tried to fight the rope. His knees slid in the scuffed dirt. The post held. The knot held. The village held.

Then he forced his breath to slow. He fixed his eyes on the well stones in front of him, damp with night. He thought of Miriam's cold fingers gripping his wrist, asking not to leave Isaac unnamed. He thought of Walter's rough hand on his shoulder by the river, furious and loyal. He thought of Essex fields, of hands in soil, of a different kind of land that had felt possible once.

A blade flashed. Not a clean executioner's blade, not justice. A butcher's knife, held in a shaking hand.

Edmund saw the tremor and knew the man did not want to do this. Or perhaps he did, but his body still remembered the old boundary and shook at crossing it. Either way, it made no difference to the cut.

The knife drew a line across Edmund's throat. Heat, then pain, then a wetness spreading too quickly. Edmund's breath left him in a harsh, gagged gasp. His body jerked against the rope. The cloth in his mouth drank some of his blood and turned it thick and sticky.

The crowd roared, a sound like release.

Walter shouted something, incoherent, and threw himself against his bindings until the rope scraped his wrists raw. A man struck Walter's face and his head snapped sideways, then lifted again stubbornly, eyes burning.

Alice's jaw clenched so tightly Edmund saw the muscles stand out beneath her skin. She did not scream. She did not beg. She watched Edmund as if she could hold him in place with her gaze, as if watching could be a kind of fidelity.

Edmund's vision began to narrow. The torchlight blurred into halos. Faces became smears of fire and shadow. The well wavered, then steadied again as if the world could not decide whether to fall with him.

Rob's voice floated above it, triumphant and loud. "There," he shouted. "See? The rot bleeds like any other. The lord is only meat when God wills it!"

Father Griffiths murmured something, a prayer or a pronouncement. Edmund could not catch it. Sound was fading into a low rushing, like the river when it widened into marsh.

Edmund tried to draw one more breath. His throat gurgled around the wound. The gag prevented any last words, and in a strange way he was grateful. The village would not get a final sentence to twist into their story. They would only get what they had always wanted: a body.

As he sagged against the rope, the last thing he saw clearly was Alice's face, pale in torchlight, eyes steady and unblinking. Not broken. Not pleading. Still herself.

Then the world tilted, and the square, the well, the posts, the priest, and Rob's hungry grin slid away into darkness.

The village cheered as if the cheer could keep death from noticing them.

And in that cheer, Edmund Harrow's defiance ended, not as a surrender, but as a silence forced by hands that did not understand they had only killed the one thing that had tried to name what they were becoming.

Chapter 15

Nothing Left to Blame

Edmund's body hung slack against the post, the rope holding what the man no longer could. For a few heartbeats the square was all noise and torch-smoke, the crowd tasting its own power like strong drink. Hands clapped shoulders. Some laughed too loudly, as if laughter could prove the act had been necessary. Others stood with their faces turned slightly away, their mouths tight, their eyes fixed on anything but the dark wetness spreading down the wood.

Rob Baines lifted both arms again, riding the roar. "You've seen it," he shouted, voice raw with triumph. "It bleeds. It dies. It ends. The Lord has shown us the path!"

But the roar did not settle into peace. It did not become relief. It stayed sharp, searching for another place to land.

Walter's hoarse voice tore through it. "You've killed him and it still won't stop!" he spat, straining against his bindings until the rope cut and his wrists shone slick. His face was swollen where he'd been struck, one eye narrowing to a slit, but the fury in him was clear enough to be its own light.

A man rushed forward and struck Walter across the mouth with the flat of his hand. "Quiet," he hissed, like Walter was an ill-behaved animal. Walter's head snapped to the side and came back again, stubborn as a nail that would not pull free.

Alice said nothing. Her jaw was set so hard the muscles stood out. She stared at Edmund's hanging head, the cloth gag darkened now, clinging to his mouth as if the village wanted even in death to keep him from speaking. When she finally looked away, it was not toward the crowd but toward Rob and Father Griffiths, as if measuring the distance between them and the nearest blade.

Thomas knelt a few paces back, not tied to a post yet, held by two men who gripped his arms like they feared he might vanish if they blinked. He was shaking so hard his teeth clicked. His eyes darted from Edmund to Rob, to Father Griffiths, to the crowd that had become a single face made of many mouths.

Father Griffiths stepped forward, cross still in hand, and raised it as if blessing a harvest. "May God receive the soul," he intoned, solemnly, and a few voices answered with a mumbled "Amen," more habit than conviction. The priest's gaze slid over the crowd and tightened. He could sense it too: the hunger did not leave when it was fed. It only learned it could be fed again.

Rob pointed at Walter, as if the next part of the lesson had already been decided. "His man still spits," he called. "Still curses. Still defies the village even after the Lord has shown His judgment."

A woman's voice, thin and high, rose from the edge of the ring. "My boy died," she said, and there was no sense to it, only pain looking for somewhere to be placed. "And you stand there talking about judgment. Where was judgment for my boy?"

Rob's head turned, his smile stiffening. "Judgment is what we're doing," he snapped. "It takes time."

"Time," another voice echoed, bitter. A man stepped into the torchlight, shoulders hunched, eyes bright with sleeplessness. "Time for what, Rob? Time for more ropes? More burning? My wife's got fever in her bones. She can't stand. Is she a mark too?"

A ripple moved through the crowd. Not sympathy, not yet, but something like irritation. The plague had a way of making every grievance urgent. It made patience feel like mockery.

Father Griffiths lifted his hand, palm out, the same gesture he'd used to tune them. "The Lord tests us in stages," he said, voice smooth. "He reveals, and we obey. That is our protection."

"Protection," the man with the sick wife said, and he laughed once, a short, ugly bark. "We killed cats. We killed dogs. We burned our own. And now rats run in my pantry in daylight. Where's your protection in that?"

Someone hissed at him. Someone else muttered, "Careful," as if anger itself might summon a rope. But the man did not stop. He had the reckless courage of a man whose fear had been overtaken by exhaustion. "You told us the beasts carried it," he shouted. "So, we slaughtered them. Now the beasts that do carry it are everywhere. You can't club a rat that lives in your walls."

The crowd began to shift, bodies rubbing together in impatience. Torches flared as hands moved. A child coughed somewhere, a wet sound that cut straight through talk, and for a moment heads turned as if the cough had direction. The mother hushed it quickly, too quickly, pulling the child's face into her skirt as though hiding sound could hide sickness.

Rob's voice sharpened. "We don't question now," he shouted. "Not after what we've done. We hold fast."

But something in the crowd faltered at that. Not after what we've done. It was meant to be a rallying cry. Instead, it sounded, to some ears, like a trap. A reminder that turning back would mean facing the pile of bodies behind them.

A man near the well, older, with hands like knotted roots, stared at Edmund's corpse and whispered, not to anyone in particular, "He didn't look sick."

The words were quiet, almost lost, but they landed anyway. A few heads turned. A few faces tightened. Alice heard it. Her eyes flicked toward the speaker, not with gratitude, but with a weary recognition of what would come next. Doubt did not free a village like this. Doubt only demanded a new sacrifice to crush it.

Rob heard the whisper too. His gaze snapped like a dog's. "He hid it," Rob said immediately, loud and sure. “That’s what corruption does. It hides, and then it spreads.”

“It spreads anyway,” someone muttered.

The mutter became another mutter, and then another, until it was no longer a single voice that could be struck down. It was a current.

Father Griffiths stepped closer to Rob, his voice low enough that only those nearest might hear, but the square had a way of catching even low words when fear sharpened hearing. “We must keep order,” the priest murmured. “The village must see firmness.”

Rob’s nostrils flared. “Order is what I’ve given them,” he hissed back, and there was something childish in the insistence. He had tasted command too long to imagine setting it down.

A scream rose from a lane off the square.

It was the kind of scream that did not belong to punishment or argument. It was pure alarm, high and tearing. Heads turned. The crowd’s ring broke at once, people surging toward sound, as if pulled by one nervous system.

Edmund’s body swayed slightly as bodies brushed past the post. No one looked at him now.

The lesson was complete; the corpse was already becoming part of the square's furniture.

Rob shouted, "Stay here!" but his voice did not hold them. It was hard to command a crowd whose attention had found fresh terror.

They rushed down the lane, torches bobbing. Alice and Walter were left at the posts, bound, half-forgotten in the shift. Thomas remained with his captors, who hesitated, uncertain whether to drag him along or keep him for later. Uncertainty, once introduced, spread faster than any illness.

From where Alice stood, she could see the lane's mouth and the bodies jostling toward it. The torchlight revealed what the scream had meant: a man had collapsed in the mud, his legs folded wrong beneath him. Two women hovered over him, hands out and then pulling back, not daring to touch. The man's face was swollen, his lips dark. In the brief flare of torchlight, a lump showed beneath his jaw like an egg gone bad.

"Plague," someone whispered.

The whisper ran through the crowd with the speed of a match through straw. Not as a distant concept now, not as rumor on the road, but as a shape in the mud, breathing in short choking pulls.

"Get back," a man shouted. "Don't touch him!"

The women recoiled. The man on the ground tried to speak, but only a wet gurgle came out. He clawed at his own throat as if he could pull the sickness free with his fingers. A child began to cry, thin and terrified, and was hushed too sharply.

Father Griffiths pushed his way forward, face set in the expression he used for sermons and scaffolds alike. He lifted the cross. "Stand firm," he called. "Do not fall into panic. The Lord—"

The man on the ground convulsed, and a dark spray flecked the mud.

The priest's words stopped. Not because he ran out of faith, but because the sight was too honest to be turned into rhetoric quickly. The crowd took that pause and filled it with instinct.

Bodies began to move backward. Not in orderly retreat. In shoves and stumbles. People pushed past each other, eyes wide, mouths open. A woman fell, her basket spilling, and someone stepped on her hand without noticing. A torch dropped and hissed out in the mud, sending up a puff of steam that looked, in the half-light, like something leaving the earth.

“Go home!” someone shouted.

Home. The word was a knife. Home meant doors, meant families, meant closeness, meant hiding. It meant bringing the unseen into the one place people still pretended they controlled.

The crowd broke into smaller crowds, each one turning toward its own survival. Men who had stood shoulder to shoulder now shoved each other aside. Women who had cheered now clutched children and glanced at other children as if measuring which cough belonged to which house. The patrol staff with its rags stood by the church steps, forgotten, leaning like a weary soldier. The rags fluttered anyway, pleased with themselves, signaling to no one.

Rob tried to regain the square with force. “Back!” he shouted. “Back, you fools!” He grabbed a man by the shoulder and yanked him hard enough to turn him. “We don’t scatter. We don’t—”

The man jerked free with a violence that surprised even him. “You don’t tell me now,” he snapped, and his eyes were bright with something close to hate. “Not after you made me burn my neighbor. Not after you made my boy watch.”

Rob blinked. The crowd's obedience had always depended on the belief that obedience bought safety. Now safety lay in flight, and the belief cracked.

Father Griffiths stood at the lane's mouth, cross raised, eyes scanning faces that would not meet his. He had framed murder as duty and duty as holiness, but holiness did not keep a man's lungs from filling. His lips moved, perhaps finding another verse, another interpretation, another way to turn the collapse into proof of God's will. But the village did not wait for scripture. It moved like water seeking the lowest place.

In the square, the posts remained, and at them the village had left its true work unfinished.

Alice pulled hard against her bindings until the rope dug deeper. Walter did the same, his breath coming in harsh grunts. Their wrists bled. Thomas, seeing the crowd's attention turned away, made a small, desperate sound and tried to wrench free. One of his captors struck him out of reflex, not with purpose but with the panicked need to keep control of something.

Edmund's corpse hung between them and the well, a silent center in a world that had finally run out of story for the moment.

The village had killed its last voice and expected quiet afterward.

Instead, the plague answered, close enough to smell.

And with that answer, the order Rob and Father Griffiths had built from fear began to crumble, not in a noble awakening, not in repentance, but in the ugliest truth of all: without a scapegoat to hold them steady, the villagers remembered they were fragile animals in a narrowing world, and they turned on one another not for righteousness, but for space to breathe.

No one went back to the well.

The man in the lane lay on his side, knees drawing up in a child's curl and then jerking out again as cramps seized him. When he tried to inhale, the sound was not breath but a wet pulling, as if his lungs were stitched shut and someone was trying to tear the thread. In torchlight the swellings beneath his jaw and in the soft hollow of his armpit shone with a slick, bruised sheen.

A few men hovered at what they judged a safe distance, hands half-lifted as though they might help and then remembered what help cost. The women who had first bent over him backed away until their shoulders struck the wall of a cottage, eyes wide and shining with the animal terror of being caught too close to the kill.

"Don't touch him," a voice insisted again, harsh with certainty, as if repeating it could build a barrier in the air.

But the sickness did not care about distance measured by fear. It moved in breaths, in fleas too small to see, in hands that had already touched door-latches and shared cups and wiped a child's nose. It moved in the grain stores where rats now ran bold in daylight because the village had slaughtered the mouths that once hunted them. It moved in bedding that had been kept because burning it meant admitting the plague lived in cloth and not in a neighbor's eyes.

The crowd that had cheered Edmund Harrow's death broke apart not into repentance but into frantic geometry: each person calculating the quickest line to their own threshold. "Home," they had shouted, as if the word itself were medicine. Doors slammed. Bolts scraped. Windows were shuttered so fast that fingers were caught and bloodied without being noticed.

The man in the lane tried again to speak. His mouth opened wide, lips dark with swelling, and only a bubbling rattle came out. A splatter of blackened spit struck the mud. Someone screamed, and then that someone ran, tripping over a dropped torch and leaving it hissing out in the wet.

Father Griffiths stood at the lane's mouth with the cross lifted, the gesture rigid now, not serene. The torchlight picked out the pallor around his mouth. He looked from the convulsing man to the retreating backs of his parishioners and seemed, for the first time in days, uncertain where to place his words.

"The Lord—" he began again.

A woman's voice snapped back from behind a half-closed shutter, high and frantic. "Keep Him in the church, then!"

The shutter slammed.

Rob Baines lunged after a knot of men who were shoving each other toward the square, trying to force their way past bodies with the kind of urgency that did not wait for permission. Rob grabbed one by the collar and wrenched him back, face inches from his.

"You don't run," Rob hissed. "You don't scatter like rats."

The man's eyes were rimmed red with sleeplessness. He shoved Rob's hand away with sudden strength. "We learned from you," he spat. "We learned what to do when we're afraid."

Rob flinched as if struck, not by the shove, but by the truth inside it. He raised his hand, ready to call men back into line with the familiar threat of force.

But the men who would have obeyed were already gone, sucked into the lanes and the dark mouths of their own doorways. And those still near him looked at his lifted hand as if seeing it clearly for the first time: not a command, but a weapon he used because he had no other power.

In the square the posts stood waiting, ugly and patient, and Edmund's body hung slack in its bindings, a shape already losing the last heat of life. The cloth gag was dark and stiff. Blood had dried in streaks down the wood, and below, the earth was trampled into hard mud.

Alice and Walter were still tied. Their wrists had been scraped raw by struggling; the ropes were wet with their blood in thin rings. Walter's head was bowed, breath coming in short harsh pulls through split lips. Alice held herself as still as stone, not because she had surrendered, but because she understood stillness could be a kind of endurance. Her eyes kept moving, measuring, listening.

Thomas remained half-held near the edge of the square, the men who gripped his arms unsure now whether to keep him for later or abandon him to the chaos. Their faces had changed. The righteousness that had lit them earlier had been blown out by the sudden gust of the real plague. They looked like men waking from a drink and discovering what was in their hands.

From somewhere down a side lane, another cough rose, wet and close.

A child's cough.

It carried differently than an adult's, thinner, more helpless. It cut through the night like a blade sliding into cloth.

For a moment the square paused. Even those who were running faltered as if pulled by the sound. Then the mother's voice came, pleading and furious all at once. "Hush, hush, hush," she hissed. "Do you want them to hear you?"

As if the danger was not the sickness, but the hearing.

The child coughed again, and the sound turned into a choking sob. The mother's door slammed with such force the frame shook.

Alice watched that door and understood, with a cold certainty, what would happen now. The village had been taught to hide sickness the way it hid guilt. Not to seek help. Not to isolate with care. To bury it under silence and hope it did not crawl out.

The coughing did not stop.

It multiplied.

A man staggered into the square from another lane, one hand clamped beneath his jaw as if he could hold his throat together. He moved as though drunk, but there was no ale in his eyes, only panic. He tried to speak and gagged. When he lowered his hand, torchlight caught the swelling there, round and livid.

He saw the posts, saw Edmund's hanging body, and something broke in him. He turned sharply, stumbled, and ran, leaving a dark smear of spit on the stones.

The plague was no longer rumor. It was no longer a story that could be shaped and aimed. It was walking.

It was inside.

And because the village had spent its strength chasing phantoms, there was nothing ready to meet it. No ordered quarantine, no care for the sick, no stores guarded with clean hands, no animals left to keep the rat tide down. Only bolted doors and a thousand terrified minds repeating the same prayer: let it be someone else.

In the lane where the first man had fallen, his convulsions eased into a trembling stillness. His eyes rolled, showing white in the torchlight, and then fixed on nothing. The women who had hovered earlier stared at him with the stunned relief of people who think the worst part is over when a body stops moving. None of them stepped closer to close his mouth, to cover him, to do the small dignities that used to make death bearable.

They backed away and left him in the mud as if he were already poison.

The next day did not arrive cleanly. Dawn came, smeared with smoke and the sour smell of waste. When the sun lifted over the roofs, it shone on a village that had locked itself into hundreds of small prisons.

In one cottage a man lay sweating on a straw mattress while his wife sat in the corner with their children, refusing to touch him, refusing to leave, whispering prayers that became curses when the children began to sniffle. In another, a grandmother hid her own fever under blankets and told everyone she was merely cold, because to admit heat in the bones was to invite abandonment. In the priest's own house, a young acolyte vomited dark bile into a bowl and sobbed when he realized no one was coming to empty it.

Rats moved through the lanes in daylight, sleek and unafraid. They darted beneath doors, squeezed through cracked boards, climbed sacks of grain that had been left unguarded. Without cats, the rat bodies multiplied until the village seemed to ripple in corners with small movements.

Those who had once carried the patrol staff with rags did not gather. The staff lay where it had been dropped in the night, rags damp with dew, its authority dissolved. Men who might have lifted it again remembered the swelling in the lane, the black spit, the way the sickness had answered the village's violence as if mocking it.

Rob tried, at midday, to call people back to the square. He rang the church bell once, twice, hard enough that the sound hurt. Only a few came, and they stood apart, watching one another more than watching him. Rob's voice cracked with fury as he shouted about resolve, about unity, about cleansing.

A man in the thin crowd called back, "Cleanse what? The air?"

Rob's face reddened. "We need order," he insisted.

A woman, hair unbound, eyes hollow, answered, "Order won't bury my husband."

No one laughed at that. The old way, the cruel way, required a crowd. It required the warmth of bodies pressing together until individual doubt melted. Now bodies were the danger. The plague had done what Edmund's words could not. It had made proximity frightening enough to break the mob's shape.

Father Griffiths appeared on the church steps late in the day, robe wrinkled, cross in hand. He spoke of faith and endurance, but his voice did not carry the way it had when the square was full and hungry. It fell into the empty space and died. People watched him from doorways like wary animals, listening for coughs more than sermons.

Behind him, inside the church, someone began to weep.

In the square, Alice and Walter were still tied, left where the village had placed them and then forgotten in its scramble for breath. Their mouths were dry. The ropes had loosened slightly with the night's damp and the day's heat, but not enough. Walter's head lolled forward and then lifted again, stubborn even now, eyes bloodshot and burning.

Thomas managed, at some point, to stumble back toward them. No one stopped him; no one cared what happened to traitors when everyone was busy fearing their own lungs. He moved like a man walking into a dream he could not wake from, one hand clutching his side where he'd been struck. He knelt near Alice, fingers trembling as he reached toward her bindings.

"I'm sorry," he whispered, voice ragged. "I'm sorry. I didn't mean—"

Alice's eyes snapped to his. "Then cut it," she said, and her voice was flat, stripped of comfort. "If you can."

Thomas looked around wildly, as if expecting someone to leap out and accuse him again. Then he fumbled at his belt and produced a small knife, the kind used for cutting twine, not throats. His hands shook so badly he nearly dropped it.

He saw Edmund's body hanging above them and made a sound like a swallowed sob. He did not look long. Looking long was a luxury.

He put the blade to Alice's rope.

The knife was too small, the rope too thick, and his hands too weak from fear. The fibers resisted him with humiliating strength.

From somewhere nearby, a door opened a crack. A face appeared and then vanished. The village was watching even now, not to intervene, but to decide whether helping was dangerous.

Thomas pressed harder, sawing at the rope until the blade bit into his own thumb and blood slicked the fibers. He cursed softly, then kept going.

Walter rasped, "Hurry," and it was not a command but a plea he hated himself for needing.

Thomas worked until his shoulders shook.

In the lanes behind them, another scream rose.

Not the scream of accusation this time. Not the scream of a crowd making itself brave.

The scream of someone discovering, too late, that there was nothing left to blame and nowhere left to run.

The disease had been invited in by hesitation, fed by slaughter, and unleashed by panic. And now it moved through the village like water through broken earth, finding every crack, every hidden pocket, every bolted door.

Edmund Harrow was dead, and still the plague came.

The village had demanded a visible enemy, and the plague answered by reminding them of the oldest truth they had tried to outrun: that death does not need permission, and it does not need a story.

It only needs time.

Thomas's little knife worried at the rope like a mouse at a sack seam. The fibers had been soaked by night damp and warmed again by sun; they tightened and loosened in stubborn rhythm, refusing to part. Blood from Thomas's thumb smeared dark into the twist. He sawed harder, jaw clenched, breath coming in quick, shallow pulls as if he feared to inhale too deeply in the open square.

Alice did not look at the blade. She looked past Thomas's shoulder, tracking the lanes. Every few heartbeats her gaze snapped to a doorway, a shutter crack, a window where a face might appear and vanish again. She had the stillness of a trapped animal that has decided it will not waste itself on panic.

"Hurry," Walter rasped again. It came out raw, as though he had swallowed smoke. His wrists were swollen around the rope; the skin there looked torn in crescents where he'd fought it through the night. He kept lifting his head, as if refusing to bow even to pain.

Thomas's hands shook. "It's not cutting," he whispered, and the shame in his voice was almost as loud as the fear. "It's too thick."

"Then cut your own belt," Alice said. "Wrap it and pull until the knot shifts. Do something."

Thomas stared at her as if he had forgotten belts could be used for anything except holding up trousers. Then he fumbled at his waist, tore the belt free, and threaded it awkwardly between the rope and the post, trying to make a lever. His breath hitched as a cough sounded from somewhere close, behind one of the cottages bordering the square. It was not a single cough, not the casual clearing of a throat. It was wet, persistent, followed by a whine of a child being hushed.

Thomas froze, belt half threaded. He looked over his shoulder, eyes wide.

"No," Alice said softly, as if speaking to a dog that might bolt. "Don't listen for it. You'll hear it everywhere soon enough."

He swallowed and forced his hands back to work.

Across the square, Edmund's body hung slack, head tilted. The cloth gag had dried stiff, a dark band across his mouth that seemed obscene in daylight. Flies had come, bold in the heat, landing where blood had crusted at his throat. A few villagers crossed the edge of the square with heads lowered, moving quickly as if the open space were a danger all its own. No one went close to the posts. Not from respect. From fear that the posts had become a kind of infection, not in wood and rope, but in memory: a place where people had stood together and shouted, and now standing together felt like an invitation.

The village had collapsed into rooms.

It was quiet in a way Edmund would have recognized as wrong even in healthy times. A village's quiet was never true quiet; it was always filled with animal noise, with carts, with quarrels, with work. This quiet had the hollow quality of a church after everyone has left, when the air feels heavy with what was said inside it. Only now the church itself could not hold the weight. The sound came from houses instead: muffled crying, the slam of a door, a burst of coughing, the scrape of a bolt being thrown.

In the lane where the first man had fallen the previous night, someone had dragged his body toward the side of the road and left it there like refuse. The mud around it was darkened by what had leaked out of him. Two boys, faces pinched and pale, tried to pass without looking. Their mother slapped the back of one boy's head for slowing, not in cruelty, but in terror, as if a lingering gaze could invite the same fate. The boy stumbled forward with his eyes squeezed shut.

By mid-afternoon, the sickness stopped arriving like a visitor and began to rise from within the village like water from the ground.

A woman staggered out of a cottage near the smithy, hair loose, hands pressed to her neck. She was barefoot, feet black with soot and dirt. She made it three steps into the lane and then collapsed, knees folding. When she tried to push herself back up, her arms shook violently. Her mouth worked, lips swelling darkly, as if she were chewing on words she could not speak. A neighbor opened a shutter and watched her from behind wood. The neighbor's eyes met the woman's briefly, then slid away. The shutter closed again with a soft, final sound.

No one went to her.

A cart creaked somewhere behind the church, the slow complaint of wood under strain. Edmund could not hear it, but Alice did, and her head turned. Two men had harnessed themselves like oxen to a small handcart and were dragging a bundled shape toward the graveyard. Their faces were wrapped with cloth, absurd little masks that would not stop what crawled in breath and flea. They moved with quick jerks, like men trying to keep from thinking. When they reached the churchyard gate, one man let go and retched into the grass, shoulders heaving. The other man stood holding the cart handles alone and looked around as if expecting someone to accuse him of weakness.

No one came to accuse him. There were too many other things to fear.

Rob Baines tried once more to make the village into a crowd again. Near evening, he appeared in the square with a few men at his back, their faces tight and uncertain. Rob's voice had lost its easy triumph; it sounded scraped raw.

"Out!" he shouted toward the nearest cottages. "Out, all of you. We need to see who's sick. We need to keep order. We need to—"

A window above a cottage snapped open. A woman leaned out, hair in a braid gone loose, her face blotched with heat. "Order?" she shrieked, and the sound was sharp enough to make Rob flinch. "My husband's dead in the bed and you want order? Come in and fetch him then, Rob. Come in and kiss his mouth and tell me what you see."

The window slammed shut. A moment later the sound of furniture being dragged across the floor came, a barricade made by shaking hands.

Rob stood in the square staring at the closed window as if he had been struck. He looked smaller in daylight, less a prophet and more a man who had shouted too long and found his voice no longer carried. One of his companions coughed into his fist, then tried to hide it by wiping his mouth quickly on his sleeve. Rob's eyes snapped to the movement.

"Don't do that," Rob hissed, stepping back. "Don't you do that near me."

The man's eyes widened with the same offended fear the crowd had once shown when Edmund spoke. "It's only dust," he said too quickly. Then, quieter, "I'm fine."

Rob backed away another step anyway. The instinct was immediate, unconsidered. It was the village's new language speaking through him: distance is virtue, closeness is danger, and anyone who brings danger near is an enemy. It would have been laughable if it had not been so predictable.

Father Griffiths did not come to help Rob this time. The priest appeared only briefly on the church steps, cross held in white fingers, eyes shadowed. He began a prayer for fortitude, but his voice drifted thinly across an emptying square. A few heads turned toward him from behind shutters, not in reverence, but in irritation, as if his words were another kind of noise that might draw the wrong attention. When a cough erupted somewhere in the lane beside the tavern, Father Griffiths's prayer faltered mid-sentence. He tightened his grip on the cross, looked toward the sound, then retreated back inside the church as if the building could still serve as a wall.

It could not.

Thomas's belt trick shifted the rope enough that the knot moved a fraction. He grunted with effort, pulling hard until his shoulders trembled. The belt bit into his palms. He leaned back, using his weight, and the rope creaked against wood. For a heartbeat nothing happened.

Then one strand gave with a soft snap.

Thomas almost fell backward. He caught himself, eyes bright with sudden hope, and lunged back in, sawing at the loosened fibers. The knife finally bit deeper. The rope frayed, then parted.

Alice's hands came free.

She did not waste a second rubbing her wrists. She snatched the belt from Thomas's hands, wrapped it once around the remaining rope still tied to the post, and yanked, forcing slack. Her freed fingers moved quickly, untying what could be untied. She had the efficiency of someone who understood that salvation, when it comes, is never gentle. It must be taken.

Walter watched with bloodshot eyes, breath scraping. "Alice," he croaked.

"I know," she said, and crossed to him. Thomas followed, nearly tripping in his urgency, and together they attacked Walter's bindings. The knot was tighter there, soaked with sweat and blood. Walter flinched when the rope shifted, and a low sound escaped him, half pain, half relief that he tried to smother.

As they worked, the village continued to die around them.

A door opened suddenly on the far side of the square and a young man stumbled out, shirt hanging open, chest slick with sweat. He took two steps, turned his head as if searching for someone, and then vomited dark fluid onto the earth. He stared at it in horror, swayed, and collapsed onto his side. From inside the house came a shriek, then another voice shouting, “Shut it! Shut it!” as if closing a door could erase what had spilled into the open.

The young man’s fingers clawed weakly at the ground. He made a sound like an attempt at a name. No one answered him.

Alice’s gaze flicked toward him only once. Her face did not harden further; it had no farther to harden. She returned her attention to Walter’s rope, pulling it free with a final jerk that left fibers stuck to his torn skin.

Walter sagged forward, hands immediately cradling his wrists, teeth clenched. He looked toward Edmund’s hanging body and made a sound that might have been a sob if his throat had not been too dry for it.

Thomas followed Walter’s gaze and stared at Edmund for a long, helpless moment. “I didn’t mean—” he began, voice breaking.

Alice grabbed Thomas’s collar and shook him once, hard. “Not now,” she said. “If you want to be sorry, live long enough to carry it.”

Walter forced himself upright, swaying. He took one step toward Edmund, then stopped. His shoulders shook. He looked at Alice, eyes full of something raw and furious.

"We can't leave him," he whispered.

Alice's jaw tightened. "He's already been left," she said. "By everyone who cheered. By everyone who hid behind shutters. By God, if you still believe in that sort of watching."

Walter's mouth worked. He looked back at Edmund and took another step, then another, as if pulled by a rope no knife could cut. Alice did not stop him. She followed, close, ready to drag him back if someone surged from a doorway with a club. No one did. There were no clubs now, no righteousness, only the quiet frantic guarding of thresholds.

At the base of the post, Walter reached up with trembling hands and touched Edmund's leg as though confirming what his eyes already knew. Edmund's body was cold through cloth. Walter flinched at the touch, then pressed his forehead briefly against the wood, eyes squeezed shut. His breath hitched. He did not speak. There were no words left that could make sense of the shape hanging above them.

The village around them continued to buckle, cottage by cottage, lane by lane. The plague did not strike like a single blow. It poured. It seeped under doors, climbed into beds, sat in lungs, swelled in throats. It moved with the patience of water finding every crack.

Death in the flood did not look like one grand moment. It looked like a woman too frightened to open her door even when her sister screamed on the step outside. It looked like a man dragging a bundle toward the churchyard and not knowing if he was carrying his wife or his own future. It looked like children learning to hold their breath when anyone coughed, as if breath itself were betrayal.

Alice stepped back from Edmund's post, scanning the square again. "We go," she said, voice low.

Walter lifted his head, eyes hollow. "And the others?" he whispered, and Edmund knew he meant Miriam, the boys, the moneylender and his son, the widow whose tapping stick had been taken.

Alice nodded once, sharp. "If they're alive, they're in the marsh," she said. "If they aren't, we can't bleed ourselves into the square for ghosts."

Thomas wiped his bloody thumb on his trousers, leaving a dark streak. His eyes were wild. "They'll die here," he whispered, and he did not mean Edmund. He meant all of them. The whole village. He said it like a discovery, as if he had only just understood that the machine of blame had stalled and now the plague could move unchallenged through the silence.

Walter's gaze lingered on Edmund one last time. Then he stepped away, limping, shoulders hunched as though carrying a weight no one could see.

They moved out of the square without anyone stopping them.

A shutter creaked open a finger's width as they passed. A single eye watched them go, cautious and unreadable. The shutter closed again.

Behind them, Edmund Harrow hung where the village had placed him, and the well stood at the center of the square like an unblinking witness. The posts remained, waiting for the next lesson that would never come, because the village had run out of enemies it could name.

Now it had only the flood.

And the flood did not care what anyone believed.

Chapter 16

Ashes and Echoes

They did not go far before the village's sounds began to change behind them.

At first, it was only the thinning of it, the way noise fell away in patches. The square had been a mouth, and now that mouth was closing. As they moved along the back lanes toward the fields, cries rose and stopped too quickly, as if cut off by hands clapped over lips. Doors slammed with desperate care. Somewhere a bowl shattered, and no one swore at it. A dog would have barked at the flight of three figures along the hedge line, but there were no dogs left to speak the alarm into the air.

Walter kept looking back.

Alice let him, because looking back cost him nothing but pain, and he had little else left to spend. He walked hunched, one hand pressed to his ribs where he'd been struck, the other wrapped around his scraped wrists as if he could hold the skin together by will. His eyes were raw, and each time he blinked it looked like an effort.

Thomas followed close, breathing through his mouth. The cut on his thumb had stopped bleeding but left a dark smear down his palm. Every few steps his gaze skittered toward the cottages as if expecting a shout, a command, a rope thrown from a doorway. But the village had turned inward. It no longer hunted. It hid.

They slipped past the last outbuildings and into the ragged edge of the fields. Grain stood in uneven patches, some trampled, some untouched. A cart lay half-tipped near a hedge, its wheel sunk into soft ground. The village would have fixed it once, would have cursed the poor workmanship, would have grumbled about the cost of a new axle. Now it was simply another broken thing left where it failed.

When they reached the reed beds by the river, the marsh wind met them, damp and cool, carrying the scent of rot and green growth. It should have felt like relief.

It did not.

The marsh had been hiding. Now it was beginning to feel like waiting.

They found Miriam where they had left her, deeper in the reeds than before. She had moved the children twice, perhaps three times, leaving false beds of flattened grass behind like skins. Her younger boy slept fitfully against her, his face hot, a sheen of sweat catching the pale light. The older boy watched Alice and Walter approach with eyes too old for him, tracking Walter's injured gait, Alice's bound wrists now freed but chafed and red.

The moneylender was there too, pressed against a stunted willow, his son tucked into his side. The boy's fingers worried at a strip of cloth until it frayed. The candle widow sat apart, rocking slowly, her hands empty now that Walter had taken the tapping stick. Her lips moved soundlessly, as if she were still making the sound in her head.

When Walter saw them, something in his shoulders loosened and then locked again. Relief, quickly punished by the next thought.

"They're alive," he said, and his voice broke on the word as if it had been too long since he'd been allowed to say it.

Miriam's eyes flicked to his wrists, to the marks, to the way his mouth moved with pain. Then past him, to the direction they had come from. She did not ask what happened. The marsh had already answered it in the set of their faces.

"Edmund," she said quietly.

Walter stared at the reeds as if he could find a clean place in them to put the word. "He's still there," he managed. "In the square. They left him."

Alice sat down hard, as if her legs had decided without asking that they were done. For a moment she pressed her palm to her face, not to hide tears, but to steady herself against the shape of what she saw when she closed her eyes: the well stones, the posts, the gag gone dark, the crowd's roar swallowing the sound of a throat cut like an animal's.

Thomas dropped to his knees. "I freed you," he said to no one, then to all of them. "I did. I cut you loose. I tried."

The moneylender's gaze pinned him, sharp and frightened. "You led them," he said, voice low.

Thomas flinched. "I didn't mean to." His hands opened and closed. "They were going to burn my mother's cottage. They said they'd do it with her inside. They said I'd already chosen Harrow, and I had to prove I hadn't. I thought…

I thought if I gave them a direction, not the true one—"

"Stop," Alice said. Her voice was flat, not gentle. "Save your explaining for the dead. The living need water."

She reached for the skin they'd brought and drank once, then held it out to Walter. He drank and handed it on. It was a small ritual, clean and simple: share, do not hoard. It was the opposite of the square.

Miriam took only a little. She pressed her fingertips against her younger boy's cheek and frowned. "He's hot," she said. "He's been hot since morning."

The words made the small group tighten without moving, like a net drawn in a fraction.

The moneylender pulled his son closer instinctively. The widow's rocking stilled. Walter's eyes went to the child and then away again, as if looking too long might make it true.

Edmund's rules in the marsh came back to Alice with cruel clarity. Do not measure each other for risk. Do not abandon. Isolate with care.

"We do it here," Alice said. "Not like them."

Miriam's mouth tightened. "Here," she repeated. "In the reeds."

"Here," Alice confirmed. She looked at Walter. "Can you walk?"

Walter nodded, though his face said otherwise.

They moved, not far, but far enough that the reeds thickened, that the ground softened and swallowed their footfalls. They made a small separate place for Miriam and the child, close enough to speak, far enough that breath did not mingle. Alice carried water. Walter carried a strip of cloth torn clean from Thomas's shirt. Thomas did not complain. He watched the tear as if each ripping sound was a penance.

That night, as they huddled in their separate pockets of marsh, the village's bell rang once.

A single toll, dull and wavering, carried over the reeds.

Then nothing.

No second toll. No pattern. Just one sound, like an object dropped in deep water.

Walter raised his head, eyes narrowing, listening for more.

Alice did not move. She stared into the dark where the village lay unseen. "That bell won't call anyone," she said quietly.

Thomas whispered, "Father Griffiths."

Alice's gaze remained fixed. "Or no one at all."

The marsh wind shifted. It brought smells now and then, faint and wrong: smoke, waste, a sourness that sat in the back of the throat. On the second day, a pale haze stood above the village roofs even from this distance, the kind of heat-warp that did not come from sun.

"Burning," Walter said.

Miriam's older boy asked, "Are they burning the sick?"

Miriam closed her eyes. She did not answer. There were too many possible answers, and none were safe.

On the third day, the village became quiet in a new way.

Not the quiet of doors shut against danger, but the quiet of a place that has stopped making decisions. The cries that rose now did not carry anger. They carried need. They were shorter, weaker, as if the lungs behind them had less air to spend.

And then, even those thinned out.

The marsh held them through it, damp and cold at night, swarming with insects by day. They ate what they had and what Alice could snare. The moneylender's son began to cough, a small dry cough at first. The moneylender tried to hush him, then stopped, remembering the sound of a woman in a cottage hissing at a child as if silence could change the air.

"We're not them," Walter said once, hoarse. It sounded like a vow he was afraid to break by speaking too loudly.

The fever took Miriam's younger boy on the fifth night.

He did not swell with the great black lumps they had seen in the lane. He simply grew hotter and hotter until his breath became a rapid flutter like a trapped bird. Miriam held him and rocked, not like the widow, not mindless, but deliberate, as if she could move death back out of him by refusing to stop touching.

Alice sat near enough to speak but not close enough to share breath. "He knows you," she told Miriam, and her voice was the nearest thing to prayer she could manage.

When the child's breath finally stuttered and stopped, Miriam made a sound that did not belong to any word. It tore out of her and then she swallowed it down, pressing her mouth to the child's hair until her lips went still.

They buried him at dawn on a strip of higher ground where the reeds thinned. Walter dug with his hands and a broken piece of wood, because there was no spade and no time to find one. The earth was wet and clung to his fingers. Alice watched the edge of the marsh while he worked, knife in hand, scanning for movement that never came.

When it was done, Miriam did not leave at once. She sat with her palm flat on the raised mound, as if anchoring herself to something that would not run.

"I told you not to leave Isaac unnamed," she said to Alice without looking up. Her voice was quiet, the quiet of a person speaking to the only part of herself that might listen. "I said it like it mattered. And now he's in mud with reeds."

Alice swallowed. "He's not unnamed," she said. "You spoke him. That's more than the village did for anyone."

Miriam's mouth twisted, not quite a smile, not quite a snarl. "The village," she whispered, and finally looked toward the place beyond the reeds. "Is it gone?"

Walter answered without hesitation, because the certainty was the only clean thing left to him. "It will be," he said.

A week later, when the smoke above the roofs thinned and the bell did not ring again, Alice stood at the marsh edge and stared toward the road.

Walter came to her side. His wrists had scabbed over. The skin looked new and tight, like a scar still deciding what shape it would keep.

"You're thinking of going back," he said.

Alice did not deny it. "They left him," she replied.

Walter's jaw worked. "If we go in there now, we don't come out."

"We might," Alice said. "Or we might not. But if we don't, he hangs until he drops apart, and they'll say even that was God's will. They'll make a story out of the rot."

Walter's eyes closed briefly, a man holding back an image that kept forcing itself forward: Edmund's head tilted, the gag dark, the flies. When he opened them again, his gaze had the distant look of someone walking through ruins in his mind.

"What about them?" he asked, nodding toward the reeds where Miriam sat with her older boy, the moneylender, the widow. Thomas. A handful of shaken survivors held together by the marsh and by the rules Edmund had spoken.

Alice looked back. Her voice softened a fraction, not in warmth, but in necessity. "They stay," she said. "They stay hidden. If the village has any teeth left, it will bite at movement."

"And if it doesn't?" Walter asked.

"Then it's already dead," Alice replied.

They went at dusk, because dusk had become their habit for dangerous things. Alice took her knife. Walter took nothing but his stubbornness and the memory of Edmund's voice trying to make a crowd remember itself. Thomas followed them, pale and desperate.

"I can help," Thomas said, as if the words might change what he had already done.

Alice did not answer him until they reached the edge of the fields and saw the village for the first time in days.

It looked smaller.

Not physically, but as if something had been drained out of it. The lanes lay empty. Shutters hung crooked. A roof had collapsed on one cottage, sagging like a broken back. Smoke stains streaked the church wall. The square, glimpsed through the gaps between buildings, was a patch of dark earth where no torchlight moved.

The silence was not peaceful. It was thick with absence.

Thomas stopped walking. He stared at the village like a man staring at a mouth that had once spoken his name and now held no sound at all.

"Ghosts," he whispered.

Walter's eyes narrowed. "Not ghosts," he said. "Just what's left when people run out."

Alice watched the lanes. In the fading light, the village's emptiness played tricks. A shutter creaked, and for a heartbeat it sounded like the tapping stick the widow had lost. Somewhere inside a cottage, something scratched, and it sounded like fingernails on wood, like a person trying to get out after being barricaded in.

They moved anyway, stepping carefully, not because anyone might see them, but because the ground itself felt contaminated with memory. They passed a house with its door hanging open. Inside, a table had been overturned. A bowl lay shattered on the floor; dried gruel smeared like pale vomit. A blanket was bunched near the hearth, and beneath it a shape lay too still.

Walter did not go in. He could not bear to turn any more bodies into proof.

At the edge of the square, Alice stopped.

The posts stood where they always had. The well stood at the center like an eye that refused to close. The ragged patrol staff lay on the ground, the cloth strips limp and dirty, no longer a banner but litter.

And Edmund was still there.

He hung slack, lower than before, as if the rope had stretched under his weight and under time. His head lolled at an angle that made Walter's breath catch in his throat. The gag remained, stiff and dark, though the cloth had begun to fray at the edges. Flies rose in a slow cloud as the three of them approached, and the sound of them was the only living thing in the square.

Walter made a sound and stepped forward, then stopped, swaying slightly as if the square itself had become unsteady.

Alice's voice came low. "Don't look at his face," she said, not as an order, but as a mercy.

Walter looked anyway, because grief does not obey instructions. His eyes shone in the dim light. "He shouldn't be here," he whispered, and the childish simplicity of it broke something in Thomas, who covered his mouth with his bloody hand and began to sob without sound.

Alice stepped closer to the post. She rested her hand against the rough wood beneath Edmund's bound wrists, feeling the dried streaks, the gouges from the knots. The village had made this place into a lesson. Now it stood as a monument to what the lesson had cost.

"You wanted ghosts," she said to Thomas without looking back. "This is how they're made."

Walter reached for the rope with shaking fingers. He did not speak. He simply began to work at the knot, clumsy at first, then more focused, as if the only way to keep from falling apart was to give his hands a task they could finish.

Behind them the village remained silent, but silence in a dead place is never truly empty. It is full of echoes the mind insists on hearing: a cheer that is no longer there, a bell that will not toll, a child being hissed into quiet.

And beneath it all, in the cracks of the square and the seams of doorways, the rats moved unseen, the true inheritors of the village's choices, carrying their own small, relentless life through the ruins.

Walter's fingers worried at the knot as if stubbornness could soften hemp. The rope had been tied in haste, but it had been tightened by time, by rain and sun, by the slow drag of Edmund's weight. It resisted at first, then gave a fraction, the fibers creaking against themselves.

Alice kept watch without truly expecting anyone to come. The village had no patrols left. It had barely any people left. Still, she listened for the scrape of a shoe on stone, for a cough too near, for the soft thump of a door closing. Silence, she had learned, could be a trap as easily as shouting.

Thomas stood behind them with his hands pressed over his mouth, shoulders jerking with a sob he would not let out loud. His eyes kept sliding away from Edmund and then returning as if he were compelled to check that what he saw was real, that his own choices had weight and shape.

Walter finally freed the knot enough to slip a loop loose. He climbed onto the low crossbeam of the post, bracing himself with his forearm against the wood. His wrists trembled, not from weakness alone but from the effort of making his body do something gentle after so many days of violence.

"Hold him," Walter said, voice raw.

Alice stepped in, close despite everything she knew about distance and breath. The dead did not cough. The dead did not plead. She put one hand under Edmund's arm and the other at his shoulder, feeling the stiff give of cloth, the wrong looseness beneath it. She had carried sacks of grain, dragged snares from thickets, pulled a child from a ditch once, years ago. None of it had prepared her for the way a man's weight changed when the life was gone from him.

Walter tugged the rope free, inch by inch, then lifted it off Edmund's bound wrists. Edmund's body slumped forward into Alice's arms, head lolling. The gag was still tied behind his skull, the cloth stiff with old blood.

Walter jumped down, boots striking the packed dirt. For a moment he only stood there staring, hands lifted and useless, as if he expected Edmund to right himself and speak. Then he stepped in and took Edmund's other side.

Together, they eased him down onto the ground at the base of the post. Thomas made a small sound and knelt, not touching, only hovering close enough to be of use if asked. His thumb, still cut, left a faint smear of dried blood on his own palm as he clenched and unclenched his hands.

Walter's fingers went to the gag knot. He hesitated.

Alice saw it. "Do it," she said quietly. "Or I will."

Walter swallowed. His hands shook as he untied the cloth. The gag came away with a soft tearing sound where it had stuck to skin. Edmund's mouth was slack. His split lip had healed into a hard ridge and reopened again in places; flies had found the edges and left their work.

Walter turned his face away sharply, jaw clenched so hard the muscles jumped. He did not weep. He looked as if he had run out of that ability days ago and only now understood what the lack of it cost.

Thomas leaned forward, finally touching Edmund's sleeve with two trembling fingers, as if asking permission from the dead. "I'm sorry," he whispered, not to Alice or Walter. To the earth. To whatever might still be listening.

Alice stood and looked around the square. The well's stones were stained in places with old damp and newer filth. The rags on the fallen staff lay limp, their strips darkened and frayed. A crust of ash clung to the edges of the square where fires had once been built. It was all so ordinary in its materials. Wood. Rope. Stone. Cloth. And yet it had held a village's madness like a bowl holds water.

"We can't leave him here," Walter said, and his voice cracked on the word here.

"No," Alice agreed.

Walter looked toward the churchyard gate beyond the square. "There," he said. "If there's ground left that isn't... this."

Alice did not argue. She bent and took Edmund beneath the arms again. Walter lifted his legs. Edmund's body was stiffening, heavy in an awkward way, and they had to move in short, careful steps.

Thomas stumbled after them, reaching out once to steady Edmund's shoulder and then snatching his hand back as if he'd touched a brand. He kept close anyway, like a dog that knows it will be kicked and stays near because leaving would be worse.

They passed the church steps where Father Griffiths had stood. The door hung slightly ajar, the wood swollen from damp. A chalked cross had been drawn and redrawn so many times it had become a thick, smeared X. Walter stared at it as they went by, and Alice saw the moment in his face when hatred tried to rise and found nowhere to go. There was no priest to strike. There was only a building that had watched and said nothing.

In the churchyard, the gate stood open. No one had bothered to close it.

The ground inside was wrong. Not only because of fresh mounds, but because there were too many and they were too shallow. Dirt had been thrown back with haste and exhaustion. Some of the mounds had sunk already, caving in at the center where bodies collapsed and the earth followed. In places, boards had been laid over the worst, not coffins, just planks as if to keep the living from seeing too much.

Walter stopped and lowered Edmund's legs to rest for a breath. His eyes scanned the uneven ground.

"They didn't mark them," he said.

Alice followed his gaze. There were no stones. No crosses. No names scratched into wood. Only lumps of earth in shapes that blurred together. If someone had once set a crude marker, it had been knocked aside or stolen for firewood or simply fallen and been forgotten.

"They couldn't," Thomas said hoarsely. "There were too many."

Walter's head snapped toward him. "They could have tried," he said, and the anger in his voice was immediate and clean. "They had time to tie knots. They had time to cheer. They had time to kill cats in the street until the rats ran bold. But they didn't have time to put a stick in the ground and call it a name."

Thomas flinched and looked down.

Alice stepped between them without touching either. "We don't fix it by breaking him," she said. Then, to Thomas, "Find a spade. If there is one."

Thomas blinked as if not understanding why she would ask him for anything. Then he nodded too quickly and ran, stumbling toward a shed near the far wall. His boots slid in soft ground. He caught himself and kept going.

Walter and Alice carried Edmund farther in, past the oldest stones that leaned like tired men. Here and there, names still existed, carved into weathered rock. Half-letters. Dates worn smooth. Proof that once, the village had believed a person's name mattered after death.

They found a patch of ground at the edge where the earth looked less disturbed, where grass still grew in a thin stubborn skin. Alice lowered Edmund's shoulders. Walter lowered his legs. Edmund lay on his back, face turned slightly as if listening.

Walter stared down at him for a long moment. "He deserved better," he said.

Alice answered honestly, because lies had become another form of theft. "So did they all," she said, and swept her gaze across the yard. Better for Edmund. Better for Isaac in the reeds. Better for the strangers burned. Better for the animals slaughtered and left to rot. Better even for some of the villagers who had cheered, because many of them had died behind bolted doors without anyone to close their eyes.

Thomas returned dragging a spade with a cracked handle. He held it as if it weighed more than iron. His face was streaked with sweat, though the day was cooling. He thrust it toward Walter, then toward Alice, as if unsure who had the right to take it.

Walter took it. His hands were swollen and raw, but he wrapped them around the handle anyway. He drove the blade into the ground with a short, hard motion. The earth gave, damp and reluctant. He dug again, jaw clenched, breath loud through his nose. Dirt piled at the edge of the hole. The work was ugly and sacred at once.

Alice knelt beside Edmund and folded his hands over his belly. The wrists still bore the deep marks of rope; dark bands pressed into skin. She touched them briefly, then pulled her hand back, not because she was afraid, but because she knew she would start counting every bruise and never stop.

Thomas hovered at her shoulder, hands twisting. "I should dig," he said.

"You will," Alice replied. "When Walter can't."

Walter dug until his shoulders shook and the spade handle creaked. He paused only to spit and wipe his mouth with the back of his wrist, leaving a smear of dirt. Each time he straightened, his gaze went to the unmarked mounds around them, as if he expected the dead to rise and demand their names.

"Do you think any of them are still in their houses?" Thomas asked suddenly, voice thin. "Dead in the beds?"

Walter did not answer at first. He drove the spade again. Then he said, very quietly, "Yes."

Alice looked toward the village beyond the churchyard wall. Shutters hung crooked. One roof had burned through and collapsed, leaving a black gap. The air smelled faintly of old smoke and something sourer beneath it.

"They locked themselves in," she said. "And when no one came to open the doors, the doors stayed shut."

Thomas pressed his hands to his face. "It wasn't meant to—"

Walter's voice rose, sharp. "Wasn't meant to what? Kill him? Burn strangers? Hang the weak? Slit throats at the well? You don't get to say what it meant when you did it."

Thomas made a small choking sound and dropped to his knees, not in drama but in collapse. "I didn't cut his throat," he whispered. "I didn't. I didn't."

Alice's voice cut through, low and firm. "Then help," she said. "Dig. Carry. Bury. Do something the village refused to do."

Walter stepped back from the hole, chest heaving. He handed the spade to Thomas without looking at him.

Thomas took it as if it might strike him on its own. He began to dig, clumsy at first, the blade biting and skidding. Then he found the rhythm: lift, drive, pry, throw. Dirt flecked his trousers.

Sweat beaded at his hairline. He did not stop to wipe it away.

Walter watched him dig, face tight. Alice watched the yard.

Somewhere beyond the wall, something scratched inside a house. It was a small sound, like nails on wood. A rat, perhaps. Or a door swinging on a loose hinge. Or nothing at all, only the mind insisting that quiet places must contain movement.

When the hole was deep enough, Walter and Thomas lifted Edmund again. They lowered him into the earth with care that felt almost obscene after the village's hands. Edmund's head rolled slightly. Alice reached down and straightened it.

Walter's breath hitched. He did not speak any prayer. He had no words left that felt clean.

Alice looked down into the grave and said, "Edmund Harrow," plainly, as if naming him could keep him from joining the faceless earth around him.

Walter's voice joined hers, rough. "Edmund Harrow."

Thomas swallowed hard. "Edmund Harrow," he repeated, and the words sounded like penance.

They began to fill the grave. Dirt struck cloth with soft thuds. A few clumps hit harder, and Walter flinched each time as if it were a blow. When the earth rose to cover Edmund's face, Alice looked away. Walter did not. He watched until there was only ground.

No marker remained but the shape of the mound. They had no stone. No carved cross. Only what they could carry.

Alice broke a thin branch from a nearby hedge and pushed it into the soil at the grave's head. It was a poor thing, already brittle. It would not last a season. But it stood upright for the moment, and that mattered.

Thomas stared at it. "It won't hold," he whispered.

"I know," Alice said. "But we did."

Walter stood over the mound, hands hanging at his sides, fingers curled as if still holding rope. His eyes roamed the churchyard again, taking in the unmarked graves, the sunken mounds, the places where bodies had been laid without names because naming had become too heavy for frightened hands.

"This is what's left," he said quietly. "A village of dirt."

Alice's gaze moved across the yard one last time. "No," she said. "This is what they tried to make of it. Unmarked. Uncounted. Easy to forget."

She looked at Walter, then at Thomas. "We remember," she said. "Even if no one else does."

Walter nodded once, small and final. Thomas did not nod. He simply stood there breathing, eyes wet, hands filthy with earth, as if the dirt had finally taught him something his fear had refused to learn.

Behind the churchyard wall, the village remained silent, full of doors that would never open again and houses that held their dead like secrets.

And in the yard itself, among the unmarked graves, a single thin branch stood in fresh soil, defiant in its frailty, marking one name against the weight of all the unnamed.

They left the churchyard as the light began to fail, stepping back through the open gate as if crossing a boundary that would not let them return unchanged. The thin branch Alice had planted stood behind them in the fresh mound, already small against the field of unmarked earth. Walter looked back twice, then forced his eyes forward as if looking too long would pull him into the ground with Edmund.

The village did not stop them. It did not even seem to notice.

A shutter moved once, a cautious lift and fall, and the sound of wood on wood made Thomas flinch hard enough that he nearly stumbled. He caught himself on the churchyard wall, fingers scraping lichen. For a moment he pressed his forehead against the stone, breathing in short pulls, as if the wall might lend him some of its age and steadiness.

Alice did not touch him. She had learned that people could be steadied and also broken by a hand at the wrong time. Instead, she stood a pace away and listened.

There were sounds in the village now, but they were not the sounds of living work. They were little noises that came from emptiness: a loose sign creaking against a post, something shifting in a collapsed roof, the soft scuffle of rats that no longer cared to hide. The air still smelled faintly of old smoke and sourness. Under it all was the sweet-rot smell that clung to places where too many bodies had lain too long and no one had been left strong enough to carry them out.

Walter's voice came rough, as if the words had to be dragged out past bruises. "We should have taken something."

Thomas looked up sharply. "Taken what?"

Walter's mouth tightened. "Something that says he was here. Something that lasts longer than a branch."

Alice understood what he meant: a stone, a plank, a cross. Something that could not be blown down by the first hard wind. Something that could defy the village's forgetting.

"There's nothing in there that isn't soaked in it," she said. "If we start pulling at what's left, we'll be carrying the village on our backs. And it will still fall apart."

Walter's eyes flicked toward the square as they passed the edge of it, though they did not step into it. The well sat at its center like a dark mouth. He swallowed and kept walking.

Thomas's hands were still stained with earth. He kept rubbing his fingertips together as if he could grind the dirt away without water. "They'll say it never happened," he whispered, and the words came out with a child's fear, irrational and sincere. "If anyone comes later. If anyone asks. They'll say the plague did it, and that's all."

Walter turned on him, sudden and fierce. “It did happen.”

“I know,” Thomas said quickly, too quickly. His eyes darted toward Alice as if seeking permission to be forgiven and not finding it there. “I know it did. But the village is gone. There’s no one left to answer for it. Rob. Father Griffiths. Anyone. They’re either dead or hiding behind doors that won’t open again. So, what happens to the truth?”

Alice watched the lane ahead. The fields beyond were darker now, the hedgerows thickening into silhouettes. “It doesn’t go away just because no one’s punished,” she said. “It stays in the people who lived.”

Walter let out a breath that was almost a laugh and almost a sob. “And in the people who didn’t,” he said, and his eyes went distant for a moment. Edmund, hanging by the post. Isaac in the reeds. Names swallowed by mud.

They moved faster once they reached the fields, not running, but walking with the urgent economy of people who knew daylight had never truly meant safety. Dusk had become the hour of decisions, of doors opening and knives being drawn and crowds gathering. Even in a dead village, the habit of dread remained.

Thomas kept glancing back. "No one's following," he said, half statement, half question.

Alice did not turn her head. "If anyone's left to follow, they've learned to fear breath more than footprints."

Walter touched his scraped wrists, then let his hands drop. "Still," he murmured.

Still. The word held everything that lingered: the sense that the village could rise up again, that voices could return to the square, that Rob could step out of a doorway with that satisfied smile and call them traitors. Memory made corpses into pursuers. It gave the dead a way to keep walking.

When they reached the reed beds, the marsh wind met them like a cold hand. It carried damp and green and the soft rot of water plants. It also carried something else now, faint but unmistakable: the village's smell, thinned by distance but not erased. Smoke had a way of traveling. So did sickness. So did what people did to each other when they were afraid.

Miriam saw them first. She rose from the reeds with a movement that was too quick, too sharp, as if she had been holding herself ready for days. Her older boy stood beside her, thin and watchful. The moneylender appeared behind them, his son tucked close as always. The widow sat with her hands in her lap, rocking without rhythm. When she saw Alice, her rocking slowed until it stopped.

Walter lifted his chin, and Miriam's eyes searched his face for the answer before he could speak.

"It's done," Walter said quietly.

Miriam's mouth tightened. She did not ask what done meant. She had learned that asking did not change what was waiting. "You buried him," she said.

Alice nodded once. "In the churchyard," she replied. "With a name."

The moneylender swallowed. He did not look relieved. Relief had become a dangerous emotion; it invited punishment. "And the village?" he asked.

Thomas's voice came out hollow. "It's gone," he said, and Miriam's older boy flinched slightly at the certainty of it. Gone was a big word. Children understood gone in pieces, in missing faces and empty beds, not in the collapse of an entire place.

Walter sank down onto firmer ground and sat heavily, wincing as his ribs protested. He stared at his hands as if he expected to see rope still wrapped around them. "There are so many graves," he said, voice low. "They didn't mark them. They just piled earth like it was the only thing left they could afford."

The widow made a small sound then, something like a breath catching. Her eyes stared past Walter into the reeds, and Alice realized she was hearing the square again. The tapping stick had been taken from her, but the rhythm remained inside her. People kept their habits even when the objects were gone. Fear did not need tools. It only needed a mind that remembered.

Miriam's voice turned flat. "They'll do it elsewhere," she said. Not a question. A statement carved from bitter experience.

Alice looked toward the black line of the distant village roofs, barely visible beyond the marsh's edge. "Yes," she said. "If it finds the right mouths."

Thomas flinched, as if Alice had named him without using his name. He stared at the wet ground and whispered, "I tried to warn him."

Walter's head lifted. His gaze pinned Thomas, not with rage now, but with something colder. "You warned him," Walter said slowly. "And you still brought them."

Thomas's shoulders hunched. "I didn't bring them to the marsh," he insisted, and his voice was raw with the need for some part of his story to be less ugly. "I lied. I told them he'd gone the other way. I— I only—"

"You only led them to him in the square," Walter finished, and the quietness of it made it sharper than shouting.

Thomas's eyes went wet. He wiped his face with the back of his hand, smearing marsh grime across his cheek. "I'm here," he said, desperation spilling through. "I'm here now. I dug the grave. I said his name."

Alice watched him for a long moment. Then she said, "Names don't undo knives."

Thomas's mouth opened, then shut again. He looked like a man who had been given an equation and found he had no numbers left to balance it.

Miriam shifted, pressing her palm briefly against the reed-stem braid she'd made around her dead son's small grave. She had tied reeds into a ring and set it there, a fragile crown that would not last long, but would last longer than bare mud. "Then what do we do?" she asked, and the question was not only about the marsh, about food and water and where to sleep. It was about the thing that had followed the plague like a shadow: how to keep being human when everything around them rewarded the opposite.

Walter stared at the damp earth. "We remember," he said, and the words came out as if pulled from a place in him that still bled. "Not like the village. Not only the fear. The names. The choices. The moments when we could have turned and didn't."

The moneylender's son coughed once, a small dry cough, and then froze, eyes wide with sudden alarm at his own sound. The moneylender tightened his arm around the boy instinctively, then forced himself to loosen it a fraction, as if remembering Walter's earlier rule: no one is volunteered by another man's fear.

Alice looked at the boy, then at the others. "This is how it lingers," she said quietly. "Not just in stories. In flinches. In how you hold your child when he makes a noise. In what you hear when the wind moves through reeds."

Miriam's older boy stared at Alice. "Will we ever stop hearing it?" he asked. His voice was small but steady, as if he had decided crying was a waste and questions were all he had left.

Alice did not lie to him. She crouched so she was closer to his level and said, "You'll hear it less some days. You'll hear it more on others. But you can learn the difference between a memory and a command."

The boy frowned as if trying to understand what a memory could command.

Walter's voice came rough again. "The village made a command out of fear," he said. "They made it into a religion. They made it into a rope."

Thomas stared at his hands. "And now there's no one left to blame," he murmured.

Miriam's mouth twisted. "There's always someone left to blame," she said, and looked toward the dark where the roads ran beyond the marsh. "If not in that village, then in another. If not a stranger, then a weak one. If not a weak one, then a child with the wrong eyes."

Alice stood slowly, her joints aching with exhaustion that felt older than a day. "Then we carry something else with us," she said. "Not the village's story. Edmund's."

Walter lifted his head. For a moment the hardness in his face cracked, and grief showed cleanly. "He'd hate that," he said, and there was a hint of bitter affection in it. "Being turned into a tale."

Alice shook her head once. "Not a tale," she replied. "A warning. There's a difference."

The marsh wind shifted again, and the reeds whispered against each other like low voices trading news. In the dark beyond, the dead village sat with its unmarked graves and its silent well and the memory of a crowd's roar. But here, in the wet breath of the marsh, a handful of survivors sat close enough to speak and far enough to keep each other breathing and tried to do the one thing the village could not.

They tried to live with fear without letting it choose their hands.

And even as the night settled around them, the memories lingered, not only as pain, but as a thin, stubborn thread that held names against the dark. Edmund Harrow. Isaac. The strangers turned to ash. The weak hanged as purification. The beasts slaughtered until rats ruled the walls. The priest's soft voice making murder sound like duty.

The wind carried it all, and they listened, not because they wanted to, but because forgetting was how it began.

Chapter 17

Epilogue: A Town Without Names

The road that led toward the village had been rutted by carts once, by hooves and bare feet and the steady press of trade. Now it was only a line cut through hedgerows and low fields, and even that line seemed to hesitate as it neared the place, as if the earth itself had learned to skirt it.

Two travelers came with the afternoon light at their backs: a man with a pack strapped tight across his shoulders and a woman leading a small mule whose ribs showed through its hide. They had the lean look of people who had learned to eat sparingly and walk far. Their boots were caked with old mud that had dried and cracked, then been soaked again. A strip of cloth was tied around the woman's hair to keep it from whipping into her eyes. The man carried a staff cut from a branch, not as a weapon so much as a habit, something to test ground ahead when the road turned slick.

They had passed three hamlets in two days where smoke rose from chimneys and children's voices carried, thin but real. Each time they had been turned away with the same words, spoken through a crack in a door: "No room. No strangers. Go on." In one place an old woman had thrown a crust of bread onto the road as if feeding a dog and shouted, "Keep your breath to yourself."

So, they went on. And when the land dipped and the hedgerows opened, and the roofs of the village appeared like a cluster of broken teeth against the sky, the woman slowed the mule without meaning to.

"Is this it?" she asked.

The man did not answer at first. He stared as if waiting for something to move, for a figure to cross between houses, for smoke to curl from a hearth. There was none. The village sat under the light like a thing held underwater.

"It should be," he said finally. "The last place marked on the steward's list. He said there were stores here. Grain. Tools. Anything left, we could trade for." He sounded like a man repeating someone else's certainty because his own had worn thin.

The mule snorted, uneasy. Its ears angled forward and then back again, as if it could hear something the humans could not. The woman patted its neck, but her hand lingered too long, fingers tense against the animal's hide.

As they drew closer, the silence sharpened. It was not the peaceful quiet of fields. It was the absence of ordinary interruption. No dog barked. No chicken clucked. No hammer rang from a smithy. Even the birds seemed to skirt the place, cutting around it as though the air above the roofs tasted wrong.

They reached the first cottage at the village edge. The door hung open on one hinge, swinging slightly with the breeze, the soft wood-on-wood sound like a quiet knocking that would never be answered. The man stepped up, careful with his footing, and peered inside.

"Hello?" he called.

His voice fell into the cottage and did not return. The air smelled of old smoke and something sour beneath it, a sweetness that made the back of the throat tighten. The woman shifted her weight, holding the mule's lead with both hands now as if it might bolt.

"Leave it," she said.

The man swallowed. He moved away from the open doorway, scanning the lane. Farther in, shutters hung crooked or were nailed closed from the inside. One roof had caved in, leaving rafters exposed like ribs. A cart lay tipped on its side near a hedge, wheel half sunk into the earth, as if the village had dropped what it was holding and never bent to pick it up again.

They walked deeper.

Their footfalls sounded too loud on the packed dirt. The man lowered his voice without realizing he was doing it. "There should be people," he murmured, as if this were a riddle that could be solved by stating it plainly.

The woman glanced toward the church steeple rising above the roofs. The bell rope hung slack through an open belfry window. No bell sounded. If there had been a toll, it had already been spent.

They passed a house with a shutter cracked open a finger's width. The man halted and leaned closer.

A face looked out.

It was a child's face, pale and still, eyes too large. The child did not speak. The crack widened just enough for one eye to blink, then narrowed again.

"Wait," the man said quickly, stepping toward the shutter. "We mean no harm. We only want water. Food, if you can spare it."

The shutter snapped shut with a sharp sound. A bolt scraped. From inside came a rustle and then nothing.

The woman exhaled slowly. "Someone's alive," she whispered.

The man's mouth tightened. "Then why—"

He stopped. The answer was everywhere. The absence of sound was not emptiness. It was hiding.

They continued toward the square, and the air changed again. The smell thickened, more rot now than smoke. Flies drifted in slow clouds near doorways and along the edges of the lane, rising and settling with lazy persistence. The mule's hooves clopped unevenly; it wanted to hurry but did not know where.

When they reached the square, the woman's hand tightened on the mule's lead until her knuckles blanched.

At the center stood the well, its stone rim stained darker in places. Beside it, the posts still rose from the ground, two upright timbers scarred and splintered where ropes had bitten and hands had gripped. The earth around them was trampled hard, scuffed as if by many feet, as if the village had danced here.

The man stepped forward, eyes fixed not on the well but on the rags.

A staff lay on the ground near the church steps, strips of cloth tied to it. Once, those rags might have snapped in the wind as a sign of patrol and order. Now they were limp and dirty, a broken banner that meant nothing.

"It's like they fled," he said softly.

The woman shook her head once. "No," she replied. Her gaze had gone to the posts. To the dark streaks on the wood. To the way the square held itself, waiting.

The man moved toward the church steps. The door was partly ajar. He put a hand on it and pushed gently.

The hinges complained, a dry, aching sound. Inside, the church smelled of damp and old wax. The light that came through the narrow windows fell in pale bars across empty benches. The altar cloth was gone. A few candles had been melted down to stubs. On the stone floor near the front, there were marks: drag lines and dark stains that had soaked in and been scrubbed badly, leaving shadows.

He backed out again, swallowing.

"Nothing," he said.

The woman did not answer. She was staring at a corner of the square where the ground was darker, where ash still clung in a thin crust along the edge of the hard-packed earth. Near it, a small object lay half-buried. She stepped closer and bent, careful not to put her fingers directly on it.

It was a broken piece of rope, stiff with old dirt and dried dark stains. She let it fall back as if it had burned her.

"Not fled," she said, voice flat. "Not all at once."

The mule stamped, and the sound jolted them both. The man patted its neck, but his own hand trembled.

From somewhere in the lane behind the square came a faint scratching, like wood rubbing against wood. The man turned sharply. His eyes searched the emptiness between cottages. He saw movement low to the ground.

Rats.

Not one or two, furtive. Several, sleek and unafraid, slipping along the base of a wall and vanishing into a gap beneath a door. The man's stomach tightened. He had seen rats in ports and barns all his life, but these moved as if the village belonged to them. As if they were the only ones left who understood how to live here.

The woman pulled the mule closer, instinctive. "We should go," she said.

The man's eyes kept scanning. "There must be stores," he insisted, but it sounded weaker now, like a man clinging to a plan because hunger did not allow for uncertainty.

A sound came then, so faint at first it might have been the wind: a cough, wet and deep, from somewhere close, behind a shutter.

The man froze.

The cough came again, followed by a ragged inhale. A voice tried to form a word and failed, turning into a choke.

The woman's face tightened. She took one step back, then another. "No," she whispered, and it was not refusal of the person coughing, but refusal of the trap the village had become. She had seen illness before, had walked past bodies in ditches along the road, had smelled death in summer heat. But this was different. This was a sickness still breathing behind walls.

The man's gaze flicked toward the sound, and for a heartbeat he looked like he might step toward it, like decency was trying to rise through his fear.

Then another sound answered the cough: the scrape of a bolt being thrown, quickly, desperately. The same door that hid the sick also hid itself from help. The village had learned that opening was danger, and now it could not unlearn it.

"Come on," the woman said sharply. "Come on now."

They turned to leave the square, and that was when the man saw it.

On the church steps, half tucked into the shadow where the door had swung, lay a small wooden cross. Not hanging, not held, just dropped. It was worn smooth by touch, its edges darkened by oil and smoke. It looked like something a hand had carried for years and then let fall when the carrying no longer mattered.

The man stared at it, then looked away, as if afraid the object might demand meaning from him.

They moved quickly down the lane, the mule eager now, pulling them. As they passed the house with the cracked shutter, the shutter did not open again. No voice called. No one begged. If anyone watched, they watched in silence, measuring distance like morality.

At the village edge the woman stopped once, turning back to look.

From here the roofs looked almost normal again, just poor cottages clustered around a church, a place that might have held laughter once. But the silence pressed out even this far, following them like breath they could not shake.

"What happened?" she asked quietly, not expecting an answer.

The man shifted his pack. He did not look back a second time. "Plague," he said, as if the word could contain everything. Then, after a pause that felt like thought trying to break through habit, he added, "And something else."

The woman nodded, because she had smelled the something else in the square. Ash. Rope. The stale echo of many bodies pressing together in a frenzy and then scattering into locked rooms.

They walked on, leaving the village behind.

And as the road rose and the hedgerows closed again, the woman glanced once over her shoulder and saw, just for a moment, a figure in a doorway at the village edge. A man, thin as a fencepost, watching them go with a face that held no welcome and no threat, only the blankness of someone who had survived by becoming smaller than notice.

Then the figure withdrew, and the doorway was only a dark rectangle in a dead place.

The travelers did not speak again until the village was hidden by land.

When the man finally broke the silence, his voice was low, as if still afraid of being heard. "No names," he said. "No markers. Nothing."

The woman's hand rested on the mule's lead, steady now. "There were names once," she replied. "They just didn't survive the fear."

The wind moved across the fields, ordinary again, carrying the smell of damp earth and distant smoke from other places where people still tried to live. Behind them, the village sat with its silent well and its scarred posts and its unmarked graves, holding its story in rot and rubble.

A town without names did not need gates to keep people out.

It only needed memory.

They did not stop until the road dipped and the hedgerows thickened, until the village was no longer visible even if they turned and tried to force it into view. Only then did the man ease his pack down from his shoulders and let it thump into the grass. He rolled his shoulders once, grimacing, as if pain were preferable to the strange lightness of walking away from stores he had promised himself existed.

The woman kept hold of the mule's lead. The animal's ears were still angled back, listening for the sounds that had not come: a call, a bell, a dog's bark. When there was nothing, it snorted and lowered its head to tear at grass with greedy relief.

"Plague," the man said again, as if testing the word in his mouth. "And something else."

The woman watched him. His face was drawn tight in a way hunger alone did not explain. "You saw the posts," she said.

He nodded without looking at her. "And the rope. And the stains. That's not plague. Not by itself."

They stood in the lane for a time, listening to their own breathing. Behind them the wind came steady across the fields, and for the first time since they had stepped into the village's silence, it felt like an ordinary thing again. But ordinary wind could not scrub away what the place had pressed into them: the shutter snapping closed, the wet cough behind wood, the rats moving like owners.

The man shifted his weight. "We should go on," he said.

"We should," the woman agreed, and yet her hand did not move on the lead.

His gaze flicked to her. "What?"

She hesitated, and for a moment he saw not stubbornness but calculation, the kind of careful accounting people had learned when the world stopped being generous. "If there is anyone left," she said slowly, "they'll die in there. Alone. The way they've chosen. Or the way fear chose for them."

"And if we go back," he replied, voice low, "we don't come out. You heard it. That cough."

She nodded. "I heard the bolt too. They won't let help in. But there might be something else worth taking."

He frowned. “Grain?”

“No.” She looked toward the hedgerow, toward where the road turned back if they followed it. “A reason. A warning. Something to tell the next door we knock on, so they don’t think we’re only mouths asking for their bread.”

The man’s face hardened. “Warnings don’t fill a belly.”

“No,” she said. “But lies kill faster than hunger when they spread.”

He stared at her for a long moment. Then he glanced at the mule, at its narrow ribs, and made a sound that was half surrender and half irritation. “Quick,” he said. “If we go back, we go quick. We take what we can carry and we leave.”

They turned the mule, leading it reluctantly back along the lane. The animal’s hooves slowed as if it remembered the smell. The hedgerows opened again, and the roofs returned in the distance like broken teeth. The man kept his staff in his hand now, not to test the ground but as if wood could be used to push away an invisible presence.

They did not go back to the square first. The woman drew them along a side lane where cottages leaned toward each other, their thatch darkened by smoke and weather. The air was thick here, trapped between walls. Flies drifted in idle spirals near a doorway where the door had been shut from inside and never opened again.

The man turned his head away. "Stores," he muttered, as if repeating the word might make it true.

The woman stopped at a cottage where the shutter had fallen off one hinge and hung like a broken arm. "If a man survived by becoming smaller than notice," she said, remembering the figure she had seen at the edge, "he might have survived by staying near what he knew. Near his own house."

"You want to knock?" he asked, incredulous.

"No." She touched the door with two fingers. The wood was cool. The latch was broken, either forced or rotted. "This one's already open to the world."

He stepped past her and pushed. The door swung inward with a soft scrape.

The smell hit them at once, a sweet rot that made the back of the throat tighten. The man froze, hand still on the door. The woman's grip tightened on the mule's lead, and the mule snorted and tried to back away.

“Stay,” she whispered to the animal, and the word sounded like a prayer.

Inside, the cottage was dim. Light came through a gap in the thatch and fell in a pale stripe across a table that had been set for a meal that never finished: a bowl with crusted porridge, a cup tipped on its side. On the floor near the hearth, a shape lay under a blanket.

The man swallowed hard. “Don’t,” he said.

“I’m not touching,” the woman replied.

They stepped in anyway, careful, their boots quiet on the packed dirt floor. The man’s eyes darted, searching for movement, for a breath. There was none. Only the soft hum of flies.

The woman moved toward the table. Her gaze caught on something half hidden beneath it, pushed back as if someone had tried to keep it from being seen. A small chest, the kind used for linens or church offerings, sat with its lid askew. Dust had settled thickly on it, disturbed only by faint trails that could have been made by a rat’s whiskers.

She crouched, holding her breath without meaning to, and lifted the lid the rest of the way.

Inside were scraps of cloth, a broken wooden spoon, and beneath them, wrapped in oilcloth gone stiff with age, a thin book.

The man leaned closer, eyes narrowing. “A ledger?”

“Maybe,” she said, and slid it out carefully, as if it might crumble in her hands.

The cover was plain, dark with grime. When she opened it, the pages stuck slightly, not with blood but with damp and time. Ink marks ran across the first sheet in a hand that was controlled even when the lines slanted as if written by candlelight.

The man exhaled. “Read it.”

The woman hesitated. Reading was not rare, but it was not common either. Her father had taught her letters in a winter when the roads were impassable and boredom had been more dangerous than cold. She had not thought of those lessons in years. Now the shapes on the page felt like something both fragile and powerful.

She sounded the first line quietly.

“My name is Edmund Harrow.”

The man’s eyes widened. “Harrow?” he repeated, and the name stirred something in him like a half-remembered tale. "I've heard it. In Dorset, years ago. An Earl's son who walked away."

The woman turned the page carefully. The writing continued, and as she read, the cottage seemed to tighten around the words.

"I came here believing men could be made better by being treated as men. I believed that if you gave a person dignity, he would not need cruelty to feel strong."

She glanced up at the man. He had gone still, listening as if the voice on the page had filled the room.

The next lines were darker, the ink pressed harder.

"They have found a new kind of faith. It is not in God but in certainty. They want a cause they can hang. They want a name they can burn. They think that if they make their fear into a knife, the knife will keep the sickness away."

The woman's mouth went dry. She turned another page. Dust lifted in a faint cloud, making the light from the roof gap look like smoke.

The journal did not describe the plague in the way travelers did, as a distant thing that crept from port to port. It described the village's reaction like a slow possession. Names appeared in the margins, scrawled as if Edmund had been trying to hold them in place: Miriam. Walter. Alice. Thomas.

The woman's voice stumbled on Alice's name. She pictured someone with a knife and bound wrists, a woman whose calm would look like defiance in torchlight.

The man leaned closer, his breath shallow. "What does it say?"

The woman kept reading, quieter now, as if afraid the cottage might hear and object.

"They blamed the strangers first. They called them poisoners. They called it protection. Then when protection did not work, they called it purification. They hanged the weak. They slaughtered beasts until rats moved through their walls like shadows. And each time they did it, they felt the brief relief of doing something, which is the worst relief a frightened man can taste."

She swallowed and turned another page. There were smudges here, where a thumb had dragged through ink. The lines wavered.

"I have argued until my voice became another kind of target. Reason has become a mark.

Compassion has become proof. If you find this, and there is anyone left to find it, know this: the sickness did not teach them cruelty. The cruelty only gave the sickness room."

The man's hand went to his own throat unconsciously, as if feeling for the rope-stain that lived on the posts in the square.

The woman reached the last page that was fully written. The ink had run in one corner, as if touched by water. The final words were pressed deep, carved into paper.

"We were not destroyed by the plague, but by the fear that made us deserving of it."

She stopped. The cottage seemed to breathe around them, not with life, but with the settling of dust.

The man looked at the book as if it were a hot coal. "He wrote that," he said. "Before he died."

"Or knowing he would," the woman replied.

From beneath the blanket by the hearth came a soft sound, a shift that might have been fabric settling. Both of them froze. The man lifted his staff slightly, useless. The woman held the journal tighter to her chest.

They waited.

Nothing moved again. Only flies, only the faint scrape of something in the wall.

The man's voice dropped to a whisper. "We take it."

The woman nodded once. She wrapped the journal back in the oilcloth as carefully as if swaddling a child and slid it into her satchel. It made the bag heavier in a way no loaf of bread could. Weight with meaning. Weight with consequence.

As they backed toward the door, the man's eyes flicked one last time to the shape under the blanket. "No names," he murmured, the words he'd said on the road. But now they sounded different. Not observation, but accusation.

The woman stepped out first, drawing in air that still smelled wrong but was at least open. The mule jerked away from the doorway, ears pinned back, and the woman soothed it with a low sound. The man followed, pulling the door mostly shut behind them without latching it. A small, pointless mercy.

They did not go back through the square. They cut through a gap between cottages and reached the road with quick steps, shoulders hunched as if the village could reach out and pull them back.

Only when the hedgerows closed again and the roofs vanished did the woman slow.

The man glanced at her satchel. "What will you do with it?"

The woman's fingers rested on the bag's strap. "Read it," she said. "To anyone who still opens a door. To anyone who thinks the sickness is the only thing to fear."

The man's jaw tightened. "They won't like it."

"No," she agreed. "They'll call it a lie, or a curse, or a provocation. They'll say it's dangerous."

"And it is," the man said, and his eyes were grim now, not with hunger but with understanding. "Dangerous to people who need a scapegoat."

The woman looked down the road ahead, where fields stretched toward other villages, other doors, other frightened faces. She adjusted the satchel higher on her shoulder as if bracing herself beneath it.

"Then let it be dangerous," she said quietly.

Behind them, the wind crossed the hedgerows and moved on, carrying with it the dust of a cottage floor, the ink of a dead man's hand, and the thin, stubborn possibility that a town without names might still leave one name behind, if someone was willing to carry it.

The journal rode in the woman's satchel like a second spine, stiff and insistent. As the road pulled them away from the dead village, she kept reaching back with her fingers to touch the strap where it crossed her shoulder, as if to make sure it had not slipped out without her noticing. The man walked beside her with his staff tapping at stones that no longer needed testing. His eyes moved constantly, not scanning for wolves or thieves, but for shutters and doorways, for the small signs of human fear that had become more dangerous than any blade.

They did not speak much after they left the hedgerows behind. Words felt loud now. In the distance, smoke lifted from somewhere living, a thin gray thread against the sky. Smoke meant people. People meant warmth and bread. People also meant suspicion, and the question that always came first now: where have you been, and what have you carried with you?

By late afternoon they reached the next village, smaller than the one they had left to rot, but busy enough that a pair of children still ran along a lane with sticks in their hands, chasing a hoop made from bent willow. The sight struck the woman hard in the chest. For a moment she hated them for being able to run without looking over their shoulders. Then she hated herself for the thought.

The children stopped when they saw the mule.

One of them called, "Da!" and sprinted toward a cottage with a tiled roof. A woman appeared in the doorway, wiping her hands on her apron, and the moment she saw the travelers her posture changed. Her smile did not fully form. Her eyes dropped to their boots, to the mud, to the satchel at the woman's side.

"You can't come in," she called before they had spoken. Her voice was firm, practiced. "We've had enough of strangers."

"We only want water," the man said. He held both hands out, palms forward, empty. He had learned that empty hands were a kind of language. "We'll pay."

The woman in the doorway laughed once, without humor. "Pay with what? Breath?" Her gaze flicked to the mule's ribs. "Go on. There's a stream a half mile west. Drink there."

The traveler woman took a step forward before her companion could answer. "We've come from a village that died," she said, and the words landed wrong immediately. The doorway woman's face hardened as if she had been struck.

"Then you should keep walking," she snapped.

"It died because—" the traveler woman began, then stopped, realizing how foolish it sounded to offer a because to someone whose first instinct was to bolt their door. A because asked to be listened to. Listening was risk.

The man murmured, "Not here," warning, but the traveler woman could not leave it. The journal in her satchel felt like a hand pushing at her ribs.

"There's a warning," she said, forcing steadiness into her voice. "A man wrote it. Edmund Harrow. He kept a journal. He—"

The name did nothing for the doorway woman. Her eyes narrowed, not in recognition but in suspicion of any name offered too confidently.

"And why," the doorway woman said slowly, "are you carrying a dead man's words?"

"Because the living won't," the traveler woman replied, and regretted the sharpness the moment it left her mouth.

A second door opened down the lane. A man stepped out, thin, hair uncombed, a cloth tied over his mouth like a crude mask. He did not come closer. He stood at a distance and watched, hands on his hips as though he were bracing himself against anger.

"Who are they?" he called.

"Passing through," the doorway woman said quickly. "They're leaving."

The traveler woman swallowed and reached into her satchel. The oilcloth-wrapped book resisted, as if reluctant to be exposed to another village's air. She pulled it free anyway. The man beside her inhaled sharply, as if the act itself might invite trouble.

The lane's attention tightened. Two more faces appeared at windows, then vanished again. A dog would have barked once, but there were fewer dogs now. Even animals had begun to learn the shape of fear.

"I can read it," the traveler woman said. "Just a page. Just enough to tell you what happened. It wasn't only the plague."

The masked man down the lane shifted his weight. "It's always the plague," he said, voice muffled by cloth. "Unless it's poison. Unless it's strangers. Unless it's sin." His eyes flicked to the journal. "Unless it's a story someone wants to sell."

"It's not for sale," she said. "It's a warning."

The doorway woman's mouth tightened. "Warnings bring trouble," she replied. "Trouble brings crowds. Crowds bring sickness. You want to read, read to your mule."

The traveler woman's fingers tightened around the journal's edges until the oilcloth creased. She looked at the man beside her, searching his face for permission to try harder. He gave her none. His expression said only: we are hungry and tired and not worth dying for.

But the journal had been written by a man who died because he would not hand over names. The memory of that, carried through ink, made it hard to retreat.

She opened the book.

The pages fluttered slightly in the wind, thin and stiff. She wet her lips and began to read aloud, keeping her voice low but clear.

"My name is Edmund Harrow."

A woman at a window across the lane made a small sound, like a cough swallowed. The traveler woman continued.

"I came here believing men could be made better by being treated as men. I believed that if you gave a person dignity, he would not need cruelty to feel strong."

The doorway woman's face did not soften. It tightened further, as if kindness itself were an accusation.

The traveler woman turned the page and read the lines she could not forget, because they described the shape of the dead village more precisely than any mention of swelling or black spit.

"They have found a new kind of faith. It is not in God but in certainty. They want a cause they can hang. They want a name they can burn."

At that, the masked man down the lane barked a laugh that was too sharp to be amusement. "And what does this dead lord know about us?" he called. "About what it's like to watch your child cough and not know if the next breath will be his last?"

The traveler woman looked at him. "He knew," she said simply. "He watched it. He tried to stop what came after."

A movement at the edge of the lane drew her eye: a boy, perhaps twelve, standing behind a fence, staring at the journal with an intensity that made him look older. His face was smudged with dirt. His eyes were bright with either curiosity or hunger, and not only hunger for food.

"Read more," the boy said softly, too soft for bravery. The words slipped out before he could call them back.

His mother, unseen, yanked him down behind the fence. "Inside," she hissed, the sound carrying. "Inside now."

The traveler woman's throat tightened. She read anyway, turning to another passage, one that felt like it belonged to every village, not only the one she had walked through.

"They blamed the strangers first. They called it protection. Then when protection did not work, they called it purification."

A face appeared at another doorway, an old man this time, leaning on a stick. His eyes were cloudy, but his attention was sharp. "Purification," he echoed, tasting the word as if it were already in his mouth. He looked at the doorway woman. "You remember what they did in Coleford," he said quietly. "When the fever came and they said the midwife was marked."

“Don’t,” the doorway woman snapped, too fast. The word had hit something in her that she could not afford to examine.

The traveler woman took a breath and read the line that had felt like a nail driven into wood.

“And each time they did it, they felt the brief relief of doing something, which is the worst relief a frightened man can taste.”

The lane held still for a heartbeat. It was not agreement. It was recognition fighting with the need to deny.

The masked man down the lane took a step forward despite himself. Then he stopped, as if realizing he had crossed an invisible boundary. “You think we don’t know fear?” he demanded. “You think we need a dead man to teach us?”

“No,” the traveler woman said. Her voice was gentler now, because she saw in his anger the same shape the journal described: a man desperate for control. “I think fear teaches quickly. It teaches you to find a target. It teaches you to call it duty. And it teaches you to believe you are clean because someone else is burning.”

The old man with the stick made a sound deep in his throat, like grief. “It spreads anyway,” he murmured, not to anyone in particular. "It always spreads anyway."

The doorway woman lifted her chin. "Enough," she said, and now her voice carried the tone of someone reclaiming authority over her threshold. "If you've read your warning, then go. We'll not have strangers stirring talk."

"Talk is not the danger," the traveler woman replied, and her frustration flared again. "Silence is. Silence is what turns a village into bolted doors and unmarked graves."

At the words unmarked graves, the doorway woman flinched, just slightly, as if she had seen earth piled too fast somewhere in her own mind. Then her face hardened back into place.

"Go," she said again, and this time there were murmurs of agreement behind shutters, the soft rustle of people choosing distance over doubt.

The traveler woman closed the journal slowly. She could feel the lane closing around itself, like a fist. She had not brought revelation. She had brought a mirror, and mirrors were hated by those who could not bear what they might reflect.

The man beside her touched her elbow, a gentle insistence. "We tried," he said quietly.

She did not answer him. She slid the journal back into her satchel as if putting a blade away. The oilcloth rasped softly against the worn fabric, a small sound swallowed by the larger quiet.

As they turned the mule and began to walk on, the boy's face appeared again for a heartbeat through a gap in the fence slats. His eyes met the traveler woman's. He did not look afraid of her. He looked afraid of his own village.

She wanted to tell him to remember the lines. To remember that fear could be taught to do better things than kill. But she had learned, in the dead village's square, how easily a child's mouth could become a liability.

So, she only nodded once, the smallest gesture, and then the fence gap closed as the boy was pulled away.

They left the village behind to its doors and its careful distances. Ahead, the road rolled toward other chimneys, other thresholds.

The traveler woman walked with her hand gripping her satchel strap. The journal thumped faintly against her hip with each step, not heavy enough to slow her, not light enough to forget.

Behind them, in the village they had just tried to warn, a cough rose from somewhere inside a house and was smothered quickly, as if silence could stop breath from betraying its owner.

The warning had been spoken.

But like Edmund Harrow's voice in the square, it landed too late in ears already trained to hear only what fear allowed.

And the wind, indifferent and patient, kept moving on.

Chapter 18

Afterword: The Wind Moves On

Three weeks after the village with the silent well fell behind them, the road turned stony underfoot and began to smell of salt.

It came gradually at first, a faint sharpness that threaded through the damp stink of ditches and the smoke of cooking fires. Then it strengthened with every mile, until even the mule seemed to lift its head and breathe differently, nostrils flaring at a scent that promised water too wide to cross. The woman felt it in the back of her throat, that clean bite that belonged to tides and open air. She should have been relieved.

Instead, the taste of salt only made her think of ships.

She and the man had learned to read the world in smaller signs than they used to. A village that hung rags in the lane to signal caution. A church bell rung once and never again. A door opened only a finger's width so an eye could measure risk. A cough swallowed behind wood.

Now the signs changed. Carts crowded the road, their wheels banded in iron, their axles groaning with the weight of barrels. Men walked beside them with hooks and ropes. Women carried baskets with fish laid under damp cloth, silver scales flashing in the sun where the cloth slipped. A boy ran past with a coil of twine slung over his shoulder, and when he laughed the sound seemed wrong for a moment, like hearing music in a place you expected silence.

The port rose ahead not as a cluster of cottages but as a low sprawl of warehouses, taverns, and roofs pressed close together. Masts stabbed up in rows beyond the buildings, a forest of wood and rope. Gulls turned above it, white and gray, dropping their cries over everything like a constant argument.

"Here," the man said, and his voice held a hunger that had nothing to do with bread. He had spent too long walking past shutters and being turned away by fear. A port did not belong to one village's suspicion. A port belonged to trade.

The woman did not answer. The journal in her satchel had become a steady presence, as familiar as her own ribs. She could tell, by the way it thumped against her hip with each step, when she was walking too quickly. She could tell, by the ache in her shoulder where the strap rubbed, when she was clenching too hard.

At the gate, a man with a tally board looked them over. His eyes went to the mule first, lingering on its narrowness as if thin animals were as suspect as thin men. Then his gaze flicked to their boots and the caked mud. "Where from?" he asked.

The man started to answer, then stopped, choosing his words the way a person chose where to step on ice. "Inland," he said. "We're looking for work. And food."

The tally man snorted as if those were the same request. "Work is for those who can prove they won't fall dead in the street," he said. It was not cruelty, only the bluntness of a place that dealt in bodies the way it dealt in cargo.

The woman felt her mouth tighten. She could have said, no one can prove that. She could have said, proof is what fear demands when it has already decided what it wants. But she had learned, on the road and in the last village where the journal had been called trouble, that truth spoken at the wrong moment did not become wisdom. It became a spark in dry grass.

"We're healthy," she said instead.

The tally man looked past her, toward the road behind them. A cart creaked through the gate piled high with sacks. "Everyone says so," he replied. Then he waved them through, not because he believed them, but because the gate could not afford to be choosy when trade was moving. "Keep to yourselves. If you start coughing, you take it to the church house and you stay there. No quarrels. No stealing."

No stealing. No coughing. Two commandments for survival, as if the second were a sin a person could choose not to commit.

Inside the port, noise hit them like a hand. It was not the roar of a mob, hungry for a scapegoat. It was the constant grind of a place that never truly slept. Barrels thudded. Ropes creaked. Men shouted measurements and prices. Somewhere metal rang against metal, the quick bright sound of a hammer on a nail.

They walked through it with the mule close. The animal's hooves clicked on stone, and more than one person glanced down at it, gauging whether it could carry anything worth paying for. No one looked at their faces long enough to read anything like guilt. The port did not have time for that. It had different fears.

The man's shoulders loosened as they passed a tavern whose door stood open. Warmth rolled out with the smell of ale and sweat. Voices inside rose and fell in argument, not about poison or marks on skin, but about whether a captain had cheated his crew. The man's stomach growled audibly. He grimaced as if ashamed of the sound. The woman's own hunger answered it like an echo.

"We can sell something," he murmured, glancing at her satchel. "Not that." He did not need to say what that was.

She shook her head. "We'll find work," she said, though the words felt thin.

By the docks, the air shifted again. It carried tar and seaweed, fish guts and wet wood. The river mouth opened out beyond the quays into gray-blue water flecked with white. Ships sat at anchor, some with sails furled, some with men climbing their rigging like insects on a web. Rowboats darted between them, loaded with crates.

The woman stopped without meaning to.

Along the far quay, a merchant vessel was being unloaded. Men passed bundles hand to hand. A clerk stood with a wax tablet, marking tallies. The work was brisk. No one wanted cargo lingering. Cargo meant profit only when it moved.

And there, under the hull's shadow, she saw them: rats.

They scurried along the edge of the quay, quick as water, slipping between stacked crates and vanishing into gaps beneath boards. One ran bold enough to pause and sniff at a bit of fish offal, then snatched it and darted away.

Her stomach tightened. She remembered the dead village's lanes after the cats were slaughtered, the slick movement in corners, the ownership the rats seemed to claim. Rats did not announce plague. Rats announced only rats. But she had learned that danger did not need to announce itself to be real.

The man followed her gaze and cursed under his breath. "Every port has them," he said, trying to make it ordinary.

"Yes," she replied. "Every port."

A boy in a dockworker's cap ran past them carrying a coil of rope. He nearly collided with the mule and swore, then laughed. The laugh turned into a cough. Just one. Dry. He slapped his chest once and kept running as if nothing had happened.

The woman watched him go, and in her mind she heard another cough, wetter, smothered behind a shutter. She felt the old urge to chase the sound, to grab the boy by the shoulders and tell him to stop laughing and start fearing. But fear was not a medicine. It was a match.

They found a place to sleep that night in a loft above a cooper's shed, paid for by carrying barrels until their arms shook. The cooper did not ask their names. He asked whether they could lift. When the man said yes, the cooper nodded and that was the end of the matter. In the corner of the loft, other bodies lay wrapped in blankets, strangers pressed together because warmth still mattered more than suspicion here, at least for the moment.

The woman lay on her side with the satchel hugged against her chest. The journal's oilcloth pressed into her ribs. She did not open it. She knew the words too well now. They were written inside her like scar tissue.

Below, in the street, a bell rang. Not a church bell. A ship's bell, marking the hour. It sounded clean and practical, meant for the sea, not for the dead.

The man whispered in the dark, “Do you think they’ll listen here?”

She did not pretend to misunderstand. “To the journal?” she asked softly.

“Yes.”

She stared into the loft’s darkness until her eyes picked out the shape of a beam, then the faint line of moonlight through a crack in the roof. “Ports listen to coin,” she said. “And to hunger. That’s all.”

“That’s not fair,” he murmured, and it was a strange complaint from a man who had watched villages turn away water to strangers.

“It’s not fair,” she agreed. “But it’s true.”

He shifted on the straw, then fell still. She could hear his breathing. She could hear the breathing of others. She could hear a distant shout from the docks, then laughter, then the constant whisper of the sea.

In her mind, the dead village rose again, not as buildings but as acts: a rope pulled tight, a child’s cough hushed like a crime, names swallowed by mud. Edmund’s voice, insisting that dignity could make men better, drowned out by a crowd's certainty.

She reached into the satchel and touched the journal's edge through the oilcloth, a small reassurance that something had survived besides fear.

At dawn, she went down to the quay alone while the man bartered for stale bread. The tide was out, leaving slick mud and weed-slick stones exposed. Men already moved cargo in long practiced lines. A ship had arrived in the night, and its deck was busy with activity.

She stood at the edge of the crowd and watched faces. She watched hands. She watched the way a dockworker wiped sweat from his brow and then rubbed his nose with the same hand. She watched a sailor spit into the water and laugh when it splashed. She watched rats slip between stacked barrels as if they were part of the dock's machinery.

A voice behind her said, "You looking for someone?"

She turned. A dock official stood there, not in fine clothes, but in a better coat than most, with a leather pouch at his waist. His gaze was suspicious and bored; the gaze of a man whose job was to keep trouble moving along.

"No," she said carefully. "I'm looking at the ships."

He followed her gaze to the newest vessel. "Trade must go on," he said, as if reciting a creed.

The woman's mouth went dry. She thought of another place, another time, when officials had hesitated to quarantine because they would not disrupt trade. She thought of rats vanishing into streets unnoticed.

She nodded once, slow. "Yes," she said. "It always does."

The official narrowed his eyes. "What's that mean?"

She could have lied. She could have said nothing. But the journal's weight seemed to press against her back like a hand insisting on its own purpose.

"It means," she said quietly, "that the wind doesn't care what you need."

The official snorted. "Wind is wind," he replied, and turned away, already done with her.

She watched him go. Behind him, cargo moved. Rats moved. Men moved. The port breathed in and out with the tide.

She stood there until the salt air made her eyes sting, and then she walked back toward the cooper's shed, toward the man, toward the mule, toward the road that would lead away again when the time came.

Above the rooftops, a gull rode the air and cried out. The sound was sharp and ordinary, like a nail struck true.

The wind shifted, coming in off the water, and carried with it every smell of the port: tar, fish, sweat, smoke. It lifted the hem of the woman's coat and tugged at the satchel strap across her shoulder as if testing its strength.

It did not matter that Edmund Harrow's village was dead. It did not matter that his words had been read and rejected in a lane of bolted doors. It did not matter that a thin branch marked his grave for a season and then would fall.

The wind moved on anyway.

It always did.

And where it went, it carried more than weather. It carried the same old human hunger for certainty, the same fear that wanted a name to burn, the same refusal to believe in an enemy too small to see and too indifferent to hate.

A new port. A new beginning.

The same breath in a different throat.

The woman did not sleep well after that morning on the quay. In the loft above the cooper's shed, surrounded by strangers whose breath rose and fell in the dark, she lay with her eyes open and listened. The port's noises bled up through the boards: the distant clack of hooves on stone, a shout, laughter that turned sharp at the edges when it carried too far, a bell from the water marking time in a voice that pretended time was still honest.

In the village they'd left behind, time had been counted in ropes and coughs, in doors bolted from the inside. Here time was counted in tallies and tides. It should have felt safer. It felt only busier.

When dawn came, the man returned with a heel of stale bread and a handful of dried fish heads he'd bought cheap. He tried to smile when he handed them over, as if hunger could be made into a joke that did not matter.

She ate, because she had learned that refusing food did not make a point. It only made the body weaker for the next argument. The journal sat in her satchel, and the words inside it pressed against her like the memory of a hand on her shoulder, steady and insistent.

By midday, they were back at the docks carrying barrels again. The cooper paid them in coin so small it felt like an insult, but coin was coin. The man accepted it without complaint. He had learned, too, that complaining made you noticeable, and noticeable people were the first to be blamed when something went wrong.

They passed the same merchant vessel she had watched that morning, and another besides it, newly arrived, men swarming over its deck like ants over a carcass. A clerk stood with his tablet, calling out numbers that floated away on the wind and were lost before they could become meaning.

There was a smell near the second ship that made the woman slow. Not salt or fish or tar. Something sourer, trapped and stale, like bedding that had never been aired out.

The man noticed her hesitation. "Don't," he murmured, and tugged her sleeve lightly, warning her back into motion.

She kept walking, but her eyes stayed on the ship's rail. A sailor leaned over, his face gray under the sunburn, and vomited into the water. It was dark and thick, splashing against the pilings. He wiped his mouth with the back of his hand

and laughed weakly at something someone said behind him.

Laughter here came easily. It was one of the port's tricks, the way it made fear seem childish because there were too many mouths and too much movement for any one cough to matter. But she had seen coughs become verdicts. She had seen a village teach itself to hear sickness as guilt.

The dock official from earlier stood again near the quay, arguing with a merchant whose sleeves were too clean. Their voices rose and fell, the merchant's sharp with frustration, the official's slick with patience.

"I told you," the official said, loud enough for passing men to hear. "No delays. Not unless a man's corpse falls on my feet. Goods move. People eat."

"A sailor died on the crossing," the merchant snapped. "Two were sick. We've got word from Marseille. Whole districts shut. You want that here?"

The official made a dismissive gesture with his hand, as if swatting a fly. "Word," he said, and spat the last syllable. "There's always word. And there's always someone who wants to use it to stop a ship and seize a cargo cheap."

A dockworker nearby muttered something and crossed himself. Another laughed and said, "If God wants us, He'll find us." He said it the way men said weather phrases, as if God were a raincloud and not a hunger.

The woman's fingers tightened around the barrel's rim. Edmund Harrow's face rose in her mind, not as she had never seen it, but as the journal described him: a man who had believed reason could stand in a square and hold. A man who had been gagged and left hanging because his village had decided words were more dangerous than sickness.

She wanted to step toward the official and tell him what she had watched on the quay, what she had smelled in the village, what Edmund had written with ink pressed so hard it tore the paper's patience.

Trade must go on, the official had said. Officials had said it before. They had said it on a southern European dock when a merchant vessel drifted in under unnatural stillness, when bodies lay below decks and rats ran free. She knew that story too now, not as a legend, but as a pattern. A beginning the world kept choosing.

The man cleared his throat beside her, a small sound, ordinary. She flinched anyway. He saw it and looked offended for half a heartbeat, then remembered what they both had learned.

"I'm fine," he said quickly.

"I know," she replied, and forced her shoulders to loosen. She hated the way fear lodged in the body and refused to leave even when the mind tried to push it out. She hated how easily a sound became a question. She hated most of all how that hate could turn outward if she did not watch it.

That evening, they found a tavern willing to sell them thin stew. It was mostly water and onions, with a bone floating like a joke. They sat at a corner table and ate anyway. Around them men argued about coin and captains. A woman with red hands and tired eyes carried tankards from table to table, moving fast enough that no one could trap her in a conversation.

At the next table, two sailors talked in low voices.

"They say in the inland villages," one said, leaning close, "they're killing folk to keep it away."

The other snorted. "They always say that. They always say inland folk are savages. And then they come to port and beg us for bread."

"I heard it true," the first insisted. "A priest leading it. Said he could see marks on people. Said some were unclean."

The word unclean drifted into the woman's ears like smoke. She stared down into her bowl. The stew's surface trembled slightly, reflecting the tavern's candlelight in broken pieces.

Marks, she thought. Marks of the damned. Blue eyes, fair hair, birthmarks. A village that ran out of sense and started measuring bodies for guilt because it could not measure the air.

The man saw her face tighten. "Don't listen," he murmured.

"I have to," she said, and it came out harsher than she meant. Then she softened it. "If we don't listen, it happens again without anyone knowing why."

He stared at his bowl. "Knowing why didn't stop it."

"No," she agreed. "But it might slow it. It might make one door open instead of bolt."

He did not answer. His silence was not refusal; it was fatigue. Fatigue had its own logic. Fatigue made survival feel like the only honest religion left.

They left the tavern and walked back toward the cooper's loft through streets that smelled of fish rot and wet rope. A group of men stood near a warehouse door, talking too loudly. The woman heard a name repeated in their laughter.

"Ramon," one said. "That foreign rat. Came off a ship last week. Now look."

"What happened?" another asked, delighted in advance.

"He's got the swellings," the first said, drawing the words out like a story told for sport. "Under the jaw. Like a toad's pouch. They say his kind brings it. They sleep in filth. They rot from the inside."

The man beside the woman stiffened. She felt it through the air more than she saw it. The shape of the talk was familiar. Not the specifics. The hunger beneath.

A third man spat. "Should throw him in the water and see if it takes."

The woman stopped walking. Her heart beat hard enough she could feel it in her throat. She turned toward the group, her satchel strap biting into her shoulder.

"Stop," she said, and her voice carried more than she intended.

The men turned. In the streetlight their faces were crude with drink and certainty. One of them looked her up and down and smiled, slow and unfriendly.

"Look at that," he said. "A preaching woman."

The man beside her murmured, urgent, "Come on. Not here."

But she could not make her feet move. The journal might have been a stone in her satchel, anchoring her in place.

"You don't know where it comes from," she said, forcing her voice steady. "You don't know what brings it. You just want a name."

The man's smile widened. "We want it gone," he replied, and the simplicity of it was the most frightening thing. "You got a better way?"

She did not say quarantine. She did not say cleanliness. She did not say rats and fleas and ships' holds. Those were words for people willing to hear an enemy they could not see. These men were already reaching for a face to hit.

"There was a man," she said, and her hand went to her satchel without thinking. "He wrote—"

The men's eyes flicked to the satchel. The smallest shift, and the street felt narrower.

"What you got there?" one asked. His tone was casual, but his feet moved half a step closer.

The man beside her stepped in front of her slightly, not brave, just protective in the way exhausted people sometimes were when something in them snapped and decided that fear could not have everything. "Nothing," he said. "We're leaving."

The first man laughed. "Everyone's leaving," he said. "Everyone's always leaving, carrying their curses with them."

Curses. The word was a hook. It did not matter what the journal was. In their mouths it could only become something dangerous.

The woman swallowed. She thought of Edmund again, gagged because his voice made fear feel uncertain. She thought of a village that had needed to burn strangers and hang the weak and slaughter animals because those actions could be seen, could be counted, could be felt in the hands.

The wind moved down the street, carrying the port's smells and stirring the men's hair. It did not care what they believed. It did not care what names they threw at it. It moved anyway, slipping between bodies the way sickness did, indifferent and patient.

Her voice came quieter now, because she understood something she had not wanted to understand in the last village, the one that had turned her away when she tried to read. People did not refuse warnings because they were stupid. They refused because warnings demanded change, and change demanded giving up the brief relief of certainty.

"You're doing it already," she said softly, and the men leaned in as if softness was permission. "You're making a story so you don't have to admit you can't control it."

The first man's smile vanished. His face hardened, offended, as if she had accused him of cowardice. "Careful," he said.

The man beside her touched her arm again, firmer. "Please," he whispered, and she heard in the word the sound of bolted doors, the sound of people choosing survival over truth.

She let him pull her away. Her feet finally moved. They walked, quickly, not running, because running drew attention, and attention was a spark in dry grass.

Behind them one of the men called, "Keep your breath to yourself!" and the others laughed, the same phrase the old woman had shouted on the road, the same ritual of distance spoken like wisdom.

In the loft that night, the woman sat with the journal open on her knees and did not read it. She stared at the ink until the letters blurred.

The man lay down on the straw and turned his face to the wall. "You can't fight a whole port," he said, his voice muffled.

"I'm not fighting the port," she replied.

"What then?"

She closed the journal gently, as if not to wake the dead man inside it. "I'm watching," she said. "So, I know what comes next."

He was quiet for a time. Then, very softly, he asked, "And what comes next?"

She thought of the rats she'd seen slipping between barrels. She thought of the sailor vomiting over a ship's rail. She thought of men in a street choosing a foreign name because a foreign name was easier to drown than an invisible thing carried in fleas.

"The same lesson," she said. "And the same refusal to learn it."

Outside, a gull cried, and somewhere on the water a ship's bell marked the hour again, clean and practical as a knife.

The wind shifted, and the loft's thin walls did nothing to stop it. It moved through the cracks, across sleeping bodies, across the satchel strap, across the oilcloth-wrapped journal, and went on toward other streets where men were already building their stories.

It carried no moral. It carried no mercy.

Only motion, and the human habit of believing that this time, the old rules of fear would finally keep them safe.

The next morning the port looked the same from the loft window: the same muddle of roofs and masts, the same thin ribbon of smoke rising from cookfires, the same gulls circling and arguing as if nothing in the world had ever changed. That sameness was what frightened the woman most. Disaster never announced itself with trumpets. It arrived wearing yesterday's clothes.

She went down early, before the cooper's boys began rolling barrels, before the streets filled with men who did not want to think. The air held the night's damp and the sour edge of fish left too long in baskets. Somewhere a woman was already scrubbing a doorstep with a brush so worn it was mostly wood. She scrubbed hard, as if force could turn filth into safety.

On the quay, voices rose in their usual commerce, but the woman began to notice how often certain words repeated, passed from mouth to mouth like a coin.

“Marseille.”

“Genoa.”

“Quarantine.”

“Foreign.”

The man found her near the pilings where she could watch the ships without being in the way of the work. He had bread again, harder than yesterday’s, and his eyes had the flat look of someone who had dreamed badly and woken with no time to recover.

“You didn’t sleep,” he said.

“I listened,” she replied.

He followed her gaze toward a knot of dockworkers gathered near a warehouse door. One of them was speaking too loudly, showing off to the others. A few laughed on cue, then glanced around quickly as if laughter itself might draw notice.

"They say a sailor collapsed in the lane behind the netmaker's," the loud one said. "Coughed up black. Like he'd swallowed soot."

"That's just rotgut," another man answered, but his voice held no conviction. He spat into the water, then wiped his mouth with the back of his hand as if remembering belatedly that hands were treacherous.

A third man crossed himself. "My cousin in Colneford wrote," he muttered. "He says they hang rags on poles there and won't let anyone in. They beat a peddler for trying to sell lace."

Rags on poles. The woman's stomach tightened at the familiar image. She saw again the village square that had become a mouth for shouting, the fallen patrol staff with its limp strips of cloth, the way authority had been reduced to a gesture in the wind.

The man beside her kept his voice low. "We should leave," he said. "Ports are worse when they turn. Too many bodies."

"Where?" she asked.

He hesitated, because the honest answer was nowhere. There were only degrees of refusal. Inland villages shut their doors and cursed strangers. Ports kept their gates open because coin demanded it, and then tried to punish sickness as if punishment were medicine.

A cart rattled past loaded with sacks. The clerk walking beside it held his tablet close, eyes down, as if numbers could protect him. Behind the cart, rats slipped along the quay edge and vanished beneath boards.

The woman's hand went to her satchel strap. "It's starting," she said.

The man's jaw tightened. "Everything is always starting," he replied. But his eyes did not leave the dockworkers. He was trying to decide what a beginning looked like, and whether it could be outrun.

They did not speak again until they were back in the street that led away from the docks. There, a cluster of people stood outside a tavern even this early, faces turned toward a man perched on a barrel. He had the posture of someone who had discovered that attention felt like strength.

"They won't say it," he was calling, voice bright with indignation. "But we all know. Those ships bring it. Those sailors. Those foreigners with their rotten teeth and their filthy prayers. We feed them and they repay us with death."

A few heads nodded, hungry for certainty. Others looked away, not disagreeing, only unwilling to be seen disagreeing. The crowd was not large. It did not need to be. A spark did not require a bonfire to be dangerous. It only required dry grass and a wind that did not care.

The woman stopped at the edge of the knot of bodies. The man with the staff stopped with her, then shifted as if trying to pull her onward without making it a struggle.

“Come,” he murmured.

She did not move. “Listen to him,” she said.

“I am listening,” he replied. “That’s why I want to go.”

The man on the barrel raised one hand, and his ring caught the light. “We need order,” he declared, and the word order was a familiar poison now. “We need a list. Who came off which ship. Who sold bread to whom. Who took coin from foreign hands. We mark them, and we keep the rest safe.”

Mark them. The woman felt, with a cold clarity, the old chain of thought clicking into place. In the dead village, marks had been blue eyes and fair hair and birthmarks. Here, marks would be accents and ship names and skin darkened by sun. Fear always found something visible, because the invisible could not be beaten.

A woman in the crowd called out, “And if you’re wrong?”

The man on the barrel smiled as if he had expected the question. “Then we’ve still done something,” he said. “Better than waiting to die like sheep.”

The woman’s mouth went dry. Better than waiting. She had read that line in Edmund Harrow’s hand without knowing it would follow her into another place.

“And if you’re right?” someone else asked, a man with red eyes and a cloth tied at his throat. His voice shook on the last word, right, as if rightness itself were a plank over deep water.

“Then we’ve saved the port,” the barrel-man said, and the crowd made a sound that was half approval, half relief. The relief was the most dangerous part. It tasted clean. It made people feel virtuous in their fear.

The traveler man touched the woman’s elbow again, urgent. “Please,” he whispered.

She turned her head slightly toward him. “This is what Edmund meant,” she said.

He flinched at the name, as if names carried their own contagion. “Don’t,” he warned. “Not here.”

But she could not keep the thought from forming. The journal had become a lens, and now the port's faces slid into the pattern it described. Not identical, never identical. Always the same shape beneath different clothing.

They walked on, leaving the little crowd behind them. The barrel-man's voice followed in fragments, carried by the wind between buildings. The woman felt each fragment land in her mind like a small stone.

Around the next corner they found a doorway marked with chalk. Not a cross this time, but a crude circle with a dot at its center, drawn again and again until the plaster was scored. A woman stood there holding a bucket of lye-water, her hands red and raw.

"What's that mean?" the traveler man asked, though his voice suggested he already knew.

The woman with the bucket looked at them as if they were slow. "Sick house," she said. "Or foreign house. Same thing, if you ask me." She jerked her chin toward the street. "Move along. Don't stand breathing."

Sick house or foreign house. The woman's fingers tightened around her satchel strap until her knuckles ached. There it was, the blend of categories that made violence feel logical.

Sickness became identity. Identity became blame. Blame became permission.

They moved on. A cart went by carrying straw. A boy threw a handful of it into the air and laughed. His laugh turned into a cough, and his mother slapped his shoulder sharply, not cruelly, but with the quick panic of someone trying to discipline sound itself.

“Quiet,” she hissed. “Quiet, you fool.”

The woman’s throat tightened. She thought of the child in the dead village being hushed into a skirt, as if the sound were the crime. She thought of doors bolted from the inside, of sickness hidden until it filled the whole room.

At midday they passed the church house the tally man had mentioned at the gate, the place where coughers were meant to go. A guard stood outside with a pole in his hands and a cloth wrapped around his mouth. He looked bored, but his eyes were too alert.

A man sat on the church house steps with his head bowed. His shoulders shook. His wife stood a few paces away, not touching him. She held a bundle of cloth that might have been bedding or might have been a child’s blanket. Her eyes were fixed on her husband, but her feet would not move closer. Distance was becoming a kind of prayer.

The traveler man slowed. "We could help," he murmured, and the words sounded like a memory of who he had been before the road taught him caution.

The guard snapped, "No," without raising his voice. The pole tilted slightly, the gesture enough. "Keep walking."

The wife lifted her eyes to the travelers. For a heartbeat her gaze held something like appeal. Then it hardened into calculation, the same calculation the doorway woman in the last village had worn. If I accept help, I accept risk. If I accept risk, I may lose everyone.

She looked away.

They kept walking.

That night in the loft, the woman finally opened the journal and read not because she expected new words, but because she needed to anchor herself to the truth of one place while standing in another that was already trying to rewrite itself. The man sat with his back against a beam, knees drawn up, listening with his head turned slightly away as if the words hurt to face directly.

She read the lines about certainty, about wanting a cause they could hang and a name they could burn. When she looked up, the man's eyes were shut.

"Do you think anyone will carry this after we're gone?" he asked quietly.

The question was not about the journal's paper surviving damp. It was about whether people were capable of holding a warning without turning it into another weapon.

The woman ran her thumb along the oilcloth's stiff edge. "People carry what helps them live," she said. "Sometimes they carry the wrong thing because it feels lighter."

He nodded once, as if that was the only answer he had expected.

Below them, the port went on with its noises. Somewhere a fight broke out and ended quickly. Somewhere a baby cried and was hushed. Somewhere a ship's bell marked an hour that did not care who lived to hear the next one.

In the dark, the woman imagined the road stretching out like a vein across the land. She imagined other villages, each with its own square, its own church steps, its own frightened men with voices loud enough to make others follow. She imagined chalk marks appearing on doors like sores. She imagined rags tied to poles and called protection. She imagined someone, somewhere, lifting a rope and thinking it was cleaner than waiting.

The wind came in off the water and pushed through the loft's cracks. It lifted a corner of the journal's page, making it flutter as if trying to speak on its own.

The woman laid her hand flat on it, steadying it. Not silencing it. Holding it in place.

Outside, the port's lights trembled and blurred in the damp air, and the sound of the sea moved beneath everything else, patient and indifferent. The same wind that carried salt across the docks would carry fear inland again and carry the stories men told themselves to justify what their hands were already itching to do.

Echoes did not require the original voice to remain.

They only required ears trained to hear what they wanted.

And across the land, in villages and ports and narrow lanes, those ears were already turning toward the same old song, while the unseen thing that began it all moved quietly through walls and bedding and breath, needing no names at all.